THE
DRAGON
COMMONS

THE DRAGON COMMONS

TIFFANY CLAVECILLA

ARPress
45 Dan Road Suite 5
Canton MA 02021

Hotline: 1(800) 220-7660
Fax: 1(855) 752-6001

Ordering Information:
Quantity sales. Special discounts are available on quantity purchases by corporations, associations, and others. For details, contact the publisher at the address above.

Printed in the United States of America.

ISBN-13:   Paperback   979-8-89389-790-6
            eBook   979-8-89389-791-3

Library of Congress Control Number: 2024923067

For my husband,

Casey Clavecilla

who trans-formed my life

Special thanks to Casey Clavecilla, my parents Lanny and Gloria Clavecilla, Kerri Knight, and Emily Errico.

CONTENTS

CHAPTER 1

ARDYCE ~ GREAT AEGIS of the TREE CROWNS

The earth had been hollowed through, as if consumed, for there were no remnants of the ploughed marl as would be through the act of burrowing. In its impaled state, the silent knoll filled its wound with moon-glare as an unguent and found some solace in the maiden's light before a pallid shade invaded and overwhelmed the sward for a mile in diameter. Gray earth struck the region through.

From the heavens' halls, she witnessed the mar of the land and descended from the gods' heights to moor upon the vale. The trees surrounding the valley could not buffet the resounding impact of her weight, and the birds nested there frightened up out the tops of the verdant canopies before settling once more. She circled the perimeter of the rictus tunneling into the depths of the soil; vapors bannered out in gossamer columns, and the hole was sixty-feet in diameter.

She stared into the lesion, until she felt it make a reflection of itself within her: a tear that opened wide and bore trepidation and unrest into her mind. Her instincts flailed her nerves, and she took a careful step back from the grayed soil.

The early Autumn's breath had settled around her as if it were her scent and when she moved, it too came and wafted gelid

1

pheromones into the cavities of her lungs. She breathed deep, pulling at the sylvan exhalations. In her breast, a six-chambered heart hammered the phoeniceous torrents of her blood rivers, and ninety-five tons of muscle warmed with steady tidal fronts. She was a Drake, a dragon, scaled in pearl-white opulence. Upon her immense form, gathered in greater concentrations at her shoulders and haunches, was chalcedony; it glinted even in the star-driven night. A fair, gridelin hue, the cryptocrystalline silica lined the apertures of her eyes as well, those eyes of rainbow, oil-spill likeness with pupils that seemed to float to the surface as she gazed here then there. That pupil - a small, black, rondure body with crooked, spider legs of darker colors - was another trait to her kind and gender.

Her name was Ardyce, and she was the Great Aegis to the Tree Crown tribe. Her kith were few in number, amassing a mere thirty-eight Drakes, and their cognomen of "Tree Crowns" adopted for their grandiose display of three-tiered antlers. They were a breed of Drakes with females much-endowed in strength and size. Jowls wide with power and mandibles of crushing force, the female Tree Crowns were the shields to their people, and though fireless as were the males too, their hides were like hauberk and they were tusked, their maws rowed in fanged teeth.

Ardyce trained her stare to the northward lands. In the distance, miles away, she could smell the emergence of new Wyrms. A nest, most likely, was not far from where she now stood. But, this gouging had not been crafted by a wayward youth. It was the mark of a Wyrm in full maturation. Indeed, the bristles shed from the hide of the Wyrm once here were barbed as only appeared in those well-beyond pubescence, and the size of the hole alone was indication of an adult in its prime. The manner of this act was highly unusual, especial to the area, for this land was Gled Tria. It was the border territory betwixt the homes of the Wyrms and the Drakes.

The humans simply called this stretch of coastal land, and the Reigns beyond it, "non-regions" for they were uninhabitable and uncultivable. Gled Tria, in particular, had made itself detrimental to the belly of humankind. The boles of the Ever-standing Ones here were thorned, and not in the gentle loveliness as those found on rose stems, but thorns with great, razored edges, like sabers or the cinquedea. The trees wore their armament and filled, also, the dale with a nutrient substantial to animal, reptilian, and raptor life, but to humans, it made them very ill. They jaundiced and excreted all sustenance for weeks until death, if they came in contact with the grounds of Gled Tria.

So, the trees here had made a world for non-human life to survive, including the Drakes who hid in the folds of the forests. The Wyrms, however, had never any need of Gled Tria – neither for food nor protection from humankind. Their lands, too, were undesirable to human eye, being, on the whole, acres of sand traps which relented only to an invasive species of weeds that could not be felled or uprooted. The weeds, minutely disturbed, would huff like old men with pipes and dirty the air with their spores. Those spores had the truculent characteristic of being like glass finely shaven; they fell away from furred or feathered coats, but to one encased all in soft, open flesh, they settled in and deeper still with every movement. It was realized, then, that humans could die from pain alone. With the feeling of shards under their skin, cutting and scraping ever inwards, people exposed to the weeds' spores begged to be released to Death. They saw to it by their own hands, if no other would assist them. Yet, these plants were of no regard to the Wyrms, and the soil, meters down below the sands, were profitable to their health and ever-replenished by the very spores which bore such ill will towards the smooth, bipedal sponges.

Ardyce could imagine no reason for the Wyrms to breach territories.

She, and her tribe, belonged to Outer Gled Tria – tracts of land ran deep with lore, with romantic debate. It could not be agreed upon if the trees of Outer Gled Tria grew out of the earth up-ended for love of the Tree Crown Drakes, or the Tree Crowns, by mysterious nurturing, bewitched and cultivated the trees of their region to outre aesthetics. Even Time, fatherly and stoop-backed, was beside Himself in marking the origin of the first Up-Ended Tree; the rows of wooded sentries had grown in this manner for so long that not even the Tree Crown tribe could accurately account a time when the trees flourished right-side up.

Their roots were in the sky – delicate, frail-white, with a sheen of viscid moisture – and they burgeoned in an oblate form of calculated shape, almost as if an over-simplification of what the flourish of trees looked like. The trunks held their masses of roots most punctiliously – in the wind, the rain, and sun - just as reverential to the equations of Nature, despite the lawlessness of their design. And, the trunks, also, shied not from the soil of Outer Gled Tria which was equally abandoned to mutinous structure. The marl was bound, by fibers too miniscule for the unaided eye to see, thus creating one, expansive organ, like integument, and it was semi-translucent, as skin is. This was how those treading the lands of Outer Gled Tria saw the leaves beneath the surface of the valleys, like peering through ice at filigree artworks unending.

Every Tree Crown Drake became enamored with the beauty of these trees, of the leaves galloping like frozen-motioned herds through the vastness of the soil, who wore a glassy carapace. Why a mutual enchantment existed between the habitat and inhabitant was unknown, but it was undeniable to all Drakes a simple, unerring fact: the Tree Crowns slept near to their Up-Ended Trees, with their tiers of antlers touching those exposed roots, and if a Tree Crown did not, especially in their formative years, the limbs of wings would forsake that Drake, never emerging. Or, a tree neglected the adoration of these Drakes blackened at the roots and the leaves browned as if to Autumn and became soil. There were not more legends and tales authored by Drakes that did not begin with this enigma to set the stage for profound escapades.

Yet, here – here was Gled Tria of the armed boles. It was not Ardyce's domain, thus, by Code of Comity, she had crossed into her neighbors' heartland. But, she knew the Mungkr (*Muhng-kuhr*) nation, Thai Drakes, in amiable terms and anticipated no quarrel. Behind her, having finally caught her lead, a flock of smaller Drakes anchored the terra. They were each a Tree Crown, as she herself. All of them male – they were, individually, every tone of azure and rhodopsin. Their antlers were slender and lightly comose, and by comparison, they were far weaker than Ardyce, being only a third her tonnage. Males of the Tree Crown tribe were ever-beautiful, never outwardly manifesting their age, even as they approached death. Their flights (as is the Draconian word for "wings") were vitreous and patterned as leaves with veins throughout. They did not have oil-spill eyes, as were the females' common attribute, but instead, they looked upon the world from eyes milky-white, as though to match the females' dominant body color, and the males' pupils were horizontal slits.

There were seven in the newly-arrived flock. They were all brothers, and the eldest of them was Ardyce's Vow, her mate. With flights of unusual mottled distinction, his name was Mohonia, and he went to her with slow, mindful steps. The underside of him bulged against his lissome frame, making his walk delicate; he held in his abdominal folds three of her fertilized eggs. Mohonia was nervous to become a father; he was young and exercised caution beyond necessity with their unborn.

He came to her shoulder, standing close. Before them laid the abysmal puncture and the afflicted lea. *It is the greatest empty I've seen. Like a gouged eye socket. Why must you leave our tribe to trifle with these Wyrms?* His tone was pleading, and typical to their breed, Tree Crowns preferred telepathy. Their fanged jaws hindered physical speech.

Ardyce answered him, *I am our dwindling tribes' Great Aegis, Mohonia. No other should be in this hamlet. Return home; you are over-exerted in flying this far with our family unborn.*

Like wet clay, the hoary marl gave beneath their clawed hands and feet; they had impressed their prints, encircling that bottomless wound. The second eldest brother came forward and peered into the malice brought upon the land. *Earth fallowed by a Wyrm's hunger - how could that be? Even the few, reckless ones who have before gorged themselves to this excess, never rendered the soil blighted.*

Mohonia was venturing to the mouth of the hole. *Something resides within,* Mohonia began, but Ardyce was nudging him away from the rictus as the first Mungkr of Gled Tria alighted the terrain.

Ardyce and her favored retinue made obeisance to the Thai Drake as she came down from the sky with wisps of clouds trailing to thinness across the breadth of her scaled body. Ardyce knew her as Sasithorn *(Saa-see-TAWN)*. She came from a people of some 200 Drakes, and this was their Reign. To them, she was their *Ngaw (Nn-gow)*, an Offensive Official of surmounting martial skill. As pups, she and Ardyce had been fast-tied as Sworn Kindred, but now primed, they were loose ends to one another. The Past echoed betwixt them, for there extended a long stretch of years where neither had so much as glanced face of the other. Ardyce was found disquieted by their unforeseen reunion.

"*Sawadee kah.*" Sasithorn's jaws remained still, yet her chiming voice blossomed, then seeded the air behind her, as if she were walking away though she stirred not from her place. "I trust you have been well, dear friend."

Greetings, Sasithorn. Ardyce dipped her helmed head in time with the Mungkr's formalities. *Yes,* she answered her. *My hope is the same for you as well.* She stood taller, with neck rigid, after her bow to the Ngaw and sought a reflection of her preponderate size or laurels in the other's eyes.

But, Sasithorn was relaxed, comfortable in her presence. She said, "I am a widow. Same as before." Her gaze flitted from one face of the brothers to the next, then she blinked away her attention, returning it to Ardyce.

The Great Aegis snorted to herself, pretending it as a casual release of air. *You are no such thing.* Ardyce corrected her gently, a tone given practice for the times before where they had made discussion of the very same topic.

"I am entirely veiled in the emotions of one bereaved," Sasithorn was not insistent, but declared her facts. Ardyce shook her head to herself, for she would have known if her former friend had been paired. The five nations of Drakes would have spread word, undoubtedly. Yet, Sasithorn continued: "She was there. In a time or space separated by dream barriers, or something akin to color-blindness, or between the overlap of musical instruments. You never helped me search for her. What became of her before she died? I had these things to say, but you didn't listen." Sasithorn's tone was neutral, detached.

Ardyce felt uncomfortable for having to continue upon an issue so absurd, and this, when she meant to treat Sasithorn as a stranger – this, when there were more pertinent matters at hand. She attempted to sound reasonable, but her tail flicked acutely with agitation. *You've no memory of one at your side, marital Ceremony, or the death of that Vow. I've no memory of her either, or any other Drake who knows you.* The Great Aegis could not think why someone should wish to fantasize of deceased spouses, but Mohonia had once told her that perhaps it was that she felt half of her was missing; something had happened which they didn't have knowledge.

"My love story is a ghost, so when I close my eyes and see nothing, still I am haunted, and I feel her breath against me, like feathers through the skies of my dreams."

Ardyce sighed. *You are a ruinous poet and not much else, friend.* She was reminded of the years she'd spent at the side of the Mungkr, who was given to her whims and daydreams, her intuition and her reading of the elements. She was ever the unconventional choice for her post, yet she was exalted by her people, and the Tree Crown wondered how she kept their regard as so plainly herself. She stared at the Thai Drake, and Ardyce realized there burred a nostalgia in her breast for Sasithorn, but they were no longer those roaming juveniles from before.

They stood across from one another, the Tree Crown waiting for the other Drake to speak first on the event that brought them to this locus, as was the custom for one who has happened upon a visitor to her country.

The male Drakes waited, too, and let confusion nip at their brows, for Sasithorn was silent, speaking not more of her spouse, who might also be a mirage. Nor did she appear to remember the spoiled crater and why they had gathered here.

Ardyce shifted her weight. She was sorrowful for her old friend and ashamed.

Sasithorn sustained her silence. She swayed in false answer to a breeze that was not there. Ardyce gazed at the revered Ngaw. In many respects, she was structured as a Long, a Chinese Drake, with a body of fish-scaled, snake-like immensity. Yet, differing were her plates of gold, like a sallet over her skull and mandible, emerging as shimmering growth out of her virescent scales. A fourth the way down the length of her was a golden encirclement, augmenting her appearance of royal grandeur. The collar and her head plates were developed in equal measures of intricacy and beauty. From the back of her head – a skull short for that of a Drake's - to the tip of her snout arose a peaked elaboration of curving chitin with the twists and dagger-points of flames. It tapered to rough skins that ended in a blunt rounding off, like an elephant's trunk. Undulating was the mane, which hung from Sasithorn's chin, and mimicked her motion of a cobra under charmed flute. The Tree Crown remembered all this from years much passed and saw that adulthood had taken a striking youth and transformed this she-Drake to elegant expression.

She was, however, still odd.

Ardyce continued in due silence. But, impatience edged her stare and stiffened the bulk of her person. The Mungkr took no notice, her maw parted and witch-hour eyes of blackness dazed – she gave no indication of further remembering Ardyce's presence. Sasithorn seemed almost an inanimate object.

The Great Aegis' frustration flared. *Sasithorn. These Wyrms--!*

Mohonia weaved in between the two, and he had nearly begun a vain attempt to placate his angered Vow when Sasithorn spoke.

"Tree Crown. You are swift to this tragedy of the lands."

Ardyce stitched her composure. She and Mohonia exchanged affirming glimpses and subtle gesture which only lovers do understand in detail so slight, and he left after consideration, so that she may proceed to counsel. Again, Ardyce and Sasithorn's past as youths together murmured between them, but was obscured by the Present's contingency. The Tree Crown made explanation: *A tremor seized the Gled Tria to its outer realms, and I pursued it to its source—*

"It *smells* here. Like fire set to the history of all dross expelled from every Wyrm that ever and never was. Rather pungent." Sasithorn blinked after her words had long since finished.

My Honored Mungkr, we must convene with your clan's Great Aegis—

"Do you not perceive that mephitis?" She pendulated in the same, serene draft which belonged only to imagination.

I do not. Ardyce itched for more words, but they would not come. It seemed she could never lead their conversations.

Sasithorn was quick to affirm: "No. Tree Crowns have the olfactory gifts as those tall, branched sentries they are named after. Come away from this fetor with me. It drowns my appetite."

The Mungkr turned and threaded her way towards the center of the clearing. Her species' gait was to weave side to side – indeed, Thai Drakes exuded a serenity of one lost to the pleasures of sweet, meditative music with their every movement, and through this, Ardyce shed her brief peevishness at the other Drake. She trusted her. She and Sasithorn had known one another for many rotations of the seasons, even before either had acquired the titles they now bore.

"Tree Crown, delay no further this conference and shoo away your pretty kickshaws. Attend these matters with *some* determination for there is much to discuss. It is not every hour we discover a crater of demise."

Ardyce elected patience as her governor, understanding that all would come to pass as Sasithorn intended. She moved towards her Vow and bowed low to tenderly bring an antler tip to the underside of Mohonia's chin, where she scratched him with gentle endearment.

Assume a guarded formation with the others, she told him. *This Wyrm troubles me, and I shall hasten our return to Outer Gled Tria, once Sasithorn and I have concluded the measures to be taken.*

He agreed to her wishes and reciprocated the affections before departing her presence to join his brothers, who were rapt in their own speculations of the earth's lesion. The second eldest brother, Salaris, hurried out to Mohonia's side once more, as if walking alongside him could ease the pregnant male's laborious condition.

Ardyce lingered eye upon the two brothers, watching as they reared to lock antlers in play. Salaris gave only a bout or two before ignoring his older brother's challenges out of concern for the eggs nested in Mohonia's abdominal fold. He urged his older brother to the midst of their siblings. To Ardyce, the band of them seemed younger than they were yesterday, and Time was somehow older than it was.

The cold had stiffened, ushering in the caballing clouds. She turned to the Mungkr, and again her nerves writhed near her heart and in the thick of her throat. The sky was awakening; it hung over all and shook the world with one breath. Ardyce felt it unfamiliar – not the empyrean of yester-night. It was as a great alien organism hovering.

From above Gled Tria came the westward winds, descending from the mountaintops of Wymira, which neighbored the home of the Mungkr's dale from across the great River Orb. Saffron and sakura notes tinctured the air, resigned to act as quiet bystanders, whilst the Tree Crown's Great Aegis approached the Mungkr's Ngaw. Behind them, the Orb made heartbeats in wild procession.

Like billions of eyes blinking out of sleep, the River Orb reflected every lighted thought and every shadowed face who came to her mirror-like visage. The river was the central vein to Drakes and Wyrms alike, cherished by all for the nurture it pulsed through each region of draconic abodes as well as the dune-lands belonging to the sightless Wyrms. Its proclivity was due North, and the River Orb danced on light feet out to marine reaches. The river served also as gentle demarcation between draconic domains.

As known, to the Northeast was Gled Tria that harbored the Mungkr, and at its hinterlands, the Tree Crown tribe of Outer

Gled Tria. Below this realm, and Southeast, stood The Eye Backs, an appellation bestowed for the reasons that the backs of one's eyes are unerringly near to sight, yet behind perception and a link to the mind's light. Accordingly, this terrain of gullies and gorges was veiled. The Eye Backs were shrouded in a nimbus of argentine light and rain droplets which hung in the air, never to touch the ground. It was here that the Tianlong lived. Crossing Orb, and tracing Southwest, lay the holds of The Nocturnes, forever in umbra that was the likeness to eternal night. Inhabited by the Pyrolites and the Fire Craws, here was the realm of the firebreathers, who were finely attuned to their sable world by tailored sight – unusual to any other Drake species - and drew course and direction same as one on a jaunt at the height of day. Finally, Northwest was Wymira: home of the scented groves and sky-piercing mountains which cradled the lives of the Japanese Drakes, the Ryuu. Frequented by all other nations, Wymira brought congregations of Drakes together by means of having the most lush and bounteous of fruit. These lands sprawled below the dominion of the Wyrms, and were far, far South of the humans' nations.

Without the intersection of one species upon another, harmony prevailed. It was not so much decree as it was customary deportment that the Wyrms and Drakes did not intermingle.

Sasithorn stood at the lip of the rutted earth, and Ardyce knew she felt too the lazar-like torment of the soil. Yet, the Thai Drake looked as one does upon a mountain peak which has yet a name or a new star peeking through the night sky. She was intrigued.

"What do you see in this, Ardyce?" Sasithron dipped her muzzle towards the destroyed glebe.

The errant behavior of a Wyrm, nothing more, Ardyce answered gravely. *What else should the eye take of it?*

The Mungkr's silence chided a subaltern grin, which fluttered at a corner of her mouth, near the hinge of her jaw. Inwardly, Ardyce sighed to herself, knowing this look. Sasithorn answered her, at last: "It is a wormhole." The Great Aegis wore her expression of stone. Sasithorn continued, "One, blunderous movement too close to the mouth of it, and we may be transported. To foreign dimension. To a universe running our parallel. To a space-time Other. A *wormhole*." Her smile crept to the foreground.

Ardyce's face of sourness would not find saccharine pacification. *What?* she asked.

"A physics joke," Sasithorn tried once more. Then, she muttered to herself: "Astronomically squandered upon your ears." But, Ardyce had never laughed at her japes. The Ngaw straightened, grew taller, and addressed the anomaly. "Ardyce, this condition is unprecedented. Nothing may yet be determined, and in that, all answers balance themselves. Why has the marl turned shade? Did the Wyrm intend this destruction? And, by what means could a Wyrm architect this?"

Ardyce's variegated eyes narrowed, and she tossed her head slightly as if to put tears in the Mungkr's words with her antler tips. *A Wyrm is a beast of its belly. To fill it, the creature wakes, and when that hollow is filled, the Wyrm sleeps. Some perform through miscreant devices to eldritch result, yet by conclusion, what is more to be said than 'The Wyrm ate,' as Wyrms have ever done? The Sun will not witness a Wyrm with merit or comportment higher than a digesting tube sack, and now, we've no other task than to shepherd it back to the dunes from whence it's strayed away.* She wore her breastplate of haughty irritability to scold the fear inside herself. The Great Aegis and Ngaw stood silently in the gaze of each other. At the ends of the dale, the gathered Tree Crown males hushed, too. Finally, the white Drake continued, *I feel your old theories, from when we were ignorant youth, swelling up, Sasithorn.*

The Mungkr pretended to shift herself in absorbed cogitativeness. In so doing, the gold ringlet which clasped her body met in angles with the brightness of the full moon to pitch an intrusive glare into Ardyce's eyes, for the Ngaw felt annoyed with the fusty bearing she now recalled was always Ardyce's hallmark. Sasithorn went on with their discussion, seemingly unaware of Ardyce wincing and backing away. "The Wyrms may be more than they seem. We fill the emptiness we can, even if we must start with our appetites."

These theories, Ardyce regretted, as she blinked the return of her unaddled sight. *What good will your whimsical sentiments do, my friend? Let us continue to your people and consult your Great Aegis. We have still to courier news to the Tianlong.*

"The Tianlong have been here."

What—what did they confer? Ardyce stumbled in her words, wondering if she should, too, have known this.

The Chinese Drakes were the oldest, living breed of dragons. Like wisdom, they were silent, until Peace turned her back and showed her chaos-wings. If they were here, then left, this matter of the Wyrm may already be in procession to an end.

Sasithorn drew closer to the grayness of the valley. "Do you know what odor this is, which heckles my senses and rankles my mind?" She stooped her gold-plated head and took the fallow soil into her mouth, swallowing it.

Sasithorn! Ardyce wavered with shock.

The Ngaw's eyes were a darkness the Tree Crown felt she could not see into. Sasithorn's voice came as from the depths of instinct, a clarion to horrors impending: "Wyrms touch not my sense of smell, not 'til their jaws break open and their throats have been washed in blood, with life putrefying in the catches of their mouths. Then, do they emerge on the map, stained in dark crimson."

What are you goading forward, friend? Wyrms are earth-eaters. They have been known to strike down peripatetic goat or deer at times, but this matters little—

The muscles of the Ngaw surged as one pulse and with that sudden effort, she rammed the battered lip of the hole with the curve of her long body. The hamlet broke away at the impact, and tumbling loose from grit and pebbles, something shook up out of the land.

"This malodor stiffens like crusted blood in my veins, for the flesh so consumed by the Wyrm ... is Drake."

The skull of a Mungkr revealed itself, half-sleeved in skin. It had been mauled.

Ardyce went to it, as if peering into a loose seam between realities. It seemed the threads of logic blew in the wind like the tails of kites flying on a windless afternoon.

Wyrms generally rivaled the lengths and girths of the Ryuu, smallest of the Drake breeds, but a kill made of a Drake by a Wyrm was not possible.

They've no teeth, Sasithorn. Ardyce looked to the other Drake. As if the obvious should ever need be said. It was preposterous. *Some other creature stalks the land.* She gave herself a step's worth of distance from the rendered Mungkr. The only eye she could see of the beheaded Thai dragon was punctured and stared after her from around its erupted body. Blood and a whey-colored liquid ringed the eye socket.

Ardyce had never seen a mangled Drake.

The Wyrms had their territories and kept to them, uninterested in nearing even the boundaries of draconic habitat. They were not a species endued with speech, and their mouths were empty of teeth. They had, instead, hard gums and an acrid bile which they ejected during feeding that eroded rocks, sinew, and bone. Ardyce had seen but a handful of the sightless creatures while on sentry flights over Gled Tria, and those instances had yielded two sightings of the Wyrms as they sated hunger. In this, the Tree Crown had acquired an ill taste for those whose domain laid just beyond her home. Wyrms gnashed the fields which they feasted, and if they happened upon some other vitality of brain and heart rhythm, they sought it down in fury. Sonorous hunters, they utilized a mockery of sight by detecting vibrations, even wingbeats upon the air. With their screaming wails that made crescendo to a pitch which surpassed the ears' capacities, but that rung throughout the confines of one's skull, the eyeless ones chased down their prey, like relentless nightmares. They utilized the weight of their brawn, first, to knock the goat or deer to the ground, and next, to be a crushing momentum over the legs or over the back end of that animal. And, then, they circled their suffering meal and with great indolence. In time, they ate. It was the low, rumbled grating of the shelves in their mouth which Ardyce could not withstand. Whether earth or life, that sound of the Wyrms consuming strummed her nerves with discordancy.

"Ardyce."

The Great Aegis turned her branched head. She had not taken notice of Sasithorn, who had become rigid in surveying the open veld. *What is it?*

But, still, the question hung upon the muted air as the Mungkr's eyes grew wide. She bent suddenly in the direction of the herd of younger Drakes. *"Beneath! Take flight--!"*

And, in that instant, Ardyce saw the loam make the head of a volcano and discharge violence. Mohonia, with his full belly, twisted sideways as he fell away from the upheaval of soil. His jaws were locked in pain as one of his back legs was shorn from his body. The first arcs of his blood were descending towards the vale as Ardyce ran towards him. A wild fear and the maelstrom which is wrath thunder-clapped her being. Vocally, she shook the vaults of heaven. *"MOHONIA!!"*

Sasithorn made fervent arrival to the smaller Drakes first and aligned herself between the threat and the bewildered males, who clenched into a tight group around Mohonia's suffering. The Ngaw rose tall, nearly to the last third of her body, then bore down powerfully in place and, like the stomping of a titan, she caused the whole of the valley to reverberate. *"Not the Tree Crowns, Wyrm. Answer me the reasons of this onslaught!"*

The Wyrm flung out of the ground, screaming and writhing, and much affected by the Mungkr striking deep, blustering pitch through the soil. It, the creature, was the proportions of ancient monsters, heavy-dark in pigment, and a mouth bladed with long, clipping teeth. It was ringed with muscular scoring along the entirety of its body.

Salaris, the only one to break from the enclosure of his brothers protecting Mohonia, lost his footing in the quakes made by the Mungkr, but regained himself to dash towards a copse and strike the bole of a tree with his antlers. From the punctured wood, the tree offered sap, and Salaris gathered this with his tongue. He felt nearly thrust out of his body by Fear, and his will to remain – to help or to fight at the side of his family – grew blurred around the edges.

At the corners of his sight, he saw the sun-glint of the great Ngaw's golden head as her jade-colored body careened from right to left and back; she staved off the Wyrm's further advance towards them. With a howl, the Wyrm plunged under-earth once more, and Sasithorn urged for its life. She struck with her open maw at the ground where its body could be seen, but she could not ensnare the creature in the trammels of her jaws. Wounds were seized along the length of the Wyrm's body, but not enough to end its rampage, and the Mungkr shattered teeth where she foiled strikes. Her jaws bled.

Ardyce now was upon her herd and swept Mohonia into the coils of her tail with ardent care, bringing him against her tremendous body. He was staring into her eyes with his words repeating inside her thoughts: *Our daughter, Ardyce. Our daughter.* She saw, then, that fluid crept out the folds of his abdomen; it burned his skin, but he seemed unaware of the pain. The shell of eggs, once splintered, turn the fluid inside to mild acids, in order to assist the hatchling in breaking down the barrier to outside life. Ardyce made herself gentle to nudge the one egg from his warmth, where he had housed their unborn for twenty-nine months. The other of the two shelled young were undamaged and remained within Mohonia. Treven, the third eldest brother, helped to ease the cracked ovoid from their eldest brother to the cushioned grass. As he did, Salaris returned and applied the salve from the tree to his elder brother's cleaved limb to clot the blood and interrupt the draining of his life. Salaris was shaken, but cut reeds may howl in strong winds, though never be felled by storms, and such was his Fear brought to composure. Though not long acquainted with Time, Ardyce's family fit themselves to the crisis in quiet, due order.

Mohonia turned his gaze for Salaris and spoke to him: *Hasten home with my daughter. In time, ages from now, she will be the succeeding*

Great Aegis to our tribe, like her honorable mother. This day will deny her nothing. Salaris gained clarity at his brother's words. He was the swiftest of his siblings, no other should be nurse maid to the newest Tree Crown of their tribe.

Mohonia left the protection of his Vow and shed the halves of the shell away from the newborn, who was no larger than a foal. Though there was no way he could have known the sex beforehand, the others saw that the youth was an opulent white – a she-Drake.

Ardyce thought of the times a many she had chided her love for his wishes and insistence on bearing a daughter. With the last egg given unto him, he had professed his yearning fulfilled, and knew always the egg which concealed his dream-given, though the three of them looked precisely the same.

In his eyes now grew a doting fondness that augmented every moment he beheld the hatchling in his stare. He was quick to cleanse her of the birth-fluids and traded her off to Salaris' custody, who stole to the winds in a gleam of glass wings before Mohonia could begin to miss her. She had not stirred in all the commotion, and Mohonia knew, dead before living might she be, having been brought out her egg three months premature.

Follow after, brothers all! Ardyce charged the Wyrm who veered for her tribe-members. This Wyrm would not be ran off, though it was twice out-weighed by the Great Aegis. She swung her mantle of antlers in efforts to spear the behemoth, unnaturally fast for its magnitude, but the Wyrm clattered all its teeth at once and, as it burst past Ardyce's head, the left side of her antlers were hewn, and half the proud crown of the Great Aegis fell to the ground.

Mohonia moaned and moved towards her, blundering, as he forgot the absence of his limb. The other brothers could not look away at the kindling made of Ardyce's seventy-two years of antler growth, but she was yelling after them, and her cries made shape in their minds: *Ascend the firmament, my tribe. Ride home.* Angling her head low to the earth, Ardyce drew in a breath to the utter limits of her lungs. She minded no regrets for her fallen branches and reconfigured strategy in expeditious succession to provide rescue for the young males. The Wyrm had cut back on its own tracks and submerged into the earth once more. It could not be seen.

Mohonia pleaded with her, *No, my Vow. We are one. Let me stay with you, Ardyce!*

But, with explosive force, the Tree Crown of pearl-white scales expelled gales from her great organs and made billows of the smaller dragon's wings. They caught the skies in flight and were swept out of reach of the brawl betwixt Drakes and Wyrm.

Ardyce watched after he who possessed the whole of her loyalty. He and their unborn should now be safe, guarded by the dark of the wide sky.

Gled Tria seemed to tremble once more as the Wyrm bellowed with rage. It had been uprooted, torn out of the soil like a weed, and Ardyce gave her back to the vision of Mohonia to find that Sasithorn had seized the Wyrm in her jowls. The Mungkr was coiling herself around the length of its body, unmindful of the thorn-like bristles which pierced her skin. She meant to crush the invader, wrung between the might of her muscles, but the Wyrm thrashed as a bass out of water, and Ardyce was an instant tardy as the eyeless creature bent back perversely upon itself.

When the sea's surface is pounded by the highest waves, such was the sound which drummed in Ardyce's ears as Sasithorn's mandible broke at its hinges, forcing the Ngaw's jaws to hang slack and open; her tongue lolling over the injury. Yet, was there only a thin gasp from the throat of her friend as she fell away from the Wyrm's blow. Like a ribbon carelessly tossed, the Mungkr fell with crescent-moon curves in her body to the sward below. From her emerald scales, blood wet the glade.

That orphaned skull of the other Thai Drake, already-deceased, seemed to lay, staring in direction of Sasithorn. Again, its weeping, exploded eye seemed still wet.

Ardyce's chambered heart drew sharp contractions then, and her pupils submerged completely into the depths of her oil-spill irises as anger blazed her every emotion now. The Thai Drake laid in the grass, without motion. The Great Aegis' thoughts harkened back to the times shared with the Mungkr, and boiling rage at Sasithorn's injury compelled Ardyce forward. The Tree Crown dove for the Wyrm, and bit into its face with savagery. The mickle pressure exerted by the she-Drake's bite shattered teeth out the gums of the Wyrm. It swung round its body to her right side, but, with a thrust, the Great Aegis javelined its innards through with her antlers, and she pinned with one claw that enormity of the Wyrm. To the azure empyrean, Ardyce threw back her head and rent the anguine torso, and by tatters, it slopped to the ground before her. Its skull still in her fanged hold, she would not cease the mastication, until the head of the Wyrm suppurated in gore and brains in her mouth.

The Wyrm of night-hue relented motion and spirit. Beneath the carcass pieces of its destruction, which continued bleeding a saffron-tinted ichor, the Tree Crown could see the turquoise hide of the devoured Mungkr.

Ardyce vomited hotly from the rear reaches of her throat to rid the foulness of death from her being. With rabid panic, she surveyed her friend fallen.

Sasithorn.

Ardyce went to the prone Drake and saw now the glistening circlet once enclosed around the Mungkr's frame in three fragments, resting in her blood and the dirt. With horror, the white Drake realized the Ngaw's spine must be snapped. Her scaled hide and muscle kept her as one, but to her bones, she was two. Ardyce nuzzled her and with the gentle touch of one who arranges flowers, she determined where the backbone had given. With the panic still thrumming through her, she whispered how she would transport the Thai Drake, how Sasithorn would let time and Nature rebuild her.

But, Sasithorn was deaf to her plight. She struggled to craft her words upon the air. They came faint as the summer breeze across an open field, "Overtake your family, Great Aegis. This Wyrm—"

Find quiet, noble Mungkr. I will ferry you home and reunite with my tribe in short while. The Tree Crown gingerly took the Thai

Drake into her claws and her wingspan crowded the veld. It wasn't, yet, that any of this felt wrong, but that it felt like a dream to Ardyce, and the way one's consciousness pricks at dreamscapes, attempting to influence change or action to one's benefit. And, the failing of it, but through that anxious failure, the knowledge that wakeful reality was near, ready to undo the crowded night.

"*No.* Ardyce, leave me here." Sasithorn's breath would not catch metered rhythm; the pain rifled her through. "That Wyrm--! It is not the one who parched the glen of its verdancy! Its size!" She racked the air for breath, her lungs clawing but catching so little. Finally, she finished: "Its size matches not the crater."

As the Mungkr's voice echoed to dissipation, Ardyce gave attention to the rictus once more, and back to the corpse she had made.

Peace seemed then, to her, the finest glass. Inherently fragile. With no more effort than that to pluck a daisy, Peace, in the duration of one-quarter day, may once a valley of wildflowers be, then meet transformation by havoc to empty grass. Did it not wonder at who it was but yesterday, so deceitfully close, yet erased in a black night?

Ardyce felt Sasithorn lose consciousness in her grasp. The rest of the world was hushed in soft quietude with only the quotidian habits of the careless weather to make stir upon the draconic lands. The dale had returned to sleep, like a wild pack after blood-frenzy. It took to slumber with blood at its muzzle. The Tree Crown made cardinal priority in seeking out care for her friend; the moments to come afterwards seemed very far away. She stared at the gray hollow in the valley and the skull, not yet mourned. The trees largest of Gled Tria escaped not the leaning in the whirled winds created as the Tree Crown mounted the skies. She drew up high into the welkin to catch glimpse of her tribe's realm, yet all was wrongfully silent. There was no movement to garner clue where her Vow and his brothers may be. Droplets of Sasithorn's blood fell back to that bellicose scene of bitter revelation.

Ardyce sailed through the brume of clouds and the downcast currents to the riverfronts, where the Mungkr people grazed and made community. As she neared, a smokestack to her left climbed the heavens to stain the mounting dawn in an ashen haze.

Fear made avalanches in her heart and a sensation of ice arrested her nerves. Ardyce called below to the Thai Drake nation as she neared; she left them Sasithorn, propping her friend on the banks of Orb – yet, a part of her remained with that selfless warrior. For her prescience which turned the passe-partout on chained worlds and her martial skill, unanswerable to fear or hesitation, the Ngaw lay broken. In the history of Drakes, she and Ardyce were the first to engage in lethal combat with a Wyrm. Sasithorn had shouldered burden for two. And, only by the fortitude of the Mungkr was Ardyce's young family given means to escape the fanged adversary.

The Great Aegis returned to the heights from whence she had seen the remnants of an inferno. Below her and shrinking by distance, the Mungkr Drakes had enveloped Sasithorn and care of their Ngaw had begun.

Ardyce could guess as much that the Wyrm she sought had headed Salaris off – the blind beasts with hearing unerringly acute, were known to track birds in flight and throw themselves upwards into the skies for their bounty. By concatenation of the brothers seeking to stanchion one another, all seven of them might be ran astray before they could seek refuge in the domain of Outer Gled Tria. It would be Salaris' strategy, she knew, to alter course for the River Orb. Traversing great bodies of water was a bane to the Wyrms; they disoriented in a pandemonium of foreign sounds and, being unable to swim, they drowned.

And, yet, the River Orb – most trustworthy and venerated throughout the land – brought qualms in an instant too-soon transpiring to the Tree Crown overhead. Ardyce observed the plowed banks of the river, and upon its opposing shore, the same curdled ravaging, though the width of the Orb was well past two miles.

"Mohonia!" The Tree Crown screamed. She felt then the fire-lit shadows of doubt and their barbarous cadence that proclaimed the farce which had endowed her as Great Aegis to her kind. She

had worn deep silence to that ceremony to name the next guardian of all Tree Crowns, while another had yearned conspicuously for the duties and bearing of that coveted station. That contender had been a cerise she-Drake, of the lineage of a Tree Crown and Pyrolite crossed, and honed in the tactics of battle; she was older and stolid of character. Long had Ardyce admired her, even from her days as a hatchling, yet their people had chosen Ardyce as Great Aegis – chosen her for her kindness and compassion and exceeding physical strength. She wondered if the many could be so wrong, and if the veracity known by two – herself and the red Tree Crown – would come to reveal itself this day.

Whatsoever the truth, she wanted not her Vow, their young, his brothers, nor Sasithorn – nay, no others – to pay coin to the sun-forgotten Ferryman of the Buried Realms for her inaptitude. She wished not to see Death glut Himself of this day.

What haunts you, Wyrm, she thought unto herself, *to shift Peace out of a day? A day which threatens to become many a night in the manifestation of war.*

The trail of that interloper wove pits and channels towards The Nocturnes, and again, a flare of scorching element briefly illuminated the shadowed lands from whence the firebreathers resided. When brightness returned to dark, a frenzied jet of racing tar-colored smoke issued out of the shaded territories, and the Great Aegis had in her heart a feeling of surreal disorientation, yet of it, too, something cyclic and familiar, as when Summer impulsively becomes Autumn. Ardyce rejected the evaporation of her pools of knowledge within, which made up who she was, so that they would not condensate and cloudburst as heavy rainfall within herself. She plunged blindly into the umbra nation, wings on aim for the descent into the Southwestern reaches.

She stone-set what she knew. The Wyrms had grown weapons in their mouths, thus their minds had turned to war, and if they rested strength upon that bugle, she would answer as was her crown, that of the title *Great Aegis.*

CHAPTER 2

THE MOON and the NIGHT

He held her 300th letter to him under the bright eye of a full moon, immersed in the spiny, scented thicket of a treetop, so that he may see far – to the wall that ran between them: a fixture to demarcate human civilization, the Tiered Nations and where he resided, from the remainder of the world. That wall was known as The Merlons. It had existed as simple, meshed fencing for a number of generations, then it had been reinforced with cement and bricks the year she'd left the Nations.

"Beyond The Merlons" - that was the phrase denizens, those of the Nations, coined to name their fears of going out past that simple construction of crooked pieces and plaster that had not set well. It was what was left of the lands uninhabited by the shoe-print of humankind, and she lived there by choice, by her convictions and usually without protection between her soles and the loam of Nature. He could not say as much for himself in the Districts, the mansions, and the astroturf of the Tiered Nations.

Hadryn rested the unopened envelope in his lap. Upon their arrival, he came to this same tree with her letter enclosed in scrap fabrics and secured with twine. Pieces were sometimes sewn together to create a proper rectangle in order to enclose the pulpy paper. Paper was hard to come by, she'd told him. She preferred to save what little she had for their billets exchanged than use it for envelopes, and the people beyond The Merlons were much more inclined to invest their hours of labor in clothing for one's back, so there were always the remnants from wardrobe or sacks, once completed.

The envelope he held was coarser than usual. It was mostly composed of burlap, woven straw, and old leather. It was so prickled, so textured, that he felt the etched sensation of it along his fingers and palms even minutes after he'd rested it away from his questioning skin. Not for its lack of aesthetics did it discomfort him, but something else. Usually, as he held her reply in hand, more and more came to him that he should converse with her. But, this night, under the same moon, was not one of those nights.

He wavered in the gruff night breeze. He didn't like how her letter sat upon him. It'd come too early, only a day after the letter he'd sent. It was too light; it should be at least twice-more tied, as they usually were to constrain together the accordion of many pages containing their journaled thoughts, unbridled to one another.

Hadryn clasped between the paddings of two his fingers an end of the singular strand of twine. He pulled it, and the binding simply stared back at him, in quiet, and limply undone. The pages were not yawning open, like one trapped in couchant position, then suddenly released and stretching wide their limbs and stiffness.

He gazed at the innards of the envelope, then he began to read.

2048. 08. 228th.

To: The Orb in a flatland of Squares.

Sir Circle,

As I struck the match to set aglow the wick on my waxen night-sentry and sat at this four-posted pallet which makes parody of finer escritoires, a hasty calculation ran through my head. If I am right by it, it would seem this letter is our 300th. The effect of that cognizance created desirous in me to attach some distinguished importance or event to it, this letter, for it is an emblem of the nine years we have written our innermost thoughts and records of our deeds or misadventure to one the other. I know of no others to continue and sustain the childhood together, albeit cleaved and distanced by paternal hands and unassuming fate. Peculiar and exceptional I find this, even still, that there exists our tie and affection for each other when you and I are not only divided by the width of a nation, but by societal classes, ethnicity, and gender. Solely, the pen reveals how very much alike we are. Alas, though, to what end, but tied bundles of precious envelopes? We are a conclusion in limbo, I suppose.

In any instance, there is purpose to this missive, namely 3 in count. The first: to further our collective knowledge of curious deaths. I have investigated the body found in my village to the best of my ability, given the inadequate means and instrumentality at my avail. The body was, in fact, eaten — though there is nothing within poor Mr. Stabel's dwelling to indicate a struggle, nor did anyone hear him cry out. He was undoubtedly awake at the time of misfortune, for there was a freshly brewed pot of tea, still warm, near the body when he was found. And, now, you say there is a possible, similar death in the Nations? If you go to it and peek, I would be most fascinated as to what you may find. If, indeed, there is something to be discovered. I must not fail nor forget to mention: before we could lay to earthly rest Mr. Stabel's body, it went missing. A bird, not little, has told me he's seen murders and disappearances of the nature same. They cannot, I feel, be unrelated occurrences.

Secondly, I have something for you, and I shall send it within the folds of these pages. It is a thing I have stubbornly held onto for a long while, even though those of my village do press me to give it to another. Tell me, what do you think of it?

Of the third item: I will make you aware that this letter to you, from me, will be the last. We've penned flighted parchment to one another for so very long. It is time to make an end of it, for we are not children, lonesome for the sweetness of our past. We are matured - helped on, no doubt, by the words out of our veins, translated into ink, for one another. Yet, leagues of footfalls are what they are. You are not here; I am not there. Of each our outward dissimilarities, I recognize that none matter, save the absence created by long roads never traversed, which rest between us. You never told me why it was that you persisted living on in the Tiered Nations, even though you despise it, as I do. I suspect it is because of your mother and the care of her. Or, your military career? Anyhow. We are something more or less than ghosts to one another. I have grown away from the bitter haunts and seductive memories of myself when I was but 18 winters old. And, you, neither, are that child of 15 summers. I trust that. Thus, you will not see another written word of mine.

How to properly end these nine years as confidantes and, with it, the three years prior of when we were youths to first kiss and be each other's infatuation? Honestly, I know not how. I think it best to let it hurt, as piercingly as it will for all the time that it should. For, it will do no less.

No longer an eidolon, but, an

Oshin Rysing

By an errand runner he'd hired, they usually wrote twice a month – alternating weeks – and a letter extra once a year on their birthdays.

Hadryn shut his eyes. He questioned himself whether or not he had expected this. The answers returned to him were salted and stinging with verity.

She had always been there; she'd always been somewhere safe to rest his thoughts and a deeper expression of who he was. He realized, mistakenly, he had thought of small pieces of themselves being interwoven to one the other. Very small pieces, just threads or shreds, but perhaps, from the innermost well of themselves.

He opened his eyes. Hadryn stared at the wall.

He thumbed the pages of her letter, written front and back, but couldn't find the thing she had sent him. He looked thrice through the envelope and the leaves of words. Still, there was nothing. Hadryn sat and worried. He feared that, at the last moment, she had decided to give the thing to another, after all.

Hadryn stared out, far from himself.

On the other side of that wall encircling the city was a society free of everything for which the Nations stood. Most distinct of that life outside: pedestrians, people who still walked – feet upon the ground. Those beyond the walls were not half-bodied, as Hadryn thought of the denizens, here. He, himself, was an oddity in the Tiered Nations, to have still his legs and feet about him, those limbs warmed by racing blood. The upperclassmen though of the Nations were overwhelmingly their torsos with mounted heads. They were like worms.

And, Oshin had resisted that. It had been she who had begun that life, the "anarchy" as denizens called it, beyond the border. Oshin was the first denizen to leave the Tiered Nations. She'd fought for it. She'd fled upon her legs to land anew, unknown. He should have gone with her, yet, if he had, she would not have scribed herself in letters to him or tell of her reestablishment – to speak of the fear and grunt-labor, the rallying against the denizens who came to undo the thatched homes and new sprouts of their first crops. He felt the record of her, from her, was vital. But, she'd always wished for him there.

He'd kept himself from her. Now, she had severed their tie with nothing more than the darkness of ink.

The tree limbs around him nodded in the winds, and he unclasped the gauntlet of his right arm, rolled the letter from her to fit his forearm, then returned to place the glove. A part of him had expected this, a dreadful anticipation realized. Even without it scrawled by her hand, he felt he knew her reasons why.

Hadryn stared at The Merlons a moment longer, then dismounted the tree. He tried to bring to memory how she looked when they were but children upon the first steps of maturity, but her features were muddled, and he saw only the red birthmark she bore which ran along the left side of her neck. The pattern of it was of scattered rain clouds. In his thoughts, the color was more scarlet than he knew was true of her mark, like pain recently inflicted. Hadryn knew it to be reflection of his own regret. He ran to his dormitory at the military base. He spent the entire night writing letters in return to her. Hours and leaves of papers filled his small room and the cramped cot that was his bed.

Only once was his feverish lapse of writing broken by a distraction at his window. Like a twin to the echoes of his scrawling pencil, something outside scraped and thumped beneath the sill on the other side of the only wall to have an eye out onto the night. He sat staring for a moment. With writing bodkin still in hand, he went to the bottom lip of the wide panes and threw open the mouth of the window to lean out. Hadryn searched for anything which may have made the sound he'd heard. But, at the feet of the wall, all he saw was dirt, loose and disturbed though the rest of the yard extending from the dormitory was orderly and unbroken.

He closed the window and sat again upon his bed. Nearly without his consent, the pencil in his hand began on a fresh leaf of paper. It was his reflex to write to her. Every letter that he thought he still had time to write came from him during that night. Finally, when the sun began to wink open its rays of golden eyes, he tore to shreds every page meant for her and went to sleep.

When he awoke that afternoon, he checked to see that the parchment from her was still there in his glove. He checked to see if her words had changed. Then, he left, in a hurry.

CHAPTER 3

HADRYN ARCHIDUX: KNIGHT, RANK 3

2048. Month 8. Day 229.
Corpse recovered: 2048. Month 8. Day 227.

Last witnessed alive: 2048. Month 5. Day 122.
Otruna M. Plodd.
Tier 7. Male. Aged 47.
Residence: Parameter A45.

Hadryn Communis Archidux read from afar the window monitor projected on a pane of one-way glass, mounted as a bay window and looking in upon the autopsy room from the intake vestibule for all cadavers of Parameter A45. The enclosure was arranged as a hallway: half of it carpeted, a brightly-lit office with mobile hologram computers - monitor screens and keyboards which could be moved to walls and furniture for convenience - and the rest of it a paved, inclined driveway for emergency vehicles to back into and unload bodies. Every corner in the morgue which made a protruding edge was gouged like the rotted smile of one inclined to the pleasures of sugar without care towards proper dental hygiene. The walls were battered, tarnished roughly at waist-height, and it seemed that the wheeled gurneys were temerarious, possibly due to those steering the dead, possibly due to the burden of the dead.

The theme of the room seemed to be pastel and gold-trim. Unsightly, but perhaps, it fetched a distraction from the odors of the profession. Hadryn leaned somewhat, in his concealed compartment of the janitor's closet, to see the entirety of the victim's file. He held open the door and by a sliver of sight, observed a sheeted body being pushed upon its metal slab by two men into the autopsy room. A mortician, with clipboard, followed after them.

Otruna Plodd, the newly-deceased. He had amassed a fortune four years ago by concoction of a pill. He needed the millions in wealth to eat, like every well-respected denizen in the Tiered Nations. Plodd wanted his plates filled. The priority of his actions, once he acquired his first million-dollar profit, was to purchase a cabinet's worth of plates.

Spending money and eating money were one in the same for those of civilized society. The objective was to consume. Denizens had forgotten if there was any other way or any reason why they should not consume. Somewhere along the continuum that was *Homo sapiens sapiens,* we became verbose in wanting, unconquerable in acquiring, and lastly, presently, insatiable.

But, there were side effects. People who ate out of the hunger of greed are a people who would, inevitably, become inert. Physical weight could only tally so much before it overthrew one's frame, or frames, and equated the loss of one's volition and the footprints therewithal. It left people in a brackish mindset, where they ate still more to have, at least, the familiar pleasure of the tongue.

Thus, joy was not valued, yet sought, and no one spoke of the absurdity of it all. Plodd was a businessman, and he proclaimed the pill he had constructed gave the consumer a flare of happiness and positivity. He withheld the knowledge that the affects were for a block of minutes which a cinematic feature could outlast.

Thus, "Great Again!" – that was what Plodd called the little, red tablets -- was bought, believed, packaged, then re-packaged thrice at the ever-increasing expense to the public. When he spoke of it, he said the name of the pills over and over again, as if it were a mantra or summoning. He smiled forcefully through his teeth made of plastic each time he exclaimed "Great Again!"

Thought of in the same vein as those products that deliver a boost of energy or wakefulness, Plodd's warehouse-experiment was assumed innocuous, and the media publicity, while not clever nor catchy, had an Alice-falling-towards-Wonderland tone about it. Happiness was exotic, not because it had been fought for and robbed from history, but because it had succumbed in muted quietus millions of times with no one noticing. It was an extinction that made no sound anyone could hear, except the eventual and deafening silence of its absence. The pills were enchanting for those deprived of enchantment.

Testimonials in favor for "Great Again!" suspiciously arrived only a week after the product was released to the market, and later, it was found that the reviews – heavily touted and exploited in entertainment and even a few newsfeeds – were made by relatives and business partners of Plodd's. This dubious occurrence was noted and filed away just as quick as money changes hands between one who is wealthy to another who is equally burdened by riches and marked, also, with an uniquely rapacious disposition.

Before the end of a year had cleared, "Great Again!" sat on the countertops of half the nation and rattled out contentment and a sense of well-being many "hadn't realized they'd been yearning." More remarkable: the pills began a trend of belief that they relieved After-Meals-Melancholy, AMM, and gastric pains as well. AMM was the country's foremost concern, also referred to as one's "daily sickening." It wriggled up and flared, like an internal rash, when a splendid course of dining came to close, and napkins had been lowered as masts are, to give way to a nausea like seasickness. Denizens lied in bed with knotted bowels or served meditations on the garderobe during their "sicking periods," which is the hell that comes with the heaven of over-eating. Not resigned to merely a salubrious cure for exploits in consumption, the pill continued to gain popularity for a number of other reasons as well. A pair of twins – prosperous, grandly obese, and of the society's First Tier – were even so bold as to come forward and detail the resurrection of their sex lives with their wives. This, in a time where no one regularly had sex, set a blush upon consumers' cheeks and tripled sales.

Plodd's edacity for fame and the public's tender multiplied with each new commercial and advertisement. In each segment or photo for his product, Plodd grinned, as if the stretch of it would increase accordingly his profit income. He winced through each advertisement, lips drawn so far back to reveal gums and fifteen artificial teeth. He was not loved, just desperately needed.

Hadryn had watched the spread of Plodd's gimmick and his subsequent rabbit-hole descent into not wonders, but bankruptcy. The only inconcinnity of Plodd's development, in Hadryn's mind, was the people's endorsement of "Great Again!" from a man who, whenever witnessed in public, was forever in the midst of acrimony and all things presented to him became his anathema. But, perhaps, when one sells mirth, it is by catalyst of one's own enduring wretchedness.

Restaurants and clothing manufacturers convinced themselves they would traverse all lengths to please the man resistant to pleasure, yet by the end of their encounter with Otruna Plodd, no business solicited his return, regardless if he emptied his wallet into their profit margin. He was seen too, habitually berating his wife, and once struck her down, for all to see, outside of his favorite, most-detested dining establishment. She had fallen down the three, short steps leading to the terraced entrance of the restaurant, and when she looked up at him, he had waved her away with an air of deep regret.

She had walked home. She had walked when people no longer walked.

That was where the half-bodies came in that Hadryn couldn't help but see all around himself: the paraplegics who had all their limbs that Oshin had ran away from to reap and harvest an extinct way of living.

Denizens who lived by the coin and were substantial in moneyed affairs considered themselves analogous to royalty, and that aristocratic mentality called for "thrones." Thrones were lavish seats, motorized by whirring engines installed beneath the backrest of the throne and towards the underside of the mobile chair. They operated in every imaginable pitch to grate the sense of hearing. Thrones were wide with the maneuverability of the lowest-ranking chess piece, the pawn with its griping pace, and thrones smelled like bodies and engine oil. The odor was not quite human sweat which arose from the elaborately patterned and textured cushions that made up the seat of the chair, but it was a different wafting into the nose, the smell of breaking down something which was once alive. Be it that denizens thought in terms of their prestige and rank among others, eating and eating away their dollar, the truth which none of them cared to speak was that their gluttony would allow no other way for them to still have mobility, other than by thrones. Morbid obesity was normalized in a society which lived by the stomach.

So, Plodd's wife had been struck to the ground by his hand, then left her throne in the midst of recording cameras and bystanders to walk back from whence she'd come. Not Plodd's home, but her home before that. She had, still, a surviving mother, and the mother was not a denizen, but employed to a family of them.

Plodd had turned to the reporters gathering.

Lamentingly, Plodd explained her abstruse nature; she was "as frustrating as the common cold and just as hard to remedy." Then, Plodd dabbed at his eyes, saying that by all misfortune, her appearance compounded her mystical personality. He said, "I am apologetic for what I have done, but as you can see, gentlemen, the woman hasn't a curve to her, until I send her into a spin, as you so witnessed." The men recording his remarks, who were rich and annually forgot their own wives' birthdays, laughed and clapped Plodd on the back. Everyone else left and felt that Plodd should not have said what he had, yet following those thoughts were ones of how they would never have wealth and clout as Plodd so enjoyed.

Yet, glory is a firework and rises loftily into the sky, bursts light and color, then leaves the night appearing blacker than it looked before. Sustained use of "Great Again!" resulted in hospital appointments, brain scans, and symptoms of dementia in some as young as their mid-20's. Plodd pleaded ignorance when investigators revealed the pill to be made predominantly of fluoride and a tincture of opium – both highly-illegal. The effects of "Great Again" were placebo, the neuronal damage: a veracious reality, which drove Plodd into isolation. It is said that he fled even from his wife, that she would have remained at his side if she could only locate him, for her heart was made of forgiveness and it had been quoted of her, in reference to him, that he "never knew what he truly wanted, so he achieved everything else." In time, she re-married.

And, Otruna M. Plodd was now here.

Outside, the sun was rapt in its daily duties, touching everything, like a child in a shop prominent with porcelain and glass figurines. It left its thoughts upon all surfaces, each conjecture well-intentioned, so that when the hours turned to shades of dusk, heat was released and those figures of Earth would reflect back to the parental sun his teachings and, maybe even too, his consideration.

But, the planet had gone mute. Even the shadows were sterile.

This building, *Morgue A45*, hung like an abandoned nailhead upon a wall entirely white and void. Down the street, on either side of it, were formidable shopping complexes, kept lighted to every corner and well into early evening. The sky-seeking towers each emitted their own themed music, all the songs equally bland and composed by contract workers who bore no background nor necessarily gifts in the art of composition. For those employed to the morgue, it was preferable to submerge into the building that was partway underground and be among the silent dead, walking in and out of lights that were adequate only near the autopsy tables.

Hadryn waited, watching.

The dismal lighting was almost like curtains arranged in erratic design, and Hadryn could not see, from his place of hiding, the body. The gurney came to a stop and its contents were transported to the long countertop of the examination table. One of the men who had helped to wheel the cadaver in made a deft motion, and Hadryn caught a flicker of white sheet as he unveiled the once-living. There came a sharp clanking at this, as if someone had struck a shelf of glass vials. The other man assisting the delivery became concerned, and his voice could be heard muffled with the words indistinct, like the voices one sometimes thinks they hear while washing under the hot spray of showers, the water loud with nymphs or ghosts in their ears. The mortician was rushing from the room, and Hadryn stepped back into the shadows whilst she hurried past the cabinet he occupied to paw at the egress door with one hand – her other hand over her mouth. She brought the door open and darted down the long corridor to the toilets to vomit once more.

As the men talked between themselves, debating attendance to the mortician but noting, too, the time needed to make their last rounds, they came to decision and returned to their truck.

Hadryn entered the deserted morgue from the closet and passed the monitor screen to the room beyond. The transport vehicle was already warming and pulled out onto the road in the next moment. It was gone and had left the scene to its own cryptic silence; every four corners and their adjacent walls stood stoically, as if waiting.

Hadryn gauged the time he should have before the mortician returned, then slipped into the adjoining room with the corpse. The air was noticeably cooler in the autopsy room, like an artificial Autumn, and sharp instruments laying on the surgical tray near the body seemed to keep an aged odor to them of dried blood and stale pus. He felt the finest of his hairs prickle, and he glanced up at the lighting as it stuttered before drawing brighter the closer he came to the dissecting table.

Hadryn snapped on a pair of thin, latex gloves as he approached the corpse. He stood over what was Otruna Plodd and regarded the body with some sympathy. Plodd's success had been unusually despicable; his end reflected the same, for the cadaver was without limbs and rested half-contorted, as if still experiencing pain. The torment left the body partially raised and bones of Plodd's spine shown with their warped curvature. The static expression of the body's face was one of a bruised ego and the opposite shape of the unnatural cleft his mouth had made whenever he yelled, "Great Again!"

In his days of lucrative comfort, Plodd had been as the rest of affluent society was: corpulent, skin stretched nearly to the bounds of no longer being able to contain the excess underneath. Not to be confused with being desirable, but the mark of prestige was one's girth; being rotund meant riches adhered to one's name and the sensibility to consume all that one could. To be sated of hunger were the ways of the past. "Beyond satiation" was the only philosophy of the times now, and consumption was the new religion.

Yet, sequestration is not only an empty room, but a room made all of mirrors, and it could be that Plodd was humbled by who he saw in himself. The former-businessman and creator of the pills - which bartered memories for early dementia and receded IQ – was curiously emaciated in the face and upper torso. The bones of him made ridges and sunken gullies of his skin's topography. Otruna's belly still protruded, but not to the measure Hadryn could remember, having seen him in the news-circulatories.

Hadryn bent down to eye-level himself with the ruined stumps of the body-trunk. He circled to all portals where an arm or leg should have been and pushed aside draperies of flayed skin and hanging muscle for closer inspection. The bones, he determined, had been broken and carelessly so by blunt, crushing force; the corpse's integument ripped at the location of dismemberment. Half-kneeling on the morgue's floor, Hadryn found a lower shelf to the flatbed Plodd's body rested upon. Blanketed by a sheet, more diaphanous than not, Hadryn swept back the thin cloth. Some of the missing extremities were there, but the better count of toes and fingers were absent, and the bones resembled tree branches in Fall: mostly bare and reminiscent of more bountiful times. Hadryn replaced the coverlet. The limbs were aged past the remainder of the body and were both odorous and discolored by decay.

He thought of what Oshin had discovered of the corpse beyond The Merlons. And, here, was another person mauled for their flesh. Hadryn glanced at his right vambrace of the pair that he wore and concealed in that armor was a short dagger, as Oshin had implored him arrive to the morgue with, in the case that defensive measures were needed. But, there was only the deceased man and the monsters of him long-fled away.

Hadryn stood and spoke clearly, without the strain of having seen his first deceased person. "He's eaten." Being of the knighted order, it would prove detrimental to Hadryn's office to be caught sleuthing through unsavory lots like the district's morgue, so he began to retrace his actions, in order to erase evidence of his presence. As he did, Hadryn repeated, "He's eaten. Does it sour your gall as well? You may join the mortician in the ladies' room, if you so wish."

From out the small room, which arrayed the myriad of chemicals used by those in the trade of the dead, came Thaddius Merlone. She was dark-skinned, short-haired, and like Hadryn, of admirable height and leaned through with muscle. She belonged to the Royal Guard, Rank 9, a subsection to the military, as was Hadryn, too.

The military department of the Tiered Nations enlisted three classes of soldiers: Foot Soldiers, which presently numbered over 3,000 individuals, Knights belonging to different ranks which ascended accordingly from 1 to 12 based on one's martial skill, and Royal Guards who were the most elite class and ranked from 1 to 10. As it was, only three individuals were allowed for each level of rank.

The purpose of the military was law enforcement, or more commonly, the threat of law enforcement. Arresting thieves was the customary duty of soldiers, but much more frequently, Foot Soldiers were preoccupied with retrieval of the dead, Knights were assigned street patrol, and Royal Guards were hired by the richest denizens to protect their material wealth. Each soldier was trained in the use of weaponry, firearms included, but most carried only lightweight tasers. Violence was minimal in the Tiered Nations, and Death came quietly, usually as a cessation of the heart or the soul departing under the sickness of cancer. Violent deaths were nearly unheard of, making Plodd even more of a rarity than when he was alive.

Thaddius was swallowing with difficulty and kept her nose raised, as if to escape the body's odors or retain her breakfast. She had insisted on coming, so it was her mask now to appear equally casual about the state of the dead man.

"Yes. He's eaten. It fattens his gullet, remains even in his mouth, pr-protruding." Thaddius looked to the corners of the room, anywhere but the corpse.

Hadryn was leaning over the parted lips of the body and used his fingertips to feel along the unnatural swelling of the throat. He inserted his fingers into the mouth and pushed around things. A bit of meat peeked out the corner of Plodd's mouth. "I hadn't noticed, Thaddius. True, you are--!" Hadryn was not one to show excitement and did so only in the expression of his voice becoming louder, but it was inopportune for their situation. Thaddius struck a palm over her friend's mouth.

"Idiot."

"Genius." Hadryn pulled her hand aside to smile. "I had meant 'been eaten.' A queer coincidence it is that Plodd ate, gratifyingly so, even though his limbs were torn away and his parts themselves consumed before he perished. Imagine the struggle: arms ripped away, wrenched right from their sockets, then it appears as though the legs were next. See the variance from the arms to what is left of the thighs and calves. Days in between. It stayed there with him, that which feasted of him. Yet, blood-loss should have delivered him to death. And, pain. And, horror. How could he have withstood so much? Did Plodd survive for so very long that hunger set in? One would think the pain would not have allowed the thought of food. Thaddius?"

Thaddius was swaying now. Hadryn went to her and held her upright with one hand. She was attempting to gesture at him to pause sharing his conclusions, but to no avail. "Hadryn." She made her focus breathing. "Humans disease, are murdered, or aged 'til they become dirges. They are not eaten."

Hadryn shrugged. "Garner attention upon the right shoulder. And, here. The bone has been gnawed."

Thaddius did not look well. She kept a palm to her chest. Hadryn had his arm around her shoulders and guided her back to the room of stored chemicals. He steadied her, and she, with a hand on his chest, steadied herself – it took the both of them. Thaddius patted his arm and nodded after a spell, then Hadryn situated her precisely beneath the ceiling where a panel had been removed and took her at the hips to boost her reach.

Thaddius climbed upwards, nonplussed and almost argumentative. "'Gnawed,' you say? And, in that pedantic tone. Overwhelmingly annoying."

Hadryn leaped and crawled into the air duct, after first hitting his head. "Ow." They continued escape.

"Your proposal, then, is that Otruna Plodd, locked away in his ill-kept estate, came to end by horrors of – what? A beast? A creature?" Thaddius' voice was breaking with incredulity.

Hadryn was crawling, content with his discoveries and answered her with only an ear half-attentive. "A beast is one who was or wants to belong to society, yet was dismissed, and holds in place an acrid heart. A creature has her own cherished world, and if she imposes or wroughts havoc upon another's sphere, takes heed no more than a child which steps on a dandelion in running by."

Thaddius never enjoyed Hadryn's philosophical meanderings, but they oft seeped passed her barriers to task her learning. "A monster, then?" she ventured.

Hadryn perpended, "Yea, a being who cares not for any other life, itself not existing for living or dying, but a mechanism operating to staunch its own simple avarice. A hollow being."

Thaddius turned a number of corners, and Hadryn followed. She said, "So, an animal? Something out of chapters of dead books? What, then? A thing of fur, of claws and teeth! A thing whose locomotion is by the ends of all its limbs?"

"Even as we now are."

She kicked back at him, but he dodged, then Thaddius ceased movement abruptly, and Hadryn's face collided with her buttocks. She noticed not and was pensive. "Were they not called … 'bears?'"

Hadryn shoved his face between the corridor wall and her thigh, so she would look back at him. "You think bears were the only animals of the past, Thad?" The laughter was in his face, not bubbling out yet.

Thaddius glared, "Ever flaunting your schooling. An asshole, you are, like one after piles." Hadryn nudged her on, with the top of his head. She continued, "Your definitions. To hell with them. Something killed this man. Something by some archaic word exiled to other histories, and yet somehow here. Now. In our Tiered Nations."

"Panic is not an action, Thad, but a feeling. And, only actions accomplish the moment."

Thaddius was now muttering to herself. "All this. Tweezing at things, which are not our province. For a paramour from long ago. She and her lurid amusements. You would do well to come to close with that feverish romance of her. Though I think you have not, you should be considering ending it with her."

"In her last letter, she said she would never write me again." His voice had lessened, and for a moment, Thaddius did not recognize it.

"*How's this?*" She paused to look over her shoulder at him. "The Lady Beyond the Merlons? The Lady of Red Gorget? You jest."

Hadryn stopped crawling as well. He was silent, with his chin down, then he was decided. "I'm going to her, Thad."

Thaddius was immediately depleted of sympathy. *"You can't, you dolt! Besides, she is a lesbian."*

"She loved me once," Hadryn offered.

"She was confused."

The Knight made a face, unaccepting of her words. "Were you ever confused?"

"Never." Thaddis sighed. "But, you were children then. And, especially now, it is impossible for you to leave. You know that." Thaddius was not looking at her friend. She missed the pinch of confusion at his features. "Besides all, I do not think she is sorted in the head. It may be she takes hallucinogens."

"That is an entirely confounded statement, Thad."

"Is it? A sound mind does not go on about the things told to her by a talking 'bird'—"

"'A bird, not little, who tells me things' are her words exact." He was smiling. "It is an expression from the Past World. She receives visions, I believe."

"Or, she is lunatic." With the climate in her tone as if to make a point. "And, how does she know it is a little or not little bird when you've told me that she has never seen this informant? Or, deity. Or, mental disorder. Whatever it may be."

"He leaves behind a raven-hued feather the length of one of her arms," Hadryn answered.

"Fairy tales." Thaddius rolled her eyes, then asked, "Again, the things which this 'bird' tells her? Remind me once more."

Hadryn was silent a moment. "You are not fair to her. You condemn unusualness as if it were a disgrace. Yet, every one of us is unusual in some capacity or another. It is how we learn from one another."

Thaddius was shrewd and resumed her way down the last hall of the ceiling tunnels. "She claims the bird discovers to her supernatural crafts at the loom. Monsters slipping in from the night to claim people and leaving without a trace. Silent deaths? There are better explanations for the disappearances of denizens and military personnel over the last year's course. Yet, here we are, gallivanting through morgues on our relief days because of an imaginary character fantasized by a woman who you've not seen in nine years and know only through the scratching of ink marks. Fair enough?"

Hadryn followed after the Royal Guard. "You should never to be a novelist. Such disenchantment with life would not a page turn by the reader." He laughed.

"You are insouciant as only a fool could ever be. I wish you were not. I wish you had regard for this reality and felt the tether of it."

"You are muttering again, as is your praxis. I cannot hear you, good friend."

Thaddius had reached the labyrinth's end and leaned out to ensure no others were within sight before climbing out the dusty shaft and into the deserted garage from whence they had commenced their journey. She didn't look back at Hadryn as he joined her a moment later. Thaddius hastened out a side exit of the parking structure and, once out in the sun-stained streets, she paced to and fro for some steps before threading her way back to her vehicle. There was the dew of sweat on her brow, and she walked with the great intention of one who foresees an unfavorable week surfacing, but is resigned to it.

"Thaddius," Hadryn attempted. "You are irked by a collection of things, so I cannot tab which it now is or was."

The Royal Guard stood near her throne, thinking to herself. "Actually. You are of spirits well. Like always. Perhaps, I expected even you to be daunted by this turn of events so despicable. If you are putting up a show, I tell you, drop it. We are fast-bonded and the machismo we parry back and forth is for humor alone, but this – this has not a modicum of amusement to me, nor should it to you."

Hadryn began, "What—" But, she interrupted him.

"We are late. If we make not an appearance, they will sign the paperwork and there will be nothing we can do then to save your name from becoming another's belonging." Her changshan, a tunic fashioned in the style of a culture much-forgotten (as were all cultures dismissed and only their food delicacies remained), caught wind and made slight sounds where she was otherwise muted.

"Wait. Late for what?" Hadryn came to her side and wanted to pacify her apprehension, but the unknown had tendency to drive splinters under the nails for Thaddius Merlone.

Hadryn tried again with his friend. "Thad?"

The one belonging to the Royal Guard turned suddenly, only now recalling Hadryn's question from before. "Late for your mother's banquet, Hadryn."

Hadryn scoffed. "She has banquets every second day. Never eat at them and strive to chat even less. It is a deportment which she never pines after, trust me."

Thaddius inspected Hadryn's own changshan, leveling the high collar of it. Something changed in her demeanor, and Hadryn watched her curiously. "You are ever the jester. Pretending to be ignorant of your straits?" she asked, then sternly gripped him. "You must know. The declaration was formally telegraphed to you. From your father."

Hadryn eyed her now. "His character is such to habitually send messages threatening to 'give me away,' that I am of the 'proper age to marry.' How do you know of them, Thad?"

"You, loon!" Thaddius released him and paced with angry gesticulations, then came back to him and said with determined composure: "The banquet is to declare your betrothal."

When those with minds oriented entirely towards the discipline of logic laugh aloud, it is usually with the unbearable tension of realizing something which they have not foreseen and, by respect, consider acutely implausible. "Betrothal? Mine?'" The laughter left the district, and Hadryn turned his back to Thaddius, lost to thought.

"Your hand given, as any young maiden," Thaddius continued, grimly. "That atrocious man. He forgets to be human, inclines instead to be the fever and the ague. Slithering at your back. Hadryn? What will you do? Devise it, and I shall be at it, alongside you ever."

The Knight met his dear friend with a smile, and Thaddius reckoned, now, the morgue was a place safer than where they were destined. She watched as Hadryn climbed into her throne; she'd had it uniquely structured to accommodate two people for the reason that Hadryn did not have a vehicle. He ran or walked to wherever he needed, but it drew unwanted attention, so Thaddius had this special throne and preferred to call it a "buddy-buggy" instead – one of the few times Thaddius practiced humor.

Hadryn had taken her seat, that of the driver's. She forgot to condemn him for it and went around to the passenger side to sit. He was cranking a reel near the foot rest of the buggy and music came forth as he righted himself to look out onto the road. With small, relaxed nods of his head, Hadryn kept time with the beat of the song playing. He looked to his best friend, so Thaddius added the snap of her fingers upon one hand to the measure of the bass drum, still perplexed as she was. He spoke to her, "My thanks, Thaddius. Yet, what else to be done, but dress for the occasion?"

The buggy exhaled gray fumes, thick as cotton, and made the air around them instantaneously humid. A spoke on one wheel soundly popped out, away from the rest of the vehicle. Thaddius leaned over to secure it back in place, then Hadryn drove the buggy forward, directed towards the Archidux House, which he had only last seen two months ago.

CHAPTER 4

CYSSILINE ARCHIDUX

Cyssiline Archidux sat at her vanity mirror, scrolling through recent photos of her son in her holographic gallery. Cyssiline was the color of sugar with a face sweetly beautiful. The roundness of her features explored femininity to new depths and, so truly lovely was she, that her eyes and skin needed not adornment of artificial hues; only her lips she dabbed a glimmering lavender tint. In ringlets with ribbons, her auburn tresses fell over one shoulder, nearly negating the fact that she was 43 years aged.

"Pink Skin Cerate."

The vocally-commanded vanity shook miniature bells in acknowledgement of her command, and Cyssiline withdrew a palm-sized, circular tin from the repository chute. She twisted it open, and juniper scents skirted the air. Dipping her fingers into the wax, she brought the unction to the insides of her thighs where the skin was chaffed raw by the rubbing of her thighs against one another. Cyssiline was much overweight. She regulated her bedroom to a cold clime and had one wall of her boudoir that was an enormous fan with wood panels which churned without rest. Even then, an intolerable warmth coated her and pricked perspiration from her fair skin. She could walk a few minutes at a time, but then, she felt her lungs and throat dry out by her gasping breaths, and she would return to sitting.

"Dastardly thing." She scavenged through one of the drawers at her vanity. Dutifully, Cyssiline measured her blood sugar levels and listened to her heart and respiratory functions; she scribbled quick notes on a form with her doctor's logo in the uppermost right region. He'd asked her to be mindful of these numbers, but she recorded them without regard to trend, then threw aside the form.

Her last visit to him, she'd admitted she wanted to reduce her largeness. He had laughed most heinously, thus she blinked back tears to agree with him that she had been in a mood for joking that morning. When he had pushed his glasses up the bridge of his nose before handing her her forms, she'd glanced into his eyes to see, but there was nothing reflecting back to her that she knew to be human or a kinship to her true feelings. The doctor did not feel it was his duty to keep her alive, only to dodge death or her discomfort as often as possible, until her grave. He did the same for himself. It was why Cyssiline tended to keep her head down. She hated the not-seeing, the void of humanity in human-formed things.

She wiped some of the Pink Cerate from the doctor's form and sighed. The sunstrokes coming in through the stained panes of the nearest bedroom window colored the floor tiles they rested upon an ember-emboldened orange. Orange was said to be good for one's spirits, raised them up – or, so she was told by other denizens. She'd never felt it, the intended effect of the glowing hue, and looking around at her room, it seemed neither were her chambers much impressed by orange. The tiles made a graph of her small world, here in her bedroom. Small, in comparison to the world, yet well-respected in terms of largeness in one's house.

Her room accommodated seven sofas, at least a dozen feet from one another, and each couch was unique in colors, patterns, material, and shape with their own complimentary rugs laid down in servile manner at the feet of them. She had one divan at which to sip tea and it was nearest to the windows, another for reading, and another for napping. The largest lounge with the most embracing of cushions was where she snacked before a tall monitor to watch network dramas. The other sofas she could not now remember what she had once used them for. They collected pillows with no other function. There was one New Year's Day, after the Grand Dinners at the Gutierrez's mansions – the wealthiest denizens in the Tiered Nations – where she had watched two diners die at their plates, and subsequently, came to realization, upon returning home, that her life was little more than motorizing from one of these couches to the next, when she wasn't feasting downstairs or at someone else's banquet. And, that day had had a profound influence on her since.

Cyssiline was the only woman she knew of in her Tier to be tired of sitting. If humankind no longer stood upon its own two feet – or, rarely did, as was the case, especially for those very wealthy – and became static, dormant, handicapped, or simply legless (it was one of those descriptions, but she was not certain which one); if that was what became of human beings, then Cyssiline worried that her species could no more be classified "bipeds." And, she hadn't a word for what they all now were. This troubled her.

It made her swim.

Exercising was something most affluent neighborhoods shunned of their residents. It made one sweat and smell wild, so denizens did not partake in this antiquated habit – at least, none confessed practice of it where ears could hear. But, it had been known for years that Cyssiline swam. In fact, during banquets, she sometimes encouraged her guests to view the pool room: indoors, with flower-stenciled lights at the bottom, and a tastefully-short waterfall that made the noise of light rain, not at all like the galloping hooves of Neptune's white horses which actual waterfalls were said to sound like. The pool, in its greatness, bristled unease from visitors initially. As each guest leaned forward and peered down – very foreign, indeed, to look into something – the waters gave back to them natural reflection: rippled and never quite stagnant. They felt the threat of the liquid's kinetic potential, potentially uncontrollable, but Cyssiline explained that she swam in order to calm her biting nerves. She was one of *those*. She had tried medication, and in rare cases, it was understood that certain medicines were ineffective for certain individuals. People nodded, then, and exclaimed how wonderful the pool was. Cyssiline did not mind lying. To mitigate her nerves was not the reason for the pool. In fact, she could not swim, unless she was in a good day, filled with an adequate measure of glee. To submerge into the waters with less seemed it may dirty them.

When she was alone, with the water giving way to her strokes, pushing back up against her, and becoming a moving, almost living raiment over the whole of her body, then did she feel she had some place in her own life. To swim made her feel powerful, and she felt more a mother to her son, who was the very image of strength in a culture that invested diminutive value in such pith.

Hadryn. She had chosen the boy's name.

Hadryn had ever been a child of numinous element. He had made Cyssiline feel the sun for the first time by the way he ran and ran just to run. He was an energy like that wondrous star in their sky, and he laughed and played, until night called him to sleep. It had alarmed Cyssiline to her core, at first. Being unable to keep him within sight, once he learned to walk, she had to trust that he would return to her. This was before she had had her pool installed and learned to trust water and other momentums beyond her will. After hours gone by, and miles ran, and sign posts or whatever tall structures climbed, Hadryn always retired to their estate.

There, he ate feverishly, and Cyssiline could not dam the emotion that fell in cataracts at seeing someone eat out of ravenous hunger. He had spent the day starving, in an empty body that requested food, and he had answered not. Not until he had captured the day as he intended. His stomach was no master to his joy. Hadryn ate out of need, and when he finally did, she saw him relish his food, not just for its taste, but the way a tree drinks in solar radiance to burst forth new growth. As he quaffed his thirst, he sometimes closed his eyes in gratitude, though all he ever imbibed was unornamented water. Cyssiline had before only been acquainted with water as that liquid which their housekeeps used to wash dishes. Denizens drank wine or sugared coffees, teas, and carbonated beverages. But, Hadryn, her son, was not at all like a denizen. His meals he took the time to appreciate, too, though she could hear his stomach making the call of echoes in hollow space. Hadryn would lean down to his plate, letting the aroma of food imprint memories, and sometimes he touched his food to have another sense of it. He often said that everything was wonderful, and he always offered her something from his meal.

Cyssiline had tried to control herself in watching him eat. She didn't know why she cried, except that there was the thought that he may forget for so long his hunger and die of it. It had frightened her, in the beginning, to see a person so hungry. It felt like a disease to her, and she wanted to be rid of it, see that it never returned. So, she would bring him another helping and bid him eat more, but Hadryn never took another plate. She came to love this about him. He would smile at her from across the table, and then, when she brushed at the corners of her eyes, he knew that she wept for love of him.

Though he was the first happiness she had known, Cyssiline could not bring herself to live as Hadryn did – to eat only when the body beckoned and could not be hushed. She loved him, but others – her relatives, friends, neighbors, and peers – felt the need to call him words such as "ugly" and "ghastly." She understood better than to correct them. For, Hadryn was exceedingly lean as a youth, and as he made transition to manhood, became bulked with taut muscle. Cyssiline made gentle suggestion, then, for Hadryn to join the military, for it was understandable then to sacrifice one's genteel padding. A "strained body," as denizens called it, came with the occupation. Hadryn had reacted as though she was the bringer of all sensible solutions and agreed before she could finish her words and give her motherly smile at the end.

Once enlisted and knighted, Hadryn gave slack rein to his love for all physical discipline and hardships, delighting in fierce competition and adopting three styles of martial arts, one of which he was very poor at, yet insisted all the more to continue in its study. From the boyish age of 14, Cyssiline had kept eye on Hadryn in his career in the military. He was now ten years in knowing no other rigor, but the back-break of knighthood.

And, lo, how the Upper Tiers continued on in aspersion against Cyssiline's only child.

"Unsoft to every edge of him!"

"A man should carry the size of a mountain to him, not be like the hardness of rock or stone."

"An anorexic, I'm sure."

And, nearly every day, whether Cyssiline was in attendance to someone else's feast or in her own home, from the mouth of her husband came: "He is most abstemious!" It was the worst that could be said of a denizen, as if Hadryn had not the common sense to take as much as he could. There was always more to be had, yet her son walked away from meals. He left foods untouched. Once riches had bitten any other, the mind turned flea-infested with thoughts always of more gold coins, more food, but Hadryn was not susceptible to the bite. There were things he could have, but of them, he chose very few.

Those in the Upper Tiers spoke forever in whispers of Hadryn Archidux.

Yet, no matter one's proclivities, many stared over-long at her son. He was topped in maroon locks, and Hadryn could look over the tops of most men's heights. Complementarily bewitching, Cyssiline's child was born with heterochromatic eyes: his left being of an unnatural cerulean and violet coalescence, and the right, a pure white and ringed in tawny border.

"His genes were dropped on their heads, and he is freak and Grendelian," said Hadryn's father, as though he had put good money into something, only to be met with disaster.

Cyssiline had not before nor after drove fist to another's face, being that it was wholly unbecoming for denizens. Later, she told her husband she regretted it, but mostly so that he could tell everyone else, and she would be absolved of any accusations that she might be as contumacious as her son. Let them believe she had been under Dionysus' spell. Wine drove laughter out of the very air and pulled puppet strings towards unexpected nights, so might a wife once pummel the face of her husband.

"Miss Cyssiline, my lady. Your son and Mrs. Merlone have arrived, and the dinner course has been cued for your entrance."

She turned away from her vanity to meet the gaze of her errand-runner and housekeep: Isia Blane. He was a Native American gentleman, 58 years old, who never spoke of food or eating, yet seemed more attuned to the feats of the skies. He chronicled with his deep gaze every aimless shift of the weather. His hair was of a deep black, long and tracing down half his spine. The skin of him was weathered, as tree bark which stood always in the elements, but his eyes were young and seeking, like shards of darkened glass which both reflected and revealed, through transparency, a world separate of this. Isia was a "blue card" only the past five years of his life. It was fabled that he came from beyond the Nations, outside of The Merlons, and labored for income to assist in the ails of a sick grandchild.

Imagine one living to see their grandchildren. It was unheard of. Denizens were nearly at their life's end by the age of 40. This made Isia special in Cyssiline's eyes. She asked him what he had seen in nearly six decades of life; they were awake into the night, at times, to recount his days past. Everyone else simply wondered of Isia Blane why he had not yet died.

"Thank you, Mr. Blane." She stood from her stool and began final adjustments to her hair, then dabbed at her eyes and touched the handkerchief to her nose, visibly trembling.

"My lady." Isia went to her. "Hadryn was born as such to fray the customs and the knots of old, comfortable traditionalism. He would chuckle to see us with these pressured hearts."

Cyssiline could not stop herself, once started. "Oh, I know. However, I am his mother. When he would fall down as a child and bruise or cut himself, I would be awash in guilt for his injury, even if he was laughing at his tumble." She looked to the butler. "Isia, my husband forced me to do this. As a mother is required to host a banquet for her child's engagement. I refused. He would listen not to a word I'd said against this marriage. Will my son despise me?"

"Impossible," Isia assured her. "You chose the suitor, as was the thread alone that Mr. Archidux would permit you sew, and you chose well. Hadryn will figure out the rest."

She preened a moment longer out of nervousness, then hurried to the door, but Isia kept barricade of the entrance. Cyssiline lowered her eyes, and said, "If he is here, he must know."

Isia's gaze was tender with concern, as though she were newly-feathered and had just fallen out of the nest. He reminded her gently: "My lady has forgotten her throne."

Taken aback, she went to the motorized chair and sat to remember who she was. "You'll join us at the tables this night, Isia." She slid forward one finger over a pellucid ball at the dash of her vehicle, and it rolled forward.

Isia stepped aside to admit her passing. "Many thanks, my lady." But, he knew her husband would not allow it, and that she could give no more than the caring in the thought of her request.

He stared after her. She had hung upon the room the sighs of the juniper tree that were her trademark, and the scent was weightless and striated in modest strength, so unlike his lady's features as she navigated down the ramped path to her dining hall below.

As she glanced back at him, he nodded final encouragement to her. She permitted a smile, yet more earnest emotions stung her eyes, and these feelings she persuaded conceal themselves at the backside of a clock for some other time. Her throne edged down the long ramp, engine whirring. He watched, and her hair the color of phoenix wings disappeared as she wheeled towards the reserved clamor of people waiting to feed.

Isia knew that Hadryn was ever the lady's concern, but he could not imagine the youth blaming Cyssiline for the arranged marriage. He bent low to a grain bag he had brought with him, hoisting the heavy food sack up to the platform of his shoulders. It would be churned into meals for the banquet, and he knew it best not to be late with the provisions. Cyssiline's husband had a curious preoccupation in noticing whenever Isia was a moment overdue in completing some task or daily chore. The man was wealthy and uncouth for it. Isia hurried down the carpeted ramps to begin the meal processor, where everyone waited.

Gluttony needed company, he reminded himself.

He had done fast and hard learning here. All grounds of the Tiered Nations were unfamiliar to the soles of his feet, though he had traveled widely, and was considered something of a "nomad" and "homeless" before the young woman, Oshin Rysing, established the village which came to be known as "Beyond the Merlons." He didn't consider himself a resident of her new territory, but a regular visitor, and it wasn't because he had any disagreement with the life she'd cultivated for former-denizens. It was because he did agree with her. He was individual, by nature, and that was how he needed to be.

Yet, now, he needed the Tiered Nations. And, he saw here that the individual was miscible with all others. It seemed to be their pleasure, their protection. As long as the majority played along and became an approving coterie, it didn't seem there was anything to question. Time was eaten. One's well-being was eaten. Then, denizens ate their relationships with one another as well. He'd seen it with Cysilline and her husband; he would see more of it tonight when the son of them would be given away in front of all.

Isia's reservation was to limit himself as eyes without a voice. He'd bit the inside of his cheeks as one parent does when another parent's children act out badly. Yet, they were all children here, spoiled and unlearned and congratulating one another for it. It was as if mere numbers equated truth and validity – as if enough people, millions of them, entranced by the same thoughtless conventions meant there was no other way to live life. Each sorrowful existence was an affirmation to another. Those with any ambition seemed only to endeavor in efforts to methodically satiate, augment, then aggravate the wanting and the having.

He had loathed them when he'd arrived a year ago. Yet, in its place now was a manner of grief. Isia had not expected, nor did he want to be the living amongst the dead. A dead nation had, once, frightened him. He caught glimpses of them in their graves: denizens rutting through a miniature drawer or compartment on their thrones, usually a discreet housing for a sundry of medications. Those hard, little ovoid bodies were lifelines to ameliorate heartburn, indigestion, diarrhea, constipation, and regulate blood pressure. There was a separate interior shelf for syringes to doctor more serious complications.

But, now he walked quietly with bowed head, as if through a hospital, or a funeral service, or an empty street where there was nothing but winter all throughout.

And, he didn't eat as they did. He restricted himself to handfuls of their food at a time and scavenged their trees meant for ornamentation, finding berries and underdeveloped fruit. He could not become as they were.

He was here for a purpose – temporarily, here.

That was why he'd come, staging a beggar's plea and gratitude. It was not for his grandchild, a girl, 9 years old, whom he loved just as Cyssiline loved her Hadryn – no, that child was dead. His grandchild eaten, and Isia, solely himself, had seen that beast in a night twice-cloaked by the mists before first rain and the emerging scintilla of dawn. He had wakened that night, running, it seemed, and gathering his wits about him as he sprinted for his son and daughter-by-union's sod home. The ground was cold on his bare feet, little pebbles niggled the arches of his soles, but he was running even before the girl began to scream. In his hand, he found the bone knife he kept by his roll-out mattress. His breath came quick, but in time with his steps. He was confident he had awakened in time, his dreams dismissing him by the instinct of his body, alone.

The distance, when he came upon his grandchild, was such that he could see that she was entangled with a thing of fantastical hellishness, a brutalized arm of hers nipped away by a monster all mouth. She struggled, writhing against it, and perhaps there was little more than her face left – he could remember her eyes, at least - because he could see the creature's rangy body, extended on the ground, but none of the girl's limbs or torso. Isia yelled at the thing, but he was several seconds too far of hard running to reach the murderer in time.

Her cries reached him even now, and Isia rested the food sack, over 100 pounds, down on the ground as his memory succumbed to her, and his anguish was stirred anew. His skin flinched with a cold layer of sweat, and he swallowed stiffly as he heard in his mind her screams. He felt nauseated and coughed, but tears came out instead, for his grandchild's cries had been that night the voice of an adult woman, wailing in pain and fear. It was as if she had grown in one, terrible moment from cosseted youth to adult, matured and abraded by the trauma of a long, difficult life. She had shrieked for him to come save her.

Then, her voice was severed forever. She fell over strangely, like a sack of wheat, on her side, and then, through the mist, he saw the monster twist, and the entirety of his grandchild was gone. He arrived to that creature only in time to slit open one of its nostrils, then it slipped away and he chased it, until it disappeared into a deep burrow that went under and beyond the walls. It went into the Tiered Nations.

No one else had seen her or the beast. What was left was her arm and all the dark hairs of her head, left in locks and strewn in the place of their struggle. Other villagers and the family of her had heard the child, but could not bring themselves to believe the atrocity Isia had witnessed. He couldn't blame them for wanting to spare themselves what he had seen. He set out to the Nations by himself.

Isia steadied himself, righted his breathing. Solitary, the things one needed to do required awful valor, of the type which came with no glory or accolades. It didn't taste right to many. It molested the tongue, like medicament and bitter, herbal remedy, but for Isia, there was no other path. He re-lived the girl's suffering every night, and in his sleep, he whispered, *The hair on the ground … The Hair. … --Ground, thehairontheground.*

"Mr. Blane!" The Archidux husband called for him from somewhere out of sight.

Isia wiped at his eyes, muttering he knew not what to himself, and then, he grasped the burlap of the grain sack, remembering where he was. He checked the time, turning away the glare on the face of his watch to see that it was nearly halfway into the 6th hour of evening. The feasting would begin, and then, he would leave and have his appointment in a Parameter far from here: District 11. His income earned at the Archidux House had finally found the right hands, and a woman of District 11 knew, not of another death or eaten person, but of vast supplies of food disappearing from denizens' storehouses. Isia wagered his guess. The thing he had seen that night looked like it could eat – and would eat a goodly amount. He would find it here, root it out, then punish the creature, and he would force it to answer his questions by flaying the belly of it open.

Conjuring in his mind, the sight again of that awful brute, Isia dug his clawed hands into the burlap and thrust the burden to his shoulders. He jogged down the ramp to ground level, then paused, partway between feigned duty and memory.

He said to himself, but once: *"Her hair on the ground."*

CHAPTER 5

KATSUHIRO ISHIDA

"Son?" he tried to call down the adobe hall to a stranger. He wondered who might emerge, or if there would be only the indifference of his escaped sleep, sitting in the next room, away from him.

Beyond the walls of his home, the man tried to listen. The 11th District was the only corner in the Tiered Nations where one could acquire food in its natural form, not the cubed pellets which denizens daily consumed. It was also the only piece of land left in civilized society where one could barter, and the act of trade created a lively atmosphere. Trading was better than buying. It was uncertain what exactly one would get in return for a thing offered, and the 11th District was ordinarily loud with both the possibilities and disappointments of exchanged goods and services.

The man heard nothing outside.

The house, too, stood silent.

Katsuhiro Ishida was sick.

He was alone. Perhaps, the entire district had disappeared, too. Or, were they, the residents, each in their muted houses, separated by soundlessness?

Katsuhiro moaned. He knew there was no one to turn over in bed to and ask for the grace of care.

Katsuhiro's dark hair clung to the sides of his face with sweat. He was lean, as many of District 11 tended to be. The denizens always stared at those of this area. He could remember that much. And, he could remember he'd had a wife, a son, and a daughter. But, his wife had been gone for many days now, and he couldn't remember why. He couldn't remember his son's name. His daughter was deaf. He recollected, off-handedly, that she was also an albino.

"Son, are you there?" Had his son left home as a young man? To join the military? He tried to imagine that: packing a suitcase for his boy and seeing him off. But, the memories were sun-glared and felt like scenes he had read from books.

"Chinami?" He coughed. She wouldn't be able to hear him, but she was always home, tucked into a world of her own. A child, now a young woman, so entirely peculiar that he had always told himself she was not of him. The shame of his thoughts were like gravel and glass shards under his skin, and though he loved her, she had never been one he could understand. It was nothing that she did, nor her disability – and perhaps, only partly her albinism, but it was predominately a look in her pink-colored eyes. She was less than human, yet a little more than a god. He found her sometimes whispering into tiny burrows in the ground or cracks in the walls of their house, and he heard, always, a rejoinder to she who could not perceive sound. The sounds were thin, like whispered prayers which sought deities who lived beyond the clouds.

He strained to look over his shoulder for her. There was no one, and his head fell back as the pain in his stomach began again like an ominous turbine.

He couldn't place when this illness had begun.

The man asked his memories for Saturday or Sunday, but logic sat behind a desk and, in monotone, told him that he didn't even know what today was, so Sundays or Tuesdays or Wednesdays couldn't possibly aid him, or be for him of any meaning. So, he pleaded instead for sleep.

He fought to remember his own name, but found nothing more than lightning strikes of panic, rambling on about how none of this made sense. There were tiny footsteps of rain to say how he would be drowned soon in his own small chamber of things he just barely remembered.

The man shuddered.

He listened for a storm, yet that, too, was voiceless, like District 11.

Peering beneath the one blanket over his body, he saw that seven of his toes were missing. The blood of where they'd been was still wet. *Where have they gone?* His memory made riddles and madness between his ears. He realized he was injured and not only sick. This compounded the problem. He questioned how to walk.

He saw the battery-operated clock across the room, and he blinked through his nausea. The clock seemed to be a meter, gauging his illness and telling him how far slumber laid in the distance, out of his reach. He had gone to bed eleven hours ago with every expectation to wake, unchained from this burden, but instead, he felt caught between two realities; neither world could decide to take him. He wasn't sure if he had lost his family in that space of fevered time. The passing hours had led him tumbling further down into a constricting throat of thick, congealed breathing. His nasal passage felt like a fist withholding oxygen. He tried to breathe through the clenched fingers.

It was the 18th hour. He would need to be up, upon his two feet, in a quarter hour to be at work by the 19th stroke. That was how each day was supposed to happen. The denizen he was employed under would need to be made ready for a banquet. It didn't make sense to Katsuhiro that he had become crippled without the memory of when such a thing had happened.

Ebbing Time and that merciless clock.

He blinked heavy and slow, then attempted to counter everything inside himself. But, the smells from his dreams, acrid and souring, were permeating his skin, making his sweat fill the room with the odor of excrement and stale fear. He began to shake. It began small, like a fluttering under his skin, then his joints went slack, and the weight of his bones and muscles felt as though they laid in a heap without the structure of a skeleton. Trembling, he weakly swept back his blankets with one hand to see that he had, indeed, fouled his bed. The ordure came out the leg holes of his boxers: dark yellow with milky masses.

He was very sick. The fever was rising, climbing up his cold, wet back to submerge his hair in sweat. The shaking of his body would not stop. There was a feeling of things separating in his intestines, and through his nausea, an earnest hunger that told him he would be ripped asunder by this illness if he did not eat.

"Water."

Outside, the night had nothing to say in return. His empty, rabbit-burrow home echoed the same. From the one window in his bedroom, a street light made shapes on his walls of tree branches which found opportunity to pantomime grasping hands and arms. He wanted those darkened shadows to keep away. He imagined they grew along the wall towards him. He was panicking. In an undertow of emotions that all ran from Death, he attempted to discern where he could have contracted the seed that was burgeoning his destruction from within, outwards.

Nothing came to him, not one answer.

He felt bare and displaced by a gradual, accumulating sense of being alone, yet needing to survive. If only he could breathe without feeling as though vomit were in the way.

The man groaned as a shuddering weakness swept through his body and he felt his bowels giving up again. *"Ahhhh!"* The bed filled with hot, rancid liquid that clung to the depression his body made in the mattress. He wondered now if he was dying. A blindness was coming and going as he blinked.

If he weren't alone – if there could be someone there, anyone – he might be able to sleep and find himself returned from the half-living to the wakeful world. The world where everyone else was. *"If I weren't alone – if someone else is there – anyone – anyone – I might be able to sleep ...."* He realized too late that he had been whispering this to himself, over and over again, like a chant.

And, he knew.

He knew he sounded like the things that spoke in return to Chinami when the girl's soft words seeped into the burrows of the earth and wood of the walls.

The pain and the sickness were goblins at him again. He contorted, clawing at himself. He screamed. He felt the last of his toes torn away – next, the bones in his feet shattered - and the man began to bang his skull against the bed's headboard to try to escape out the top of himself from whatever it was that he couldn't understand was happening.

Before he lost consciousness – the frames of his vision became jarring, unnatural movement, like an old kinetoscope – and he side-glanced a figure in the doorway of his bedroom. His daughter, Chinami, stood there with her skin and hair pale like eye whites, then she became a shadow. Then, all the whiteness of his failed memories turned dark, like the expanding tenebrousness of an approaching storm.

He reached for her though she was far away.

CHAPTER 6

THE EVER-STANDING ONES

The sun broke off in mid-sentence and winked away into an enveloping void. She swallowed hard in between her racing breaths, which beat at her lungs like the oceanic waves farthest from shores.

Ardyce felt muted of all senses by the abrupt blackness that was The Nocturnes. She trembled, but could not slacken her speed. Like mold appearing on the best of her memories, something within told her she was much overdue in bringing her family home.

"Mohonia!" She continued her bass-like bellows for him and groped for any means to give her direction. Finally, like passing through wind-borne spider webs, she caught threads of warmth against her right cheek and the edges of her right wing. She had just begun to lead in that direction when beneath her a miasma of stramineous plasma came as the low tide to sweep at the sanded shore and nudged away the darkness.

"Hie to your left, Tree Crown!"

The light, pinpricked in that fourth-matter, lingered as fog over marshes. She recognized it as the curious substance which Drakes of this region could emit to allow passage for other Drakes who had not their eyes crafted for blinding darkness. The plasma, though, sapped vitality of the firebreather and was only ever used sparingly. For Ardyce's light-starved eyes, it filled her vision with the world again.

She collided into the tower-like trunk of an old Tibetan cypress tree. The sound of a thousand whip-lashings rent the air as the arms of branches splintered and dislocated. Then, the whole of the tree collapsed and groaned like a cyclops cast to the abyss. Over 400 years fell all at once and held the alabaster Tree Crown with half-shattered embrace.

Ardyce sun-flickered in and out of consciousness for a moment. As sylphs of the world's first blackness covered and uncovered her eyes, she scented her family. The warm, cotton smells of their bodies and the more tacit walnut and smoky fragrance of their hyaline flights beckoned her, and she fought for vision. Somewhere, her limbs were making more progress and gathering her enormous body.

"Salaris. I'm here." The Great Aegis rose up out of the cypress tree. Her oil-spill eyes were blank with head injury, and she disengaged clumsily from all the broken wood. "Salaris?"

Behind her, an intruder began to lope into those familiar scents she was still struggling to grasp. A brutish wafting slid into her nostrils as her sight resurfaced and the Earth gave up the view it seemed to wish to protect her from.

Here, lied Salaris.

And, Treven.

The other four brothers were there as well, and beside the six of them, a fire-breathing Drake.

The odor of a mass gutting now stained all color out of the other scents which marked the hesitant wind. The body cavities of her family laid open to the skittish flurries and the dirt. The stillness of them haunted her to her bones, and she went to each their sides to rest her cheek and forehead to that of theirs.

Ardyce bit into her deep groans. Her gullet vibrated with the lamenting that came from her throat, and she wept out of the crux of herself. She had tended, sheltered, and provided for these striplings since her betrothal to their eldest-born, being that they had no other relations - the likewise for Ardyce, herself. This had been their family, oddly creased together, but the un-aged bucks were as much her brothers as she could daydream kin of her own. She had caught Mohonia in her head anon, like the impulsive, innate ardor for a melody which speaks to every cell of thee, but the younger males, too, had brought to her lyrics of hearty fullness. They had chased out into the light her loneliest hours. Every gesture to augment their well-being, they had returned in kind, and her devoirs to Outer Gled Tria were never wanting, for they endeavored in her name. To Ardyce, the entitlement of 'Great Aegis' meant to her and her people these six youths as well.

Yet, now, they were strewn like battered dolls whose once-childish owner was dispatched to an adult world too erringly fast.

Ardyce walked through their dried blood.

It was not something one who is a protector, a shield to her people, did. She had been elected their defensive force; they had submitted to her care.

Not in thousands of possible scenarios could she have fathomed that this was what failure would mean, what it would look like. Ardyce, as she knew herself, was torn away, like old bedding.

Each of thee, like a chamber of my heart. With this horror in my eyes, the Earthly shell of me feels as Death. I renounce this diadem never meant for me and swear to you the only peace I can now grant: your brother will I safekeep 'til every sinew of mine body erodes to soil. For, if I cannot, then I've forfeited my heart by the loss of your six arete and absent, too, will be the soul of me, if Mohonia is no more. Then, let Ardyce Breckensine be despised of all the universal spheres.

Unable to attend to them more than her sparse words, the alabaster Tree Crown regretted this hasty farewell. She sought to draw memories of them, yet presently more forceful were the manner in which they had left her. In the diminished light, she was seized by the petrified curios they had become. The youngest of them was supine, chest to belly rendered, with every organ stolen and shadows settling inside him. His tail was eaten away, and his maw remained agape, as if he had screamed until he was no more. Ardyce knew he would have been the one most afraid. Hardly more than a child, he had never to be brave with his six brothers so joyously courageous in his stead. The second youngest hung from a tall tree, like an interrupted kite. He was entangled by his limbs and by a thick bough through his gullet. His jawbone held the weight of him. The Drake's rib cage had been crushed and his flights sundered of his body. The wings of him were set to sail, fully expanded, and pinned through by branches above his head. Ardyce saw black blood in his claws and traced about his mouth and chin. Born with audacity, with defiance, she knew he had fought the Wyrm. She harvested him from the tree and laid him close to his siblings. The fourth and fifth-born of the brood were twins and died together, as if huddled for an afternoon's passing under the sun. They would have looked as she had known them, but that one of them had only his upper torso remaining and the other's head had been pulled beneath ground. When Ardyce went to him and unearthed him, he was decollated.

She wept. But, the grief was not yet done with her.

Ardyce found Treven a little way's off from his brothers. She had ever known this convivial beau an enduring and impish male-coquette. Gregarious to whatever reckless end, Treven had a fair number of envious enemies, an increasing count of dear friends aplenty in every draconic region, and nearly as many suitors of either sex. He rested now in an unnatural midden of himself. There was no other color left to him besides the pink of his muscle and the dark hues of his blood which oozed from the heap of him. His carcass steamed still, for he had been stripped to pieces, swallowed, then retched back up. Ardyce was selfish. She turned away from him. This could never be Treven; she denied it.

Approaching now shy Salaris, forever reserved and much too serious, she saw that lacerations attired him from angles too many to count. He had fought the longest with the Wyrm, she guessed, and most tenaciously – not out of valor either, but she knew, from desperation. Salaris had been most attentive to Mohonia's carriage of the unborn, for he wished himself to be a sire soon as well. Lacking the mettle to proposition his love interest, Ardyce had been his messenger and arranged for their Ceremony of

Vows. Thus, Salaris belonged to that night six sunsets from now, and not this – this bleeding-out in a sight-ridden darkness. She licked his face to clean him of the gore as best she could. It was then that someone put voice to her thoughts.

"If the little one lives on – your daughter, I presume, it is because of him. He fought as never I have seen a Drake bear arms. Magnificent." The Drake still-living, one of the firebreathers, appeared to be just past the mid of his life in years, scaled in coral tones with seaweed-colored speckling. His eyes were fuscous and large-set. The body of him was, like hers, proportioned more as a mammal – a reptilian bull – than uraeus-like as was the nature of the Drakes descended from extinct Asian territories.

The only light in The Nocturnes was ebbing – the light he had emitted for her. Ardyce went to the Pyrolite quickly, apologizing through her grief for being stunned out of remembrance of his presence. He declined her self-reproach.

"I spent my last day with these whom you love, and it was good to know them in an hour most heinous. We went to combat – together. They flanked that *thing*, ominous creature, and warred with it, drove it away from myself many a time, like heroes out of legend. *I loved them in that violently-brief time.* The Tree Crown race would I leap to the donnybrook once more in defense of your kind. Alas, my intentions amounted to no more than this grotesque hirculation. *I am sorry, Tree Crown.*" He grew quiet. Each breath of his was another small obstacle as Death began to catch up to him, and Ardyce shamed away her tears.

"You gave your life for something I failed to stop," Ardyce confessed.

"*To the refuse pile with those thoughts,*" he said, stubbornly. "This is my fault. A single puncture by a single tooth, and I could stand beside your family no longer." He lost himself for a moment, blinking out of their conversation and said more to himself: "My Vow was here. He would be *so upset* if he saw this."

She saw that all but one chamber of his heart had been destroyed. The Wyrm they'd fought had bitten into the chest of him.

"Let me save you, cherished stranger." Ardyce brought a talon to her breast.

"Do not!" With such passion he cried out that it made him to cough weakly the next instant. Ardyce tried to soothe him. "Do not," he repeated. "For, now, I must issue you my most selfish plea."

"It shall be granted, I swear." She wished for him not to die. She wanted to hear his voice more. He was kinder than she could remember of most Drakes. He could stay with her; they could exchange more stories of her bereaved darlings.

"Good," he wheezed. "Good." He reached out and touched her talons. There was blood, too much of it, from the goring of his chest. It suited not his river-calm voice, and Ardyce braced a palm over his wound to attempt an end to the essence of him running like hourglass sand. He was blinking with difficulty and seemed not to notice her touch. "First, I must sting your ears with this vital recount: during the affray, that ugly, wailing, stretched mammoth caught the head of the sire – your Vow, yes? - in its mouth and screamed a piercing ululation. It burst the eardrums of that poor parent. *He's deaf. I'm sorry.*"

Ardyce fought for composure. Immediately, though it was ridiculous, she began to peer into the distant blackness for Mohonia.

The Pyrolite continued. "Unable to hear and doubly confounded by many minutes without vision as well – the firebreaths of our fight coming and going - he wandered off in search of his child. *I told my husband 'After him at once! And, take with you the moppet who hides behind the far parasol tree.'* And, that is what my husband did. Now, Tree Crown. Now." He bid her closer and she bent to him. "My own Vow: full of skull density and every ounce of dashing bravery and genuine purity of heart which comes with it, I have not been able to cease thinking of. So, my dastardly request is this: please, save my husband, my Dreyon. I have been trying to find sleep in this death, but the thought of him joining me binds me to this world. Keeps me all awake. He does not belong with the dead. Can you understand?"

Ardyce reached up and snapped clean one of her antlers. The Pyrolite made a soft, surprised noise as she did, for there was no gesture of deeper respect a Tree Crown could bestow upon another Drake. She gifted it to him. "It is promised to you. May you relish the sweetest of dreams." She nuzzled him, and he gave a chuckle, closer to death now.

"Such heartfelt people, those with branched heads. I understand to my center why the Tianlong urge us to safeguard your delicate numbers. A parting token then: let me be your lantern for as far as my gratitude reaches." And, he expelled all breath, emitting again that plasma – this time, in a thin stream which elongated into the far distance - for which she could see by, and Ardyce watched his eyes fall closed.

She called to him, but he did not respond. She sought to gently nudge him out of Death's grasp, but he seemed to sleep, as if trusting wholly in her promise given to him. Ardyce wished to hold him awhile longer, but the light he had created with the last of himself would not keep indefinitely, this she knew.

The Tree Crown rose and flew by his luminous guidance, tracing that glowing thread, deep into The Nocturnes. She was forced to put behind her those who had imbued her days with the deepest ambrosia of happiness her life had known.

She knew they were cold, and that it would no longer be her nights to draw them in close and blanket them in her wingspan.

The plasma, rich and thick, coiled and un-coiled as the light therein glinted and made accessory of every estival hue. It illuminated a trifle, dozen feet on either side of it, but by it, Ardyce could see that she tracked the course true of which her Vow must have gone before. Unnatural trenches gouged the land where the leprous Wyrm had made its pursuit, and they followed specks of fallen blood that smelled of Mohonia, casting Ardyce to the depths of aberrant intentions for when she would be upon the Wyrm.

She could still scent on the trail of that fourth matter the Pyrolite Drake, who had come to know her precious brood as she had never known. A shred of her was sick with relief and self-loathing of herself for not having to carve at her psyche the knowledge of them as desperate warriors. Disparaged by waiting Death, who had Time substantial to claim them, this Wyrm – the earth-fallowing hellion – had persuaded the Reaper to bend their lives into an early Winter. It, that Wyrm, put the snow in their bones, and they were chivvied out the homes of their bodies. For that, she would waste the Wyrm to annihilation, bit by bit.

She raced on, and the illumination she traced grew timid. The plasma, once swollen and arching when first emitted, was now thinning. In faded sight, the trail offered her an unwitting yield. Ground into the soil, thin fragments with freckles so familiar slowed her endeavor. Ardyce left flight to walk towards the pieces so thoughtlessly discarded. She peered at them.

They were the shattered disunity of eggshells.

She went from one deconstructed egg to the next. At the close of their destruction, she saw a small face. Extraordinary in the likeness to Mohonia's beauty, the hatchling differed only in miniature size and that there were no antlers, only peach-fuzzed nubs to crown his head.

She tarried not in that presence. She didn't want to think of what their names should have been.

Away, on her wings, Ardyce let any motherly-gentleness fall away.

She quelled her hatred and fed the coal of it to her burning velocity, 'til an ache fierce and demanding dam-burst through her veins. As she flew, the cold of The Nocturnes swept in against her with the likeness of an elemental deity seeking to bully her course astray, but Ardyce was fed by fire. Her mind had narrowed to scythes. Of her thoughts, no longer were there mores or the leniency to compassion parley.

No. She would have death for death.

And, the love in her turned hideous.

In her storm-swept flight, she passed the trees of that midnight realm, and they, with so many arms outstretched and fingers in the wind, perceived her bellicose wrath. They shed and withered.

The leaves and berry-like buds dashed up into the welkin by the force of her celerity, and the trees made themselves frail.

Ardyce gritted her teeth at this. She could see them, even by the faint light. And, as she knew the meaning of the trees, she felt the first leaf emerge upon one segment of her antlers. It awakened green and of perfect symmetry. Her head, heavy-tusked, she tossed in refusal of the actions of the ancient, silent sentries. Yet, within moments, each their boughs of leaves and branches that had atrophied in her passing, burgeoned upon her brow in full bounty. The side of antlers she had had cleaved in the battle with the first Wyrm manifested in fresh rebirth, ripe with matured size and much-weighted.

Ardyce roared in fury. She was grounded, mercilessly, by the new weight of her antlers, and, chin leading, she was rushed into the dirt. The soil flew up all around her massive frame. With cries of rage, the she-Drake, tremendous in her tonnage of strength, lifted a forest with her mickle neck. She may have trembled, but it restrained her not from lashing talons out at those rooted cousins within her reach.

She tore them up out of their homes, the trees which wished to cease her hateful flight. Their roots were suddenly exposed to the winds, and their trunks laid to ruins. Ardyce screamed at the Ever-Standing Ones, "*Leave me!! I am of you no more! Stay, in your sanctuary of foundational Earth – remain rooted, not swept or drowned in the tides of momentum. But, I! I must be upon this chessboard, strategizing checkered tiles to move into and out of whiteness and darkness! And, with me, my loved ones. With flesh that bleeds and bodies razed by enemy hunger, they were lost in the blackness. Thus, to the hands of antipathy with your forbearance, your benevolence! Do away with your sagacity! Wisdom ransoms not one life!*" She bared the land before her. As the roots upturned and grew sick in the eyes of the firmament, she ran from them and from herself, for never existed there a Tree Crown Drake who would commit intentional harm to her elders as she had.

The plasma, and its glow, failed. She was again blind. And, because she would author no vision of her actions now, the Great

Aegis threw down her branched diadem. Upon the floors of Earth and rung through the halls and up to open space, she crushed the new formations with heart-consumed rancor. Blood burst from that deforestation she wrought, and shed of that weight, she would have shot again through the dark, but from a distance, she caught sight of a plume of flames with hurled direction.

Ardyce drove at that luminance.

In that burst of sight, she saw a Wyrm – flesh-colored, overwhelming in the hulk of its body, and its head that had a snout made of bone. With skin attached to that skeletal maw, it seemed to have an impression of a face, the eyes were much elongated, bloodshot, and roaming without conscious means.

The Wyrm caught fire just behind the jawbone and needled was its cry. It thrashed with the pain. Aloft, in the air, was he who had administered the attack: a Firecraw of unusual coloration. He was silver-scaled like fish who acrobat into the daylight to gleam their arched bodies. Upon his back were cervine plates, which she knew their warrior class to develop for armory. His eyes were as all firebreathing-Drakes were who resided in this obsidian domain: over-large in the absence of light, yet receded far back when there was the presence of any soft brilliance. When the eyes retracted, firebreathers wore skull-faces, which unnerved or aroused other dragons, there being no mid-ground in regards to their eyes. Ardyce watched him, so fleet of foot in the gale forces. As he twisted away from his adversity or dove sharply, he reached to his backside to brace a small figure close to his person, so that she would not fall away from him.

The Tree Crown lost sight of them as the Wyrm rolled into the marl and extinguished that burning of its skin. In the eyeless night, she heard the gnarr of the haunted beast and with it a short scream. A tree collapsed with finale, and Ardyce meant to rush it, but another sunburst of fire came again. This the Wyrm evaded, but it caught aflame a tree of nearness, and by that burning torch, she saw the hatchling clung to the back of the Firecraw.

An hour known to this world, no more, yet still the newborn erupted a hiss and cry at the Wyrm in answer to that soil-destroyer's piercing bawl. She was entirely white of body. The antlers belonging to her were already twice-tiered, and upon her back, rested at the peaks of her shoulder bones, were blunt outgrowths – her wings had not developed. Ardyce realized it must be for that untimely rupture of her egg; her daughter had been stunted.

But, she was here. She lived.

CHAPTER 7

PROFESSOR GRO

The House of Archidux was, in itself, a perfect symptom of a greater disease. Where the fulcrum of the Tiered Nation was a dependency on technological advancement, particularly in the fields of locomotion and food production, the Archidux estate mimicked this by being entirely erected in metals and strong plastics – the hallmarks of human convenience. Its architecture had the intention of a castle, but there were odd, oblate modules composed of plastic and built into the mid-sections of turrets, towers, and the central keep. If ever Hadryn could imagine medieval history sick with dishonor and pustules breaking out with that illness, it would be the home where he grew up. What bothered him most was that it didn't look aged in the least bit, as castles were when they'd long been stages for fairy tales. The estate was always immaculately-kept. It was very much like a wall-mounted sword, decorative and a replica of historical glory.

Inside, the grooved steel walls and high ceilings released all warmth. This pleased every denizen who was guest to the House of Archidux, for a home where one could see their own breath as they spoke was fashionable. Sweating was ever a social nuisance and cool skin kept one from feeling languid or breathless.

The halls, archways, and rooms were built wide and sprawling to allow the navigation of dozens of thrones at a time. Doors were, here, antiquated for the sole reason that they tended only to be an obstruction to thrones entering, exiting, or turning corners. Only Hadryn's mother insisted on a door to her bed chambers. Everywhere else, the rooms were barely distinguishable from one another. They tended to open as long gullets through the length of the house.

There was not art on the walls and what color there was ran a terse palette with no more complexity than that of a grayscale. Hadryn's father though, who customized the mansion, grew indignant at anyone who implied this. He was convinced that there existed blues and "forest greens," though Hadryn was certain his father had never seen a tree before. The man seemed oblivious to aesthetics. Every light source could only be considered that, and not a "lamp" or "chandelier" or "wall sconce." The modular tables and counters, located in each room and great hall, were functional, yet nearly comical in their efficiency. When the guests gathered for a banquet and sat in their designated place at the oval Feast Table, they looked to Hadryn like toddlers in highchairs. A tray, crescent-shaped, was brought in towards the belly of the diner, and carved into that tray were shallow shapes to distinguish where one's hors d'oeuvres should reside, and likewise, their wine glass, Courses 1 through 6, and dessert plate with an adjoining groove for a tea or coffee cup.

Constructed into the center of the table was a stacked machine; retractable chutes made octopus arms from the bulk of it and carouseled along the mid-section – indeed, it even played music once it was set to motion. The machine was called The Chef[3]. This was the pride and the darling of any denizen's home. No easier means existed on how to look upon a neighbor, than to judge her or him by which model of Chef fed them. With a voice in decimals like tractors hauling debris from cleared lands, The Chef[3] permitted no others speak as it worked. It was the dominance of the evening, and its vents sighed with labor as it utilized the pelleted food inputted, usually by the housekeep or errand-runner, to 3-D print cubes of food.

A cube of food.

A box. Humankind had a long history with the shape; there could not be a more comforting construction than the box. Whether holding the array of human whims and trinkets, or being the dice rolled for games, or as the pedestal for revered statues and marbled figures, or the packaging of food and various product, the box was much utilized. Multitudes of paper documentations asked people to check boxes about who they were and what they needed. "Check the box that applies to you." Humans loved four corners, six sides, and just enough room to fit a fraction of themselves.

Thus, food became cubed. Of course, there was variation. Who wouldn't expect to tire, at times, of so many cubes? Food dyes were sometimes added, and to outlandish effect. Neon cake cubes and pastel, scrambled eggs of smaller cubes never failed to please guests. Some cubes were encased in a sausage casing or a clear, vegetable gel; these cubes could be split open to reveal custards inside or any delightful sauce or cream. The Chef[3] was upgraded yearly with new features, new gimmicks – lights could be added or the music it played changed. They served no function other than to present a newness. The cubes, though, were ever the same which the machine produced. Recipes varied annually, yet lies tend to develop all the same shape, no matter how we label them individually.

But, the cubes were why everyone gathered. The rich spoke of very little else than what they would next ingest and where to attain the next dining. Their schedules were oriented around consuming and doing so in the presence of others.

"6:45 post-meridian! Set The Chef for hor d'oeuvres and the wine--! Pour each glass with the label facing the guest." Mr. Archidux felt the need to yell to his employed staff though they were instructed days in advance for each banquet. He made eye contact with none of them and left in a motorized whine upon his throne, headed for the dining hall.

Hadryn and Thaddius entered the House of Archidux through an alcove that recessed to a brief archway and led to a door once used only by the housekeeps and runners of the estate. It was now obsolete, and the pair of them journeyed through in casual custom, as they had since their youth together.

Hadryn and Thaddius walked the narrow hall, and they were properly-attired, by their standards and intentions, having not disrobed of their military uniforms for dining-robes. "To do war," they had said at the same instant and laughed.

Between the two of them, they traded to and fro a graphic novel, one reading a page, then giving to the other the book to read of the same page. Thaddius, however, left the book on a wall-shelf as they passed through the door. To this Hadryn nearly objected, but was stopped by his friend's tacit demeanor.

Hadryn stretched his muscles and sighed. "How very difficult you've made this guessing game, Thaddius. I've one or two guesses left, then I shall be stranded on the ait. Why this brooding silence? It can't be whether to send Plodd's former-wife, now-unknowing-widow cypress and marigolds or snapdragons and hydrangeas – of course, we'd send the latter! Perhaps, you worry how to tell Mrs. Merlone what we've done today." He pretended he was not soon to be wedded off, and Thaddius was his perfect distraction, especially, he knew, at the mention of the Royal Guard's spouse.

"Idiot!" Thaddius pulled at one of the earrings on Hadryn's right ear, until he winced.

"Enigma." Hadryn rubbed at his earlobe, once it was returned to him.

"Last would be my thought to tell LeShawn of our gruesome excursions through the morgue!" Thaddius began to speak fast, a barometer of how quickly she knew the current of events would unfold. "She is royalty; I, her guard. It would be her obligation to alert my Command that one of their Rank 9's donned the cloak of a common thief and snuck into – of all things – a house of the freshly-departed to poke at – of all people! – the body of Otruna

Plodd. Then, would they need to know how LeShawn came to know what I had done. Well, I am her guard. Yet, upon the media's further investigation: I am her wife. And, like trick-or-treat candies thrown into the pails of children, she would be devoured on the spot. The noble House of Gutierrez, Tier 5, the youngest of their succeeding generation and (we should not refrain from honesty now) their most beautiful of cousins married to a guard which – no less! – is a union outside of endogamy, a union betwixt those owning of the same likes of genitals!"

"Thaddius, everyone knows of your marriage to LeShawn. She has your last name."

"How could anyone know! We acquired our permits for a homosexual, bi-racial marriage under the most discreet means. And though, she is a 'Merlone' on paper, the Nations still know her as a Gutierrez. Furthermore, the public would come to ask why I went to examine Plodd's body and who I was with! Ah, then the Big Top arrives. After 10 years of quiet, you would be chum-baited again to the seas of gossipmongers and all fish of exploitation. This arranged marriage helps nothing, in tow. People have not risen high enough to resist those stories, Hadryn. They are vastly ignorant still. And, by 'vastly ignorant,' I mean 'completely shitty.'"

Hadryn smiled and admired his closest friend. "Paranoia for other people's sake is a big heart, my friend." He rough-housed with her. "But, you needn't gray your hairs over us. LeShawn tells all ears who would listen that you are hers and that you are above all Earthly wonders, with kitten-smitten eyes, and so on and so forth. So, I assure you, your marital status is well-known. And, I am no longer that child made weak by how 'bizarre' others saw me." Hadryn drew his friend close. "Besides, why this ever-fantasizing of the public sphere, which belongs to no one, when you've your own private globe replete with a wife who adores you and a best friend who is ever the idiot to your better qualities?"

Thaddius became quiet, so quiet that the insides of her shown to Hadryn. The way her face carried those tiny, familiar creases and tension at certain planes nearest her eyes and mouth made her skin seem pellucid. He liked her this way, except that she was only ever so when she was wanting the past to run far from herself. In another breath, she regained her color and the deep hue of her armor returned. "I never asked you. Then, a decade went by like a corn snake shedding its skin – so slow, but all in one day." She looked to Hadryn. "When your father told the masses what would become of you, and everyone who had a public platform spoke of you, saying sometimes the most horrid things," Thaddius hesitated, "What did you feel?" She was, also, honest: "I could not fathom what you have endured. The denizens do eat and gossip no less. LeShawn and I, thankfully, married in private, and her father's name of Gutierrez restricted most of the media, like a restraining order. Even now, I don't believe one reporter knows my face – just a name and that LeShawn is 'unfavorably' tied."

Their boots trod the vinyl flooring which was blotched and gray, in a mimicry of stone, so that it should seem in accord with this pretense of a castle. The walls they walked by were wallpapered with the imagery of ashlar, and the recessed lighting from the high ceilings put a sheen to every boundary. Hadryn shrugged. It brought confusion to Thaddius' face, and she wondered if she shouldn't have asked. A wending quiet passed between them, not uncomfortable. It was the muted thoughts of those, closely bound, when they stand with one foot in their own world, and the other in that of their companion's – out of concern, out of sympathy.

Hadryn came to an oriel window, strangely set at the first level, instead of located at an upper floor as was once the tradition, when fortresses were long-ago built. The Knight leaned out towards the night. He peered upwards, and his eyes, particularly the one like kaolin, became an aureole surrounding the pupils of his eyes in the evening glow of the moon and her star-populace. Thaddius watched him for a moment, suddenly aware of how she had never noticed the sky, or subconsciously assumed it could not be seen from the Tiered Nations. She edged forward to join him.

There it was: the sky in dark, oceanic hues. Hadryn was undoing the clasps of one of his gauntlets. When he removed it, a half-curled paper creased at the midpoint, rested on his arm. He handed it to her.

"This is the only thing which has hurt me."

Thaddius took it and looked the paper over. She sighed, "The parting letter from that girl." Thaddius began, "This—" She sighed again, burdened and annoyed. "Why do you mellow for her? You have not seen her for many years. She may look like a troll's foot."

Hadryn laughed silently, mostly a smile, shaking his head at Thaddius' words.

The Royal Guard returned the letter to Hadryn, and he tucked it away, this time in his robe upon his chest. She clapped him on the back. "Is this not a fronted chest-thumping? Or, do you truly not bear the eschar from the public slandering?"

He answered, "There were lenses without eyes and flashes without lightning and questions as if, in asking, I would steer back upon myself and abandon the fracas I had become. Yet, that was all. I emerged a man and a knight. That rather bored everyone." He smiled. "Will you tell me now what troubles you?"

She had listened to his words with care, but made a face at his question. "The obvious, idiot."

"Where we'll put the cubes of food we pretend to eat?"

Thaddius whispered harshly, pulling Hadryn down to her level. "That you may be wedded to a stinky, old man, and that we, being military, shall have to hunt the thing which ate Plodd!" She released him. "Yet, you will not be a Knight much longer. Undoubtedly, the Nations you will leave, thus escaping the name and bed of that unknown man, who sits, even now, at the dining table, waiting to be served your freedom." Thaddius scowled, and Hadryn walked close beside her, their arms at their sides, leaned into one another. "If only this were like the times before. More people had love, and marriage came from it, like the emergence of a third being. As LeShawn and I have. Additionally, I believe they had animal policemen and women for when the beasts roved the streets." Because, she didn't want to have to ask, she waited before asking. "You will be leaving, won't you?"

Hadryn nodded, then said, "They were called 'animal control,' Thad." They made their way deeper into the castle. He thought of the 'stinky, old man' with whom he might now be engaged. His father would choose no less for him.

Thaddius continued, "Yes, that. And, we've no training for beasts. Our weaponry is nothing more than a paralysis-inducer, which takes 17 seconds to fell a human. Will it even illicit a response on a savage mind?" The Royal Guard was silent for missing her best friend already, knowing he would need to make a play soon for his independency. Perhaps, tomorrow or the following day. She vowed she would see him away.

"So, you are worried something will eat you, Thaddius?" He seemed unconcerned, and she often wondered of him what he believed: that nothing could be of truly fantastic nature, or if everything was of fantastic nature, and he was accepting of it all.

"It ate a human being, Hadryn. Why shouldn't I be concerned?"

"Hunger urges one to eat. That is all. The stomach is our warlord. It terrorizes the rest of the body with its incoherent demands. Yet, the ruler of us is the one who sits at the very crown of us, and each our minds govern the violence which shall be wrought."

They were upon the lobby now, which used to be a ballroom, and a few clusters of chatty guests loitered. In the Tiered Nations, denizens were expected to be caparisoned in stately robes from waking moment unto sleep. Habiliments were no more designed for rest or casual affairs, and this being a celebration of engagement, guests had arrived in stroboscopic hues and bijoux. The hair of the women was done up high, and the men vested tightly, despite the heat it inspired. They wheeled about in their thrones, feet dangling to note their footwear, equally elaborate and adorned.

As the two soldiers descended into the lobby, Hadryn's head of maroon arrested conversations, and he was recognized as the, supposed and traditionally, honored guest. Yet, no one dared congratulate the betrothed, as they had the daughters of their neighbors, or acquaintances, or family. Hadryn and Thaddius both ignored the staring and the fingers, supposed to be subtle, that drifted in their direction, then away again. Rather straight-faced, Thaddius bowed very gentlemanly to those who met their gaze and likewise, Hadryn offered his best curtsy. To one another though, Thaddius curtsied to Hadryn, and Hadryn made a deep bow to her. The denizens, confused, edged closer to the walls, even if the walls were far from where they stood. They were here for the meal and the spectacle. All else would have to be endured.

"What is our strategy to deal with your father?" Thaddius continued, not yet through with their discussion. She thought she might be able to speak reason to the Knight. "Also, I don't want to be eaten. I don't want to see a thing that would eat a human."

"Dogs could eat us. Or, ravens. And, mosquitos take a little blood, but never ask permission."

At their backs, Thaddius and Hadryn caught a snippet of one pairs' conversation before egressing the lobby:

"He is an anorexic, I believe."

"Anorex? What business is that?"

"Oh, you simple ninny. An anorexic. People with a phobia of food. They resist cubed food, believe it to be evil and diseased, which is *so very backwards*. Food is food, after all."

"Yes, food. The taste of it. And, if it is there, why shan't one eat – indeed, eat plenty, I'd say!"

"Agreed, my friend. It is only as nature intended that we eat. Why refrain or guard what one consumes, such as that fool carries on?"

Pity seemed to touch the other man. "It is remarkable. How do you suppose he survives?"

"I've not one idea how. I must admit, I don't know if he even should – begging one's pardon for my bluntness. But, to live afraid of eating. I can't fathom it. He, and those of his thought, think of our food pellets as 'polluted.'" He sweated lightly, being that a pain had begun in his bowels, but it had been there, intermittently, since this morning. He continued, "Even the seeds sprouting in our hydrophonic gardens an anorexic will believe are modified and devilish. Anorexics, like him – like them both, that woman as well - waste away; they are living skeletons. I should guess they consume nothing, and wait simply for the rain to fall, only then opening their mouths." He shook his head with seeming intelligence. "Not I, though. I *will* have my food. For, food is meant to be eaten."

And, they in their knowledgeable exchange, regurgitating the popular opinion, did not take note of Hadryn nor Thaddius, until the Knight and the Royal Guard had come to rest their folded arms and chins upon the back rest of either the guests' thrones.

"He is right, you understand?" Thaddius told Hadryn.

The pair of them in the thrones were flustered, attempting to look behind themselves, but it was difficult for either of them to turn back very far.

"This one or that one?" Hadryn asked, pointing from one to the other of the denizens.

The man of lesser confidence stuttered, "M-Mrs. Merlone. Sir Hadryn."

"Food," Thaddius mused, *"is* meant to be eaten. However, gentlemen, there is a somber tale I must scar thy mind with, a tale in the vein of that thought."

Hadryn alerted – or played the part so. "Oh, Royal Guard, good Merlone. Refrain from this tale." He looked to the older men, whispering, *"I have heard it. It stains thy dreams at night."*

The denizen, more pompous of the two, said, "Away with your prankster youth. I care not that you overheard our discussion."

Thaddius was already gone, trekking through the story she had fabricated. "'*Food is for eating,*' thought he, who was strong, brave, powerful... He is the protagonist of the story, you see. Yet, he is also hideous and *teethed,* and no human knows exactly what he is. He is giant in form with *claws* and a hide of thick, dark fur. Whenever he fights the enemy-evil, he soon becomes *hungered* and the pangs of it twist him through. *So, he eats.* And, what he eats is what is tiny and helpless to him. He plucks them from the ground as they run, and they have two hands, two feet, clothes, and manicured hair atop their heads. They are us, human beings. But, to him: just morsels. Thus, it is, gentlemen, that *what* is food depends upon *who* one is. If I were this creature, I know I would choose the fattest, softest meats to go *pop* between my teeth."

Hadryn feigned being appalled rather well. "For shame, Thaddius. You are forgetful of the saying. How does it go?"

"I know no sayings, if I am this beast with the cud of humans in my jaws." Unerringly, she was matter of fact.

"'You are what you eat,'" Hadryn quoted. "And, the stink of it will linger on thy breath." He waved an admonishing finger at her. She nodded and went to him where they joined each an arm over the other's shoulders. They sauntered off together. "Be, instead, a carful, discerning monster, Thaddius. 'Quality over quantity,' that is another motto."

At their backs, the denizen with the bigger mouth, the bigger appetite, slammed a fist on the arm rest of his vehicle and yelled, "This marriage will do you good, boy! It will tame you. It will see you domesticated."

The guests of the lobby chorused like a string of birds through a row of trees, startled. But, they would have been startled by any exchange Hadryn had made with that of a denizen. Gradually, there were the final wing-flaps of lips snapping their expert opinions, and one of the helps had witnessed the scene and hurriedly sent out waiters with wine and appetizers.

"That will be the last you must hear of *that*," Thaddius groaned.

Hadryn considered, "I would not think so. For, there will be the times I will, again, walk the streets of the Tiered Nations. How else will I come to stay at yours and LeShawn's house?"

"Oh, inviting yourself over already?"

"I am, for I will be godfather to the child you and LeShawn may someday have."

"I do not recall ever having asked you, Hadryn." But, she was relieved to think of him returning, though he was not yet gone.

"Ask Oshin to accompany you, so that we may make her family, as well."

Hadryn laughed. "I can't, Thad. There is nothing saying she will even consider me a romance." He fidgeted, attempting to seem logical and possessed of himself. "I imagine she has dozens of suitors. Women."

Thaddius was exasperated and turned to her closest friend. "What have I been trying to say to you? Lesbian. I should think I am a competent judge in that. You *could* court a heterosexual woman."

"No," Hadryn rubbed the hairs along his chin, thinking. "Well, it's because--..."

"True," Thaddius agreed. She mused, "But, Oshin is not what I had in mind for you. She, literally, holds gruesome things under a little microscope."

Hadryn was wooed. "She made that herself." Then, he explained. "It is to examine the body they've found outside The Merlons: eaten, like the one we've just come from."

"That is her influence upon you: picking at corpses. Highly unattractive."

"The manner of deaths are rare, you agree. I know it intrigues you as well."

Thaddius was quiet a moment. "No. That could not be the sort I had in mind for you."

Hadryn wore a smile, big on his face. "I believe I love her."

Thaddius scolded, "Do not speak like the little mermaid out of water." She paused, boots clicking the flooring. "Hadryn. Hold a moment."

She had keen-eyed one of the guests, and Hadryn attempted to trace her line of sight. Whoever it was, that attendee was somewhere just outside the half-mouth archway, which led to the feasting hall. It was a considerable distance from where they now stood, and denizens in their vehicles passed as slow obstructions. They were like pasture animals, motivated to movement only by the promise of another mouthful.

The servers had appeared, one by one, in bright orange robes like poppy flowers, and each of them wheeled a silver cart, laden with petite dishes. Arriving with those polished carts and courteous attendants was music. The entrance of stringed instruments seeped from an expensive intercom system which threaded through the halls of the Archidux estate. The music was classical and stripped of its body and color: the higher notes were indistinct and the lower tones muffled by static. It did not, however, affect the guests' desires for the foods. It did not affect any of them at all.

The appetizers smelled of either oil or sugar. Some of them even had edible tinsel or pickling, and the denizens could sometimes be hurried by their tongues. A sudden rasp or wheeze from their throne, and a server's calves might be struck by the low, curved nose of the motorized chair, being that the guests were excited over the dish to be handed them. The hirelings bore the infliction of bruises with mouthed, not voiced, swearings. They smiled, though, when the denizens bothered to look up at them from their seated positions.

There was but one man bypassing the carts and clusters of thrones.

Thaddius pointed him out to Hadryn. "That gentleman beckons you. Might he be the professor you've been ranting about?" She crossed her arms at this, but looked intrigued.

The man was upon them as Hadryn turned to him. "My boy, it was my ardent hope to see you again. Not like this though. Not for an ugly reason. But, I trust you shall conduct as ever the recusant and show all those here a thing or two." He laughed, then said, "I've something for you." He offered a hand to Thaddius. "And, my estimation names you 'Mrs. Merlone.' A deep pleasure to make the acquaintance of Hadryn's sworn sister. I am Professor Gro."

Thaddius glanced at Hadryn, for he did not often refer to her as such, but it always made her glad of heart to hear it. "Likewise, Professor Gro." She shook his hand, and Hadryn was all smiles.

Hadryn grasped the Professor's arm in brief affection. "An early return from your trip? This bodes well."

Professor Gro nodded and drew them both by a hand each, very close to his throne. His hair and the beard of him were far-reaching, like capes and sails; they were all crisscrossed in yin and yang colors. A pair of rimless glasses gave the impression of him looking out as if from windows. Down his back, the hair was full like cloud bundles and bound solely by one tie. He was richly dark of skin, and it seemed one could not stand very near to him, for his midsection kept all others at a distance; his head felt very far away. Yet, Hadryn knew this to be a farce. Once, while at the Professor's home, the older gentleman had greeted him without the fake belly, the suit of padding, he wore in presence of the public eye. He was a denizen, but also a charlatan: the wealth was his, however, the appetite for it was mimed. He was quick to his purpose. "Have you a room private, somewhere to counsel one's fantasies?" His face had the crinkles of expressions permanently etched there, and Thaddius realized he was quite aged. The professor's voice was low and quick, scudding with delectation.

Hadryn was the mirror of him, as though they devised between themselves. "Indeed, a room of perfect match that breathes with sun-worshippers and is confined not within mindless walls." Hadryn said and led them to the garden.

"Most appropriate," the Professor sighed with delight when they were amongst the little faces of flowers and the wide arms of shrubbery. He explained to she of the Royal Guard: "I am a recent arrival from the Western Districts, Thaddius, and Hadryn has been the only one I've managed to befriend. Perhaps, you shall be a second, if I bore you not exceedingly with my gibberish finds. I am much a hermit and tend to speak only of things from the life in my shell for which I apologize in advance to you."

Hadryn was quick to soothe his concern. "I read to her from the last item you did lend me, and Thaddius cared for it, at once."

Thaddius was hesitant to assent the claim. She remained half-involved, in case the wonder of what followed became a rash she could not be rid of. "It did make lingering melody in my mind. I appreciated it for the day." She pretended to become distracted by the garden's rooted and variegated sprites.

"We were tantalized of the very same passage: 'Lo! 'tis a gala night within the lonesome latter years! An angel throng, bewinged, bedight in veils, and drowned in tears—'"

"Hadryn, you've let your head run off again," Thaddius muttered. "He attempts to hand you something."

Professor Gro had slid back a moving lip on his vehicle, and it was revealed as a long compartment, from which he drew a satchel. He took from it a hard, rectangular shape and held it within Hadryn's reach. "Own this, my boy."

"This is mine?" Hadryn suddenly realized. He turned the book over in his hands. It was leather-bound and princely-looking. "Professor, thank you. How can I ever repay you?" He was excited now and drew the book in close to himself. The Knight swept his hand over the face of it. "What is this animal on the cover of it?"

"Ah, that. It is the serpent Uroboros. With its tail in its jaws, it makes a circle of its body around the world, thus representing the cycles, re-creation, and eternity. This story: there are knights and kings, and there are ladies who are not dangerous because they are beautiful, but beautiful because they are dangerous." He chuckled. He and Hadryn were beside themselves. "It is an adventure of epic magnitude, my boy! I thought of you immediately, once I had finished reading the last page."

"Now this is a feast to fill the heart," Hadryn idolized.

The professor's excitement seemed to be returning to a stasis, but he was still smiling and clutching his haversack. He took, suddenly, the time to stare at the Royal Guard, studying the lines of her. Thaddius saw his gaze, then looked away. She glanced at Hadryn for aid, but he was already thumbing through the pages of his new book, tasting of its contents. Thaddius cleared her throat, not knowing what else to do.

Professor Gro adjusted his glasses. "Why not borrow one, Mrs. Merlone? I have more with me. You could choose one."

Hadryn's attention had been lashed, and his head snapped up to look at his closest friend, as if the professor had offered her heavy coins and other riches.

Thaddius felt naked momentarily, then recovered. "Oh, well... That is rather---..." Her words were spilling, like the glass of wine she didn't yet have. Unexpectedly, she was shocked by the illegality of the proposition and how the word, 'No,' refused to come to her. She realized she wanted to read. "Military personnel would not—" Thaddius gave one, final effort, then she said, "What else have you?"

Hadryn took her by the shoulders and gave her a brief shake, as if triumphant. He brought her in closer to the professor's throne, using their bodies to shield from any who may so happen to be wandering by the exchange to take place. It was a precaution though. Few came to the gardens. "You can share this with LeShawn now, my friend," he said to her.

"Your wife?" Professor Gro asked, and Thaddius affirmed it. "Yes, with her, experience it, but no other then, all right?"

"I understand," Thaddius agreed. She watched him going through the tangle of his satchel and wondered what else he had in there. In the next moment, he had conjured four books from the depths of his bag.

Thaddius looked them over and felt them stare back at her. She regretted her decision immediately, but stood there, muted.

"These were recently," he winked at Hadryn and emphasized the word, "*recently* loaned to me." And, Hadryn, surprised, gathered that the professor had, here at the banquet, acquired the books from another guest. To think there were others like the educator. The older gentleman continued, "I have read all, but one of them. They are dark fantasies." He was more pleased than a denizen at dessert.

Thaddius hesitated. "'Dark fantasies?' Are they smutty?" She wanted to know.

Hadryn and Professor Gro laughed. The senior of them said, "No, those ones are at home," and Hadryn was amused, then thoughtful-looking.

"Well, what are they about?" The Royal Guard reached out to touch the edge of one.

The professor turned the spines face up for her to read the titles all at once. He pointed as he went, "Let me see. This one is about a cockroach who was once a salesman. This one is about a plant who was once a wife. Then, this is about a princess who was once a unicorn. Lastly, I am not certain of this one. I know it is about a girl who has another face – a second face."

Thaddius wrinkled her nose at them. "Wait. A cockroach?" She took the book and tried the weight of it in her hands. "Are they happy stories? Like, for children?"

"I'm afraid not," Professor Gro answered.

"Who wants to read stories which aren't happy?"

"People who aren't content?" Hadryn guessed.

Thaddius considered that. "What did he do wrong to become a cockroach?"

"Nothing. He was a model employee, son, and brother."

"Then, why was he punished?" She felt she knew how stories went.

Professor Gro replied, "He was punished only in how others reacted to his new form."

"Professor!" An unfamiliar voice interrupted from the entrance of the garden, taking them by surprise. Thaddius was the only one to have her wits enough to snatch the book from Hadryn, of which she concealed inside her robe. "Professor Gro! So, you are returned! I've messaged you plenty via the network, but what luck to find you here!" Undoubtedly, the professor ran into his students at any feast. "How the devil does one maneuver here?" His throne would not allow him down the narrow aisles of the raised garden beds.

"Just a second, dear boy," he called to his pupil, unable to bring to mind his name. Looking once more to Thaddius and Hadryn, the professor encouraged the Royal Guard, "Take it, if it is your pick, my dear."

She glanced at the student, who was leaning forward to ensure his throne was not scratched, and hastily she returned the book to the professor. "Instead, the one about the faces, please." Professor Gro waited a moment for her to change her mind, then slipped the same book about the cockroach back into her hands without her realizing. She tucked it in her robe, and he shoved the rest of the books back into his bag.

A thick stalk snapped behind them, and Professor Gro's student cursed, then apologized. "Sorry. I thought it would bend and not break."

Professor Gro was now irritated. "A truly *learned* fellow knows the limits of everything he touches." He tipped his chin to the military personnel. "Sir Hadryn. Mrs. Merlone. Happy feasting. I shall see you upon the clash of silver...ware." He laughed at his own poor joke, knowing Hadryn would not accept matrimony arranged by his father's hand, and Thaddius shook her head at his back, but smiled.

The student had finally freed his throne from tight corners and was attempting to back up towards the garden's entrance. The professor followed, and from beyond the small gate of the garden, the pupil could be heard resuming and extending his earlier intrusion.

A king protea hung with bowed head where the thoughtless student had left it. By a few fibers, it clung to the larger whole of its stem and shed two bracts in its downcast state. The hue of it was sunset-pink and its inner-head a royal purple. The flower had been three feet tall just before Thaddius' decision of books.

The head of the king protea falling to the ground drew Thaddius' attention, then she blinked to look away from it, as the classical music playing through the intercom ceased like sudden deafness. The recording of fanfare fell like stones on their ears and all the ears of those guests, waiting for the courses of dishes to begin.

The Royal Guard watched as thrones began to gravitate towards the front door or to higher levels for a view down, upon the driveway leading up to the mansion. "Fanfare. Your father might even believe he is a king with all this role-playing. Come. The trumpets herald your suitor, and I wish to see him."

C H A P T E R 8

IRYSYKTHON ~ an EARTH-FALLOWERWYRM

The Past:

Besides my name, my mother's first words to me were, "Flee. From. Here. Survive." Four words. Her first construction of a thought released to the airs.

Those sounds, the shadowy figures of them, assembled into each of these four ideas - the concepts of them – became to me pieces. I saw that some of these fragments were me, some were of her. Her voice, unknown to me all this time, came as a sinew of muscle to attach to me, to the magnetism of a form I no longer possessed.

What was I?

I was pain. I had been this for many weeks. It had become immuration to me, and though I had my body, I seemed to fall away, deep within myself. There, in the heap of my mind, in the soft corridors of my encephalon, which every thought or emotion ignited racing threads throughout like the tail ends of shooting stars, I felt my anima divide of my body. It was as if it did so to try and save itself. Yet, it was inhumed within my casket flesh, no longer the authority or a thing with its own will.

91

It – no, I – was burned and torn and un-learned.

I knew no longer myself. There was only the un-doing of me – a return of atoms to the Earth, yet this sundering would not be as the act of Death naturally proceeds. There was not the immersion into quiet, into peace, where the mind departs the body. My consciousness remained.

Every single fiber that was me, I felt it peeled away and the raw bleeding of the subsequent layers lit aflame again and again by the torture of being whittled away slowly, over the course of new moons. There was no slack, no settled moment to pant and let the abuse subside out my tattered husk of skin, bones, muscles, and organs. There was no sleep; I had not an escape of myself. My body continued, limitless, in the peaks it found of eroding nerve endings.

How do you endure metamorphosis?

My physicality, the vessel of my existence was beyond the reach of my will. I felt myself writhing and thrashing in the sand, and, impossibly, every particle of it which touched me I felt. I grew.

When the fetus develops, cell by cell: its organs and its skeleton and its moving flesh, we are thankfully unaware, immersed in a universe separate from the mind – the sphere of the soul, the gentle ocean of our mothers. But, I had been already birthed and left the sea. Thus, I endured the searing electricity as new nerves were formed and my body self-created living material from nothingness.

I burrowed, not by choice but instinct, searching for the womb where I belonged to further grow, or a tomb in which to die. Life and dying were confused, and as one.

As the sinew spread, I moaned – with terror, the murder that is rebirth – but I felt, also, the might of my width and myself extending frightful lengths back, out the back of my head. I became an enormity to equal my pain.

I convulsed violently, a specie out of my elemental environment, like land cast to sea, like water colonized by miserly soil, absorbed by this Other and turned to the treacle of mud.

The worst of it was my mouth. The gums spread and cracked, for through them pierced suddenly the finest points of ivory tusks, and each night I thought they would idle and cease their emergence, they grew another inch. I was reduced to epilepsy as the lower, then upper jaws filled with teeth.

I wished for death. And, in the lull between seizures, when my body relinquished to a throbbing exhaustion, I clawed through my stupor – at least, for enough clarity to cogitate a means to end myself. I could not remember my life, could not remember if there was any reason to continue living.

I saw the stars one night, thus to the surface of the sands, I must have returned without awareness of it. I didn't yet realize I could *see;* that would come later. I felt the questioning fingertips of a breeze, neutral in temperature, yet delicious in its banality. I realized I had slept, and it is a strange thing when sleep gives one hope. I stirred, afraid to breath and afraid of any more thoughts to come. I didn't want my body to awaken with the rest of me; my fear became that Living would find me once more. Perhaps, I could be just this: a thin skein of thoughts, herded by the winds and sometimes sleeping, but never belonging to a rooted vessel.

I slept again, mistaking it for Death, and awoke to the tremors of my muscles. I screamed for knowing what was to come, and my face ripped open to bone. My skull pulsated thick with pain as it re-imagined itself: longer to make a snout and still, more blades of teeth.

Why must we change?

Life is a potter, and all of us, clay.

"Nooo! Stop!" I shrieked, and I should not have had words or a voice.

The convulsions began sweeping my frame again, yet a new sensation arrived, too. Warm pressure. It held me, weighed me down, anchoring me so that the seizures lessened in violence.

I opened my eyes.

Now, I understand that I had claimed sight, in spite of what I was. I looked all around, alive, yet feeling it was not my life.

Images came to fill me, like the rush of water, washing away the years of sand I had known all my life.

My mother was close to my head as I lied there on my back. It was difficult, at first, to understand that I was not alone. How long had she been there? A day? Weeks? Had she been there, watching my agony – my transformation – all this time? To me, she looked the size of a child – scared, too, and concerned – but I realized it was I who had become unusually large. She had stayed the same.

I gaped through the last of my spasms and turned my head to one side so that I might look down upon myself.

There were other Wyrms.

They braced me with their own bodies against my epilepsy, slung across my immeasurable length, down to my tail. The seizure passed with me in their care, and I breathed in frayed huffs. The fear, even the pain, strayed away from me, as if intimidated by the others who had gathered. Besides the ones who held me through the fits, there were more. I didn't know if all they needed was to be witnesses, or if there was more to it than that. It took two attempts, but I righted myself, and they crept closer, like canines who want a home, but are cautious.

The ones who had held me remained near, many of them still in flesh contact with me. My breathing began to find some control, in increments.

I saw my mother staring at me. All of them there were Wyrms, just as Wyrms had ever been, appearing muted and dumb, ugly – some of them hideous.

My mother touched me, and the others gently prodded me or drew closer. I tried to move, but my body was strained beyond capacity. I blurred, struggling to think.

"I'm alright," I assured them. "Only, I cannot move." As I spoke, soil fell away from my teeth, so I came to know that I had eaten. Perhaps, my body assumed enough agency to ensure I would not starve before the growth of me was through.

I saw the Wyrms flinch, in shock, at my voice, at my capability of speech. It was then I noticed an immense rictus just beyond them and grass where there shouldn't be grass. It was eerily blanched to gray. I threw my head from one side to another, searching for sand, our home – the desertlands.

But, home would not be found.

I flung myself in abrupt desperation, wishing for my muscles to answer my command for action. But, lurching in that manner only brought war-cries of fresh pain, charging through tissue and veins. I looked across the dale.

Drake territory.

"Mother," I said. She faced me: a beautiful, terrible Wyrm. Her ghastly lips parted, very slowly, like an eye first opens from dreams. There were teeth in her mouth. She and I, always so much alike. "Mother, leave with them," I told her.

"Irysykthon," she said. I had never known I had a name. "Innocent. Irysykthon." Then, her lips sealed, her teeth were cloaked, and she came forward to me.

Contrastingly, almost as one, the other Wyrms recoiled from me. Like spiders scurrying back to their wall cracks, most of them made it back to the boundary where we should never have crossed. They gathered at the line of trees, which marked Outer Gled Tria. They were anxious and watching.

A few stayed in my vicinity, but shrank in their place, all of them facing the same direction.

I heard behind me a low hiss and breathing, too steady and facile to be that of a Wyrm's. I looked, wincing still in the throes of aggrieved aching throughout my body.

A Mungkr Drake stood a dozen lengths away, swaying nearly imperceptibly. I watched him. His aquamarine body drew breaths, and on his head were jacinthe and nacarat skins, flowing upwards, as if upon ghostly winds.

"Help me, please," I said to him.

CHAPTER 9

JONREN ARCHIDUX

Overhead, classical music came through the intercom machine of the Archidux House. It was not dignified or pleasing to the ear, as it was milked through the tin-like speakers. The music left a hollow feeling where it should have instead filled something, whether ear or awkward silence or served as an informed ambience. But, it left, rather than seemed to be arriving. Either way, it mattered not for those who had come to fill their plates.

In the feasting hall, the chandeliers that hung from the ceiling were tiered rectangles, emitting a dull illumination and most of the light that reached the diners below were from the bulbs no larger than a firefly that were connected by the dozens by thin, white cables. These connections of light were interwoven through the greater shapes of the chandelier, and one of the guests whispered that they were known as "christmas lights" in the times past.

The Chef[3], a model released earlier this year and created all of black steel, sat in the zero'ed-out space which was made by the oval shape to ring it. That oval framing was carved and engraved wood, rising and falling by segments, and tinted a darkened rose color. It was here that diners found their seats to be served a counter's worth of food. The Chef[3] groaned and coughed steam from its joints, for it had just dispensed the first meal of the eight courses to follow: a small bowl with a mound of cubes both hard and crisp. Perhaps, they were the idea that remained of what was once bread. The denizens looked strange, as they sought to get the sharpest angles of their teeth upon the food, working their jaws around the difficult cubes, yet they seemed happy enough as they chattered, and Hadryn knew the babble was for the last guest who had arrived to the banquet.

Hadryn's father sat the head of the table, upon a platform discreetly elevated a foot above where the guests sat, in their thrones. To his left was a man Hadryn had not seen before, though he knew many of the wealthiest houses and their blood-trees. The man was of complexion autumnal-brown, and his beard was overdone – thick enough to nearly conceal a mouth behind it all. This would-be groom was not a relation to any denizen, that much was evident upon his approach to the miming turrets, the imitating keep, the decorative battlements atop the mocking castle. He was something outside of the make-believe of the Tiered Nations, something a denizen could not even imagine being, for the man had all reason to be revered a prince of most peregrine origins.

This, when there were no longer princes, and only Mr. Archidux's castle, designed and built not to offend standard residential codes.

The suitor – Hadryn's suitor – had arrived with an entourage to ignite the network feeds for weeks to come. His procession of four others, women and men besides himself, was unhurried and deliberate, as it wended through the many streets, streets which were usually sterile of life and always kept much too clean.

The sound preceding this fantastical cortege, conservative in numbers as it was, was altogether unfamiliar to the ears of the inhabitants here. One woman was said to have described it as likened to the scrapping and clipping in one's fireplace when the help stirs the coals in the heart of winter. Clopping, plodding, scrapping. It was the echo of animals with singular, profound toes, cloven, that were formed of hard keratin to clack against the ears of those in their thrones. And, though the sound of that procession confused any who listened, it was not of comparison to the vision made by those beasts and their riders.

The oxen with their barbarous strength upon their shoulders and haunches – the deep muscles of their chest – elicited fear, awe, and fainting spells from the denizens they passed. They were animals so inconceivably massive that the weight of them could be felt by the eyes of humans who had, for so long, gone without the image of them to behold. Indifferent to the fascination they inspired, the oxen continued forward with easy demeanor, and sometimes gave a little toss of their horns, the power rippling in their wide necks.

Those mounted astride the oxen were attired in dark, blue robes, simple, but threaded of fine silk. Each of them was an ethnicity differing from the rest, and the denizens could not speculate the District to which they belonged. Perhaps, it was a parameter of humble population, far North. They were thinner in the Northern regions; it was the cold, estimated some of the denizens, here and now. Wheresoever was their home, the hair was kept long, even the men, and each one in the retinue wore her or his hair bound up in a clasp of white jade to half-encircle the bun of hair with a long hair pin, which dangled ornaments also of white jade.

The man at the head of their rhombus-like formation wore a robe of reflected design to his party, but the color was shaded-red with gold embroidery. He, and every one of the riders, carried a wrapped gift, so the spectators whispered, "Bridal presents. How enchantingly traditional." Yet, garnering just as much commotion as the gifts and handsome oxen were that two of the animals were harnessed – the rest of them bare of any leather straps and their riders simply directing them by foot cues and stalks of wheat against their flanks – and those harnessed had suspended between them, by chains, an oblong cabinet of smooth, dense oak. Several feet long and less than two feet in height and depth, the coffer was inlaid with hand-crafted symbols of the endless knot, which repeated, side by side, along the lengthiest walls.

At the very center of each of these endless knots was one hole, punctured through an empty space created by the natural lines of that intricate pattern.

None in the crowd quite knew from which direction this bizarre cavalcade had originated, but many thrones had followed after seeing the riders and their mighty oxen to cross the landscape of the windows of their homes. Those watching were desperate to peer into those tiny holes of the coffer, jangling by the iron handles the chains held it by. Was it riches inside? Or, gunny sacks of food pellets, exotic to the tongue? It could be silk brocades, or medicinal tablets to heal the ills of the over-taxed digestive tract. The denizens mused; excitement rarely so touched them. Again and again, one turning to another: who was this man? From where did he hail? He appeared young enough, maybe even comely, though it was hard to tell from the distance, and his paunch was firm and round, "well-set," remarked the women.

The oxen filled the narrow avenue, which ended at the entrance steps to the house of Archidux, with the scents of straw and soil and the salt upon their flanks. Incomprehensible to denizens, who never before knew a smell as this, the animals were mesmerizing to all who gathered, and every movement of them were reflected in those eyes gazing. One woman reached from her throne to touch the muzzle of one the oxen. The bull was patient and nonchalant towards her who touched him, then, he gave an easy shake of his horned head, and pleased, yet nervous laughter rippled through the congregation.

It was then that the suitor arrived before Mr. and Mrs. Archidux, both of whom sat in their thrones, a little way from the front doors to the mansion jealous to be a castle. The beau looked over the estate. He dismounted: one leg swinging in front of himself over the shoulder of his ox for him to slip down the side of the beast and land upon his feet, bowing.

The crowd leaned from their vehicles.

"Mrs. Archidux. Mr. Archidux," he said, righting himself from his courtesy. "I've come for the Knight, Sir Hadryn Archidux."

The fenceline of the garden was several yards away from the extravaganza building and unfolding at the doorstep, but it protruded slightly from the rest of the façade of the house. This gave Hadryn and Thaddius a chary view of the Knight's betrothed.

Thaddius sighed and gave her back to the scene. "The man is decidedly a *top*." She squeezed Hadryn's shoulder, as if to comfort. "So, you shall never present your split side to him. Remain whole, facing forward to him, who is ignorant of your nature, and we will yet untangle you of this mess, my friend. Come. Hurry to the Hall."

Hadryn followed after the Royal Guard, nervously holding at his "split side" for a moment.

"How very long I have waited for this day," Jonren Archidux held his wine glass as high as he could. "But, a father is patient and benevolent, and very patient to bring this day, which I share with all of you." He grinned, though the width of his mouth was already at its limit. "May I present to you, the Intended to my child: Mr. Ro."

Mr. Ro seemed uncomfortable and gave a quick wave as an applause pervaded. He met Hadryn's gaze, and Hadryn returned a stony glare. Mr. Ro diverted his eyes.

Closer now, Mr. Ro did not seem so outlandish, like his parade. He had not said much else at the front entrance, only to explain that the other riders were friends of his and not hired help, as was assumed, and that they and the oxen would be returning home as soon as he could deposit the cargo he'd brought to a room, private and adequately maintained warm. It was a disappointment to the denizens who witnessed all, for they wished for the oxen to remain.

It would not be so, and the bulls with their curving horns and sheened coats left with their riders by the next hour. Some denizens, not invited to the engagement banquet, sought to tail the mysterious riders, but the four departed each in a different direction.

In the hall, which echoed, Mr. Archidux continued his speech, enjoying the attention.

"Doubtless, Hadryn, you have my telegraph came upon. And, accepted it, as your presence here indicates. That is ...." He disguised his nervousness in a chuckle of seeming good cheer. "Well, then, there is not much else to say. Nothing from you is necessary." He attempted a joke of sorts with the whip of a parent admonishing his child. "Improperly dressed for this, but we shall sometimes ignore the fecklessness of youth for the grander scale. You are required not a word, child. Cheers to you and Mr. Ro, this fortuitous occasion. And, my thanks to those who gather with us." He went to lower his glass, but Hadryn stood from his seat and the glare came, pricking at Mr. Archidux's visage.

"Father, unseemly would it be if I did not bestow upon you that speech of propriety, which this fete requires."

Mr. Ro could be seen to turn to the young Knight, his fingers clasped and resting upon the table. The guests seemed to stiffen in their seats, as if waiting for the spotlight which would eve the main event.

"Peace, child, for I know what you should say." He motioned with his glass to their guests, yet Hadryn again interrupted.

"*My thanks*, dear sire. Glad am I to mark this milestone with you, with Mother, with Thaddius, and with all of thee, nameless faces, as you were." He took his own wine glass. "Cheers."

"Yes—cheers." Mr. Archidux drank quickly. But, Hadryn did not yet sit.

The Knight drank slowly, then let his glass fall to the floor. It clinked against the table, then shattered on the floor. The room went quiet. "Cheers, then, to this momentous, new practice. Finally, finally. Men are, now, to be shackled by the wedding finger in matrimonies not their choosing, just as women have so suffered the human-history long."

Thaddius began to clap and had rested her feet up, upon the dining table. "That is good practice!" she declared loudly. "Good practice for a bad idea!"

"Speak forth, Royal Guard. For, if there is an ugly insecurity which we have twisted into law to govern our society, let us each share in it by balanced proportion. Not one population to heft the burden upon, but let it be us all, in judicial misery."

"Hadryn, stop up your tongue this moment!" his father warned, sneering. "You know very well, the methods of union will never change. Women only have those hands to be given away by their fathers."

"Then, still? Women, alone. Not men."

Cyssiline had become emotional. "I hate you, Jonren. *Leave my boy alone."* Her husband would not look her way, pretending not to hear her.

Hadryn stood, quiet and waiting. He stepped over the table, which filled the hall with gasps, and Hadryn walked the length of the machinery at the heart of the banquet. He pulled down a lever on the Chef, quitting its power, as so rarely done to these machines, which continuously ran throughout the day's hours.

Jonren slammed his plate upon the table. *"Enough of that, you witch! Turn it back on!"*

"Ladies, why this audience, then, if not to toast the enslavement of men to strangers who shall share their beds in exchange for their wealth, family prestige, or the roof of their estate?"

Jonren sneered at his child, "Yes, side with them as is your place and by the indelible script upon your birth certificate."

Hadryn was silent. He could almost hear the pulse of the room: not really shock – no, they knew, from years back, from unending network feeds – but worse, a feeling of fulfillment, a confirmation of who he was in the presence of who he now is.

Oddly, Mr. Ro stood from his place to speak: "I don't see what any of this has to do with this dinner tonight."

Hadryn looked to his suitor abruptly, only now realizing the man had knowledge of Hadryn's transition all along.

"Mr. Ro. Forgive this impetuosity—" Mr. Archidux began, but Hadryn severed his apology.

"'Side with them?' I have never left them, Father, for my past I carry within my person and with pride. Like each our pasts, it has made me who I now am. You speak of a birth certificate as though it defines who one is. Yet, it is the most exiguous account of an individual possible – just numbers and names and a blue or pink dot in negligence of the many hues of this world." He continued to the ladies at the dinner. "In watching, madams, are happy memories stirred?"

The men went rigid at their seats. They each chanced an eye upon their wives. But, the women kept their eyelashes lowered to hide reaction. Or, some stared ahead, without expression, and tried not to think of the wide centuries in which men were commonly favored and at the expense of woman. There were, too, a few bachelor men, addled by both Hadryn's words and the reactions of the room. One lady though met the eyes of her spouse. The husband was beginning to shake his head in warning, but she folded her napkin from her lap anyway and distanced her throne from her empty plate.

"Luprinda," he scolded her.

The lady Luprinda addressed the Knight who bore heterochromatic eyes. She was tall, even sitting down. "A man who has walked, with bare soles, the road of Woman has my respect. You, sir, were never our gender, but I thank you for living and learning from it." To her husband, she said, "You are a good person in all ways, but that you asked *for* me and did not ask me. We never loved each other." The lady stared at her wedding band, then slid it from her finger and placed it upon her empty plate. The other guests gasped, chirped short sentences to one another, then waited patiently to be fed more. Softly, she said, "Ladies, we should not need a gentleman to speak for us. Sir," she addressed Hadryn once more. "People have slandered you a 'freak.'" She bowed her head. "And, I, as well, have said the same of you when beckoned by others' expectations. Can you forgive me? It is so very difficult to be *un*-like, easier to do that which is familiar, repetitious."

Hadryn went to that tall dame and took one of her hands to kiss. "Forgiveness is the natural effect of compassion, m'lady." He smiled at her. "And, every repeat is a chance to shatter the circle in exchange for an opposing revolution."

She returned his smile with one her own. "I believe I understand you a little better now. Sir Hadryn, in that your beginning was my beginning, but your course became *male*, like a string vibrating at different pitch. Perhaps, I understand a bit more of men by you, as well."

Another woman, clearly shaken and trembling, quietly directed her throne backwards, away from the dining-ware, and the eyes of everyone startled over towards her. Feeling demanded for explanation, yet fretted by nerves ran to muscle-burn, she tried to speak up. "At times, we sh-should not eat what is laid before us. I will not watch a man be treated out of custom." Her face was red, and she was perspiring. "It may be, someday, I will gain some courage as a woman as well. Like, Luprinda. Good day." She left in a hurry with a few other women admiring her and watching after her disappearing vehicle.

Luprinda, too, watched the other lady. She squeezed Hadryn's hand to look into his eyes. "You are your own gender, sir."

"A third?" He joked with her and embarrassed her.

She was good to the sport of it. "What I have seen with my own two eyes – so, I know others have seen it, too – is that sometimes, if there are two sides, they will oppose one another. A third, outside that stalemate, might be absolutely necessary." Hadryn considered it, then nodded. The lady made to leave. "I should catch up to her who departed. I never thought before today, but she and I may grow to friendship." She gave a small wave 'goodbye' to Hadryn, then navigated her motorized vehicle from the hall intended for feasting.

"This spectacle, Mr. Archidux!" the deserted spouse exclaimed. "I should have expected no less!" And, he followed after Luprinda.

Mr. Archidux yelled at his servants as he gesticulated at Hadryn, and there was Thaddius, backgrounded by the clamor of the hall, yet answering in call back chorus. "Seize her!—" exclaimed Mr. Archidux.

Thaddius responded: "He will not be had!"

"And, get that machine back on!" Mr. Archidux's face and throat were red with fury and embarrassment. "To her room—"

"You think you have shut him in and you have not!"

"Out of my sight." It seemed difficult for him even to remain sitting upright. Mr. Archidux gestured angrily for the help to begin fanning him. "She has wearied me."

"He, however, does not tire. How can he?" Thaddius concluded.

They brought silk hand-fans to Mr. Archidux, the width of one's arm span, and the light, bamboo ribs of them clattered open to full sail in blameless white with thin threads of colored paint, splattered in artistic randomness across the length of them. Hadryn watched him, he who was sure to avoid a meeting of their eyes, and Hadryn felt the old pressure of his childhood, his former skin and the girl he had worn who was an unwitting lie. It was that girl though whom his father still insisted was here, that she would live for Hadryn, instead of within him.

The servants came forward, hesitantly. They had watched the boy grow to manhood and swore in their hearts deep affection for him. "Please, Sir Hadryn." They motioned to him from across the table. He went with them, Thaddius kicking aside her chair as she left her place at the table to join him.

Mr. Ro looked from Mr. Archidux to his intended, unsure of what to do.

Thaddius was quick to her friend's side. "Well done. Bravo. I cannot tell if we've just made you immediately homeless. He is livid, like the back end of diarrhea."

"Thaddius, this rectal humor—"

"Erupts when I am nervous." She hurried alongside Hadryn as the household help escorted him towards his room in the mansion. They neared the ramp leading upstairs, but Cyssiline caught up to them, and they paused.

She trembled, at the edge of tears. "My son?" Cyssiline sat in her throne, wringing the satin gloves once on her hands. "He would not let me tell you sooner than this day. Nothing I said could dissuade him from marrying you off. *Will you understand how deeply sorry I am for not being able to protect you as a mother should?*" Her eyes pleaded with him. She shed tears, yet held his gaze. "I did not want for you what had happened to me." She bowed her head. "A sennight ago, I should have put to darkness his life as he slept! —"

Hadryn was at her side, swiftly covering his dam's mouth with one hand as a couple of denizens foremost to the foyer, where they stood, stared after them. But, then, the Chef[3] hummed to charge and stole their distraction. The food was produced and passed around.

"Mother, you could be brought in for investigation with such talk." He laughed and kissed her cheek. "I know you did everything you could for me, Mother."

"I did," she said softly.

Mr. Ro stood a few feet away from them, catching their attention. Curiously, he stood, as though he didn't have a throne. His eyes never strayed from Hadryn. "You are a natural orator, well-spoken. I did not expect that, nor your ideals. I did not expect your voice either – the quality; it is like the classical cello." He gestured in a light manner, smiling with his heavy beard just barely allowing it. "I've made it awkward." He came forward to their group. "I am Mr. Ro. From afar. We sometimes, there, cannot afford purchase of the wheeled chair." He noticed them staring at his legs. Closer now, it was more apparent how much shorter he was than Hadryn and even Thaddius. He had a portly belly which came over his waist-sash, but the remainder of him seemed not yet overwhelmed by excess. Hadryn noted that his hair was long and tied back by a low clasp. He was dressed in stately décor, but Hadryn could see the stitching at some of the seams, as if the raiment was handmade.

"Mr. Ro. We've met." Cyssiline dipped her head, respectfully, to him. "I am glad for you to meet Mrs. Thaddius Merlone, and my son, Hadryn, as you know."

Hadryn grasped the man's hand and shook it once. "Hello, Mr. Ro." He started to say more, but Thaddius was breaking their contact to stand between them. She rested a strong hand on Mr. Ro's shoulder.

"Sir, as you saw back there, you are refused. Men are not Hadryn's orientation, and to the same effect, he will never submit to an arranged marriage, for he has a sweetheart in waiting."

Mr. Ro was taken aback but wore the same congenial smile. "A woman?" He laced his fingers in front of himself, then surveyed the rooms he could see of that vast mansion. "Well, where is she?"

Hadryn stopped Thaddius from answering for not knowing what the Royal Guard might say. He spoke after a moment, "I am not, yet, where I belong, so she and I are not, yet, together."

Cyssiline blinked away from them, turning somewhat. She looked sad.

Mr. Ro stared at Hadryn. Then, he drew a brief sigh. "So, be it. I accept your refusal."

Cyssiline startled, and then, composed herself. "You've my gratitude, sir, for your understanding." She put a hand to his back. "But, stay the night. The travel back would be weary work at this late hour. It is the least our house could do for you. We have a guest room downstairs. Hadryn," she spoke over her shoulder at the Knight as she started to lead Mr. Ro towards the rear of the house. "Take Mr. Ro with you to fetch the spare blankets and pillow from the closet in your room. I've put all the extra bedding there."

Hadryn stiffened slightly, but agreed. "This way, sir. Thaddius, I've something tomorrow to tell you. About Oshin."

"I may look forward to it, if breakfast arrives on your dime." Hadryn promised it, then left with Mr. Ro. Thaddius watched him. "It is unnerving to see a man come for Hadryn."

"My hope is that he is the last," Cyssiline said. "Thaddius, I failed to mention earlier that your wife was here, invited by Jonren. I think she felt obligated to come or it was with the intention to be with you. But, poor dear, she left soon after arriving, and was flushed by fever. I think she will be fine, but I sent her home in one of our cabs."

"How was her color?"

"Faded. She complained of nausea, too." Perturbation stole over Cyssiline's features, as she asked, "Are the treatments not going well, Thaddius?"

"No, they are," the Royal Guard answered. "It is an adjustment to them, is all. Thank you for your care towards her, Mrs. Archidux. Understandably, I shall depart anon."

"Of course, love. Go to her. Though it is my last wish, I should return to the banquet."

Thaddius had just gone through the front door when Cyssiline heard a clatter in the dining hall. She was wondering if she should call one of their butlers from the other room, but a crying out broke her thoughts. On instinct, she pressed the button to accelerate the pacing of her throne and steered back, towards the great hall, which smelled of machine oil and hot, indistinct foods.

Among the diners, one of the ladies had wailed and sounded nearly singsong. She fell out of her throne and met the ground so heavily that it shook the wine glasses upon the circular table, and the denizens, in the middle of accumulating more riches to expand their belt lines, looked over one at a time, until the last quintuplet of them raised their heads in one motion. Like gulls chimed by some distraction, they waited to see if the cue was for another tasty morsel or danger and to scatter up into the skies. It was only ever one or the other.

The lady from the floor spoke, "She's bitten off her little finger." She was pointing at another guest, who had been seated to her left. The woman at the table glanced about the dining hall. There was blood at her lips, of which she seemed unknowing, and she was four-fingered at one hand.

CHAPTER 10

NANDENIA of the TREE CROWNS

When the winds' gnarled hands tattered the clouds to unraveled threads in The Nocturnes, no one noticed. Here, there were secrets, outwardly and inwardly, yet a cored honesty which amalgamated to form its own weather pattern. The shadowlands were like lonely nights where the worst of who we were could remain strangers even to ourselves, if we could promise never, in the eyes of dawn, to remember the things we became when we were without others, when we stood before ourselves, naked, in black mirrors.

The Great Aegis of the Tree Crown Drakes stepped forward, and in her eyes, she beheld one came from herself, yet distinctly of her own bearing as well: a small, white dragon. It filled her with dread and love alike. She hadn't known yet if she was ready to become a mother, but, here, in the darkness, she was.

"My daughter," Ardyce said, as if more to herself. Joy was a strange blossom to bud in the stone of her heart and amidst the ballistae of vituperation in her mind. She emerged into their presence, blood tinting her ivory scales and the havoc of blasted timber, splintered limbs still falling, upon her head.

The hatchling shied at that first sight of her dame, and the silver Firecraw, too, performed on instinct to shield that child as fear leaped in him at the enormity of her being. He flew high to elude another attack of the Wyrm, and then, his gaze settled upon Ardyce once more.

"The Tree Crowns' Great Aegis." With that recognition, he became glad. "My Lady, your daughter and I've become fast friends! Together, we've challenged this bull! I, her valiant steed, and she, the advisor at my shoulder." He flew towards Ardyce, emitting plasma directly into the sky above them to chandelier their introduction. "Welcome to The Nocturnes. I am known as 'Dreyon.'" He was casual, and Ardyce knew now that he could not have known what became of the other Drakes after he'd fled with her daughter on his back. She wavered in how to tell him of all she had seen.

However, unrelenting was that earth-fallowing Wyrm, and the report of death would have to wait. A cry rippled out from its throat somewhere nearest them, and it led with its jaws gnashing at Dreyon and the youth.

The luminance of the plasma in the sky struck the Wyrm, and its reaper-face rearing back, against the wild clouds torn at the ends by their own frenzied dance, loomed as a sick horizon before them. It was the Wyrm, Irysykthon, towering in size with teeth newly-birthed and words like first children to it, rippling forth. It was not the darkened color of the Wyrm Ardyce had destroyed. Its body was gray hued with white marbling, just as the skies are when they rage to storms, and the sleeve of the Wyrm, too, seemed calcified to a certain hardness. The head of the creature was bald of that gray coloring and, instead, wore a face of mauve and purple pigment like bruised skin, which the bone of its jaws gleamed from, in contrast.

Irysykthon said to the Tree Crown Drake, "What have you done with my mother?"

The Great Aegis' eyes widened as she stared at the beast before her. There was the blood of dragons in the grooves of its skeletal jaws, and Ardyce wished already to have the creature in her grip as ill fantasies of it soused in blood and entrails slowly unzipped a lurid grin across her face.

"A most disgusting trick, Wyrm." Ardyce leered at the Earth-fallower. "Why have you speech? It is against Nature."

Dreyon paused in the sky, his wings his only motion and the Firecraw was shocked as he held the child to himself. "The Wyrm is gifted with words. How is it possible?"

Ardyce leaned towards the Wyrm, ready to make the kill. "It is a pity you will not be able to talk your way out of death, you monster."

Irysykthon remained still. Again, was its question: "Where is my mother?"

"Shut up about your mother, Wyrm!" Ardyce's fury rattled the stones in the earth. "You are not worthy the bond of mother and child!" The white Drake fell quiet as the sneer upon her face grew to its full capacity, nearly distorting her features. Ardyce had forgotten the newborn Drake, who watched her from afar. She said to the Wyrm, "If you so wish to know, I shall tell you, and you will understand that words are not always a gift, as I shall now give to thee."

Irysykthon wavered, for it had done all it could to survive thus far as its mother had pleaded, even defeating a clan of Drakes after the first Mungkr it and its parent had encountered. "Why did the Mungkr wish to murder me?" asked Irysykthon.

The Great Aegis' eyes narrowed. She ignored the question, but felt the sting of its importance. Instead, Ardyce said to the Wyrm with a face half-skeleton: "That which you name a 'mother' is just as easily a 'father' for one of thee who subscribes to both sexes. And, that *thing* I held by the skull in my mouth, Wyrm. I, of a race who has long held teeth and words before the likes of your kind, did send the sharpness of my hatred through and through thy parent's face. You will be unable to distinguish anything of that thing you once knew from that which I vomited upon the death of it!"

Irysykthon screamed.

With swiftness unearthly, the Earth-fallower charged the Tree Crown in her path.

Yet, power, incited by grisly enmity, orchestrated the next instant and found the mutant annelid caught and thrown by wide arc of the mother Tree Crown's neck. Irysykthon had not even the awareness to cry out, so fluid and seamless was the she-Drake's counter.

The Wyrm became a projectile, a sack of flour thrown downhill to catch every harmful inclination of Nature: tree teeth made from lightning-shattered stumps, rocks who sharpened themselves when no others noted their presence, and bramble to cast burred condemnation of the lands' hordes. It was forced a surprising distance, and with a deep-throated echo of the Earth, it met the base of a mountainside, disagreeing in body with the austere hardness found there. Now, this Wyrm bled and its insides bruised and herniated. It had found its rival, someone by measure fair and sinew formidable as well as scathing hatred. Irysykthon opened its mouth and wine-poured blood to gasp in soft breath as it righted itself.

Ardyce turned to meet the Firecraw and shouldered child. Dreyon was staring at the Wyrm, so titanic in bearing, yet shoveled like dirt-clod by this Drake with three tiers of half-destroyed antler.

"You are a marvel, my liege." He bowed, in respect, yet also pricked by fear. Dreyon struggled to understand the utter disdain betwixt the white Drake and the giant Wyrm. He was afraid of the Tree Crown mother, who had admitted to the slaying of another, but he said to her, "This babe of yours I have shielded, but her father was wind-swept by the muted obscurity of this eclipsed region. He wanders. I know not mind-speak, but you, a Tree Crown versed in telepathy – might you be able to hail him no matter the width you are apart?"

Ardyce sounded gruff and unlike herself in her own ears. "Telepathy finds a channel only by sight of the intended mind to open conversation. In this blackness, he is lost to me." She took a step towards the pair, not intending threat, but Dreyon and her daughter shrank and dropped their eyes as her hugeness filled the sky. "Please, find him. With your eyes, large to perceive these nocturnal switchbacks, you'll arrive to his shape in bettered time. Take her with you. I will this Wyrm turn into catastrophe."

He hesitated. "Kill him?"

The white Drake angered. *"'It.' It is an 'it.'"* Dreyon would not speak. Like fire that burns, then finds some new fuel to devour, Ardyce's rage grew and strained its reins. *"Wyrms insult the genders by being of them both. Therefore, it is an it. It is a parade of the freak parlor."*

"'It.'" He was looking for the Wyrm, and some way's off, Ardyce heard it slip into the earth. Dreyon would not meet her gaze. "Why divide him of us? He is a third gender, but there is room enough for more than the sex of you and I. *Why murder?*" He could not understand. "This is not that world, not the northern reaches where they might sanctify death. I trust that when you go before the Higher Council to answer for his parent's death, you will have reason well enough, but answer, indeed, you must."

Ardyce felt suddenly the great weight of herself. "This Wyrm should bow low to Death ten counts, each time by means of increasing, horrid agony. Then, would there be some shred of justice done."

"Ten? That is absurd. It is but one Wyrm."

The Tree Crown knew what she must say unto him, though it was not for the soft of heart to hear or speak. "My Vow had six brothers, but no more. Two of our unborn do remain so by this Wyrm's tyranny. It killed a Mungkr Drake in Gled Tria. And, this region relinquishes another of her own to the same monstrous end. I am sorry. Of those the one belonging to The Nocturnes was he, the sweet of your marriage."

The Firecraw felt the child staring at him. He dismissed Ardyce's nonsense, returning instead to the last words of her he could comprehend. "Untrue. Untrue. A lie or misunderstanding. Well. Find the father of this stripling, then? I shall commit to this errand with her, the princess, and my husband. You came with him, did you not? He pointed you the way? No more this talk of him being gone. Come, where is he?"

Ardyce softened. "Dreyon."

"Alas, you say my name, but not this tone. What is this in your eyes, Tree Crown? Sorrow?" He glanced at the hatchling. "I beg you, do not startle us both."

She was disarmed by him. "Dreyon. Understand me. This Wyrm dies tonight for its crimes."

He was shaking his head. He walked passed her. In voice made hoarse by terror and disbelief, he cried out to The Nocturnes. *"Lynelis!"* He waited and cried again, desperate to bend reality to his favor. *"Lynelis!! Come!"* Whispers fled out of Dreyon. *"Do not break the boy-child's heart of whom fell in love with you so many decades back, for the man of him will not withstand it. This you know. Thus, no more games."* He screamed, *"Give up yourself anon!! Lynelis!"* The silver Firecraw let down the youth with tenderness, and she, feeling the grief before Dreyon could, was confused by fear and knew not where to place herself, having been dislodged from him. She stayed her gaze upon the only Drake she had formed a bond with, but her steps took the rest of her to the mother in her blood. She had no name, so Ardyce knew not who she stared down at in looking at her surviving child.

The girl said, "Please, root him, noble dame, you being an abecedarian to the Tree numina. I, too, have spoken with the trees and know it is our station to rest, in solacing soil, those who must balance at the threshold of storms breaking at every identity of themselves. Offer him some ground; he does not know himself without his Vow."

The Great Aegis stared into her offspring's eyes. Wisdom had already found this newborn. Just as older, more experienced mothers had told Ardyce would be the destiny of she who would someday succeed her as Great Aegis. Under her skin, however, Ardyce's muscles went cold, and she stood outside of Time abruptly, was wrenched into her past.

Wisdom had never come for her, never spoken to her from out the Ever-Standing Ones. Yet, Ardyce saw herself, at ceremony: thirty-seven Drakes in attendance, and one of them – an elder who would pass to death, then life anew – stood before her, and Ardyce bowed to their people, then to the Ancient who was what she would become. That matron reciprocated reverence in due fashion. At last, the older she-Drake gave her face to the vaulted realm, head held much aloft on grace of her curved crest. Now, the memory became loud and shammed reality. The ghost of that forbearer began to molt the tiers of her crown. The limbs of her antlers found the earth in forceful sound, and the crepitation of tectonic convergence spoke of her legacy. This continued, until the head of her was bare, and she was left as some strange lizard or breathing extinction from Mesozoic fantasies. Unusual were the feelings that came to Ardyce, seeing their matriarch undecorated, unburdened. Ardyce went to her and gave her her brow. She, grayed by age, rested one taloned palm upon Ardyce's forehead, and there, germinated a single, black horn – the mark of the Great Aegis. Before the past closed the door of anamnesis, Ardyce glimpsed from peripheral vision, the rubicund Tree Crown who had desired this ceremony for herself, and she, with her red dresses, was serene. She was –

"—begging you! Please! Be not of unmovable heart, lest he be succumbed!" Her child held at her, and it was their first contact.

The sapling and the silver Firecraw were to her unfamiliars. Time had not gathered between either of them and herself to make them anymore than strangers, yet Ardyce returned from the apparitions of her past with a steel-tempered appetite to be their bulwark.

It caught her unawares.

She came to sense that she had just become a mother. Yet, she didn't understand if she had, by parallel, truly became the Great Aegis as well.

"To Lynelis' end will I follow the same. *Lead on, Wyrm, though I will have some piece of you to damn in my shallow grave.*" Dreyon was forgetful of all ethics of fairness now, for love oft supersedes our principles. He sallied forth as the girl beside Ardyce cried out to him.

The Wyrm had paced its volley, spent time in observation and had recovered its ferocity. It went, headlong, to encounter the

Firecraw, its "vision" on par with the firebreather, for the Wyrms were chiefly directed by sound and vibration.

Ardyce spoke to her daughter, "Let every other inch of land persuade you not to be their visitor. To this very point will I return by count of paces in the dark. Trust me."

"*No*," said she, the youth. Then: "Name me."

The Great Aegis faltered at the gaze of her young. Ardyce knew Mohonia's heart in this instant as though he were by her side, and she breathed, "Nandenia."

The skies spoke then, growling thunder, and erstwhile, never had there struck such fierce illumination in The Nocturnes, but there came, now, arms of lightning. Blow after blow, they lit the blackness. They revealed the trees for their forms true, and those rooted giants, no longer obscured in shadow, shewn to be all pale-white and their leaves were not leaves, but mushrooms which thrived in the deep of night, the fungi of our unconscious states, growing upon dead things and eating of our more toxic impulses.

Ardyce beheld her child in her gaze and saw the firefly glow of a smile from the newborn Drake just as she wheeled direction for the rogue firebreather. She would need astute legerity to head off the silver-hided Drake. If she could not, she knew he would most likely be destroyed in a headlong assault with this Wyrm of half-bone face.

The lightning rang in her ears with the sound like thick glass being splintered - a hammer sledging at the dome of this reality from a dimension far off.

Ardyce ran, then gathered her flights for a final surge forward, to overcome Dreyon. She bodily drove the Firecraw to the ground, scuffling him from his course and bearing mindfulness of her frame so preponderant to his. It was then that the great Wyrm was upon them both, and Ardyce looked over shoulder to see it trilling and gaping as it lurched into the air to claim them.

She drew back her tail, thick with compelling might, and the winds created by her delivery shrieked at her damaging momentum as she struck down the assailant, who collapsed into the ground like cities becoming ruins all in one breath.

"Dreyon." She tussled with him and neutralized his every attempt to charge the Wyrm. "Dreyon, bring Lynelis back." Ardyce saw deep into him and recognized herself if ever she was bereft her own Vow. Forsooth, Life keeps madness at bay, but Death challenges every rank of rationale. "Return him," she instructed him.

With a curved claw, Ardyce forced entry into her own flesh. The blood fell down her body as she opened her breast to bare the chambers of her heart. Without time to exercise precision – the Wyrm had concussed from the blow, but was righting itself – the Tree Crown carved lose a piece of herself: one chamber of her heart. It pulsated, hot in her grasp, and she bestowed it to the smaller Drake. "He has not long walked with Death. With this, beseech him turn back to us. Then, I beg you, locate my Mohonia. Ward my daughter." She mane-tossed her thoughts, seemingly disoriented for a moment, and though she could not see it, Dreyon witnessed her eye-orbs retract into her sockets briefly. *"Wyrms. Worming through the apples of the trees. Impossible wormholes. Worms, why?"* Then, she was recovered unto herself and continued, as if not breaking: "Feed him this. Feed it to him." She imposed the organ, blood-sauced, to his possession.

This stilled him with fear. He told himself it was only a trick of the lightning, which surged illumination in bursts. He strained to see her true, but even he, with eyes made for the dark, seemed to see her cloaked in shadow. Or, was his vision not disturbed, and her alabaster skin less white? Her antlers glinted strangely in the intermittent light and appeared to curve to sharper ends, like blades. Dreyon struggled to his feet, unable to comprehend this reality so bewitched that Wyrms tore Drakes away from their lives and dragons grew hatred out of their own bodies. He forced words to give himself time to think. "Doctor Lynelis to resurrection, make of him an Unrested? You can't be serious."

Abruptly, she raged at him: *Go now! Or, will you survive in a world where he is not? Is that what you wish?*

Again, her eye organs receded, and she was a skull for a moment, like the annelid she fought. He scrambled away from her, calling to the child. Then, to her, he said, *"You mustn't, Tree Crown. Do not do this."* But, the words fell short, and they were hollow like glass figurines, for he knew she was flayed rope, untethered. There was no anchor he could make, so he took Nandenia upon his back, and Dreyon fled as the Wyrm sunk its teeth into Ardyce. He tried to hush the sapling, who cried for him to stop and turn 'round.

The lightning counted the rounds of those titans at Dreyon's back. He was scared, and he didn't know who he wished to see the victor of that battle.

CHAPTER 11

ISIA BLANE

Isia Blane muscled the steel door open to the cellar below. It shrieked on its rusted hinges and sent its echoes down, like tossed coins, into the basement's confines. He straightened his coarse robe and peered out. The ground was sixty feet away, being that the door opened towards the ceiling of the subterranean room, and the depth made ash of his sight after twenty feet, for there was the one light near the top, but it was inadequate and stopped after illuminating the upper holds of the cellar. He knew there was no sense in stalling. The other light waited, like bait in an animal-trap, at the bottom of the darkness. The only way to bridge the drop down was a flight of wood panels bolted at intervals in a gradual slope along the wall. Mr. Archidux referred to it as a "staircase," but since there wasn't a balustrade or even handrails, Isia thought of them as training wheels for those first learning to walk through air.

He began the descent.

Above ground, before Mr. Archidux had requested a few more dishes to be fed to the food processor, Isia had caught glimpse of Mrs. Thaddius Merlone and Sir Hadryn just entering the estate. They had been in deep conversation, unmindful of the gossiping guests, who spoke of the suitor to appear. Isia had rushed away, without opportunity to greet them.

He wondered if the two military personnel were now with Hadryn's mother. By fact, Isia had never seen happiness arise in Cyssiline for the food she ate or the things the Archidux house acquired or the praise that came from either condition. Her joy was ever her son and her pool on the lower level of the estate.

He had once asked Cyssiline, "My Lady. Did it never scare you how different Hadryn is?"

She had laughed at his question and answered with affection. "Silly. When someone so changes you for the better, fear is wholly pinched out. Like, a little splinter in one's finger. Then, we have in our hands this almost-too-much Love." She was smiling in her memories that were now 24 years past. "That day they brought him to me, set him in my arms, and I saw their faces – everyone of that room – were ghastly pale. 'You've birthed a witch, madam,' they said. Isia, they said: 'We could undo it for you, if you so wished, Mrs. Archidux.' And, then, Hadryn opened his eyes, and I saw. Such beauty. I replied – and I was very much out of sorts because of the painkillers and whatever else they'd given me. But, still, I looked at them; I held Hadryn close and said, 'You, cockeyed people. Everyone spends all their time talking about witches, what witches might look like, that you'd never know an angel, if you saw one.'"

He hadn't known what was proper to say in return, but felt her words close to his heart, especially as she concluded with saying, "Everything here is a lie."

It was a very well-decorated lie.

Isia stopped upon one of the steps and didn't need to glance at his pocket watch. His internal clock came with sound and pictures. He heard, even here in the gorge of the house, like wind-chimes jousting, the silverware against plates and brother utensils, the wine glasses' twinkling voices as they were nudged against more dinnerware or gravy boats, and the denizens' marathon-like breathing as they slopped their meals. Cubes, partially-chewed, would fall away from the corners of their mouths and confetti the floor. The conquest of the gormandizing would be in how much one ate, not what they ate, but the glorified conversation to follow would detail herbs, garnishes, sauces, and visual presentation of the perfect cubes.

The darkness below seemed to lap at the wooden step he stood upon.

Isia knew these cubes. He knew their dimensions. They all bore more or less the same base: either meat or potato, and then, a child's fistful of some artificial flavoring of onion or garlic, strawberry or mango with fats and sweeteners for added taste. Whatever it was, it was an imposter of Nature's brow-sweated toiling. There were preservatives and so many compounded chains of chemicals that no one could ever be free again to possess the wholeness of health. They were fettered to the taste of their times.

Isia winced every time he opened a sack of pelleted food and poured it into the processor. What troubled him most was that he was not a misfit in this acquired knowledge – it was common. Every denizen and blue card knew where the pellets were manufactured: laboratories. Under the precise eye of those scientists, who had become producers with such propaganda of "Advanced Technological Triumphs" plastered to the walls of their minds, the public had come to dine no longer from pastures or farms, but from the sterilized halls and equations of the "highest intellect." Meats were not livestock, as they had once been. Animal life was no more – save for those whom no one could appreciate: the rats, the birds, and fleas. The meat came from stem cells grown into patties of muscles or organs, slightly off in color: more like aged milk and less pink as meat had once been. Sometimes, complete animals were grown, but it wasn't actually slaughter any more. The lab creatures had never been birthed, so what was there to frame in terms of "death?"

Isia continued down, towards the dark. He paused at the 30th wooden plank to look back towards the single bulb of light. A moth batted its wings at the uselessness of that yellowed beacon and made monster murals of itself across the walls.

He had asked before for a hand-light: a flashlight, lantern, or candle stalk, but Mr. Archidux had his methods. He would recite to Isia, each time the housekeeper asked, his list of expenses: food, banquet décor, water, electricity, waste disposal – and always with: "You haven't the faintest inkling what it takes to keep this ship afloat, Isia." So, Isia had to make memory of the dark. He grew to know the feel of each board under the palm of his shoe and the count of footsteps across the granary to reach the light switch, like a pinpoint in the night.

There was a diminutive sound, suddenly, that made Isia miss his footing and the succeeding step flashed before his eyes. He jerked in direction of it, and some nymph of luck must have guided his hand, for he grasped that wooden piece, and he kept himself from splintering on the densely-packed dirt below.

Wild with adrenaline, Isia witnessed the dour physicality of reality come into acute focus. He glanced the interiors of the basement, coming out of his thoughts. There was a sundry of objects to maim one's self upon, and he had ever held this in first attention, except this night. In particular, the descent to the ground was the most foreboding trial, and he should have bestowed due diligence in heed to it, as he regularly practiced.

He felt himself still swaying with the momentum from his fall. He dangled like a worm on a fish hook, and one of his shoes fell. The sound of it came twice for it struck something with a padded impact, then found the floor. Isia trembled and stared down, past his feet.

That sound again, dragging at his ears, and this time, the darkness moved. He couldn't determine how far or close that shifting of blackness was, but it was undoubtedly there. Perspiration sprouted instantly, like a second skin.

"Hello." Isia wrestled with mediocrity, for it to unmask itself and reveal an evening like any other. Not this. "Hello? Someone below?" The fear was already molding his voice and the way it sounded. Isia attempted to pull himself up, but the fright in him was locking his limbs. *Come now. Lie in it – this terror. Something may be down there. But, never mind that. Lie down. As if on sweet grass.* Grounding himself, he drew breaths, steady and paced. His muscles came to on their own, and with ease, he lifted himself to the step he'd strayed from. Isia remained crouching on the wood panel as his heart caught rhythm with the rest of him.

If his hearing served him purpose, whatever was below was relatively large in bearing, and it slithered. It leaned into and traced the far wall.

He got to his feet. Did he have much choice? He was on a timely errand for an employer who would not give him a box of matches to see by, much less accept if he came back without the pellet sack on account of "having heard something." Mr. Archidux would fall into a tantrum-anger, if Isia emerged without the desired vittles. To deny this banquet a promised dish would cost Isia his employment, even if he could convince Mr. Archidux that a pilferer ravaged his treasured stock.

Isia was taking a step down and another. He imagined how a person could so taint the air with this sound. *A hungry thief shoulders behind himself a train of pellet sacks. The dark makes weary the compass in his head. He disorients, seeks out the wall of the granary and tries to follow it to light.* Isia stopped on the plank current to him, realizing that the larcenist may, indeed, be headed for the tail-end of the very thread of steps he now stood upon. Perhaps, it was mere moments before they would be confronted one of the other.

Isia's heart became loud in himself. His hands shook. His thoughts circled back to a flagrant error in his determination of this evening: a single food sack was alone 100 or 150 pounds. To caravan more than two would require the backs of many. Yet, there was not the shuffling of pairs of feet or even the whirr of a throne's motor. A personal vehicle could not move an inch down the narrow aisles of the storeroom anyhow, and the noise continued coming up out of the abyss: a slow, leaden creeping.

It would be forty steps to the light switch, once he was on the ground – perhaps, a few steps less if he ran. He would need to come off the steps and angle himself slightly right-veering to ferret passed the row of "pork" and "poultry"-flavored pellets. Then, he would trace along the longer and narrower path created by the wine barrels. Following left from there, the light switch would be on a raised column.

Isia came to the last wooden panel.

His intuition was showing him a feeling, but he didn't know how to look at a feeling that didn't have a face. Was it fear? Simply fear? A part of him that was older than his 58 years of age was speaking in his native tongue, so he didn't recognize the words at first, being so accustomed to English. He knew he heard himself speak from within, and the words were to turn back, but he couldn't. It was not solely because of duty that his curiosity became a deep yearning. It was the thought of that night, his grandchild so undeserving of pain and terror. He saw, again, the monster who had taken her – except, he could never recall the face of it or its head. He had seen, instead, only his granddaughter's eyes: her eye whites and the trembling moisture within them.

Isia reached beneath the last stair-step he stood upon and extracted a hand shovel that he sometimes used in the garden. It was the only potential weapon he had down here in the cellar.

He ran. He ran, knowing he was not alone.

Just under the flight of wooden steps, and very near to him, that sound, like fields being plowed by weighted instruments, ceased as he fled by. He had the sense – either by sound or intuition or paranoia – that the direction of the intruder's movement realigned to track him in the dark.

Isia made it passed the first row of stored foods, and as he came to the aisle of wine, a gurgle emitted out of the blackness. A rancid and charnel sweetness – the overripe state before decay - fouled the air, then came a peal of sharp intonations, like gulls crying out. The odor and those cries clung to him. He seemed to feel it on his skin and in his hair, causing the fear in him to coil into knots at his joints and in his organs, which wavered between petrification and overreaction.

He wanted the light.

As he ran in the dark, one of his feet was caught up suddenly, and he was torn back – became that much further from the small point in the room where he could indulge his vision. The muscle of his leg that was yanked filled with long threads of pain down the length of his thigh. He fell down upon his chest and cheek hard, feeling the dust of the floor come up over his mouth.

Isia froze. Then, he was lurched backwards, and the lower half of his being went into a pool of hot coagulation where his calves were lacerated. It bothered him that his mind only repeated: *I can't see! I can't see!* He tried to remember his granddaughter, for she was every reason he had spent these years in the Tiered Nations, but it was as if the darkness here kept him from seeing even his memories. He felt a warm breath, nauseating in the varying sour smells, wash over the whole of him, and Isia knew he was in the mouth of something gaping in largeness. Finally, his voice came. Perhaps, in the throat of another, his own throat had found crucial bravery.

"It was you, wasn't it? *You were the one to take my grandchild!*"

Isia raised the small, sharp hand shovel over his head, ready to strike. And, then, he fell deeper into the horrid, splashing heat up to his chest. Isia was maimed at all sides. He cried out, unable to mitigate the flayed nerves of his new wounds.

"Onii-chan, dame!" A voice rang out in Japanese, androgynous and gently coming in contact with the walls of the cellar.

Isia felt his legs curl up. He was pushed towards himself from the feet up, then he spilled forward and lied half-bent around himself, surrounded in what felt like burning glue. He panted and forced himself into a sitting position. He heard footsteps along the floor, and his eyes ached for answers.

A light clicked on. It was a flashlight.

She held it straight up, and it illuminated her face and his, but little else. She was close to him. "I'm sawry. *Sorry.*" She seemed to correct herself. Enunciation was an obstacle for her.

Isia saw that she was a young woman. Her hair was shades beyond flaxen. He could see that even in the dim light. The eyes that stared at him were pale, sunset-pink, and she was so slight of figure, dressed in the tattered robes of peasants, so much like those from District 11. He could see in her eyes the apology she sought to convey. "What are you doing here, child? What was that being which held me in its jaws? Was it the thing which took my grandchild? *Let me see it.*" He looked into the darkness, and the shape of the creature came back at him. It crept along a far wall, watching them with a rudimentary eye, the size of a serving platter, that was bloodshot.

Isia recoiled at it, and the woman lowered the flashlight to the ground, so that they lapsed again into the depths of sightlessness. He flailed instinctively for the light, but she kept it from his reach, and he reasoned with himself that, even with his injuries, he could still rise to kill the creature. Isia gripped the gardening tool in his fist.

"Just food," she said to him. "We need food." There was the faint rustle of her clothes, and Isia thought she must have gestured to the creature behind herself. She rose with the flashlight in hand and again expressed regret to him as she retreated towards the hulking shadow beyond.

A few feet of vision returned as she edged away from him. The massive being, segmented in rings of alien musculature, was swallowing pellet sacks whole and took twelve of them that Isia could count. The woman had stopped ten feet away from where Isia sat, and she placed the flashlight back on the ground, leaving it for him before she went to the creature.

"No, don't!" he called out to her, afraid the monstrosity would alter demeanor and catch her in its teeth. But, it permitted her to climb aboard its ill-shapen head, and she, every color of her absolutely white as brightness reflected in a mirror, looked to him one last time.

She placed one finger over her lips to hush him that they had been there.

Then, the slithering thing crawled into a great chasm where the opening of it was at a corner of the basement, obscured by shadow, and they were gone.

Isia heard now his own shaking respiration, and he threw himself at the flashlight, arriving to it on all fours. Desperately, he clung to it and shown it into every dark crevice of the room. Everything looked much as it should, and this unnerved him all the more. He next turned the head of the flashlight to himself and tried to rid the viscous consistency which saturated him. Isia used his arm sleeves to wipe clean one gash on his left leg, but as he did and the injury met with fresh, open air, blood erupted from the flesh and a violent, seizing agony followed with it. The lacerations were not threateningly deep, but there were many of them.

Isia gritted his teeth and fell back to the ground, holding his thigh in quivering hands. The sweat broke out on his face. He yelled and struggled against the flaring spasms that racked his nerves. With no other option, he gathered a handful of the thick, raucous gel from the floor and smeared it over his bloody leg. It placated the pain and the bleeding.

As he came to steady himself, sitting there alone in the nearly-suffocating darkness, he cursed himself for not killing the beast or, at least, following after it. Revenge had deserted him at the sight of the creature, and Isia felt the uselessness of his years spent in the Tiered Nations. He'd never killed anything before, and yet, he assumed he'd be able to now. Isia struck his own chest, apologizing to his granddaughter for his inadequacy.

And, then, because his senses had gained acumen with the threat to his life, and he heard, most clearly, a scream – powerful, then ragged with horror and despair - trail out, somewhere above himself where the banquet took place. It was that of a woman's.

"Cyssiline!" He could not tell from this distance if it were she belonging to that cry, but Isia found his feet, his strength. He made a crooked path towards the steps leading up, fearing that the beast had made its way to the diners for its own banquet.

CHAPTER 12

ERMAYA

The machine at the heart of the gala still churned. The diners remained at their seats, still in worship of this mechanical deity. It continued, even with this side attraction, to rotate its conveyor belts and the gears within turned, locking and unlocking teeth and grooves. The cacophony of it became unnaturally blatant in the sudden quietude, and though, audibly offensive, it kept at its guests to persist in due reverence, sliding another dish onto each their individual lecterns. Reflexively, two people dipped their forks into the shallow bowls and chewed as they watched the woman on the ground, the one who had screamed. Mr. Archidux was one of them, who did not break his dinner for what was clearly in his view. Still, the woman was pointing at the other diner. The rest of those in attendance looked from her to the one at the table with red-colored smearing around her lips and a bit at her chin, though none of the cubes served thus far had had any jam for filling.

"What's that she's said?" One denizen leaned in on another's shoulder to ask, just between the couple of them, but the other who'd been questioned said nothing.

The woman who'd been singled out, her hair dyed sunflower-yellow, was trembling, but otherwise forgotten by Time, for she remained as still as a hare having caught sight of wolves. In her grasp, dainty as became a lady, she balanced her fork, poised for another mouthful. The longer those at the Archidux's banquet stared at her, the more the sight of her bristled their neck and arm hairs.

Her little finger was completely gone.

The back of her palm looked peculiarly wide without the smallest member of its assembly. At the base, where that petite digit should have been affixed, blood – not much – blinked through the air, catching pinpoints of light before acquiring an uneasy home on her plate that was mostly empty, except for garnishes and a brown, creamy sauce. The blood slid into the puddles of that condiment to make ghastly neighbors, and its intrusion created a hue not sanctioned in Nature. The lady remained slightly leaned over her blood-meal, as if peering into a pond, but her eyes now were her only movement, shifting from the faces of each the other guests. She seemed flustered and frightened, but not in pain.

Cyssiline rose abruptly. She left her throne, and this astounded the crowd more so than the lady-of-the-moment. The denizens were looking to each other in an abashed way, as if to confirm with everyone present they were witnessing Mrs. Archidux upon her feet. How quickly she came to the woman's side.

"Ermaya. My dear. Are you hurt?" Cyssiline took a ribbon from her hair and wrapped the woman's hand. The bleeding made blossomed petals in the silk of Cyssiline's hair tie. The lady of the estate cast wide her gaze at all others of the table. "Summon a medical officer, please! Jonren!" Cyssiline implored her husband, but he stared at her without anything in his eyes, saying nothing in return. She picked out the grains of panic from her voice and repeated herself with force this time. "Jonren! Fetch help. Immediately." Her tone was burnished in weighted silver, and finally, he ceased mulling the food in his mouth. Fumbling the dish away from himself, he directed his throne forward, loudly striking the table and scraping at it before he was out the dining hall to do as he was told.

Cyssiline turned the woman's face to her own. She wiped scarlet from the corner of her lips. "We've help coming, Ermaya. 'Tis an accident, minor, made by haste, and the way we all become a little thoughtless with familiar ritual."

The woman on the tiled floor was rising and clutching, to no avail, at her motorized seat. Everyone ignored her.

Those residents of the highest civilization were upon the awareness that they were required a reaction in measured accordance with the event.

"She's eaten herself!" A man cried out in nearly feminine pitch. To him, Cyssiline shot a look of urgency and anger. He said no more, but his eyes grew wide as the "O" of his mouth. He would not stop pointing at Ermaya, and Cyssiline closed her eyes for a moment, expecting Isia to be at her side when she opened them. But, he was not in the hall, no matter where she looked for him.

Suddenly booming was another voice from directly across the way. "You were just eating too quickly, my dear. We have all rushed food to our mouths for the wonders of the taste of it." He was smiling to remain casual, as if to soothe the other people and in particular, those closest to him, for he kept glancing at them for credit to his words.

Ermaya began to pat her chest with her good hand. Tears slipped down her cheeks and a vein stood out on her forehead. The embarrassment was obstructing her breathing. She blanched: "But, I've swallowed it. What shall I do?"

A voice, hidden in the crowd, told her she should regurgitate it.

"Vomit? I can't." She sat there, still at her plate of food and still holding her utensil, while she and every diner there knowing it, the finger, went down her throat – skin and bone bit through so easily – and the imagining of it down in her belly, inside her.

The dining hall was tense with disbelief and disgust. Ermaya felt it upon every side of her, so she dared not turn one direction or the other. She couldn't decide what else to do, besides to do nothing. She fanned herself with quick strokes.

Someone else, who had the misfortune of sitting to her left and unable to part himself from the incident - in being that he, too, was in view of all others - tried to reassure her that he had once read how humans could snap their own fingers clean through with no more effort than that needed to bite into a carrot – one of those rooted foods of the past, facile to divide into parts. He was trying to share this mysterious tidbit with some light humor, while at the same time, knowing it was entirely inappropriate and of no usefulness to her condition. Yet, he continued because he felt a part of her limelight, and he worried how much he would be considered faint of heart, if he simply left – departed the entire Archidux estate – as he so wished. He said to her, with exaggerated gestures and his smile broad, crinkling at the corners, "Curious, isn't it? Indeed, quite so. It is only our minds which keep us from what is physically possible."

But, he was mostly made inaudible for the clamor that was bubbling up, like water brought to a boil. The guests finally parted from their meals, their thrones all abruptly in motion. Like the singular-lined procession of ants suddenly doused in water or swatted at, the diners scattered in disarray. The washbowl rooms and adjoining facilities congested, and someone was knocked out of his vehicle. The man landed very wrongly upon his left arm, and a bone in him soundly gave. He moaned for rescue.

The hysteria remained oddly curbed, laconic and hushed. As rabbits who adopt a couchant stance, eyes rounded in terror, to deceive the falcon his meal, some denizens huddled in small, protective groups towards the corners of the dining hall. They watched, riveted, and no one was quite sure how to conduct her or himself. A few guests uttered quick pardons, muttering about the hour of the clock, to Cyssiline and Jonren, who had by now returned, and they were absent of the estate in a matter of seconds.

Ermaya coughed twice, but it was not enough to undo the freakishness of the evening, and her pinky finger was indifferent to returning to its rightful plinth. She began to cry harder, yet still voicelessly. Only her shoulders shook with her body all alarmed.

Cyssiline was plying her fortitude. She asked herself for patience, but it was uncertain, like her stomach and her breath. She didn't know how to do more for Ermaya, so she stroked her hair and worried to herself that the other woman would be disfigured after tonight.

"Why would this happen? This has not happened to anyone else." The tears were escaping down Ermaya's cheeks now. Her body would not stop trembling.

Inside, Cyssiline balked. "Isia!" She searched again for him, but he wasn't there for her, even though he had always been since the first day of being hired. "He's coming, I'm sure," she told herself aloud.

Ermaya was but an acquaintance to Cyssiline, but Cyssiline stayed at that injured lady's side and sought to soothe her. She looked around at the diners she'd invited to this banquet, and they no longer appeared human to her. In their bulky caddies and pushed off to the sides of the hall, they were as furniture arranged for nothing more than storage. Only Ermaya, in her panic and mourning, felt blood-infused and somehow dear to Cyssiline – though it made no sense, nor the event, or the disregard for one's suffering by the other denizens. None of it was designed for this hour, which should have unfolded as if rehearsed.

Ermaya held at one of Cyssiline's hands. "Perhaps, I'm sick. Cyssiline, I am sick. You should not keep so close to me." She was near to questioning her, when there came footsteps from outside the banquet room.

CHAPTER 13

CHINAMI ISHIDA

Before:

She was different. And, not for the reasons most would suspect.

Chinami had known as a child. She thought it might have been why she became deaf, something to separate her from the rest of humanity – a difference which allowed her the silence to see more deeply into herself, to watch more than speak, and keep her thoughts within herself, for humans didn't expect the deaf to talk, except when necessary. She felt that those who did communicate with her were gravely serious about their interaction, as though her being deaf meant there was a greater chance of misunderstanding.

But, Chinami felt she understood more of the world without sound. She had loved, since a child, the vibration and motion of everything, everyone.

There was only her brother who spoke to her casually with a relaxed air. He joked with her and signed everything he said, even if her eyes were not always upon him. Sometimes, she would look over at him and catch him in the middle of a sentence or thought or exclamation. She felt, more so, the flow of life to find snippets of his words, here or there. He, at times, ran ahead of her, still signing what he was saying, and she would see only a bit of his words, and loved those moments. She imagined they were truer to life. Hearing people didn't always hear or listen to everything said to them. She wanted her life to reflect the unheard, even in her soundless world. But, everyone except her brother, looked so sternly into her eyes as they signed or gestured to her, as they held written pieces of paper up to her. They always wanted to confirm with her that she had understood them.

Thus, Chinami wandered away from the 11th District that was her home, and often, she went by herself. Alone, she felt more like herself, if she couldn't be with her brother. He was older and worked for the family. But, her family expected nothing of the sort from her, so Chinami was free to roam and, in doing so, to make her parents and the townspeople she passed worried for her. She knew they felt she was at a disadvantage in life, but she knew otherwise. She felt it. It hummed as a brave, trembling force beneath her skin.

She was different. She wasn't human, not entirely. Those who walked upright in her District were not her kin. Neither were the denizens who motorized in their thrones which bumped along over paved roads.

But, she knew the pull of them who were her own, and they were beyond her reach, yet waiting. There was something tremendous she would need to do. She felt it stirring somewhere near her breastbone, and if she had still been of the hearing world, Chinami knew she would have missed this essential piece of herself, unable to feel it over the noise of the Tiered Nations. She had tried, once, to tell her brother of the feeling, the tugging threads of a bizarre destiny, but he hadn't understood, asking her what she meant. She had signed back to him that she didn't know how to describe it. *It's like thunder waiting to arrive in the heavens,* she had finally answered him. He smiled at her and said that he wished to be part of it, whatever it was.

He made her happy, and she felt less alone. But, there was a sense in her that he wouldn't always be there for her, whether because of that impending fate of hers or because of typical human patterns in life. It was hard for her to pinpoint. She had these feelings, like different textures of fabric in her mind, but she couldn't see the colors of them.

Chinami waited and wandered.

One day, years ago, when she'd been wandering the 11th District noiselessly, like dandelion pappus, she'd meandered past an outdoor band playing in the town square. Then, she had found her way outside of town, carrying with her for a few steps, the faint tremors she'd felt from the instruments vibrating of the band she'd just left.

She walked on, past the imaginary boundaries her parents always requested she kept within. She knew of a place she'd always wanted to see. Their District was the only one to abut an overgrown forest that had once been a public park, and Chinami was drawn there for the scents which pricked her nose: the smell of damp soil and something of weeds with their sap milking out. As she moved through the bramble and viburnum, she realized she wasn't the only one to discover this forest returned to Nature.

Chinami paused. Instinctively, she lowered to the ground, as her gaze settled on the woman standing beneath the eldest tree of the grove: a most unusual tree of seemingly crippled growth. The branches were the thinnest Chinami had ever seen of a tree, and they hung in strange clusters without extending out into boughs. Towards the base of the tree though, she saw that the trunk was split in numerous places and here seemed to be the missing limbs of the tree. It was as though the tree were upside down, and Chinami nearly wondered, if she dug into the earth, might she find leaves beneath the soil. But, it was a queer thought, and she returned her attention to the figure beside the tree.

Chinami watched the woman. It was likely she was close to her own age. The woman's hair swept the mid of her back, dark-hued with light dancing in its depths, like the pupil of an eye. She was slender and wore a qipao the color of washed teal, which was adorned with royal-blue stenciling of bamboo and birds.

The woman stood with her eyes closed. Chinami assumed she was meditating, but the woman revealed her eyes slowly. They were heather-brown, and she began to sway slightly, as one does in dance, and Chinami watched as she held one forearm in front and across her midsection. With her other hand which she held, palm flat, the woman swept her hand back and forth over her arm, in time with her swaying. It was so unexpected that Chinami didn't, at first, recognize the signed word for "music," but the woman established pacing and a meter with her gesture, and then she began to sing in sign.

Chinami didn't know the song, but it was brought to her, felt by her. Like arriving in the middle of a dream scene with everything and everyone already in motion, Chinami felt siphoned into a cadence by force. She was made to *hear* by this woman. She watched the woman's face and the emotion of the song came through her; the lyrics told the story. In the woman's body, Chinami felt the beat. She watched as the woman drew out some words, visually elongating sound, then returned to the flow and measure of the music. The words danced through her fingers and hands, were swept through the air by this woman. Chinami felt she had been carved into this moment. Motion sickness came to her and then left. Her ears went hot as if burning to hear the song her eyes saw.

In a moment so long, which ended too soon, the woman had finished the song. Gently, the woman left Chinami's deaf world. Chinami had watched as she went to a speaker and audio-playing device as another person came for the woman who had sung. Chinami didn't hear the woman speak or say to the man who had joined her that she practiced her sign language by singing in sign, then they were gone, and still, Chinami felt unusual, and yet, no longer did she feel alone.

(*3 hours earlier and of the Present*)

"Shh..." she soothed her father. "Shh." Her hand rested on one of his arms, gently squeezing.

She had seen to the care of him the past few hours of what he thought of as sickness. His bed was befouled, but now his convulsions lasted no more than twenty seconds at a time. As they passed, his body relented to a peaceful stillness, and he would moan for his son, but Chinami was the only one left of their house whom he could speak with. She stared down at her father, knowing she had always unnerved him. But, it didn't seem to her an important thing.

He had slept with her at his bedside, and after a half hour, he'd awakened with contorted features.

"Please, feed me," he said.

Chinami had rushed to the kitchen for slices of bread and a cheese wedge for which she'd bartered her mother's last kimono from the only closet in their house. But, returning to her father's room, she found him gone and the front door swaying open. Stepping outside, she looked for him, but there was no trace of him. Just like her mother. Chinami stood, blinking into the night.

In her dreams, she knew the symptoms her father had had were spreading, touching now even the Denizens in their towering estates.

She closed the front door and made her way back to the kitchen, to the great earthen stove as it piped warmth into the room which tickled the skin of her bare arms. She peered into the mouth of it. With exceeding care and pride, Chinami maneuvered a steel paddle board into the stove to extract loaves of bread that had just finished. The scent of them was sweet grain and baked flour. Though the stove was spacious inside, it held no more than four loaves at a time, and Chinami brought the freshly-baked ones to the narrow, tiled counter in the kitchen. She rested these new ones beside eleven other loaves she'd spent the day making.

When her parents had fallen ill, she'd taken the last of their money to buy flour and yeast. Her brother had gone from home to home, too, to perform menial tasks in exchange for fruits and vegetables. They needed food, so much of it. Then, he had caught the fever as well. His body had soaked with its own waters from within, and then the rest of what was inside him had come through the planes of his skin. She remembered his eyes, brown with black flecks in them, as he stared at her by his side, until his body and breath became as silent as worms when they emerge after rainfall. She had signed to him, telling him her promises though his eyes had closed to rest. She would take care of him and all the others in the basement and the ones yet to come to their house by quiet instinct.

Chinami gathered into baskets the fifteen loaves she had baked and carried them down into the lower level of the house. The steps descending to the underground floor were aged wood, and they creaked with familiar give and had a familiar, musty odor, like cedar cradling dew for too long.

Her sandaled feet left the last, wooden step to stand on the granite floor. She wished the ground were made of something softer. Chinami took a short, Japanese chopstick from the one, inner pocket of her dirtied robe and wound her hair into a loose bun at the back of her head, securing it with the utensil. Her robe was white with emerald-green stenciling along the lower half, and it made a V-collar where the open ends came together over her chest. The quarter-sleeves were wide where they came down just past her elbows. She wore a large, pink sash at her midsection that tied just below her breasts and covered her down to her waist. The robe was short and showed her calves, for it had tattered and torn long ago. It had been her mother's.

Chinami brushed a large, breathing body as she made her way to the lamps in the room. Strands of her pale hair flitted in the many sighs that stirred the basement's confines, and she used a finger to pull free the hairs that caught at one corner of her lips which were thick and flush, like the roundness of peaches. She struck a match and set aglow the first lamp that hung from a metal hook bolted to the ceiling.

The light, with its gentle, yellow arms, reached out, and the creature nearest Chinami thrashed at that abruptness of bright, knocking her from her feet and sending the warm bread loaves in a sprawl. The beast, limbless and long in form, looked to her, and those eyes bore some semblance to a human eye, except there was too much eye-white. The iris and pupil were vague ovals of color, like water-paints that were much thinned out. Beneath the eyes, terrible in their crudeness, were nostril slits that quavered with each breath. The cartilage framing them was raised and curved, and below that, were lips that were inarguably human-like. The line of the mouth ran far back. It gaped at her, but she smiled and was calm as she recollected the food into the wicker baskets.

The second, third, and fourth lights shone at her touch, and now the cellar could be seen for its cast of stowaways. There were fifteen of them, and they were each individual in appearance – some with eyes multiple, wide and staring; others had thin slits along the head where in the depths of them could be seen eyeballs rolling. Most likely, those ocular organs they would lose altogether, as their transformation peaked, then suffused to new beings. A few had tusks or teeth in rows, all sharpness, and housed in mouths of dominant, wicked proportion. Two had mouths of rudimentary development, all molars, with tongues too large that often rested on the floor in front of them. All of them were long of form with a largeness well beyond the dimensions of anything human.

Chinami went to each of them and distributed a loaf of bread, presenting the food near to them. Yet, some, she framed the bread in the holds of their jaws, if leaning to the ground would be cumbersome because of the width of their tusks or fangs with lengths hindering.

Each the Wyrms kept respectful distance of the others, as much as the crowded enclosure would allow. But, towards the rear of the basement, was a Wyrm on its side, and the others had given to it as much room as possible. The Wyrm breathed in wheezing intakes, and Chinami hurried to the side of that overturned beast with the last loaf of bread.

"Kyranya!" she pleaded, as she kneeled in close to the Wyrm, who was of russet and scabrous integument with two sets of pale green eyes. She was not large and bore a little snout, almost porcine, and one of her nostrils was slit, a wound that had healed poorly. Kyranya had been with Chinami a handful of years now.

The albino woman touched the splatter of blood on the stone ground closest to the creature's mouth; it was congealed with phlegm-like consistency. She saw the withered body, devastated by inanition, and where there should have been vigorous muscle was instead sunken depressions along the cylindrical frame with sores yielding to cellular dissolution. *"Bread,"* Chinami said. She tore the loaf in half and went to put it in the mouth of the Wyrm, but the teeth of the beast snapped shut before she could.

She heard all their thoughts at once – the other Wyrms – and their voices were fluttering inside her mind as well as emerging as gentle mutterings against the walls of the cellar.

She dies,

Refuses all water, all food -

Refuses to rise.

Chinami turned to each the three Wyrms who spoke one after another. Whether she utilized hand-speech or spoke aloud, they heard her in return. *Why?* She asked them by sign.

Kyranya gave answer from behind Chinami. *My lady,* said she by telepathy. *My Conqueror Queen.* The albino woman gave face to her and there was hurt in her eyes and the breadth of empathy. Kyranya continued:

> *We came to you, as if by a calling.*
> *The Damned, upon our bellies, crawling.*
> *Human eyes find us frightful.*
> *And, how to go to the Drakes with advancing horror*
> *accompanying our arrival?*
> *You told us the progressions to unfold by new moon.*
> *You told us of great change and the greater commune.*
> *But, war, you said, would circle 'round as before.*
> *Led by the Angel of fire and darkness, arisen from draconic folklore.*
> *'Dramatis Personae' already cast,*
> *The ugliest face chooses their role last.*
> *So, fight we must, to survive the flighted Heroes' glorious finale.*
> *One Wyrm more is another Wyrm's only ally.*

*Thus, give my share of food to he or she whose strength we
may save
For, I die, yet one ration more may be one less occupied grave.
And, by one or two or some scarce number,
We will survive the genocide by Drakes
             and allow the race of Wyrms to remain,
                 uncommitted to eternal slumber.*

Then, her voice slipped away as two of the kerosene lamps
diminished to nothing more than crafted steel and glass. The
darkness pervaded, and here, Kyranya became absolutely
still. Chinami's visage and her tears were the sole illuminated
characters of that blackened den. She held the Wyrm who had
been starved out of life. To die by one's body in consumption of
itself for having no other means to do else – she knew it was an
agony beyond scornful imagination. A wilting to one's bones was
painful and hateful.

Another Wyrm said to her:

*For being the weaker, we die
Yet, there is a strange power in this city
and he is marked by his one eye!
We have seen him, the soldier, through the glass
If we take him, the Drakes and their Angel's wrath
will we topple and surpass*

Chinami stood, and she looked the length and width of her
treasure trove that would render any other consumed by terror.
She brought the fingertips of one hand together and motioned
to her mouth.

Eat, she told them by hand-speech, as she hastily brushed
aside a tear. *I will find you each food more and every Wyrm I can
rescue, that I swear to accomplish, but leave the boy. It is the dragons we
will come to glut ourselves upon.*

Those beasts, so hellish in appearance, were quiet as they held
at their pieces of bread. Chinami waited, but she knew they never

ate before she did. So, she took the last apple her brother had earned as payment for replacing the panes of a window shattered, and she brought it to her lips. She ate, then each Wyrm followed her manner.

Chinami stared at each of them, from her human vessel. She'd felt this day at the back of her tongue, like a certain sweet taste, and she'd left that feeling there, her entire life, since her tongue she did not often use. It made it easier for her to walk alongside human beings. She'd loved the human family to which she was born. Only her brother, she'd shared with him stories of the Conqueror Wyrm. He had seen something else in her eyes when she told him these tales, and she knew she could trust him to someday understand how she was not as she appeared. How she would be needed for this day. The protectiveness of the creatures she housed spread within her.

When they had finished dining together, Chinami called out: "Koji." One of the Wyrms came forward. She signed to him, *Father told us of the denizens for whom he once worked. Don't you remember? He mentioned one house – Archidux – which had bounties of food more than estates wealthier than they.*

And, the last two lights were blown out.

CHAPTER 14

ERYX ~ A WYRM

The dust of this lair was choking me.

Above earth, they, others like me, cried out for meat. Let the Drakes hear our keening. It would be their only siren before we pared their flesh, and this would come quick.

Anon, The Conqueror bid us peel them from the face of the world. Telepathy, triumphant over distance, seemed to make of us each the whole of our species by mind, as it was necessary. In that was power we'd never known before.

I rifled through the aphotic holds, both within myself and without. My thoughts came out hard and algid, like the confines of this cave so much like a grave or silenced womb. I was without rest or calm, pacing, so the dirt came up again and made sorrel patches on me where it settled in greater concentrations.

The ache in me stood on.

I now had teeth.

I was fearsome, I believed.

I needed to eat and would have ate the darkness out of the night, if I could.

This starvation without hunger.

I'd have the evening in my jaws, and it would be cold and thick with the year-end season, numbing the roof of my mouth and the gums in between my canines. With quick, convulsive twitches of my head, I'd tear at the moon's silent lover, rip away his arms that embraced her. I'd leave her alone in the sky and cud him between my fangs 'til his midnight rains burst forth to wet the corners of my mouth and spill over my chin. He would, then, howl the solitary gales that shock those sleeping out of nightmares, and he would call to her in broken storms before I suffocated him in my throat.

Every nocturnal villager, who daily awaited his dusk-colored arrival, would no longer have his shielding cloak. Let them try to hide without him. Let them scamp and stalk and alight or take flight without his caring, piteous pit-like eyes.

Only he would be enough for me.

And, when he was pushed down to my belly, then would I know peace for having eaten the night.

Then, would there be a sweetness in my mouth. My tongue would taste the history of existence and how this world came to be.

Only he could ever be enough for me.

Yet, damnation!

Soured, spoiled, sterile contemplation!

The night stood on.

He, a proud prince to that bright lady enveloped in her charcoal abode. The ember fragments of their heirs, that starlight overhead, seemed to giggle at my foolish imaginings.

"Hurl the great tongue of the Demon's bell,
Let it toll its cries in concentric rings
And, wake every fiend out from Hell.
The Wyrms rise with their Queen; the Drakes with their darkened King
So, let us eat of the dragon's flesh 'til our bellies swell
Eat and we will become Drakes ourselves to reign over everything!
For, the moon would not give up her knight.
Thus, we bring all Horrors to this fight."

I yelled into a wailing. My cries echoed back every crevice and outcrop of stone in this buried cavern that was my refuge.

The chant – perhaps, an incantation or mantra – was not my own. In passing one who bore my own semblance, he had gone out of his way to stop me with these words and fenced me at every angle with their cadence and rhyme. I listened. How could I not? It quickly became our praxis as speech, like contagion or catholicon, befell us each. To become suspended in the individual's interior made exterior by audible thought was a trove of depth so immeasurable that I had yet to hear one of us mention the acquisition of teeth. Let the Drakes concern themselves with our teeth. If they do not ask for our words, so long withheld, then, our fangs to them will be bared.

But, from one to another: it was this strange rhyme. He had heard it from someone else, was merely handing it along.

When he had recited to a close, I hadn't heard much of what he'd said. Ironic. We – Wyrms, that is – had spent our existence listening, given we had no other choice and could not converse. Yet, here I was, caught in a travail to both hear and understand. My mind was snagging; it was arrested at the quality of his voice, then it became stalled on the loud and soft of how he spoke, and finally, it was much distracted by the emotion he conveyed. I had comprehended very little of what he'd said, imperative as it sounded.

So, I stood there, quiet like a dumb beast.

He waited. I could feel a concern, that he fretted he had spoken and made nothing of sense. I waited impatiently for my own words. I pleaded, to no one in particular, for them to be there. I found them in holding, shuffling along the edge of my mouth.

It was something else which bridled me and buckled straps of harness at the emergence of who I was about to become.

I did not know how I should be.

Laughable conundrum! I had speech. Those dark nights as I slid through sand, so much measured Time, and passed these others – we looked at one another, but nothing more – I had been a world of one and Loneliness was capitol. And, bright days, seeing the harshness of the multitudes of us and how we were so mute; it was now gone.

And, yet, I could not determine how to conduct myself, how to present.

He was still waiting.

I dawdled on one word he had said: *night.* It was slippery and Janus-faced in my mind. Words came to us with surgical difficulty; they were pain and remedy in one, but it was certain that we loved words – each of us spoke with the care we could afford the language coming to us and up out of us. I didn't know how or if I should ask about what I could not determine. I let the water of that word escape through my grasp. Wyrms had had only this parched desert for so long. It was our home. But, we were departing it, like a rite of passage.

"Sir," I ventured, though I felt instantaneously that my demeanor was wrong. Wyrms were villains. The animals we hunted saw this, and the Drakes, too, knew us for the monstrosity of our actions. Why did I continue? But, I knew only how to be me. "Once more, if not troublesome, could you impart this knowledge of the orb and night? I found myself giddy to a fluster and unable to penetrate meaning, such is conversation a newfound delight."

He guffawed. "Ah, genteel and well-bred?" He gave pause, thinking things through. "Perhaps, we are all misled." He seemed to be considering our disposition as a species, as well, and the stage we were to grace before the eyes of Drakes. He was quiet, unable to decide.

I was not yet discouraged, and I said the facts to have them, for once, spoken. "We eat as we do, and one should think a complementary deportment must follow. If ill-fitted, I suppose it ruins the story; the serving is then viscid and grumous and unpalatable to swallow."

He considered much in his silence, and in that swath of time, a handful of curious others had come to linger at the edges of our conversation. We were a most bizarre makeshift town square, in that moment. "Hmm," he said, at last. "Unpalatable and deleterious. Certainly, it bolsters our leverage to protract this façade, however spurious."

Someone else piped up, angered and vexed. "Leverage, you say? Oh, well, it may. Or, by dice-fall, it be our fey!"

Then, came a voice more earnest, filled with hope. "'Tis truth she speaks. Now, we've the means to build bridges. We'll go to the Drakes, smolder the flame-tongues of war, and with them, through speech, we shall reach our desired peaks. They are the enlightened; let us don robes as their disciples and no more will we be constrained to the bilges."

A third Wyrm interrupted, "Ninny. Cretin. Fantasizer. Drakes loathe us. Thus. Fear is trumpcard. Become scarred. Branded. Marked. Opprobrium."

I listened, balancing their dispute in a mind that had now shapes and letters of a sort.

And, a fourth mind, besides me and him who'd originally began this, said: "Is not this the directions of the poem he's orated? War is its meaning." She turned to him who related the chant which danced familiar meter within us all. "From whom did you fetch this gleaning?"

He answered, "Oh, memory and reverie." And, he paced a brief stretch away from us, then contracted back. He, then, recollected, "As I've been told: from the First Wyrm, passed along from one to another and another, then me. She is the Queen, the Conqueror. We must trust her guidance, but of her, I know not more." He stopped and was perplexed with his own words.

Lastly, the seventh one of us voiced opinion, and he had developed but perforated language. "Sh-she. Will. Sh-shield us. From-from. The Dr-Drakes. She. Th-the Conqueror."

We gazed at him.

"Yes."

"Yes."

"Yes."

Nearly half of us chimed assent. For, this meaning of our era and how it would proceed we'd sought to define was older than us each and even so collectively. Outside our small counsel, other

Wyrms were anon gridlocked in deathly contention with the flighted dragons, and we stood here as the day became older. It seemed apparent what must be done. But, I waited for it to feel right, or at least, less wrong.

There was still so much to say; we were bewildered, but also goaded from delay.

"Please, quickly," I said to he who, singularly, I tried to feel as though I knew him. "Play minstrel and deliver the rhyme once more for me." If he could repeat it, I would know it better. I would understand.

The others were erased in the blinding of the heightened noon and left but trenches in the marl where they had been.

He discoursed again, but appeared this time less convinced or more afraid. I hastened the mantra to memory and thanked him. He grew quiet, then declared that he would commit some heinous deed. It would be an ugliness to the Drakes and smirch the pages of history. He bid me do the same.

I promised it, yet I lingered, unable to turn away from him. I wanted to ask him more. I did. "Do you know why we must end the night? I wonder at the tale of him with the command to extinguish the Drakes in the darkness of our bite."

He drew in close. "There must be reason this comes to us, as if from the shadows of the mind. We were such dumb beasts, but ancient knowledge rises and us it finds. The moon and the night. To divide them and consume the beau, supposedly will end this siege betwixt species and leave the world in peace bedight. 'Til we can have them, the Drakes we must oppose, or they will have *us* made dim."

I hesitated, yet, again: that nagging trust in him with whom I spoke. "When we find the night, it should be easy enough: we will split him from her with the following day."

His eyes widened. "Indeed, you see well; the morn's light will naturally hold them at bay!"

"But," I said, softening in tone, in character. "It seems wrong. I do not know them, but I assume they have loved long."

I saw that he became a different shade of himself, as well. An air of sadness settled upon him. "Is it our place to question? Wyrms have come to what we now are and there is war for this transgression." He appeared regretful. "If we choose not to fight, to act on what we know, we will know Death and thereby, permit our last regression."

I agreed with him. I would be a Wyrm, as Wyrms should be.

We parted and inadequately so. What was farewell to a monster-soul?

I had gone and did as he suggested. The desert-lands I kept to my back, and I journeyed far. When I came to a kingdom foreign, I tore at things. I was more violent than I had ever known myself capable. Adrenaline was my blood and breath, but I couldn't pause to sew together words for it all, so the experience came and went, and I was muddled during most of it. I had seen of that alien territory that there were tears in the sky which refused to become the act of crying. And, I had murdered, yet gone beyond even that crime. I came away with one of them: a Drake upon my back. I didn't know who she was, but the others of her kind screamed for her, as I carried her away.

I ran with her, saying nothing. I showed her my teeth, but not one word of mine.

Then, I came to this comfortless den by chance, by tracking gray grass and climbing into a punctured chasm on the face of a silent sward. I found my way down, down. Several smaller veins opened up from the central tunnel, but I sensed others, like myself, who had gone before this way or that, and avoided them. Traces of blood cave-painted those paths worn by others, and so I knew, in hauling this weighted kip, that I partook in a soldier's duty. We would catch these elements of brightness and the sea, of goodness and beauty, and in our clutches drag them beneath the world – to become as we so are: living burials. We are how night terrors begin. We are the demons beneath the brain. And, each of them, these Drakes, will we decorticate their enduring pulchritude and corrode with our appetite their august strength, 'til they are no more than their guts – a length of their entrails with teeth, who can do no more than crawl through the dirt we leave to them. Ha! And through their hideous metamorphosis will we extract from them how to capture the night and eat for all eternity. By torment, will they surrender their secrets, their coveted wisdom. They will allow us our lives; they will allow us a place beside them. We would change the order of hierarchy, by the Queen and the capture of the night.

My stentorian song, and the howling of it, filled the veins and the womb of this city, hidden. It was dark here. There was no light, save the dimness that timidly trailed after me from that mammoth piercing that, now, was hundreds of feet the distance.

To my prison.

No. Her prison.

My captive.

I had brought her here, guessing my way through the cave system, and she had not been a burden to strain my muscle or my thoughts. I dare say the act had been untroubled, no more itinerary nor craft than a trawler upon his daily riverbed. I had manipulated a few of her bones to pieces so that she might better feel inclined to accompany me here. In truth, I had crushed her under my weight. When she was forced to abort consciousness, she found herself awakened to my poem of the night.

"Who is this knight you wish for, dear Wyrm?" She was lying on her right side, since I had shattered the forms of her left limbs. In a pinched crawlspace, I had tucked her, then left to circle the perimeter of my new abode. There was not much space to arrange between us; I kept to the far side of the hollow. She regarded me with a gentleness, like the weight of pearled jewelry, nothing more, and so lovely.

I studied her, and breathed too loudly with guttural undertones, a broken rudder flailing at the marshlands. From out my mouth were only fetid odors. I could not pretend to have graced propriety. "Gather yourself to more proper order. And, panic not the confines of this tight corridor. Imbecile. Recreant. I did say 'knight.' As in, the late hours and the opposite of bright."

"Yes, of course. You did." The Drake stared at me.

She must be mocking me. Internally, I bided my anger to attack, but it was torpid and stared into the desert sun of an eternally-parched self-image of myself that thirsted for jeering insult. A validation occurred each time I sensed the Fool's cap nearer my head. *Who was I to have her?* A voice, faceless or masked, asked from out my chest. Like those chuckling stars, somewhere outside, with their selfish mother Moon, the celestial family ran me to the margins in simply being who they were and I being what I was. I told myself that my anger hadn't gone blind, that pity was the minstrel in my court, and that I was fittingly amused. It was only this, so why did I not laugh at her? The minutes leaned in on me; I should have been gloating with the bravado of a hunter with pregnant snare.

She was here because of me. May the specters of the Chinese nation portend all despair for this: the wreckage of a Tianlong *(tee-ehn lohng)*, the Heaven dragon, in my pitted den. I caught her. Still, she bled along the neck from where I fish-hooked my jaws to drag her for many miles. She was tattered like a love poem taken everywhere.

I asked her, "Why did you not take arms, resist me? Your tactics only to parry and of inquiry. Ambuscaded. Vitiated. Now, you are here, in Nosferatu's grotto. Will this be your tomb, the lowest of the low?"

She rested her head on the stone floor. "You carried me this distance to stop my breath?" The midsummer zephyr moving in and out her lungs was so entirely serene; she made it seem that injury could be set upon a stream and carried away.

Uniquely, two pebbles, no more, rattled upon the stone floor. A ripple in the sea of earth. She glanced this.

But, I was staring at her.

How she made me to stare at her! Golden, carp-like scales flourished her being. Those orbs of her face like rubies. A set of smooth, black horns above her little bovine ears and the hairs which streamed from the upper lids of her gaze were hues out of Nature – the brightest aquamarine, the sweetest tangerine, and chrome green, like sea foam from another planet. The very same likeness in colors found its way along the ridge of her, for it was her dorsal mane, too, and she, this beautiful flagship on the ocean's horizon, gave the impression of having always a dozen, miniature suns bursting at her edges. Even her two long, catfish whiskers, her feet of talons – five digits, like a human's hand or a god's – and her jaws with those rows of tiny teeth, somehow persuaded the mind to see in it a refinement, something of nobility like the emperor's seal and of civility like an iron tea set. I could not cease my staring. She was thousands of things I was not, could never be.

I drew anger into my lungs and erupted at her, "This is why you shall be my pretty tart, my rainbow confection! Even if some princely star has blessed you, he will see you lost in this sick vection! Ingurgitated. Annihilated. You shall never be as us; the heavens shrug and ignore the underworld and the providence so askew. Therefore, will you know the monster through his stomach, the stomach that created the monster!" My speech faltered of rhyme. I'd felt it.

Upon her visage, I saw now panic, but she was staring passed me at rubble that was tumbling from the roof of our buried cavern. For a moment, I was displaced by a shudder through the netherworld.

She was scraping for purchase, to come upright. "He's come," she said.

I looked everywhere for answer, but a cave hinders vision in its many walls being much alike.

The earth found stillness from its fevered trembling for a moment, then a roar like the most macabre cellos in perfect orchestra blustered into the canals of my earholes. Through rock and soil, through interlaced tree roots and layers of wrath I could never imagine possible, I heard this bellow of a creature who may have predated Time.

I gave to her my attention, for she felt the likeness of a girl's chipped music box upon a nightstand handed down by loving generations in contrast to this sudden quaking and this maelstrom of the loam. Her cinnabar eyes beheld me with something like plaintive kinship. I realized I knew nothing of what I had pillaged.

She whispered soft rhyme, as if to mend the lapsing in my own words. "He has come from out the night, the Scourge Angel. And, when he walks, what follows is the forged death knell."

Unannounced, it came to me what I had done.

"War, war. Not fables or folklore." I muttered to be gentle to myself. I had damned my life. Like simple physical laws: of course, she was protected, perhaps divinely so. I had thieved her from that rain-suspended realm, never realizing I had begun my own hunt, and now, what came for me might well be as much legend as it was unfathomable power. She was not singular, not a leaf in the fitful wind. The dragons were a garden, and from the rows of azalea, primrose, and gentian, I had snapped the stem of the one peony and carted her away. I felt again foolish, like a child who is presented the day, responds with every instinct, then returns home to be reprimanded. "What is he?" I asked, though her words were adequate. A meter in me was faltering, like the heart – if I had that organ – or my blood was stalling. I felt windless at once.

"He is older than thought, so he will never change."

The rubble became a rockslide, all dust and grit, then a boulder near my lower half gave, and that awful barrage above ground grew ten-fold in strength. The ceiling above us fissured and split; it cracked like the ribs of Earth being snapped open.

I kept my back to it, so that when the rostrum of that monstrous dreadnought careened into the rooms of my supposed fortress, I needn't have to bear witness to the teeth, ordered and calculated like the pikes of a disciplined army, or see the hearth fire resting at the back at his throat, just beyond the jaws searching for me.

I turned to her, edging closer. "You, the Heaven Drake, with beauty gilded and the empyrean your chariot, favored by all favors. And I, this: a featureless, beige, and wrinkled appendage without body and subjected to all anguished labors." I wanted to blame her. I wanted for what I had done and this beastly consequence to be her blunder.

She was upon her feet, or rather, barely hovering as Tianlong do, and she drew closer to me – or, closer to that primordial horror just beyond me. "This, you've done for yourself, and I, myself as well, shall create my own." She was watching the crust of earth come apart. Now, her breath thumped in her chest, and she looked left to right for a channel that would air-pocket and rise to breach the surface of the enclosed shell where I had brought us. Exceedingly fair to look upon, I was enchanted by her radiance again and those colors which lined her back, each of them tumbling over the others at every minute fluctuation of her aureate being.

The thing at my back cleaved away the passage I had followed to reach our grotto, and in so doing, crushed and dismantled numerous other arteries chasing out of this great hollowed cave. I heard the cries of my kith – needlepointed with vibrato, some mewling with pain – and assumed they had been crushed in the detritus or half-smeared out of existence: just a bit of kitchen scrap in the drains.

I smelled innards. How many of us had crept passed the fallow soil and into this veined tomb? Were they any I had known in that brief exchange of how and why we should have come to this?

The Heaven Drake had been ghosting in and out of the remaining tunnels still left to us. She moved quick, like incense tendrils being swept by the passerby. I watched her, for in these last, eroding moments, she was still mine. She turned to me: "Why do you not flee! Escape, my Wyrm!"

She puzzled me. Then, I recalled how I was but a fool to her. "Stagehand. Wasteland. You are cunning and full of deceit! You angled for me to take you: a lure for our defeat!"

There was only a flap of roof overhead now. I shrunk from the sudden sky, on instinct, and blinked dilated vision to see an arm like gnarled, fallen timber driving into the recesses of this stomach. The claws were overgrown, and I questioned myself for feeling that the hand looked human. I thought I saw brutish knuckles – and a crooked thumb.

I had not wished to know him, but the gates of my gaze let him in.

I choked, a few infantile hiccups emitting, then vomited out of fear. The discharge rolled and splashed out; I was coughing for breath. I wheezed, and it tasted sour.

She had called him an angel.

But, he was, every inch of him, stygian black, except that his skin was made of irregular tiles which fit as jigsaw pieces, then bulged with muscle underneath to show embers popping and crackling in between his armored plates. With each movement, that untamed fire beneath his flesh hissed like a tangle of serpents. I blinked dumbly; the heat of him was stinging my view. Above him and mottling the sky were a sheet of insects – no. They were Drakes as well; he had brought his rabble to this spectacle. They kept their distance as he ravaged through the intestines of the Earth.

The Tianlong was still attempting persuasion into my ears. She confessed, "One part Truth, yet of the whole, entirely wrong. You've teeth, you've speech. There was every reason to meet minds with you. Yet, The Angel. I didn't think he'd find eyes out of sleep. He has to see me." It seemed things were not unfolding as she had wished either. She lunged forward to flag his attention, demented as it was. And, it was in that instant that he yelled once more.

Fire, white like an explosion, and from out the angel's crag, burst into our vision. I was thinking to myself, as it happened, but I couldn't hear my own thoughts. In the absence of my governing mind, the body was responding.

"Don't, Mei Xian." (May She-uhn) How calm I sounded. I snaked out in front of her, that golden mistress, with timing infinitely impeccable. The flames paint-splashed me in open wounds upon my head and underside, from rearing up, became charred and stank, but she was unsinged for my actions.

"Wyrm! Wyrm!" Was she hyperventilating? I had shocked her with my heroic gesture. Now, she was crying.

She didn't deserve my comforting. Except, I knew I wished to give it to her. "Fly, fly. Bid a final farewell and goodbye. Trace the fourth tunnel from the right. Then, dip down before you'll come above to light." I had always known the way out, but it was plain this thing I would not be able to outrun.

"Come with me!" she urged.

Why this panic? Wyrms die. From what I understood of this age now upon us, our aim was to try and take a few, pretty Drakes with us, if we could. But, that was to be the extent of our togetherness with them. "Hmm." I mused to myself. The stinging lacerations were distracting me. A playful dizziness was beckoning, and I drew debate on whether to follow it or my body that was in the scholarly throes of comprehending this unimaginable, blistering pain. Unable to commit, I took simply to muttering to myself. "Who am I to steal her?" I asked myself. "Who am I to carve a forbidden door?"

I looked over my shoulder. The Scourge Angel was gaining a face, peering in.

The talons of that Heaven Drake hooked me by the snout and yanked away my view of him. She ran like falling silk to the fourth channel, dragging me – how dare she! – and plunged the pair of us into suffocating darkness. We flew at her lavish speed for only a short distance, then the artery constricted, and both our bodies would not pass together farther.

I screamed at her, "Leave me, Heaven's daughter!"

"Nay, you will be with me and thespian no martyr."

I dug at the hard, packed dirt with the spearhead bristles that lined all angles of my body. My voice came weakly, "Escape. Too late." Behind us, the grotto must have been flayed wide, for a harsh brightness was beginning at the end of the passage we had just fled from, and it seemed to be a small minion in league with that disgraced god. It ferreted after us, nipping at our tail ends.

She was clawing with only one hand and doing more for us than I could. The marl here was half rock; where we labored at it, it made new walls to again bar us from escape. The debris fell in her face. "Tell me how you knew my name," she said. Perhaps, she meant to distract my attention or her own. The luster of her wheaten hue became irreverent and obscene in the dust and the loam shedding. I realized at least one thousand years had passed since human hands had fell to the ground statues of her likeness. Those casts of once-sacred art had probably looked as she now did when they were uprooted from the history of the world.

I answered her, "'Mei Xian' was cried by many, the moment I had you lame."

Softly and whispered, I thought I heard her say. "Fate. This date."

I threw my strength at the parsimonious burrow, spurned by another bellow of the angel and the uncomfortable heat that threatened to drown us in blisters and the baked clay of the earth surrounding us. She was leveraging a bit of herself and gained a foot in our perilous strife. Alone, I may have thrown my bulk at all sides of this asphyxiated chamber, for I was constituted of muscle and fats with very little bone. Yet, I felt her against me, and she felt frail with too many smaller bones and other pieces that could glass-crack at calloused handling. I paced myself and rid every breath from my being to allow her an inch or two of spared room.

The Tianlong suffered silently her mangled left side but freed us with her determination. She cascaded again through the earthly reaches with me. Me, a wind-swept Wyrm – like flight. Stewing in me came bashful thoughts: I felt unlike myself being near the opposite of me. She had confronted my death with me, then plucked me from the flames. "What is your name?" Her voice, unstrained, made honeyed notes in my earholes.

I had believed for so long that I no longer had a name, but my memory suddenly jarred awake. "Eryx," I told her, even though I believed I shouldn't have. With my name, emerged into this macrocosm, I felt then that I had a face.

Mei Xian smiled at me. The layers of the Earth, who She was inside, were tumbling away in blends of color; I smelled the roots nearest us drinking water.

"A return to your homeland, then?" I asked her.

"Nay, your home or mine would mean our end."

What could be done? And, did she mean our deaths? She may have meant the cessation of what we now had: the one of the other.

I daydreamed. In my thoughts, I wondered what should be done. *To separate? Or, consummate?*

But, she interrupted my fantasies. "The River Orb nurtures the five demesnes – this count inclusive, too, of the Wyrms' sanded plains. Where it touches the four draconic sectors and at the joint, also, of Drakes' and Wyrms' abodes, there live those of a wholly different reign. They are known as 'The Higher Counsel.'"

I had heard the myths, whispered most infrequently, but there if one paid heed. "The Shenlong. The Dilong." They were Chinese Drakes, like her. The Shenlong were the spirit dragons, and the Dilong of the Earth. The fables endorsed them as peacekeepers, and it might be that they, above all others, would not be moved by the nascency of this war.

She looked to me, this knowledge of mine demanding her attention and her astonishment. "How could you have known? It is a fact so shrouded that certainly not the commons, nor even the prestigious do own."

I gained some pomp or a coat of minute self-respect as we neared the edges of light and the breaching of the ground. "My beauty, when one endures such Time to acquire this simple speech, it is a given that she has listened and learned for a lifespan each."

She chuckled and drew me closer as the aperture narrowed slightly. "To live in a world where poets may be thought of as 'simple.'"

I thought on her words, yet in a matter of beats, we no longer heard the Scourge Angel at our backs. Only hurtling distance could make small something so unnervingly goliath. I laid dirt over what I had seen of him and wondered at myself for having so long-wished to gluttonize the night. Perhaps, we had survived and fled from one who had achieved just that – I was convinced of it the next instant. He was what one became by consuming the Moon's love.

May I never wake to find myself as him. He had not eyes, the orbital basins recessed so far back that they may not have housed sight, and that angel – powerful, terrifying, and unmindful of palaver or any language to collar brutes and sit them at the table – he, I knew, was not enlisted to a god of higher order. He was a commander solely to the teeth of him and that inferno basking just beneath the tiles of his blackened skin.

But, there would be time enough to think on all of it. Presently, this Tianlong seemed to know where to find answers. For me, she felt an answer enough. Gone was my simple philosophy to gut the Drakes, that demeanor I'd fantasized as an indestructible version of myself, then later built up in the eyes of others to my kind. It was gone and by mere experience: a quick hour beside the one I'd imagined as my enemy.

I wondered what the Conqueror had experienced in her time. I wondered who she truly was. If some version of her ran the tongues of us, and it was falseness, yet no one knew.

I stared at Mei Xian, realizing I could not know the answers to any of this yet. I would need to follow out this wind-swept journey.

We came up out of the ground, and I stared at Heaven.

CHAPTER 15

MR. RO, THE SUITOR

When Jonren Archidux had asked Mr. Firth – the Firths being a family line who were financially situated a tier above his own family - for his daughter's hand in marriage, he had assumed what would follow was the old patriarch's acceptance. Which, it had, for he was nigh dead with no one to look over the last of his blood. Then, Jonren felt it unquestionable that a child should arrive. And, the child had come. Lastly, it was his belief that Cyssiline would love him. Which, she did not.

Over the years, this angered him increasingly, much of which he laid the brunt of at Hadryn's feet. He vituperated his child, to which Hadryn was phlegmatic, but never Cyssiline could he revile. She had her quiet way of defying and denying him that put a coldness to his nerves. Thus, he was left to silently abhor the murals he had hired a contractor to paint onto the very walls of his estate of himself and Cyssiline in jocund splendor. The knot in him was not about the many scenes never enacted, but the weighted coin he had departed of to see to its completion, for the money invested was his own before Cyssiline had legally acquired his family name. Even when she did, and he, therefore, had her riches added to his own, it did not compensate for his loss. It was revealed that, as Mr. Firth's health declined, the Firth's reputation presided their bank account. Jonren wished, even to this day, for Cyssiline to sell some of her mother's heirlooms to requite his damaged wallet and pride, but in the 24 years of their marriage, he had yet to determine how to word his request so that she would not cast verbal stones and refuse him.

These murals extended with Hadryn and Mr. Ro's tedious walk towards the rear of the property. The bearded man grimaced at some of them, but the Knight went by them without attention.

As any other estate would, the Archidux residence had its servant's quarters at the rear of the house. Nearest to the front double doors was the feasting hall as the focal point of the mansion. Needlessly expansive with a ceiling nearly as far away as the sky, it was the largest room. Beyond it were wine-tasting rooms, afternoon tea rooms, dessert rooms, and sicking-period rooms which were lavish restrooms with network monitors and connections, and divans in the adjoining lounges.

Upon entry to his military career, another thing against his father's wishes, Hadryn had acquired the luxury of living in the dormitory at the military base for half of the year. The other half of the year, the dorms went to the new recruits as they were disciplined for the last and most trying stage of their advancement into the ranks. When Hadryn had left his first year for training, his father had promptly had their house staff throw everything he owned from his upstairs chambers, where he had grown up, into what was formerly the help's bedrooms: adequate rooms, and shameful only in the eyes of denizens who had so much more. After six months, Hadryn had returned to the Archidux house and had been pleased to see himself so far distanced from where his father slept.

It was this distance, now, which muted the clamor of the banquet, and Hadryn continued walking the reticent corridors, passing rooms with Mr. Ro at his shoulder.

The Knight did not feel Mr. Ro was a damnable sort. He had done as men were expected: thoughtlessly and selfishly intruding. No, not damnable. However, brought to Hadryn's memory, whenever a woman was handed over from one man to another, like a document or a glinting gem, was folklore from Mr. Gro's books. There was once a mythic villain: immortal, devouring of blood, and shearing away the souls of whom he desired, yet even he, this nightmarish afreet, had first to be invited into one's home before he could begin to drain the life of his victim, making the parasitic offender a thing with more an understanding of consent, deceitful as it was, than the practices of their modern society. Hadryn was not above sharing this archived information with Mr. Ro, partly in hopes that it would persuade the shorter male to stare less or, at least, less obviously.

The suitor realized how uncomfortable the Knight was. "I assure you, I am not a vampire," Mr. Ro said, chuckling and hoping to affect a playful air to their encounter. He noticed, too, that he failed at this. They walked a couple more steps. "Were you really, once, female in appearance?" the suitor asked, abruptly.

Hadryn sighed, bored, and mentally detached from their conversation, answering the other man simply with: "I was."

"But, you've shed all that. Long ago."

"I prefer the truth, so this is how I stand in the world."

As they neared the tighter halls that led to the former servants' quarters, Mr. Ro cleared his throat. "I apologize, Sir Hadryn. I had not considered your sire would make the engagement public."

Hadryn turned and faced the suitor. "Why did you ask for me?"

"I-- ... for? For a transgender man, you mean?"

They neared the limits of the Archidux mansion, and there was furniture and more light here, things denizens didn't feel they needed. At the end of the hall stood an empty bookshelf.

Hadryn frowned at the man with a paunch. "I meant, me, as a person. Why would you ask for me when we've never met, when you know nothing of me or who I desire? What makes a man to partake in a tradition so entirely belittling of another person?"

Mr. Ro considered the question. "I suppose, men do it because it is their privilege. How is it you intend to wed the lady you have mentioned without the father's consent?"

"She is not a denizen."

Mr. Ro scoffed, "Everyone is a denizen. Even those in District 11. Do you mean that riffraff, stick-built lot of people outside the Nations? What are they hoping to accomplish anyhow?"

"They are looking simply to walk their path in life, not eat it, being that we, humans, were born with two feet and not, one enormous, unsightly ass to sit upon."

Mr. Ro could see he had struck a chord and fell silent for a space as they came to a room, and Hadryn went to the closet. "You could tell me about her," he offered. "We could get to know one another."

"Why should either of us wish for that when you shall be gone by day's light?"

Mr. Ro thought on that and scratched along his lush beard. "Perhaps, for that reason. We have these hours and nothing more. My entrance to your life has been caustic. It may be, though, upon my egress, we might ameliorate the acidity of the evening." The older man faced Hadryn squarely now. "I meant you no ills, Sir Knight, in accepting your mother's request."

The younger of them drew a deep breath to let the weight of the event fall away upon exhalation. "Father was determined to disguise me a bride. My mother must have chosen you for a reason."

Mr. Ro was sympathetic. "A pity she could not have asked the woman you love."

Hadryn was quick to shade his feelings in laughter too loud and awkward. "'Love?' I did not say I loved her."

The suitor was quiet.

Hadryn shrugged. He tossed to the bed the pillow he had been holding. "There is no need to lie to you. It would make no difference." He went to the only chair in the room and sat. "I believe any reasonable person, like my friend Thaddius," he smiled to himself, "would not trust that which I name 'love.' *Yet, I love her.* She and I have not had a physical closeness, but our bond carries the fortitude of emotional, intellectual, and mental depth due any two people who enjoy a nearness to one another." Hadryn realized he had never spoken to another about Oshin like this. He folded his arms, still smiling with the gentleness induced by the heart and no other mind. "Oshin and I have written one another for nearly a decade."

"'Ocean?'" Mr. Ro questioned.

"Spelt O – S – H – I – N," Hadryn explained.

"Interesting," he nodded. "You wrote to her as you transitioned, I assume."

Hadryn did not know why he felt this open honesty with this unknown person, but the words had found his lips and would not cease. "No other did I feel security with in revealing my fears and frustrations. To all others, those who questioned why I must do this - who judged me, who 'psychologically evaluated' me, who sought to convince me to turn back on my decision – I had to appear unwavering and proceed with indestructible conviction. I could not allow one weak point. But, to her, I could be," he searched for the word, "*human*, I suppose is the only way to say it."

"I would imagine a metamorphosis to such a degree would be a journey of most unexpected discovery, trial, and reward," Mr. Ro said.

"Yes," the Knight agreed, thinking back. The surgery to remove his breasts and the recovery afterwards had been the most wearisome and frustrating. He admitted to the other man, "Only she knows that I balk at the needle. There is no other way to administer the testosterone, but something about the thinness and sharpness of them sets the hammer to my heart."

Mr. Ro was contemplative. "In the buttocks?"

Hadryn laughed. "No, the testosterone would only sit in the fat, if one were to inject it there. Muscle, though, releases it slowly to the body, thus the thighs are best to receive the needle."

"Fascinating." Mr. Ro looked pleased. Then, he said, "This is why you loved her, for she was your listening ear through all of it."

"She comforted me, encouraged me, and sought solution for my difficulties. Oshin has always a remedy to propose. But, my transition isn't the sole, or even predominant, reason of my feelings for her." He hesitated. "Maybe I should not tell you this, but she is the foundational leader of that life Beyond the Merlons."

"Is she!" Mr. Ro gasped and held at his large belly for a moment.

"Some may disagree with the lives lived outside the walls, Mr. Ro, but *think*. She was not afraid to shed the known and reach out, past the barriers others had constructed and begin, from the level of the soil, *life anew*. Then, she did this for hundreds of others. She changes the lives of any to know her."

The suitor rose from his place on the bed, and Hadryn watched him, suddenly aware of the room once more. He could feel again the presence of the walls and the one window at his back, like a dark eye. The older man treaded the length of the room, looking thoughtful.

"I've gone on for so long." Hadryn confronted the settling tension. "It was not my intention, but I thank you for speaking with me, Mr. Ro." He, too, stood. "You must be due for rest."

Before Hadryn could say more, the man with the paunch clapped his own belly. "I was thinking, Sir Knight, you've asked nothing of me. I am not boring, I'll have you know." He hefted the belt, partly obscured by the overhang of his protruding stomach. "There is a little, personal tidbit I could share with you. It is not virile competition to that which you've shared, but it is my own – a thing to say." He winked at the Knight.

"Forgive me for not asking, sir." Hadryn felt himself amused. "Do, please, tell me."

Mr. Ro gave pause, for anticipation, Hadryn supposed, then the shorter man said, "Ere you, women, and solely women, had my eye and interest. You are the only man to stir me. By habit, I am usually much opposed to the thought of, in any manner, joining with a man, yet, here, I am. Here, I *was*, asking for you, handsome Knight."

Hadryn was caught unaware. He was not certain he wished to ask, but he did. "And, why should I move you from your propensities, good sir?"

Mr. Ro had a hand in his pants, and at first, Hadryn was disgusted. Yet, he realized the next moment that the man's hand was in his pocket. The suitor took a little, velvet box from the inside of his garments and threw it easily to Hadryn, who caught it in one hand. "I believe, Sir Hadryn, often once we are firmly decided about a thing, Life un-decides it for us. Life teaches us where we never expected nor asked to learn."

"Mr. Ro?" Hadryn was left unable to do more than stare at the box in his hand.

"Well, do not look at it, for its purpose is no longer beauty, but utility. Sell it to help build a life with this 'Oshin.' Consider it a gift from a kind stranger."

"Stranger and stranger, by the moment," Hadryn said more to himself, but Mr. Ro laughed at his words. "Sir, I cannot accept this generosity." Without gazing upon it, Hadryn knew the object's shape inside the box was small and circular.

"Oh, but I insist. How else should I partake in a love story?"

"I could not possibly."

"You are welcome to it."

"It is too much. Surely, you should keep it for another."

"It was made for you: by size, by color. It knows no other name but yours."

Hadryn swallowed. The suitor had insisted beyond Hadryn's three attempts to decline, thus it was customary now to accept. Stiffly, the taller male bowed. "I thank you, kind sir."

A wide smile found its way out from the deep maze of Mr. Ro's black beard. "Have you eaten yet?"

The younger of them realized suddenly his grievous shortcomings as a host. "Forgive me for not yet offering you the tea and table due one's guest, Mr. Ro. I shall ask the help to fetch you a plate from the banquet and have it brought back."

Mr. Ro waved aside his words. "No need. Only. Show me where your help would have deposited the cargo with which I came."

Hadryn moved hesitantly towards the door of the room. "It would be the chambers directly across this room and down the hall – the only room with a fire hearth, as you asked for the coffer to be kept warm.”

The other gentleman had already stepped by the Knight, and his feet were soundless along the tiled floor. “The gifts are foods for you. Foods I think that would be much to your fancy.” He looked back once at Hadryn. “And, if you are not offended, I may take a share of it, too, for having been denied the fete of tonight.” He laughed again and patted his stomach. “Suddenly, I am ravenous.”

Hadryn paused momentarily in the hall, thinking to himself that he’d heard some pother from direction of the feast, but then, he assumed the distance was warping the sound of laughter, and he followed the shorter man. “Mr. Ro?” There had arisen, in Hadryn’s mind, questions all at once. He felt an ease of comfort towards the older man, after sharing of their conversation together. “Sir, how is it you’ve oxen?” he asked, thinking back to the suitor’s arrival. Then, the Knight almost believed he had a better question. “*Why* did you arrive by oxen?”

Mr. Ro seemed hurried, and the corridor seemed stretched long. “A semaphore to you.”

“I don’t understand,” Hadryn said.

“What is the sign of your birth, dear beauty?”

“It is the dragon.”

“Ah,” Mr. Ro paused, then continued. “This year is yours. How very lucky for you.”

They came to the room, and Mr. Ro peered in, looking right, then left. He stepped inside.

It was a room for comfort after long hours tending to the needs of the denizens of the house. The walls were comprised of actual cut stone mortared together. Most likely, the room had been the central gathering point of an old establishment, long since destroyed and the castle-like mansion erected around it. Against one wall was a simple sink and stove with chipped porcelain and blackened burners. This, Hadryn went to and began preparation for tea. He found, in its usual cupboard from when he was a boy, a tin of strong pu-erh, red Chinese tea. The other two walls of the room, not withstanding the kitchen wall or the wall with the door through which they'd entered, met at a curve, and there, at the juncture, stood a stately fire hearth. It stood as tall as a human being, and its mouth was the shape of a half-wreath, arching over the blaze currently burning and brightening the room. On the antique rug in the room, several feet in front of the hearty fire, rested the wooden cabinet Mr. Ro and his oxen had borne to the Archidux estate.

Hadryn came down to the sprawling rug with a tea tray, and the portly man was engrossed in opening the wooden boxes which each of the other riders of his caravan had carried when he'd first came to the Archidux mansion. The contents he laid out on the simple, hardwood floor.

"Eat up," he said with pleasantry, and Hadryn quickly lowered the tray to level ground to keep from spilling everything he'd brought down.

The Knight looked at all the food. "You *are* from the 11ᵗʰ District," he insisted of the mysterious denizen.

The apples and the pears absorbed the amber glow of the room and showcased their own little horizons at the curves of their pink and yellow globes. There was, in a fluted, silver dish, nuts of different varieties, beiges and deep browns – some looked as if they were glazed or sugared. Disrobed of its satin cloth enclosure laid loaves of bread: a stouter sesame bread of crisped density and softer loaves of fluffy milkbread. In bamboo steamers were cooked vegetables, their aroma of garlic and ginger heavy in the room. Palm-sized pecan tarts were the last that Mr. Ro revealed to the younger man. The delicate crusts and smooth surfaces of them appeared as perfection to Hadryn, and when the other gentleman leaned across the rug to hand him one, Hadryn's eyes were misted by the beauty of food in its wholeness: the individual shapes of each body, given thus by Nature, and nothing reduced to a cube or mimicry of what it should have been.

The Knight took the tart from its foiled base and brought it to his lips. He took a bite, and then another; soon, the sweet was gone, and he realized that they were usually reserved as desserts. *"Thank you,"* he said. Hadryn was stunned, staring openly at the other man. "How could you possibly hide oxen in District 11?" he asked stupidly, and without thought.

The suitor chuckled, but was eating, himself, a little of everything. "Continue," he said, gesturing to the lavish spread. "If you are going to eat your dinner backwards, I suggest the fruit next."

They ate, and it was a certain heaven to Hadryn – one of contentment and the divinity of memories we know we will cherish, even as we are in the midst of their experience. Never before had Hadryn consumed past the limit of satisfaction. This once, though, he ate to fullness, feeling the forms and textures in his mouth and indulging in the sensation of savory or sweet, of earthiness. They whiled away the hour with more talk, and Hadryn wondered what human beings truly needed more, beyond earth-given and hand-prepared food, beyond the swaddling of the fire's heat, shelter, and companionship.

Upon Mr. Ro's return from the lavatory, however, they both realized what more could be wished for. The older gentleman stood at the door frame, watching as Hadryn attempted to peer into the holes of the coffer, which had been at arm's length during their dining. He knew Hadryn could not see into the darkness of that cabinet, so he asked firmly and loudly, "Would you like to guess what lies inside?"

Hadryn turned sharply, upending a tea cup. He was not shamed to silence. "Yes," he answered.

Mr. Ro walked to the coffer and stood beside it. "As you will, then."

The Knight didn't pause, guessing, "Flour. Yeast. Spices." The other man was silent, thus the younger of them continued earnestly, "Cooking and baking instruments." Then: "Recipes," he concluded.

Mr. Ro snorted and pretended to adjust his genitals. Hadryn couldn't help but watch, for it was very crass of Mr. Ro to do so. The suitor asked, "Why those items?"

Hadryn felt he had it sorted. "The beginnings for a little shop. A 'bakery,' as they were known, to return goodness and health to the Tiered Nations. To change how people eat."

"Has anyone ever told you that you are terribly romantic?" Mr. Ro cut in.

"Yes," Hadryn answered. However, in response to his guess, Mr. Ro shook his head 'no.' Hadryn would not be discouraged. "Weaponry," he said next.

"Again. Why so?" The shorter man placed his hands on the casket, feeling the polish of its surface.

"To fight the beings here, who have begun to eat the residents." Hadryn stood. "Do you know her, Mr. Ro? Oshin. Did she send you?"

The look on the older man's face was solemn, but resolved and his gaze abruptly piercing. "Why did you never go to her, Sir Knight? You love her, and how she pined for you. *Nine years.* It did not have to be so."

As though it were overdue, Hadryn was not displaced or taken to offense. He bowed his head, and from his lips came one word: "Cowardice." It clung to the walls of the room and slid into the folds of the warmth which enveloped them. It was upon both their breaths, burdensome and fragile, too.

"*No,*" Mr. Ro declared. "Not from you. That isn't good enough."

Hadryn was lost to compunction. He felt the words he'd never written and the terrible weight of their omission. He told the man who'd come to wed him: "Oshin has only ever known me in the body of a girl. What grew between us nine years ago was betwixt her and another form, a shape – breasts, hips, gentle curves, and femininity by sound, by scent – which I no more possess. She has seen nothing of that which stands before you now, sir."

Mr. Ro listened, and Mr. Ro was silent for some time. "You are not such a romantic, then, to believe Love is a shape when, by the truth of the Moon, I tell you it a *pulse,* an energy, *a heartbeat.*"

Hadryn could say nothing to this.

"To hell with it! What is done has been done for nine years," Mr. Ro concluded. He clapped suddenly and went to an end of the oblong container. "I will reveal to you the contents of this crate, in the shape of a coffin." And, he slid back the upper half of the top of it.

There, inside, was indeed a body. It was a man who appeared just past middle-aged, resting upon his back. The hue of life was expired of his person and folds of skin hung unusually from the jowls of his face. Hadryn faltered backwards, and from one his gauntlets, he drew a short dagger, bracing it in front of himself. He sought to understand. *"A corpse?* Did you murder him? What happened to him!" The blood in him raced with such force that he heard it within. He demanded, "Who is he!"

But, Mr. Ro was silent and staring at the body. Then, the corpse drew breath, and Hadryn's eyes widened. Mr. Ro turned to face him.

"I will tell you who he is. But, first, you must answer me: who am I?"

CHAPTER 16

LeSHAWN and THADDIUS MERLONE

LeShawn Merlone was chauffeured home from the Archidux banquet. She'd gone to the banquet, knowing her wife was to be there, and she'd gone to berate Hadryn's father for a heart unloving to have so treated his only child.

But, the illness had come most abruptly.

She had been forced to leave, knowing it may again be the fallout of her cells, which everyone else knew as "cancer."

Outside, the night seemed like a cavity waiting to be filled by something young and sweet. The queasy restlessness inside her belly mirrored the yearning, and she stared at the night slinking by, stalking her, from the window of the Archidux's personal carriage, which she had been sent home by. In the reflection of the window, she could see herself: long, dark eyelashes, hair sorrel with her front locks falsely blonde, and her skin the color of nutmeg - taking benefit of her father's Mexican blood. From her French mother, she had eyes of pastel blue. She wore her hair curled, just above her shoulders, and LeShawn was not as most denizens were. She was not deprived of womanly curves in the least, but her frame was lacking in largeness. Her waist could be considered undefined, yet the rest of her was but soft all over – not tremendous with adipose bulges - and beneath those gentle lines, a subtle tonality of utilized strength. It was by grace of her bosom alone that she gave the impression to other Tiered citizens that she had, too, their wideness and weight.

LeShawn watched herself a minute longer. It was as if her face were outside in the night and disowning of her, who sat in the driven cab. She felt the motorized vehicle jar with the shifting of its gears, then the evening lapsed into a strained quietude, like when one sits alone in a room with their back to an open door. She wished the interiors of carriages weren't quite so dim.

Carriages were enclosed vehicles that were flat-beds inside, the floors of them a thick metal, and the chains, which held the thrones securely in place, darted with sharp sounds against the metal flooring. The chinking sound bit at LeShawn's ears, and she felt strangely powerless, as if the chains and metal would continue on forever, dueling just within the folds of her ears.

Surrounding her was a heavy emptiness. There was room enough for the transport of six denizens in their thrones, but no more than four thrones were ever loaded into a carriage at a time. To have more than four denizens traveling together at a time cast an eerie sequence, like days out of old when there were nursing homes and elderly patients with paper-crinkled skin who sat, as if half-hung by noose, in wheelchairs that were hefted by anyone else younger than those listless seniors into the backs of specialized buses or vans. Denizens ever sensed the past, but never commented directly upon it. They performed with splendor to escape miming of the ages when people were primitive – when people walked and ate out of the ground or from abattoirs. Thus, carriages were carriages, and not shuttles arriving at nursing homes.

The carriage glided to a halt within a dozen feet of the entrance to her mother's estate. LeShawn held a silk handkerchief in one hand and dabbed at the perspiration on her upper lip and neck. Her hair was damping with the illness she felt. Overhead, the three-leveled mansion she had always lived in, but which never felt like home, leaned over her and the carriage she'd arrived in.

She glanced at it – the house - breaking her stare with the night. Even after 22 years, it still gave her the impression of a precarious tilt, beginning at the mid of it and moving up towards the highest floor. It hunched, not from old age, but from deformity. When she stood at the side of this chateau, as her mother referred to it, it was perfectly erect, wearing every straight line she could imagine – with the exception of the decorative accents - and she could never understand why she thought of it as some distraught suicidal leaning over the edge of a wind-racketed escarpment.

LeShawn tried to look over her shoulder, as the backside of the vehicle opened mechanically, and the driver from the Archidux house approached her.

"How fairs the lady's sicking-period?" He asked it without emotion. Sicking-periods were as common as sneezes. He didn't meet her eyes as he worked around her to disengage the chains nearest the back of her throne.

"Sicking-periods occur after dining. I've not eaten yet," LeShawn answered.

This man, here, was well into his mid-thirties, but he breathed with patience and great ease. He was too thin, but his skin had luster and was not the color of old cream or the pale yellow of cubes made from egg yolk, as most denizens were thus hued. He paused at her words. "Not your sicking-period?" He almost turned away from her, but something steadied his indifference. "Well. Ignorant as I am, I might suggest seeking your physician's advice, being that nausea is out of the ordinary, unless one is submitted to her sicking-period." Though she was well and capable of operating the steering device at the front of her throne to reverse out of the carriage, he proceeded to do it for her, as was the duty of his occupation.

LeShawn was silent, until her vehicle had eased down the ramp out the back of the carriage and she sat in the stillness of the cold air. She was not light in speaking next, but firm and resolved. "I am Beset," she told him, using the term for "cancer," which denizens and their help knew best.

Immediately, the man bowed low and spilled apology; his face had pinked with it. "Sincerely, I regret my thoughtlessness in speaking, my lady. I would never have expected for you to be afflicted. You are so young with such a life so well-rounded." He said everything which was customarily said to one Beset. "Of course, I wish you health – more and more of it. The treatments these days are sometimes miraculous. I have known others who were 'Set. They came away from it, aglow with health, eating just as yesterday." His words suddenly ran dry, and he waited.

LeShawn stared away from him, but asked, "What is your name, sir?"

The man raised his eyebrows. Denizens never addressed those employed to them with respect. It simply wasn't necessary. He wondered if she would speak to the Archidux's and have his employment terminated. "Fairen," he answered in an altered, softer tone. He looked her in the face now.

She tried not to pant audibly, but the fever was wringing profuse moisture through her pores. She felt a great lack of control. "Fairen," she began. "It is true I am Beset. Yet, if I may share a secret with you: this feeling inside is not what I've known of the ways of cancer. It feels different. At the academy I attend, another woman in my class became quite ill. There was nothing familiar about her malady. She said her stomach felt set to purge. She was weak nearly to the point of collapse, and then, in a matter of minutes, a paroxysm had consumed her, for she was biting at herself in a most inhuman way." LeShawn quieted her fear to remain casual and polite, but her words stung her own tongue. "Her own teeth. She mangled her skin. Her blood warmed her mouth."

Fairen watched her with clear eyes. He took a handkerchief from inside his robe. "May I?" He motioned to her forehead.

"Yes. Thank you." She was grateful as the perspiration was dabbed from her face and neck. Yet, she grew quiet, wondering why he wasn't unnerved by her account. Then, she assumed he must not believe her.

"Madam," he said, and then a brisk breeze cut all around them and seemed to hush him to silence for a spell. "Have you seen your food grow old, become useless?"

"'Useless?' No. The help clears our tables after each meal. I've never –" She felt embarrassed at this sudden confession and the obvious shallows of his face and frame, inarguably from being underfed. "I'm sorry."

Fairen laughed. "Do not apologize for your lot. Here. Let me show you my night's dinner." He went to the front of the cab and leaned in through the open window on the driver's side. He returned to her and gestured for her to hold out her hand. In her open palm, he placed a withering globe of bright, sunset likeness. On one of its sides, it was browning with soot-colored spots.

LeShawn nearly dropped it, feeling a shock of disgust at the unusual object, but she sensed it was precious to the driver. "You were going to eat this?" She was in disbelief and unable to look away from his one sphere of food. "It is terrible, in appearance – forgive me for saying so."

"It is half-rotted." He touched it briefly. "By tomorrow, the life of it will be all but expired." Fairen shrugged. "It's all I could afford for tonight. Perhaps, its true gift lies in the metaphor it may present, if you'll allow me." He waited for her to answer.

When she realized he was waiting for her permission, she nodded quickly. "Yes, of course." She held out the fruit for him to take it back, but he didn't.

He explained: "This is an orange – sweet and imbued with health for whomever should consume it. But, our times have been a formidable hardship to it. The soil, everywhere, is bad. So, the orange's youth is fleeting. It dies before its time. It grows mold."

LeShawn wrinkled her nose at the fruit. "Is the mold contagious? Should I be holding it like this?"

Fairen laughed. He took the orange from LeShawn's hand and rolled the sphere down the length of his arm. When it reached his bicep, he made a simple, quick movement to bounce the globe off his muscle, sending it to the air where it came back to rest in his hand. LeShawn smiled, despite herself. "My lady, this fruit is us.

Once we are peeled, we may show some hidden heart beneath of health or strength. But, might we also be bruised and destroyed beneath this skin. At that turn, the seeds are all that's left. How terrifying. For, this will mean, a new body must grow in place, and how often do we war to remain familiar and unchanged?"

LeShawn was speechless before him, forcing merriment or polite intrigue – now, she couldn't remember which had been her aim to present – then, she had left him. She felt the tangle of his revelation in her hair and on her hands, like a ball of yarn unraveling all around her, and she was of nothing more than ant-like size to become lost in it.

He returned to his employment – one of four, he had told her before driving away – and, she was but a denizen again, someone who never spoke of the way time brought Change, and the garden of the Earth, which burgeoned fresh life, ate up the Sun, then dried to crackled and fragile browns, withered, died, and burst forth anew. She was not someone who spoke of the living soil beneath the cemented city's thoroughfares. She did not speak of oranges decaying to the seeds of them.

She felt hungry and nauseated of the same instants, and as her throne motorized passed the arched double doors of her mother's mansion, then came that matron – face crusting with too much make-up and the remainder of her uncomfortably contained in a ball gown of the fastest trend though she had spent the evening at home. She came instantaneously to LeShawn's side. It was not to inquire her daughter's condition or why she was arrived home when she'd left no longer than an hour ago. There was some gossip to be had, and Pelena Franquios had no other metier.

"My goodness, child! Have you not heard the network feeds going on this past half hour? Everyone is saying that Otruna M. Plodd was found dead! Dead in his own estate! Which I thought, all this time, was abandoned. It certainly looks that way. And, so say the feeds as well that his body was taken to those houses which prepare the dead –"

"Morgues, Mother." LeShawn steered by the other woman's throne with difficulty, for the divorced woman followed so very close to her. LeShawn felt that she should focus on her breathing. Her throne felt tight around her as well as the dress she wore. She was disoriented in her own body as it fevered, and her stomach pitched. She was thinking, still, of Fairen, who ate prohibited fruit, and she thought of spheres that putrefy.

"*Morgues,*" her mother emphasized. "Yes, dear, taken *there. And, then, that his body simply disappeared!*" Pelena was succumbed to her storyteller-self, and she was an atrocious storyteller. She whispered low and fast. The "S'es" she pronounced were drawn a half-beat too long and slithered in LeShawn's ears, even after the sound of them had surely stopped. "It very much reminds me of that member to the Government Body. You remember her? A few years back. She was so well-respected –"

"She wasn't, Mother. No one knew her. We knew only that she was an official, thus belonging to our highest social class, and that she was rich and she was morbidly obese."

"They all *are* of our Government Body, dear." She tried to sound as if she'd cut in on LeShawn, but her daughter had already finished what she had to say. "Besides. That isn't the point. The point is that she, too, went missing!"

"Military personnel went missing too, Mother. Thaddius' comrades –"

"Oh, pish posh, LeShawn! The military are not on the order as members of the Government Body! Or, rich men, like Plodd! They are only -- ... soldiers. Not at all like officials."

Unexpectedly, she felt her anger corrode the ill-feelings, and there was less of the fever and queasy frames of mind. "Done." The finality in her tone was searing. She didn't bother to look at her mother before picking up some speed in their thrones that were so slow-moving.

"How dare you, child!" The madam's voice rose with fear. "LeShawn!"

She ignored her mother who had divorced her father – the father she rarely saw: Mr. Gutierrez. LeShawn made for her bedroom.

"LeShawn!" The older woman called to her again, and LeShawn could feel her behind herself. The French woman had resolve and a sense of herself thin as paper unwritten upon. "LeShawn, wait. I'm sorry." Now, Pelena was beginning to cry. She was 41-years old, and the smallest wrinkle in her day set her to tears, for she was told that life as a lady to the reigning class would be as smooth as a plate in waiting for a meal. "You are an awful child. To turn your back to me. Your father was awful, too." And, he who had loved Pelena, was the one who Pelena had turned from and given up her marriage.

The young woman who was part-Mexican came to a halt in her throne. "Mother, you would do well not to listen so much to those terrible network feeds."

"Well, what else, in the Tiered Nations, am I to listen to, LeShawn!"

She was quiet, for she had an answer she wished to say. She wanted to tell her mother to hear from unlikely sources, from men who drove carriages for the wealthy and ate rooted foods and knew how to look at those foods anew as they spoiled.

But, they were denizens, and denizens belonged to the social strata of mouths that ate plentiful substance, but rarely spoke it.

The wealthiest denizens were the Government Body. Curiously, they lived beneath ground in two U-shaped rows of cells, one set atop the other, said to be very vast and luxuriant and of which were called the Alveoli. The Alveoli were at the heart of the Nation, and atop the underground vaults, where the Government Body lived and never came to surface, was the structure representative of and the only entry point to the Government: the White Face. Indeed, it was the center of control for Tiered life, and the construction of it was an expansive domed building with two entries at the front that were unloading docks. There were 32 vans, one for each official of the Government Body, which were in constant circulation to and from the White Face in perpetual effort to keep the plates of each official full and exactly as they wished.

Yet, none had laid eyes on any the members of the Government Body, save for the Royal Guards who were employed to secure the premises of the White Face. They patrolled the grounds, as was their duty, but were often rotated back to the military to undertake civilian matters, such as domestic disputes and robbery, as was the chore of every military personnel.

From the Royal Guards, who had long-served these mysterious figures, it was rumored that each member of the Government Body was bedridden, for they enjoyed the most exquisite of cubed food and more of it than any mere denizen could fathom. Upon their backs, fleshed in 400 to 600 pounds, they crafted and enforced the laws of society, and they approved or declined each and every permit the denizens submitted. And, one needed a permit for every undertaking or milestone of one's life.

With the White Face its core, the Tiered Nations then gave up land to the aristocrats, who could afford a residence of sprawling grandeur. These were often denizens who owned corporations and profited from all others – like LeShawn's father, who owned The Gutierrez Line which was responsible for every Chef in every home of denizens who could afford them.

Those employees to the denizens' businesses became the next social hierarchy, and these people were housed in replicating structures which were constructed with lavishness in mind, but were exactly the same from one to the next. They were flats, stacked in stories sometimes fifty-floors high. Some were like museums in splendor, and yet, it was known, that all of them belonging of this Tier wished for the Tier above them. Likewise, their employers desired nothing more than the Tier above themselves. It was only the hired help who seemed content to remain as they were.

LeShawn realized that denizens never heard of hired help becoming denizens. Then, she was interrupted of her thoughts.

"Well, haven't you more to say? Do you know what this means?" Pelena persisted. Her tone still had hurt in it. She had always felt that LeShawn despised her, and she was ready to despise her child more than be despised, if that were the case. Yet, she longed for the young woman to never leave her alone. She studied her for a moment and now realized the sweat upon LeShawn's brow and her daughter's color grayed, but Pelena said nothing of it.

"Mama, I think I'm sick."

"I wish you could see what I'm saying, child!" She was certainly adamant and circuitous about the whole thing. "You never can see what is right in front of you!"

"It's because I'm too fat. And, whatever else I don't obstruct, you do." She often put that look of bewilderment and anger on her parent's face for no other reason than she enjoyed it. She thought that, somewhere inside, her mother enjoyed it, too.

"We do not use that word, LeShawn Gutierrez!"

"'LeShawn *Merlone.*'" The younger woman sighed. "Come now, Mama. It's funny." She edged a smile at the older woman, and it was not returned. Pelena was in a huff to herself. LeShawn waited.

Pelena didn't know how to feel towards her child, in that moment. She felt she had something of significance to say to the young woman. "You should listen to me, daughter. The living went missing, now even our dead ebb out of sight as well. It's as if we can't be buried, the way Death calls for. As if, there is no end. No end of which we'll know. I don't like things going on like that, without knowing the end." As best she could, she said it.

LeShawn stared at her mother. She fidgeted. "Well, Mama. I don't know what to say." They were both wordless for an awkward lull of seconds, and LeShawn felt that she should be more than this – that she should have her thoughts in order enough to make a reply that would garner respect for herself. Pelena began to speak, then, and LeShawn saw her chance slipping away, so she blurted out before her parent: "Mama, what if it just looks like people disappear when they've found themselves? Could not that be possible?" She regretted wording everything as questions, but that was how it emerged, and she could accept that. She was shocked to see the horror on the older woman's face.

"You mean to leave me, don't you? You ungrateful girl. After I've raised you alone in this cramped dwelling just barely fit to have

banquets with no more than a few dozen denizens in attendance." She took her handkerchief from a compartment on her throne as she began to tremble. Pelena regulated her tone to disdain and detachment. "It's because of that melanistic girl-swain."

"Mama, I won't leave you." There was a need to comfort the haughty French woman. To LeShawn, her mother suddenly looked aged and sad. "Families belong together. But, you must not speak of Thaddius in such a manner." She didn't want for the conversation to go any further. "Goodnight, Mother."

But, Pelena's feelings had been injured. She would not let LeShawn leave her to the silence, where her hurt would grow. She told her daughter: "You are so young, my daughter. It is never too late for divorce. Please, find a man."

LeShawn's voice hardened, as it always did when she gave to her parent this same sentence repeated over the course of four years. "Mother. If not to Thaddius I am married, then marriage has no meaning to me."

"You have lost weight since being her wife."

"It is because we love to dance together, Mama. I cannot dance in my throne."

Pelena wished herself to say no more, but she could not seem to grasp her will, or the part of her which treasured LeShawn. "Dancing is just kicking at time and in an insulting manner." She busied herself with things that were already done, but that she was now re-doing. She slid open a palm-sized door on the tray of her throne and begin to rearrange her pills and medication which were housed in an interior compartment below the flat surface meant to rest dinner plates and tea cups upon. "LeShawn. You know I mean to talk with you about that woman. This is gravely serious. I've allowed it to go on long enough."

LeShawn sighed, but not out of irritation. Her features had become sad. "Say it, then, if you must."

The French woman glanced at the sorrow of her child's face, then told herself she hadn't seen it. She continued, even knowing that the 22-year old woman was happy and fulfilled by the choices she'd made for herself. "LeShawn. My daughter. You've used a permit approval to marry one of your own sex. You've used another to marry the same who is not your ethnicity. A denizen is only allowed three approved permits in his or her lifetime." She looked her child in the face. "Do not use what's left to you to submit for a mongrel child. Use your last allowed permit to file for divorce." When she had said the last word, she sighed deeply and waited.

LeShawn wanted her bed. She didn't think though that rest would help, but she felt it was what people did when they felt ill, and the nausea was swelling with sour notes on her tongue. "Never," she said.

LeShawn steered her throne away from her mother. This time, her mother was silent and didn't look after her. LeShawn heard capsules being extracted from that little drawer on the older woman's throne and knew that the lady of the house had chosen an induced sleep over the things they'd said to one another. In this, she could agree that sleep proved welcoming.

LeShawn's vision seemed waterlogged, and the brightness of every light was pushing deep into her eyes. She saw odd angles of the halls she usually passed, so she couldn't be sure if her head was lolling down, then up and back against the head cushion of her vehicle. There was gray dust along the door jamb to her bedroom, but mostly it accumulated in one corner. She saw next a forgotten nail high up one of the walls that was closest to her bed.

All these unknown angles.

LeShawn stepped down from her throne and closed her bedroom door. She meant to get to the bathroom, but her legs redirected her, as if they could not be trusted for having so little been utilized since reaching puberty and that rite of passage of being made to locomote predominantly by throne. LeShawn wondered why she stood at her bed before falling into it. There, lying prone, more things made sense. She stared at nothing, feeling everything. The sheets beneath her grew warm. The mattress and its inhabitants of blankets and comforter were much too soft, but it made her heady with gratitude. When she closed her eyes, she felt herself in a hot bath with the waters gently swaying her. When her eyes opened, she was again in bed.

The cinnamon incense she had burned earlier in her room beckoned her appetite, yet she swallowed firmly, as if to keep her morning repast from ejecting. LeShawn half-curled on the large bed. She couldn't remember being so blissfully warm and teased by balmy slumber. There was only a slight prodding of discomfort in her calf muscles feeling tender and swollen. She reached down to rub gently at them.

Then, her heavy lashes came to a close. She laid still, and twenty, compassionate minutes tiptoed passed her consciousness just barely there. The upset in her stomach had ceased action and motion. She became nearly joyous, but it was subdued and clung to her through her deep breathing of dreams and sleep.

In the darkness, still wandering through netherworld hues that had never so pleased her this much before, LeShawn's nostrils quivered at the introduction of another scent in the room. She inhaled, expanding her lungs with that aromatic coloration of crisp cologne and cedar-fresh inflections of men's body deodorant.

Thaddius.

She heard her wife's voice, not feminine but ever-beautiful like the ambience of Summer in full force – the heat unrelenting and the drone of voices gently conversing all at once. Thaddius' every other word came to her as if through the wall of an adjoining room, and the words in between were contrastingly close, as if whispered against the lobe of her ear.

"How do you feel? What can I do for you, LeShawn? My beauty." Thaddius had checked her temperature, changed her out of her evening gown and even put on her favorite, fuzzy socks. She lifted her in her arms to orient her correctly in their large bed. She was beside LeShawn now, kissing her shoulder and neck.

LeShawn swooned. She had never seen someone care for another or express tender adoration as Thaddius did. It was said that the military trained soldiers to their breaking points, to make them as strong, LeShawn guessed, as denizens were weak.

Soldiers were the Nations only contingency plan. It was a great burden to rest upon any group of people, so they were honed as if catastrophe might someday strike.

Eight years ago, when Thaddius had been introduced as the new errand-runner to their estate, LeShawn had met with an insecure and austere personality, yet also, exceedingly gallant and devoted, sentimental and always ready with affection for her. She had loathed her mother telling Thaddius that only a personal Royal Guard would be at her, LeShawn's, side forever, for Thaddius had, the following day, enlisted. LeShawn felt sure that the three, strenuous years of training would abrade and scrap away the tenderness she knew in the African woman.

LeShawn had waited. For three years, she turned away all other suitors, and Thaddius' awkward and bashful smile were her dreams at night.

Then, Thaddius had returned. She wore armor as she walked up the steps of the house belonging to LeShawn's mother, and on Thaddius' face were etched lines LeShawn couldn't remember. Her mouth was set like the impassive, chiseled features of sculptures and her eyes brought the brewing of suns – like anger that had just recently been pacified and fear that troubled her gaze with nearly imperceptible shifting to and fro. Thaddius' hair was somewhat longer, and a scar that had healed poorly made a ridge on her skin, running over her collarbone and down to the top of her left breast.

That wound, now old, had put LeShawn to tears. She had cried at Thaddius, *"You should not have gone!"* for, she despised the change she saw in the girl who was so precious to her. But, Thaddius had laughed some, apologized, soothed her, and presented her with a bouquet of flowers from behind her back. From inside the chest plate of her armor, she revealed a ring box. The soldier before her was conditioned with hard muscles showing through smooth, brown skin. She was fittingly handsome, no longer adorable at all; she was not the same and yet, she was. Upon one knee, the Royal Guard, rank 9, sang to her a rhyming poem she had composed in ode to LeShawn, which rhymed but occasionally, and was terribly crafted. LeShawn's mother had endeavored vain attempt to shoo away Thaddius, who serenaded very loudly, then she had resorted to ordering her own two Guards to escort Thaddius from her real estate. But, Thaddius had out-ranked them both, and they bore deep respect of her, thus no arrest was made.

And, that was the day LeShawn's wish, made as a 14-year old girl, came to light in this reality and was no more the things of fantasies.

"What is it you feel, Pimento? You must talk to me." The concern in her voice was stippled with desperation. Thaddius felt that many things were her code and duty, of which righting all matters in LeShawn's world was paramount, and LeShawn loved her for it.

"Draw in close beside me," LeShawn requested of her. The denizen rested on her side with Thaddius at her back. "I assure you, I am well – better now, my Peanut." To this day, she still laughed inwardly that their pet names for one another was the other's most favored food. LeShawn most adored cheese cubes with pieces of pimento diced into them. Thaddius' penchant was more unique: she desired peanut-flavored sauce over everything on her plate, often times on dishes which had no business being adorned with sauce or were not things that peanuts were capable of complementing. Like, pineapple-flavored cubes with peanut sauce. It still made LeShawn cringe. She wished she hadn't thought of it, for her stomach ached a moment before steadying again.

"Let me fetch you your tea first."

But, LeShawn reached behind herself and held her wife at the wrist. "Keep me warm, Mrs. Merlone." That Thaddius was now here drove out the last oppressive feelings of disquiet that had settled just beneath her skin, and LeShawn could not imagine what would become of herself, if the Royal Guard were to leave, even for a brief space of time. "You always come for me. Did Cyssiline tell you I wasn't well?" She listened as the

African woman pulled back, but only long enough to remove her clothing, then she found LeShawn under the thick blankets and embraced her.

"Yes. I was so worried for you. This evening – it was terrible and wonderful, LeShawn. Hadryn's father is a flagrant ignoramus. And, how he paid his due tonight. Hadryn would not be silenced. It was a verbal, and very public, flogging."

"Tell me everything," she tried to look over her shoulder at Thaddius, but LeShawn felt tired. She laughed lightly. "I'm certain you were not a passive spectator. I know you had your hand in the thick of things." The taller woman was quiet behind her. "What happened, Thaddius?"

"No, my love; 'til morning, it will wait. I'll tell you then. Sleep. You'll feel better soon." The Royal Guard's leaned body came in, against LeShawn's back, and she sighed as the familiar weight of her spouse brought her closer to the tranquil hum of the realm of dreams. Thaddius was whispering against her bare shoulder – something about how she had arranged not to report in tomorrow, to be with her – but, LeShawn's senses went to the honeyed warmth of love in her tone, and that caressing breath. Her mind brought images of Thaddius' lips, vinaceous and shaped for luxury and gratification.

LeShawn slept.

It seemed to her a fleeting hour which passed. Thaddius' words came to her again, like the glow of wavering candlelight. The African woman sounded erotically out-paced by her own breath.

"You need rest, LeShawn."

She opened her eyes. They were now facing one another, and the light, timid, as it snuck through the window panes, limned her wife's countenance that was handsome and exceedingly charming at every angle. Thaddius drew light breaths through parted lips.

"Wait, Pimento."

LeShawn was watching her face, engaged with the light perspiration on that umber skin. Her eyes traced the bareness of her wife's body. As she lowered her gaze to the blankets shed to their waists, following down Thaddius' taut abdomen which caught at every inhalation, she found that she had penetrated the soldier, her fingers in deep and moving quick inside the Royal Guard's vagina.

She felt the African woman's muscles, and indeed, the whole of her body, flutter around her fingers which played her spouse's body for pleasure. Still, Thaddius went on about how LeShawn needed the night's respite to reconcile her ailment, and LeShawn said nothing in return, for she was humbled by the beauty of the soldier.

Thaddius was gasping and reaching for her clothes to remove, but LeShawn stopped her. The hunger from her bouts of sickness had returned, but it was cast now in an entirely different light and desiring with ferocity not food or drink.

LeShawn withdrew from her lover's body. She was not herself, she could feel that, and she was more herself than ever before. She looked into the soldier's eyes, and LeShawn said, "You became a Royal Guard. For me."

She had never before said it, neither had the dark-skinned woman.

Thaddius was shocked, and her words fell away. She searched the denizen's eyes. She could say no more than, "Yes."

And, then, LeShawn had eased in to nuzzle into the heat between them. She kissed her wife, and what began as sweet and love's adoration, turned to labored breath and the calling of the body for hard release. The Royal Guard came atop her, and LeShawn knew the hot wet of her tongue and how she could never have enough of it. Thaddius was all she'd ever wanted. There was nothing else – not these riches, this house, the food in cubes, or that throne – that LeShawn had felt longing for. She hadn't known how to want things for herself. Then, she and Thaddius had learned how to dance together. The tango was their deepest pleasure, and LeShawn found herself lost to a need within that would not find quiet.

As they kissed, LeShawn reached down to grasp the African woman just below the buttocks. She pulled upwards, and Thaddius broke away to look into her eyes, knowing. "No, LeShawn." But, she wore the trace of a smile.

"But, yes," LeShawn whispered to her, and she pulled again at the taller woman. Thaddius was hesitant, but sat up, and LeShawn's hands were at her hips, guiding her. The Mexican woman moved her wife forward, until the bister thighs of the Royal Guard rested on either side her face. LeShawn entered her wife again, but with different member this time, and Thaddius rolled her hips and held at the headboard of the bed as LeShawn's tongue met her every need.

After arriving to sleep aboard the drowsy electricity that is lovemaking fulfilled, LeShawn could not say that she slept soundly. A dormancy had her body, but neglected to take with it her mind. She had an awareness of the hours coming into the room to stare at her in Thaddius' arms, then leaving, and they each left her bedroom door ajar, to her irritation. Again, her legs ached; the soreness had spread up to her thighs, and her stomach was pinching once more, but it was not specific enough to tell her what she could do to remedy it.

There were noises – she could not tell from where or what – and only a faint consciousness of the room, herself, and Thaddius in that awakened state of dreaming without slumber. LeShawn didn't like the sensation. She felt a presence, large and all the way up to the ceiling – but, even then, it was hunching, as if it were in a crowded space, and it was at the end of the bed or it was in the bed with them.

LeShawn wanted to scream, but she was asleep.

Like the abrupt violence of theater curtains swooping closed at the end of a play's act, she was hurled into blackness. A tip-toeing repose circled her in feigning innocence. There, she slept, and Time toyed with her once more.

The time it takes for someone to blink must have passed, and then, LeShawn emerged into chaos. Chaos was heated liquid and screaming – her cries – and Thaddius yelling and pleading with her, and the bed was weltering, lurching them in a tumble of limbs and competing strength.

She heard her wife.

"LeShawn, stop!! Please, no! Stop, stop this – I beg you!!" And, it was not the bed that was tossing at them, but it was she and Thaddius in fierce struggle against one another. She didn't know why Thaddius was trying to pin her to the mattress, why she couldn't when she was so obviously the stronger of them, and why she, herself, emitted such horrific cries.

Thaddius was struck backwards – at her hands, she assumed – and there was blood smeared in coats upon Thaddius' naked frontside. That made LeShawn to cease for an instant, and she reached towards the Royal Guard who was shaking, and LeShawn attempted to speak to her.

But, there was an obstruction. LeShawn swallowed thickly, and a solidness went down her throat; it went to her stomach, which she realized felt weighted and protruding.

"Thad ... dius." It was then, she saw.

The bed – it was amassed with gore.

LeShawn stared at her legs that had been so sore before. The bone of her right calf now shown. Along the tops of her thighs, the skin was absent. Strips of muscle and chunks of yellowed fat clung to the destruction that was the lower half of her. She felt confused. There was a vague sense of heaviness in her curled hair; it must be blood or more pieces of herself, even there.

LeShawn felt the need to continue to tear. Her other calf had so much meat still left. She reached for it.

"Don't. Don't touch it; don't touch anything, LeShawn." Thaddius' face, damp with tears and a low whimpering beneath her words, was so strained. The Royal Guard was working quickly to rip the bedsheets into long bandages. She wrapped one of LeShawn's legs, and the white of the sheet instantly turned cardinal-red. *"You'll be fine, my love. This can be righted. We'll get you a doctor soon."*

LeShawn put her fingers to her mouth, keeping the taste of her own blood present to her senses. Behind her head, she felt her wrist halt sharply and hard. She looked over her shoulder to see that Thaddius had made further use of the torn linens: a restraint for her. She was secured to a bed post.

LeShawn wondered about all of this that was happening. She didn't understand it, only her instincts, and she knew that still she loved Thaddius – perhaps, even more. *She didn't run from this, from me,* she thought to herself, vaguely understanding so little. It was difficult for LeShawn to come to other thoughts. Then, her spine wrung a scream from her, for it arched and felt as if it elongated in her body thrown arcuate. It, her backbone, gave her the sensation as if having a fifth limb, and it was far from her body, powerful, and writhing through the sheets.

With a cry from out another world, yet coming from the throat of her wife, Thaddius watched as LeShawn fell back into the bed. Quickly, the soldier pinned her, in effort to see that the denizen no longer wrought hateful abuse upon herself. Yet, it was this moment which LeShawn froze, as if Time would have no more of her, and her mouth was gaping and her back, crescent-bent.

"LeShawn."

The eyes of the Gutierrez daughter sunk as if into a vacuum; blackened pits without end stared back at Thaddius Merlone.

The Royal Guard recoiled. She struck the footboard at the end of the bed. Like the beckoning of strings attached to a wooden doll, LeShawn sat up, snapping the one restraint of her bound arm. Her dampened, curled hair clung in half-frame along one side her face and neck. Those lips, of every shade of pretty-pink, rasped breath and were gently parted as though in seeming disbelief. But, those gems, of sky-like blue, were lost, consumed by a visage half-resembling the countenance of Death. Crooked for human movement, the puppet of LeShawn bent over the bed, beginning now to crawl to the floor upon her fours.

And, Thaddius moaned for what was once her wife. *"Noo. LeShawn, no."* She wept, holding at herself, and upon her words, LeShawn turned sharply back her head in response to the other woman.

Her mouth was a stew of blood and bits. She cocked her head at an angle that should have broken bones, then suddenly the denizen's hair, caught up as if by unseen comber, danced in gypsy contortions and rippled with ignis fatuus before erupting in a flare of multi-tongued fire. Thus, not one strand was left to her head. The blaze evaporated to steam, so that the soldier cried but harder and suffocated her wail in the bunched bedsheets in which she hid her face.

LeShawn scrapped across the tiled floor, for now her fingers had turned clawed. Her back felt soft and the flesh churned, like creamed butter – and to the same effect, it fell away from her frame as she moved so violently along the cold, hard ground. Beneath the parting skin, a scaled hide had formed.

Will she never love me again? LeShawn grieved that thought. Yet now, she had come to the tiered balcony of her room, meant for gazing at the stars. Drawn by instinct, by the hailing of something within, as if by hundreds of voices unheard yet felt, LeShawn drew herself up to the railing.

"Wait!!"

Thaddius of the Royal Guard had run out to the balcony for her. So, then, did LeShawn turn to she whom she had pledged eternal love for all her life.

And, in Thaddius' eyes was this new creation.

LeShawn was now beyond the measure of her life as a denizen. The figure of her reached into the sky. She was incarnadine by color – a deeper red, Thaddius had not seen – and she was a monstrosity. Winged, jawed, and clawed – she was nothing Thaddius could understand. Under the full moon, reigned her eyes of black holes. Upon the crest of her neck, was a mane of smoky tendrils which wafted and caught cadence of every breath, whether belonging to the night air or the beast who stood in the place of LeShawn Merlone.

Never had beauty brought such hatred. Thaddius said nothing to the creature, then she was gone. She left on wings Thaddius never knew she had.

LeShawn reasoned that she could not stay. Yet, she listened for the name of *'LeShawn'* to be called after her. She heard but silence.

Thaddius fell to one knee, then the other, for the strength of her had quitted long ago and adrenaline, too, could not sustain itself one second more. Her face fell forward, so that she was a curved shell that stared only at the ground and the lower half of herself. There, naked and entirely besmirched in blood, she appeared to the Heavens like something newly born – and sorry for it.

CHAPTER 17

———

SASITHORN ~ NGAW of the MUNGKR and THE RIVER ORB

Sasithorn awoke at the bottom of the River Orb. A gentle cadence gradually focused her awareness of being submerged.

Above her, a paddlefish kept its distance, but observed her with something liken to interest. Its eyes were geometric shapes without feeling. It wore its scales like chainmail and its dorsal fin like a crown, seeming regal, then disappointingly trickster as the light changed minutely. It swam closer, then away, out of the field of her vision.

She closed her eyes. She listened to the way the ocean inhaled and exhaled through waves and the currents at deeper levels. All of it was strong in her ears, yet muffled, as was the tradition if one sought to utilize their sense of hearing beneath surface, in the blood of planet Earth.

Her body rested on a submerged shore of the world; she could feel the grit of sand, but there was a sleek, filmy quality to it. When Sasithorn again opened her gaze, she came to understand that she saw everything through a rosy membrane. The Mungkr lifted her head to avail a better view of her condition.

The wall of membrane which encased her was a perfect sphere, semi-translucent, but having also thick, flavescent vines pulsating throughout. She saw that the sphere was anchored to the riverbed by a meat-like growth attached by one point towards the bottom of the enclosure. It throbbed intermittently.

She swallowed, but the muscles in her neck only contracted, then relented, and there was not a sense of her esophagus and only a vague interpretation of her lungs functioning to draw breath.

The warmth of her surroundings began to fade. Perhaps, it was never warm to begin with.

Sasithorn attempted to rise in that seeping coldness. It was then that she cried out. Just past the midpoint of her body, a torture like branding burned at her. She scraped, broadside, along the interior of the organ-like cocoon and bit at it, but the membrane did not give, and Sasithorn was remembering now the sequence and the details which had led her here.

She had been chined. By a Wyrm.

The Ngaw fell back to the gritty floor and stared out the top of the strange globe, which she was housed in. From within the great river, she felt the lilt of Mnemosyne, and it was subcutaneous, yet also distending to the breadth of the waters which held her.

Sasithorn's reminiscence arppeggiated, a string of thoughts tailing each other to circular repetition. Her mind echoed the past, cycling through interrupted visions of herself and Ardyce fighting a dark-hued Wyrm, then herself and Ardyce as youths. Her vision closed, though her eyes remained open, and in her mind, she was forced back many years.

They had raced the winds together and over-eaten in the groves of Wymira – she and the alabaster Tree Crown. And, after that gorging in Wymira, they had lied beneath the roots of the Up-Ended Trees and talked of nothing of importance. The sun never cared what they spoke of; it seemed it only wished for them there. Then, the Past stone-stepped along: they had challenged the firebreathers of the Nocturnes to pellet-blaze them, it being Ardyce's theory that the draconic breeds were all cousins and that they would have natural immunity to one another's offensive traits. But, the Tree Crown's hide had scalded and Sasithorn's scales had itched for a week. Ardyce no longer indulged in her theories after a week of her skin painfully peeling as it healed from the heat of those living in the Nocturnes.

The Mungkr, presently, exhaled the silken liquids of the pod that supported her. The hinge of her jaws had healed. She wondered how she did not have knowledge of this earlier, but realized her fettle was coming to strength incrementally, though in a daze. The emerging gloam was not outside herself; it was a weighted mantle over her consciousness, and now, she was muttering to herself in her perfect isolation.

"Ardyce, stop this."

Sasithorn knew the memories would not cease. They were prowling through the darkness, passing every shining thing to arrive to a specific event.

We are the fools leaping through Time, planting our regretful misdeeds in soil we hope is used only for burying the dead, but when the first pullulation stands upright, we see that a weed makes paradise just as true as does the flower, for, without it, we've cultivated a garden of lies.

Sasithorn let go.

Her will could become her sapience, perhaps.

The lids of her eyes were at half-mast.

The River Orb became the kingdom of the sky. Back, again, to those days of youth. The azure smelled like waiting rain, and Sasithorn saw Ardyce gazing out, at the sea. The Tree Crown's third tier of antlers had come in the month before. She wore them in the stainless fashion of chaste eminence.

Above them, albatross and cormorants pinwheeled in seeming chasing play, and Sasithorn saw herself beside Ardyce. She had just become the Ngaw to her people, and the circlet on her body newly-formed as well.

The ocean they studied was xenomorphic as it entered their nostrils. It wasn't just the brine, as it juxtaposed with the mellow algae and moss scents of the River Orb. It was nettled, as if it knew too much.

The Tianlong say they will be upon the sabulous banks by next daybreak, her memory of Ardyce said through telepathy.

She had replied, "When the birds arrived, the animals and the insects, they all said the same: those who are to arrive make all others their prey." The edge in her was serrated against these strangers prophesized to appear. "We should not let them land."

Trust, Ardyce said. *The Tianlong, together with the Shenlong, will hasp The Eye Backs to their crests and wide-extend the curtain of the Suspended Rains. The reflection of those tiny teardrops will pull the veil over human eyes. They will see falling precipitation, yet masked will be the motion and presence of all living beings. To one another though, we will keep sight, like daylight, of each other. The wights, seeing nothing for them here, shall leave in quiet, back upon their ships and sails.*

"Quiet is not peace." How puberty makes one the ill-tempered hero. "Hiding," she had spat, "from mammals the length of our trunks."

"*Your* trunk," Ardyce reminded her friend, then the Tree Crown became silent – more cautious or sagacious than she.

Sasithorn bit back and sought to quell the emotion claiming now the heart in her breast. She tore with her teeth as the sclera of the sack though it would not give. The yellow veins pulsated. She felt her splintered spine becoming whole, the same as her maw now operable, but it would not subdue in her the anxiety to be freed.

Freed from her past.

"They are uglier than welts, but just as pink," Sasithorn had remarked.

And, that was the day the land of Drakes first saw humankind. They arrived in the broken spirits of trees, in boots with the smell of animal hides all about them – the odor of sugar, yeast and fermentation, and decay on their breaths.

It rained on them. They walked upright on two feet, shouting to one another. For half the day, they scouted the area, coming very close to hare, boar, or dragon, yet suspecting nothing. At dusk, one of them yelled, *"There's no meat!"* So, the captain of the mission gesticulated and from their docked vessels, they brought forth axes. "Fell the trees; the first cabins will be inland. The next row: here, closer to the shores. We'll eat the bounty of the sea." And, they set their hand-teeth instruments to the Ever-Standing Ones. The whites of those trees' insides shewn as chip after chip, the boles became less.

Ardyce had struggled with Sasithorn, had stood in her path. *Refrain, my friend. The Sentries – every one of our trees – have bid us remain hidden.*

"And, now, they are dying." Sasithorn had broken the hold of her friend and passed her, willing herself to be seen. She entered the clearing, entered the eyes of humankind.

They will not understand you! Ardyce had called after her. Already, the hominids were screaming, scattering, and moving in small, frantic waves.

Sasithorn recalled the words she had spoken, away from Ardyce's ears: "There is nothing of which to discuss."

Anger is a thing which may be checked, balanced, and assigned a rhythmic meter, given that one exercised pity for the same scene. Sasithorn told herself she had for them sorrow in her breast. They had not immensity or flights or comparable strength. Even large felines could overpower any one of them. And yet, they came, no matter the leagues, to pristine and foreign host where they nested and nursed their greed. Thus, Sasithorn determined them parasites: functional, but unthinking.

Ardyce had beseeched her stand down and trust the elders' direction. In her audacity, made swollen by youth, she had acted, unknowing that in protecting her kind, she became also their ambassador. Her choices would come to stand for the nation of Drakes, in human minds.

Sasithorn rendered them bruised and broken, but she was delicate with her strength and careful not to snap the threads of life in the bipeds. Upon that inlet, she swept at them with her tail. They were knocked down and felt the marl and mire on their faces – that earth they so wished to claim. Sasithorn mocked pursuit of this running one or another one cowering, and she flourished her showmanship as the tragedian. The lead role was 'monster,' and she plied their fears out of forgotten myths with such ridiculous exhibition, roaring and rearing to snake through the eaves of Heaven.

She would scare them away from their home, put a fright in them that would succeed into the following generations of humankind. The rain and bedlam continued in The Eye Backs. Sasithorn felt the other Drakes watching her, remaining dutifully concealed. They were good followers, but she felt she, herself, was of a different mettle, and Sasithorn filled with the elation of pride when the wights had gathered their injured to flee back to their sea crafts, leaping aboard them.

There was a cessation of sound – brief, by the measure of reality, yet feeling much-delayed and over-extended as the Ryuu, the Firecraws and Pyrolites, the Mungkr and the Long with the Tree Crowns waited. Sasithorn waited. She felt Ardyce near and watching, too.

An unassuming emphasis, like a moderate popping sound, came from the docked vessels, and there were swooping fragments through the air before Sasithorn could understand more.

The Ngaw's neck erupted in garnet cataracts at one side.

That was the initial volley from the canons. Sasithorn still stood very upright. She turned to Ardyce, who was being restrained by three other sizeable Drakes. The Tree Crown wore desperation deep into the contractions of her face, of the like that Sasithorn had never before seen.

Another wave came. These were now whaling harpoons, and as the Thai dragon veered for escape, four of them notched her at the thick of her body and another two at her tail end. The humans came forth with spears, and these, too, had rope tethered to them. Sasithorn fought, but as she did, her belly was lanced and wide became her gaze as she was reeled backwards, towards the ships. The bipeds had axes of considerable measure and cleaved at the end they had her by, meaning to deconstruct her piece by piece, if there was no other way.

Sasithorn screamed. She was low to the ground now; rain and muck were thrashed into her eyes. The hominids skewered her through the underside of her jaw. She could scarcely see – those human legs pistoned back and forth all around her, and human throats buzzed their language loud in her ears. In her nostrils was the smell of her own blood.

She clawed at the enemy, but they scampered out of reach, and Sasithorn considered how she might die this day before the eyes of her sept.

She would die a fool.

Then, arose a monumental thrumming from the ground up, elegant in it tempo and unexpectedly soothing.

Sasithorn closed her eyes, but for a moment.

What was that drumbeat from the earth? It seemed native, tribal, and its cadence was fire-dancing. A hush came with it. In that brevity, the rain became sweet-smelling, uniquely mellifluent. There were rushes of frenzy and furor, of which she was in the midst, but Sasithorn had first to clear each her senses to perceive the occurrence. She blinked into the light.

The storm became a most terrible horizon.

"A demon!"

"The Devil, 'imself!"

The humans could suddenly do no more for themselves. Sasithorn was released as an immersive din engrossed the cove, and the anchored barges cracked like rib bones of gods behind her. She turned around to face that sound.

She saw the beautiful devil in the sea. Half-submerged in the shallows, ocean walls came up at the sides of her as she ran them down – the wights with their myriad weaponry. Milky-white throughout, now dashed in the vein's crimson passions, she was the maiden's cheek after first blush. There was the cage of wooden limbs sprouted from her brow – three tiers of them. She plunged death into their numbers. The humans were shucked of life, and the bay became their last memories.

Sasithorn stared at her friend: Ardyce of the Tree Crowns, who would not allow Sasithorn to become a page quietly ripped away from the tome of Drakes. The Mungkr wished to undo everything of this day, but the stone was in her being – immovable.

Ardyce charged the nautical transports, until they floated no more. She wore the insides from pitted human bodies, and from her tusked mouth hung the rope which formerly had bound Sasithorn to odious fate. The vastness of that frosted goddess had so easily obstructed doom.

She was the angel Sasithorn had not believed in. Now proven to her was that kindred hearts were not fragile: deep friendship was its own allegiance.

As the other dragons began to emerge from the veil of blindness, Ardyce, ever-methodical and disciplined by the principles of she, had laid to quiet the horrors of the sanded beach, like a bouquet set upon the headstone. She gathered in one palm those still adhered to this life, but all of them unconscious, and brought the remaining humans to the circle of elders to receive her guilty charges. Sasithorn came in tow, her muscles finally gaining shy memory. She gazed at the Tree Crown, but Ardyce would not her eyes meet.

Those bearing the highest responsibility to their tribe or clan were known as The Great Aegis, or The Shield, to their breed. These five were gathered with those most ancient of the lands, and they waited for Ardyce and Sasithorn to approach. When the Mungkr and the Tree Crown reached that solemn council, they bowed. Mei Xian, The Shield of the Tianlong Drakes, spoke: "Return them to their realm." And, of more, she said not. Sasithorn dared to look 'round at the countenances of those most revered. She saw that they were all gazing at Ardyce in admiration.

Sentenced to the skies, and postponing care to their injuries, the two friends flew in silence. Ardyce held the bundle, made from the mast of a fallen ship, that was full of human survivors who were still unbelonging to their senses. She grasped it in one her taloned hands. Sasithorn followed her route. She let the larger Drake fly ahead of her, then Sasithorn weaved over Ardyce's back and threaded around her neck. She repeated this loving affection twice, then rejoined flight at the Tree Crown's side.

Stop that, Ardyce had said.

"You did save me, dear friend," she returned. "To you, my life I —"

"Stop."

They continued on.

Because she could not stop, Sasithorn said, "You must despise me."

It was then her friend looked over at her. *Nay. Brave is she who steps forward, out the protection of anonymity, to risk herself, so that her people may their lands and their lives keep. I am envious of such a one as she.*

Sasithorn snaked over and around the Tree Crown once more. *"But, cease!"* Ardyce growled at her, nearly fumbling the collection of wights as she tried to push the Thai Drake away.

Sasithorn flew beside the white she-Drake, drifting in and out the clearance of her great wing span. The Mungkr said, "I've blood-soaked your palms, turned you a murderer."

The Tree Crown was ever-honest. *I could not be reduced my only friend, for you are part an organ which beats in me.*

Sasithorn smiled sadly at her, then looked away. "I should never have shown myself. The legends. The history of knights, armor-clad humans, hunting us to the thresholds of extinction. I wanted to save us, but once these ones find their way home, I wish it were not, but most probable will be an army of them returned to us in due time."

Ardyce's stare was fixed on nothingness. She circled a distance from the Mungkr, who stopped in mid-flight, to watch her doubled-back course.

"Ardyce?" Sasithorn questioned.

The Tree Crown simply continued the wide circle, stalling, and unable to look the Ngaw in the eyes. Finally, she said, *We will break the cycle. Of knights with their lances aimed at dragons. In doing so, we will protect human and Drake life alike.*

"What do you mean?" Sasithorn glanced below to the ground as movement triggered her attention. She saw the wide arms of the desertlands and treading through the sands were the shape of Wyrms.

Ardyce descended a few feet. *It can be no other way,* she said.

Her friend was quick to go to her. *"No.* It is despicable."

War is despicable, the white Drake answered. *Two houses of species locked in bloody campaigns. This is what you sought to prevent. It is noble of mind and heart, but the action for completion is abominable, I know. The fact though does not annul necessity.*

Sasithorn reached for the makeshift reticule. *"Please, don't."* But, the larger Drake held it out of her reach.

This happened not, besides in your silent memory and mine. The bipeds will believe their exploring crews surrendered to the seas, and to our kin: they are delivered back to human perches. Ardyce, then, opened her hand and released the folded skirt of human beings. The sheet flapped wide in the winds, and down, the wights – limbs flailing and howling screams – fell towards earth. They became impacted blotches, soft and pulpy, upon the rigid terrain. Wyrms came, then, and chorused their frenzied ululations. More and more of them surfaced for the scavenged remains.

The grating of the hard gums in the Wyrms' mouths began, and Ardyce redirected for home. *Now, it is your turn to forgive me.* She flew slowly, such was her heart thus weighted. *Let us receive our castigation anon.*

Sasithorn could not tear her eyes from the scene on the ground. She had never wished this progression nor death to any hominid. She spoke before Ardyce was out of sight. "They will not condemn you, Ardyce. Instead, they will elect you The Great Aegis."

You are dispossessed by trauma, Ardyce concluded.

Sasithorn was beside her again in another instant. She appeared regretful. "I saw in their eyes that they had witnessed such formidable power. They saw one who fought out of all her heart." She stared at the Drake, white as the heart of winter when the season kills itself to make room for all the sun-festooned months to follow.

Ardyce, that night, said nothing more.

Sasithorn felt the veins of the mysterious sphere pulsating to tapered crescendo. *'Tis true: the past will not be slighted,* she thought to herself. *It was my fault you became The Great Aegis.*

The rachis of her had unified, so she stretched and felt the muscles revived. She wondered how long the River had nursed her. To trial the body redeemed to her, she circled the organ which housed her. The fluid within it shifted with her, like a gown most sheer, and its touch was the lightness of moth wings as she twisted and rolled in almost child-like play. If it wasn't now so cold, the cocoon would be a seduction to the anchorite, even if the toll were memories which emerged like the baying moon-serenade of wolves, undeniably filling the night.

Sasithorn turned over in the river-egg – what else to call it, she knew not – and came to marked attention of a tinted ring on the outer surface of the globe. She questioned herself, felt she could not have overlooked it, yet, here it was. It was uniform in width throughout, and at its center, the Mungkr noted that it was entirely transparent. A circle of its own and large enough for her to peer through, it had not the filmy obstruction which sheathed the rest of the sphere. She was unnerved by it, and as she was telling herself that she was not, Sasithorn nearly turned away from it, except that, through it, she witnessed something leaf-float down to the bed of the River Orb. It was grimly substantial in size, and when the complete volume of it rested on the granular floor, it was empty-feeling in a way Sasithorn sensed it should not be.

She left that lucent viewing-circle to move towards the bottom of the rondure enclosure and have a closer look, but as she peered out, the bulk lying at the bottom of the river disappeared. Inwardly, she reeled, and the disturbance in her grew, for everywhere she looked was only an extension of the irenic waters.

There were paddlefish again and other of the piscine lot, but they were all shiftless itinerants, indifferent to the sorcery of the fluvial dwelling. Sasithorn studied their paths, all the meanwhile, edging away from the agitation of her mind. She patterned their similar habits as they bent and curved their lackadaisical wayfaring, as if to avoid obstacles unknown to the eye.

The Mungkr glanced about her membranous birdcage. Those xanthous veins turned shade before her eyes, and if a hue could seem to age and expire, so then did this sickly-saffron venation turn a smoked and charred bister. Within each throbbing trunk of them, meaty clods were now forming and flowing, sometimes chunking to dam the way. She could feel a pressure begin forthwith, and no longer was the frigid temperature her concern. In that sensation, as if being squeezed, her jaw and backbone ached desperately, and Sasithorn searched a way out from the organ that was seeming to destruct.

She came again to that clear aperture, which afforded her unobstructed sight and observed once more, in hopes of something she had missed. Her throat tightened, and though she had thus far breathed that seeming amniotic fluid with thoughtless ease, now began there a drowning in her mind.

Sasithorn balked. Her heart hid from that which her eyes conveyed. The hulking mass she had earlier seen was returned. It lulled in the sway of the potamic abode, and as the face was turned to her, she saw it was a Wyrm deceased. From out its mouth, and catching the cadence of the River Orb, trailed its organs – some long and others were clustered.

But, this Wyrm was not the sole casualty housed here in the river, which before was only ever the benefactor to life. Sasithorn drew closer to that modest window, and the scene revealed was what trapped her heart.

She could see very far by function of the mysterious, translucent area, and there were other globes, dozens, like hers, rooted to the riverbed. They were, however, the pustules of corpses: blackened with frothy, discolored liquid inside. Their residents were portions of themselves – some Wyrms, others Drakes – and every one of them rotted out of life, like teeth so diseased they fall away from the rest of the breathing body.

Her sorrow was very sour. It chided her eyes and drew her in tight around herself. She saw the tribute paid to black War and knew the battling was above her. She knew the River Orb had taken the dead and was struggling to reverse this history that came with haunted hatred to make ghosts of everyone.

Sasithorn tried to leave that witnessing portal, no longer able to stare into the harshness of massacre, but that spot with its encircling dark ring would not let her turn away. It came to rest wherever she faced, tracing over the surface of the sphere, and demanding she see the suspended graveyard with its unburied dead. By now, the waters surrounding her had become chilled.

The War. To go to war and serve it made her feel both a trained hound and a brick in a wall – a wall of which was made only to stymie the view of the skies and to bloody despairing fists against it. She could add numbers to these sense-ridden masses, afloat and shuttled by glistening waters. She could increase the obstacles for paddlefish to navigate. But, perhaps, this seeing organ had brought her to memory for a second determination of the past-present thus ringed and turned back on itself.

Why is change so elusive, even under the strength of our best intentions? Yet, it is a deluge upon the sleeping village when we are most fearful of gods and sacrifice anyone for quotidian ease? Why? A crucial juncture we've missed by carrying our heads so high, believing we know wisdom when wisdom is ever-silent, like a tree.

Half-distracted, the Ngaw stretched forth her snout, not to bite anymore at the sphere pressing in on her, but instead towards that cloudless aperture.

I can change all of this, came her thoughts from before. Then, she realized the repetition. Sasithorn tailored minor adjustment: *This, we can change. For, none of us are alone.*

As she reached for that glass-like portal, she found her nostrils passed through. It was an opening. The soft trunk and chitin atop her snout was pressed flat along her forehead for a moment as she eased her head through the hatch. She wriggled to maneuver into the open waters, and then the fluid of that globe released, and Sasithorn careened into the River Orb, freed.

She looked back. The sack which healed her was depleted, and now only a wrinkled heap, entirely pale. The sinewy tendril that had anchored it had atrophied to unleash emptied skin. She thanked the river, unknowing why she continued life when so many others had not, and began for the surface with thoughts of her dearest friend leading her concerns. *Ardyce I will save; she needn't change.* As she swam, she brushed Death many a time, unable to see them who had perished in the war. Sasithorn, likewise, avoided eye connection with the traversing fish, unsure if they were instead the actual figments of The Orb.

She hadn't gone far when a voice came to her from the depths she'd just departed. The stranger's words emerged in her mind through telepathy.

Drake! Drake of jade! Drake with elephant trunk made!

The Mungkr was much surprised. She gleaned the stretch of her surroundings, wondering if she would be able to perceive the owner to that voice with the river seeming to mask realities from one another.

Here! Lean left to be right; right above me. Good. Now, come down upon me.

Sasithorn saw, then, the one calling to her. She hesitated briefly for thoughts of needing air eventually. Only the Tianlong and Shenlong had both air and water-lungs, yet the Thai Drake ventured lower, closer to the unknown figure. She could see another decreasing sphere as the one which had encapsulated her, and as she, herself, had struggled to depart. Then, she startled, unintentionally allowing to escape the air she so desperately needed.

She had been looking to make the shape of a cousin Drake in her eyes, but the figure before her would not conform. He had been trapped to lie belly up, but as the upper half of him sat up to look her in the eyes, Sasithorn saw again how the Orb seemed so much a prism, not refracting light, but refracting Truth into her myriad colors.

The head shape she saw was all wrong. A long, tapered protrusion dominated the face to stare back at her, and his eyes were wolfish both in color and mien. Shadows seemed to pace in those eyes like insomniacs, caged within lost hours, for there was movement in his gaze though his stare was granite-fixed upon her. Extending away from the face, Sasithorn could see a plume of dark feathers, and she felt her mind was slowed by being long-submitted to the watery halls of the river, but searching her memory, she could not recall a Drake breed of any kind to wear the stole of feathers. Sasithorn strived to look away from him and moved to the midden, so much like flesh or cartilage.

My, my . . . . His voice moved like warm water in her thoughts as she drew close to him. The tone in his voice was hunger.

She ignored him and didn't know what to say, for she assumed him a Wyrm, who somehow had the gift of language and telepathy both. Sasithorn shoved at the collapsed globe, losing a bit more oxygen with each exertion against the burdensome sack. He was fighting, too, to make detachment from it. As he thrashed against the sphere, which must have been his salvation as well – as it had been for herself – she felt his strength and the force of him. He whipped free of the organ, like a thorn plucked from skin with a sharp hiss, and she saw the whole of him before the cognizant thought had fully emerged in her mind that the Wyrms she had of late encountered were as vicious as they were evolved.

But, now, a creature most unique swam before her – much in a way as Drakes do, yet more so as Wyrms never have had ability to traverse waters once wholly submerged. He glided in near to her, then suspended movement to float in her gaze, and he – this Wyrm either in collusion with or locked in usurping antagonism with Nature – was mantled in thick, dark feathers. The face of him was bare, as any reptile's, and then, the midnight plumage began and covered his length to the upper quarter of him. He seemed to carry a bulk to him just before where the feathers ended, and the remainder of him was dark and arrayed in pebble-smooth skin.

She felt, within, an awe at his mutation, his beauty; he was a dislocated joint in all she thus understood. As she beheld him in her gaze, she saw again the predatory hunger in his eyes, and he darted at her to which she snapped at him in warning.

He laughed, and the River Orb gurgled froth and spume from her depths, like one chocking on hemorrhaged blood. There was a lapse of blindness, then another lapse, but this one in display of the dead once more, and Sasithorn turned 'round, like the hands of a clock, to see the gnashed bodies from before. Yet, now, they ascended like flotsam towards the surface, their various gored pieces trailing after each their wretched bodies.

The creature's voice played in her thoughts, again. *'The lady in green taffeta will be mine. Even if Time unravels me, and I wait 'til after Death for us to bind. For, loving her has sent me on most worthy enterprise, disorderly conducted. She was not my passive muse or trophy-like fresco – but, fiery catalyst for me to find another me when I had already self-destructed.'*

Sasithorn realized the Wyrm had encircled her many times, again and again, up the full length of her. He held her, dearly, in the coils of himself, and she screamed at him to be freed.

Your eyes are locking memories behind the doors of vision or you would feel me familiar, Drake. You would see me, he urged.

She screamed once more with all effort to be rid of him.

And, then, she fell away to darkness, for the last of her air had been sacrificed.

CHAPTER 18

OSHIN RYSING

Hadryn stared at the body in the wooden casket, backlit against the gently tremoring fire of the hearth. Hadryn blinked, yet still he saw what he saw: the man was breathing and with deep rhythm as though he were asleep.

Mr. Ro took two steps towards Hadryn and stared up into his eyes. The Knight faltered for words, so the denizen took the blade from Hadryn's grasp and set it aside. "Hadryn." Mr. Ro slid the backs of his fingertips along Hadryn's jawline.

The Knight held at the other man's wrist, stopping him. "Tell me who he is."

Mr. Ro's hand fell away. In his gaze was a fragility and also austerity. "I said that I would tell you, but first there is a thing which you must answer me, Mr. Archidux."

Hadryn returned his eyes to Mr. Ro, but the suitor's head was now down. Mr. Ro was picking at his face. "Mr. Ro?" Hadryn questioned. The bearded man would not answer him; he peeled at his face, leaving the soldier to gape, dumbfounded. The suitor's fingernails were lancing at his skin.

"Ow. *Ow. It hurts.*" His face was coming away, starting at the cheek on one side and down to his chin. The heavy beard hung away from the head.

The Knight gasped and backed away. His thoughts were of Otruna Plodd and the way he had died: horribly disfigured. "Stop," Hadryn said to the other man. His nerves were wavering, as a thought entered his mind that perhaps, somehow, Plodd's terrible mangling had been self-inflicted.

"Shit," Mr. Ro said. He lifted his gaze to the Knight. "Help me, Hadryn. This bloody stings."

Hadryn looked at the face, staring into the eyes, staring at the browned skin. Hadryn reeled at what his eyes beheld. He felt forgotten of language, seeing the beard hanging by only a small section from the face. There wasn't any blood. He stared at the face, now without facial hair, and Hadryn croaked, *"Oshin?"*

She chuckled a little and said, "I had to come for you." She was still struggling with the false beard, carefully easing it away. "This is made of my own hair, I'll have you know."

He saw as the remainder of the facial hair came away. The latex prosthetic ran along her jawline, down over her neck. She removed it all. Her lips were revealed. The strawberry birthmark along her throat was revealed. She was still wincing and making other faces as she pecked with her fingertips at pieces of half-dried glue on her face. Hadryn was partly-returned to his childhood, for she was at once familiar, and then absolutely unknown. He thought of her letters sent to him and felt a warmness envelope him, then he was unnaturally cool-skinned with the littlest body hairs prickling up. Her eyes were a lutescent, tawny color, like moonlit wolf eyes, and her lips their own bounty of lavender pink. He saw that her long hair was now freed and shaved upon the left side. "I had not planned," he admitted, "for you to be quite so stunning. *You are very close.*" He got up suddenly and paced away from her, unable to believe that she was here. He stared at her, then looked away. He repeated this several times, shaking his head to himself. Hadryn had never dreamed that they would meet again like this. He was disappointed, euphoric, and entirely self-conscious of his male-ness. He kept seeing, in his mind, how he once looked as a female.

Oshin's words brought him back to the present. "You thought I would be ugly? I knew you would not be."

He leaned against the door frame of the room. Hadryn tried not to breathe, for he felt he was nearly panting, then he had to breathe and was wheezing.

"Hadryn?" Oshin went to him. He was gasping. She asked, alarmed, *"Are you having a panic attack?"* She put an arm around his waist and led him to the antique rug.

"Hard … to say," he fought to answer. "I have never … had one." He regretted her being here and treasured it, too. The Knight was thrown to inward turmoil that she should see him in this frame of male-ness, no longer cloaked by the written pages of their letters to one another. He was before her, and without the body she last knew of him. Hadryn fought to calm himself, wondering what she felt in seeing him for who he was. But, she didn't seem to be aware of that at all.

Oshin was darting furiously about the room now, opening every drawer she saw. *"We need a little bag for you.* Hadryn. Pace your breaths; make them slow, deep." She became flustered. "You've nothing in these chambers, but pots and pans!"

He gestured her back to him, and gradually, Hadryn regained himself. When he had the lungs again for it, he tried laughing at himself, for she was here, and it was good to touch her and look upon her. She laughed a little with him. He held her after that, and she became soft in his arms and stroked his maroon-colored hair. Hadryn stared again at the sleeping man in the coffer. "I was going to go to you," he said to Oshin.

She followed his gaze. "The bird, not little, said I should go, instead, to you, and then, he told me where I would find Mr. Stabel."

"'Mr. Stabel?'" The Knight met her eyes, confused. "But, he died, Oshin. You saw his body, torn and in pieces." Hadryn approached the sleeping figure, seeking to understand.

"Yes," Oshin answered him. "And, then, his body … left. Left death. I don't know how this happened. But, he survived, and Dayraven found him."

"He looks unwell. Strange." The Knight peered into the coffer. He reached out to touch the man.

Oshin spoke up. "There is more to it, Hadryn. This is why I brought him here—"

But, her words dropped off, as if gravity had found them without land to stand upon. Though she didn't catch them, Oshin succeeded in netting Hadryn's fall as he stumbled backward from the wooden trunk. They gaped. Mr. Stabel's eyes had sprung open. The coffer rattled as he sat up in place. He sat up tall, nearly up to the ceiling and a vibrating clicking sound issued from his throat as he threw back his head with glazed eyes.

"What the hell is that?" Hadryn cried out.

The man who had been eaten was whole, but he was not of human construction in his return to the living. Mr. Stabel's body was rounds of fat and folds of skin. There were moles along his body with little hairs twitching and grown out the center of the skin tags. He was without limbs, simply flesh extending the length of a human body.

The unfathomable creature that was Mr. Stabel gave a short, piercing call. A thick secretion flooded from the corner of his mouth as he did. He lapped at the air with a tongue thrice the size of one human.

"Mr. Stabel? Sir?" Oshin's voice was weary as she tried to feather his attention. She whispered to Hadryn, "He asked to be brought to the Tiered Nations and has slept ever since."

"Here? Why did he ask to be brought here?"

"He thought he may be cured somehow in the Nations. I didn't understand how, but I wanted to help him."

They stared at what had once been a man.

Hadryn asked Oshin, "Did he tell you what had happened to him? The mauling. How could it not have ended his life?"

"I tried again and again to ask him," Oshin said, then quieted as the half-human in the coffer issued a short, high-pitched whining.

Hadryn and Oshin flinched as Mr. Stabel banged against the portion of the lid still closed. It seemed it was his attempt to move somewhere, then he sighed, and his head fell in their direction. The man's mouth wrinkled open, creating more creases in his face than there were before. He was toothless, all gums and a dark, wide mouth that was grunting exhalations. Mr. Stabel stared at them with a joyous look in his eyes.

"Take me to the Tiered Nations?" he requested. The consonants he uttered were rough and grating to the ears, the vowels elongated.

Hadryn and Oshin stood with the Knight keeping the woman behind himself. They clung to each other, and Hadryn answered the creature. "You are here, good sir."

Mr. Stabel blinked slowly. "Medicine? I am sick." He sighed again, sliding back into the confines of the casket. "Medicine. Sick. Something I ate. Do not allow me to Make the Ring."

"What is he talking about?" Hadryn stared hard at the creature.

Mr. Stabel smiled at them, then sorrow overcame his features. It seemed he felt the need to explain. "It is said that when the head, or the beginning, has absorbed the end which one has walked, then that one has Made the Ring."

"Mr. Stabel?" Oshin once more attempted when he had fallen still again, save for his uneven breathing. "Please, tell us who did this to you. What was it that attacked you?"

The creature stared at the ceiling, lying upon his back as a cadaver would. His eyes skittered from left to right, then dew-dampened with memory, and he craned his neck as though to have better sight of his thoughts which were in the distance. Then, he answered, "Why, me, of course. *Me.* Monster-me." The creature returned to his posture of rest and bizarrely, he then fell to sleep once more, his eyes slowly closing.

They hadn't time to catch their thoughts or breath. From without the room, voices and running steps sounded in the halls.

"Sir Hadryn! Sir! Your mother requests you!" It was the hired help, and Oshin ran to the coffer and closed the lid to conceal the man she'd brought. She turned to Hadryn. They were both wide-eyed.

"Go," Oshin told him. "I'll follow after shortly."

CHAPTER 19

ALL HORRORS

The Archidux estate was succumbed to the rawness of panic and a percolating disgust. There was talk that a disease may be unfolding and Jonren's mansion was the origin of it. Still, a portion of the guests stayed to watch what would happen next. If they went home to their network feeds, they knew they'd only be wishing instead to know how the episode concerning the house of Archidux would end. The gathering in the banquet hall had become the gathering at the foot of Mr. Archidux's winding driveway.

Medical officers had arrived by carriage for Miss Ermaya, who had surely lost her little finger. There was no hope to return or re-attach it. Ermaya insisted though that there must be a way, then sobbed hysterically the third time the foremost doctor told her once more that she would be left four-fingered at one hand. This further enthralled and entertained those who remained, yet they gave, also, wide breadth to the helpless woman.

"Is she infected with something transmissible?" the guest who had been sitting near Miss Ermaya at the dinner table asked one of the officers.

"We won't know, until she has been tested," the medical aide answered. He was doing his best to administer a sedative to the crying woman, but failing.

It was at this point that Ermaya's wailing, loud like fast wind upon one's ears, came to a clumsy halt with hiccups interrupting her cries, until her sobbing all but ended. The injured lady clawed and scratched away from her throne, and for nameless reasons, the medical officers only watched her, pausing in their preparations for her care. Almost eagerly, the crowd of spectators stared at her.

She had walked a few steps, then, like a careless toddler, Ermaya had fallen to her knees, keeping her back to everyone as best she could. They saw her figure heave and heard two, labored grunts from her, then the sound of thickened liquid pelting the ground. The diners grimaced, even as Ermaya fainted, falling over on her side. One of her plastic slippers shrugged away from her foot as she toppled over.

And, screaming amongst the crowd began anew.

Many more people vomited their dinner from the Archidux feast. They pointed at Ermaya's ejection as well.

The emergency staff hurried to the fallen woman. There, they found her dismembered finger and with it, a complete set of human toes of the left foot. There was blood in Miss Ermaya's shoe.

Cyssiline stared on, helplessly. She couldn't remove her attention from Miss Ermaya, lying there on the ground, and though it was nonsensical to do so, Cyssiline blamed Jonren for everything to unfold this night.

The supervising doctor at the scene became violently ill in the shrubbery to line the paved driveway, and denizens watched as he ran from the unconscious woman in terror.

By then, the help had fetched Hadryn from the rear chambers with Oshin soon following after and, to them, they relayed the banquet's course, not by plate, but by frightening circumstance.

The Knight and Oshin stood now with Cyssiline, watching as Ermaya was lifted in a gurney and her throne wheeled into the black interior of a carriage. The medical officers went about their duties gingerly and with a tremorous caution. They cared for Ermaya and collected her small body pieces. When the officers spoke to each other, Hadryn overheard the names of other denizens on their breath. One of them was Otruna Plodd's name, and they whispered how his body was missing from the morgue. However, to he and his mother, the staff said nothing, only stared over their shoulders at them before awakening the engine of their vehicle. They left as though their abrupt absence was explanation enough.

Mr. Archidux had gone to lie down a while ago. The evening had brought him to drink, a fast stupor to follow, and then sleep, even before the doctors had arrived to his estate.

The guests of the night then departed the evening's scene of terror, leaving behind a deserted driveway and stacked plates of uneaten food at the oval table. The Chef[3] in the dining hall was finally retired for the day by the hired help, who attempted to work quietly as they cleared the dinnerware and cubes that had become cold and hard during the tumult.

Still outside, in the night which seemed exhausted to silence, Cyssiline sat in her throne with her son and Oshin close by. Oshin and Hadryn were muted, not yet ready for the knowing that they knew. Cyssiline turned to the young couple.

"It is not disease," Cyssiline said confidently. Hadryn suspected she may have taken a pill or two to numb the past hour and a half. She continued, "It could not be lunacy; she was clear in mind, self-possessed." Her hands shook, and Cyssiline's eyes were glassed, but dulled, like a mirror very far away. "And, Isia has disappeared. I've looked. He is *nowhere* – wherever *that* place is."

"Mother." Hadryn strained within to see his parent tumbled by a freak incident. "You need your bed and sweet sleep. You were astounding tonight. Now, we must care for you, as well."

"Oshin, I am glad of heart to finally see you as you," Cyssiline prattled on. "You are beautiful and the more so with my boy. Are you surprised, Hadryn? Delighted? A little ruse orchestrated by your mother and this fearless woman." Cyssiline mimicked the sound of laughter, but the features of her face had nothing to do with her effort at lightness. Then, the denizen became pensive-looking. "Oshin. Say, my girl. Have you any idea *why* a woman would suddenly eat of herself – *her very own self?*"

"Mrs. Archidux," Oshin began, but could find no other words.

Hadryn said, "Let me get her to bed. She can bear no more of this night." But, Cyssiline had edged away from them, her throne jumping forward with the twitching of her fingers at the navigating controls. "Mother," Hadryn called after her, but she was unresponsive.

Oshin held at his forearm, and he brought her against himself as they stared at the ground beneath their feet. The Knight shook his head. He swallowed, keeping an eye on his mother, who was speaking lightly to herself as she motorized in her throne aimlessly, but wound up near to the spot where Ermaya had fainted before being carted away.

Oshin said, "I thought we would happen upon a beast out of mythology. Or, nightmares, Or, one of Nature's deep pockets."

"We did," Hadryn returned softly.

Oshin turned to him. "Hadryn. We found people. Human beings."

He met her gaze, and the white of his right eye shone with anxious urgency. "It is absurd," he said. She saw on his face, not disgust, but layers of disbelief. "People can't."

"But, they must be." Oshin decided she would be the one to say it. The skin of her arms goose-fleshed and her tongue felt heavy with the words that were due. "Humans are eating themselves to death." Then, she felt defeated for how she'd worded it. "Not death. But, eating themselves into some other animal," she corrected herself.

Hadryn looked as though he was wandering in the dark with eyes that couldn't focus. His frame took on the burden of what she'd said, went rigid with it. "I don't think it's possible, Oshin. Physically possible. The body I saw at the morgue was deprived of all its limbs." But, Hadryn remembered the putrefying meat lodged in Plodd's mouth and throat. Still, the Knight said, "Besides the strength required, neither do I think it mentally or psychologically possible to exert such destruction upon one's self."

Oshin listened to him and fell within her own thoughts, quiet to him now. The night and the artificial light of the lamp posts above them shifted in her steady, dark gaze. She was staring out, past the end of the Archidux property to the streets and the city beyond. Hadryn watched as her eyes eventually went to his mother, who was picking through an array of capsules in her open palm. After a grouping of seconds, Cyssiline hurled all of them to the dirt and wiped at her eyes.

"Then, tell me what we are witnessing, Hadryn." There was a fragment of pleading to Oshin's tone. "The woman with her missing pieces and the creature of Mr. Stabel. Why is any of this happening?"

The Knight couldn't answer her, and another voice came upon them from direction of the mansion.

"The maggots come for the dead. Giant maggots."

The man approaching them was upright, but hobbling with lameness. Both his legs were bandaged over the tatter of his pants. Dark blood shone through the wraps.

"Mr. Blane!" Hadryn rushed to the older man. "What's happened to you?"

"You are returned, Isia!" Cyssiline drove her wheeled chair to the hired help, and her eyes widened in alarm as she saw the blood on him. "*Not you, too, Isia.* Does it not stop at one's smallest parts? Does one eat the legs as well?" Cyssiline dove into the compartment of her throne though it was now emptied of pills. "Quickly, Isia!" she begged him. "Swallow the path—the pills to enter dreaming states, lest you swallow yourself instead!" But, there was nothing which she could give to him.

With gentleness, Isia stopped the denizen. "What are you speaking of, my lady? I did not harm myself." He sought to soothe her, then looked to Hadryn and Oshin. "Did she see it? Is that why she has taken to her pills?"

"Seen what?" Oshin quickly asked.

Isia sighed, some of it from the pain. "In the cellar, I came upon a most unnatural beast. You may not believe me, but it held me in its jaws, flaying the flesh of my legs!"

Hadryn and Oshin looked to each other.

"Could it have been?" Hadryn asked.

"No," Oshin interjected. "Mr. Stabel was near us for most of the night."

"You know of them," Isia said, gazing at Hadryn and Oshin. "You have seen them. Do you know who the girl is? The one who can speak to them?"

"A girl?" Hadryn asked.

Isia was becoming agitated. "She may know about my granddaughter. The girl!" He entreated the Knight and the woman at his side. "She is the color of innocence: purely pale!" He gripped at Hadryn's sleeve, partly for support as the blood ran down his legs.

Cyssiline, then, wailed. She covered her ears. "Monsters and little girls and Miss Ermaya! No!" she moaned. "We will be driven to eat of ourselves!"

The Knight was at his parent's side, holding her. "Nay, mother, not so. But soft now, shh. We have not, yet, the mark of our teeth, thus, subscribe not to doom."

"*Our* teeth?" Isia stood there, baffled.

"A woman, one of those dining here tonight; she bit off her finger," Oshin told the older man. "And, five of her toes." She said the last of her words at a whisper, so that Cyssiline would not overhear them.

Isia thought of his granddaughter's dark hair on the ground. Then, he shook his head to clear the memories before they became a wakened nightmare in his mind. "Cyssiline," he said to himself and went to her.

Cyssiline's features were ghastly with despair, and Isia released the issue of his granddaughter and the girl. He stared into the eyes of the denizen, and Isia wondered if there were things which he did not wish to know. He fumbled with his words before they came out. "It is a night too cold to be out much longer, my lady. Let me get you to the warmth of your bed." He spoke to Hadryn next. "I will escort her home." He took one step closer to the Knight and made his words low, for Hadryn alone. "We should barricade in a room to be safe. I do not know what you've seen, but in the cellar of your father's basement was a beast hideously large. I thought I had seen one like it before, but that creature five years ago was only the size of—" Isia went still before he could finish his thoughts. He said, "The size of a young child."

"How did you see one?" Hadryn asked, incredulous at this to be revealed, but Isia was shaking his head and leading them away with Cyssiline.

"To the house. Quickly," Isia begged.

Hadryn took Oshin by the hand. "He may be right. We don't know what's out here."

"It's people," Oshin said. "Like you or me, my Knight."

Hadryn turned quickly in his mother's direction as Isia fell to the ground from blood loss. Cyssiline was fretting over him and left her throne to help Isia into it. "Come with us," Hadryn said to Oshin.

"In a moment," she answered, taking from her pocket folded paper and glued to the edges of them: thin sticks. As she unfolded the material, Hadryn saw that they were miniature sky lanterns. From another pocket, Oshin brought forth candles and matches. "We need to speak to Dayraven. These will signal him. He'll see them in the sky and come. I'll meet you inside when I've finished."

Hadryn stared at her busy hands and her fingers quick and sure. His gaze went to her eyes, then lips. He glanced back once at his mother, knowing he should hurry to catch up to her and Isia. He asked of Oshin, "Your bird, not little. You believe he knows more than he's told you?"

Oshin met his gaze and there was fear in her eyes and ambition for the truth. "I believe he may be one of those creatures."

"And, dangerous?" Hadryn feared and came now close to her, unwilling to leave.

"If he wished me harm, he would have long ago indulged himself. No." She lit a match. "He knows what has befallen the condition of human, perhaps even *why*. And, this we should know as well. Don't you think?"

"I'll stay with you," Hadryn concluded.

"They need you. I will be five minutes behind you."

Hadryn was unsure a moment, for she felt both familiar to him and not. "This Dayraven. A year now you have met with him; he's chosen you to inform."

"Not 'met.' It is untrue to say we 'met' to exchange what we knew. Without exception, he has remained sheathed from my eyes."

Hadryn mused, "Leaving only a black, raven feather where you would stand and he to attend the otherwise isolated conference at your backside, unexposed to sight."

"Indeed," she agreed. Then: "What is this hounding? I do not seem to have caught the tail of it."

Hadryn looked her directly in the eyes and was firm with her. "We meet him *together.* Or, not at all."

She crossed her arms to face him squarely. A moment passed between them, then Oshin admitted, "I would be terrified to do otherwise."

Hadryn nodded with faint smile. "Five minutes," he repeated of their promise to one another. She winked at him, then he turned to hurry after his mother and Isia. He looked back at her once, and Oshin stared after his retreating figure.

Hadryn's jogging gait faded from her ears, as she knelt again to the lanterns she would prepare. The night was not imposingly cold. She felt her own warmth about her, yet it was a sudden revelation of how very isolated she now was from other human company.

Oshin gathered her lanterns now and walked to the midpoint of the street in front of the Archidux's driveway. With the candles burning within, she released them one by one to the Moon's night, and they rose, tall and up to the heavens.

If one person became a monster, we would capture and destroy she or he of us who became so unbearably different. But, if hundreds of people turned monster, we would have a war. And, if all *people changed to monsters, monsters would be allowed survival. Life.*

Oshin stood to face the mansion, as the winds awakened to the witching hours. She regretted the thoughts to have found her without her searching for them. She was quiet as she sought to change her mind about them, but they would not leave her. Oshin looked up, high above herself.

The sky lanterns were nearly out of sight now. As they seemed to evaporate from her vision, her ears caught something else in the mounting breeze. There was a noise behind her, down towards the end of the avenue, where the street lamps did not penetrate.

She turned around. "Is someone there?" But, she hadn't quite heard the last word she'd said for distraction at a siren that had begun in the sky. Oshin peered up, and it was the District's archaic emergency system: an old double-speaker mounted high atop the steeple of an abandoned clock tower. She could remember seeing them when she was still a child who lived with her parents in the Tiered Nations, but she had never deemed them worthy of operation. The monotone issuing from the tower did not seem particularly urgent, despite the singularity of the event, for the call was audible, but not the goading loudness she imagined would move one to action. Oshin wondered if, miles away in the neighboring Districts, their devices, too, had been triggered to alert, or could it be a malfunction – perhaps, a testing – of one, hobbling remnant from the past.

Oshin looked for another denizen, someone who might know what to do.

"Sir?" She spotted him near a hedge, close to the ground, as if he had dropped something. She could see only his head, oscillating – most likely, in search of his fallen possession. Although large of frame, he didn't appear to have a throne nearby. "Excuse me, sir?"

She'd caught glimpse of a face and wondered aloud. "Dayraven?" Oshin asked hesitantly. Then, she thought of Hadryn when he had gone to the morgue, and she said, "Mr. Plodd?" Oshin wondered why the denizen didn't have a strand of hair on his head, yet it seemed better to let that be, to let him go on seeking what was bereaved of him.

Oshin, who had never feared the night, tensed with the feeling that the cloaked hours battened upon the trepidation of those who'd come to the understanding of horrific transformation. Oshin shuddered, as she stared at this silent denizen now before her, and she did not another step advance towards him. With care, she placed a foot behind herself, and the cobblestone betrayed her with a gasp heard over the siren, or it was her movement that caught his eye, or she'd gasped too loudly, herself. Oshin could not figure out why he'd turned to her, but she wished he hadn't.

His face was much too large, the size of a carriage's tire, and it was canted to one side. It strained from off the ground in direction of her. Covered in viscous fluid, it inched into the glare of an isolated lamp post, and Oshin became weak at the sight of him.

The lips of him were swollen to absurd proportion, and they caught along the street's surface, if he dipped too low his heavy head. Drooling the entire time, his mouth remained slightly agape, and his eyes roamed, but his nostrils were pointed at her, sniffing the air.

And, that was not the worst of him. The beast, all folds of sarcoline tissue, had risen upon his elongated body, stark naked. His nipples were still there, splayed to the sides and distended by a form now anything but human, and farther down, she saw too a cluster of wiry hairs which could be nothing else than pubic hairs, though there was naught of genitalia.

Around them, the sirens, too soft, wailed on in the neighborhood, and Oshin came to realization that Mr. Stabel was not complete in his metamorphosis, still close to human height, when this beast by contrast was thrice his size. Oshin fell backwards as she attempted to turn and run. She looked back over her shoulder, in direction of the Archidux estate, weary that she should underestimate the speed and strength of the creature. She screamed as he came up, tall as the roof of the nearest estate, and he pitched back his awful head and was clicking and trilling to the sky. His language ended in a perverted chortle, then he was back on the ground – the whole of him – and Oshin had found her feet. He sniffed at where she stood, and the sweat was all over her; every limb and the core of her was set to trembling.

It was then that Oshin felt the road beneath her quivering, almost in sympathy of her fright, and the cause for the siren became known to her. To her right, the fencing at the perimeter of a lawn made of astroturf came up, a picket at a time, as another of the creatures passed them, relatively slow and uninterested in their presence. Another one, fast and bearing the same cylindrical shape, barreled by and seemed to make it its course to avoid them by wide discretion. In the vicinity, she could hear screams and the destruction of house and property. She sought not to see more of them, but kept her gaze on the beast before her.

"What are thee?" she asked, genuinely confused. "Not of the Past, you are, for the Past was never such an ugly baby. And, mythology would not have one as you. A dreadful rash of Nature's? Or, are you truly what we are to become?" Oshin grimaced at the smell of it. "You are like a revolting penis, I daresay," she muttered under her breath.

He, who was once Otruna Plodd, did not come closer, but inclined to his side once more, and by long, crawling seconds, he opened his mouth to her. The jaws of him fell inch by inch wider, and Oshin was backing away, but unable to tear her eyes from the creature. She gasped and stopped herself when, unprepared for it, a molding-like pungency suddenly collapsed her sense of smell. Oshin nearly retched, as the creature opened its jaws to speak.

"You have him, girl. The Orb. Where is he?" His lips made shapes and lines by delayed measure, ever more wet and slopped with saliva.

Oshin stood there with eyes wide. She knew he would be capable of speech, yet still it unnerved her to a panting quiet. She tried to get away from the beast, as another drove of Wyrms came from the shadows to pass them at either side. She watched them crawl and buckle the pavement under their weight. Her legs weakened when the last of them had passed, and Oshin knew.

"You mean Hadryn?" she asked the thing drooling in front of her.

It guffawed its abusive breath. "The Angel and the Conqueror approach, child. As I have heard it, they wait and wait…" His utterance was slow, as though he thought with difficulty. "And, they wait 200 years, or longer. 2,000 years. They wait for the opportunity to swallow The Orb – the enlightened one, the buddha, the chosen – *all of that crap!* The Lightening Encapsulated. For, it is then that one, either Angel or Conqueror, will come to power and ascend over the other and their people. That One will toll the Earth as a mourning bell, and Drake or Wyrm will be no more." He laughed, and it sounded like something between a bleating and a rockslide. "I will bring to the one of my choosing this Orb and escape the extinction either and both of them shall sow."

Oshin's terror grew. She knew she should be running. "Speak sense if you are to have words, you thing." She hoped to delay him. Her reflections came back to her, riding an instinct of understanding. "You seem to imply there is a war to come."

The Wyrm rose up in its anger. "You idiot, *they are the gods; they are Amaranthine Time!* And, Time does no other thing, but to chew us each up to digestible mush, and then, *does it swallow.* How long one lasts at their games is the only consolation prize. Call it 'war' or what have you. *Now.* Give him to me!"

It lunged at her, and Oshin evaded the blow it would serve, but she was struck from her feet, hurled into shrubbery as the animal, at the last moment, swung its lower half to find her body. She felt the dense elasticity of the creature, hot to the touch, as they met upon impact, and different odors, all of them foul, came from the beast with its every movement. Oshin rolled out from the tangle of brush, trying to steady herself.

"Oshin!!"

She saw him, then, the Knight, and he was running hard with his gauntlet rapier drawn. In his other hand was a sword. Oshin struggled to get to her feet and find the strength, again, in her legs. She watched Hadryn, so newly-reunited with her, and knew the distance between them was too great – just as she'd always felt it in penning letters to him. Why could they never be closer than to miss one another?

"Oshin, run!" Hadryn cried it so hoarsely, and he threw his dagger to lodge in the side of the beast, but she had just found her feet. She meant to run. And, that was when the creature bore down upon her and swallowed her whole.

CHAPTER 20

An Interlude: DAYRAVEN

The Past:

I do not know the reason we lived buried. Perhaps, it was to escape the shameful possibility of being seen. Imagine. Living where the dead went to rest, solely for the reason that we wished to be shadows and were not. It could be, too, that we were a truth overwhelmingly bitter and ergo, impossible to endure in the inexorable honesty of daylight.

When I thought on that, a peculiar yearning arose in me to read Archfiend literature. *The Prince of Darkness*, they crowned him. Father to the Beasts. The Devil. Satan. Every pen wrote of him with great acrimony, and every principle humankind has ever shipwrecked by our own folly could be blamed on the Archfiend. It was as if he were Damned to pay for our sins. Like a matter of convenience, so that we need not bear our own self-reproach. He was written to be entirely unlikeable, but if that were actually so, I wondered why there existed so many stories of him. A great many minds had spent time with him to write on him, to write characters consumed by him. I feel authors are comforted and take profound pleasure – sexual, I believe - in the things which move them to pen strokes.

Moreover, he lived in the caliginous Beneath – the Underworld – as I did, so a kinship was there, however remote.

I had attempted to read on the Chrises, as well. But, they seemed to me all blue-eyed with everyone attired in white, and the tales there were penny-dreadfuls which made me ill, what with the talk of blindness and boils and lepers and famine and everyone seemed to have a son who would die. So, if I saw the name "Chris," I kept away from that literature.

I heard a clatter outside my den and the tintinnabular, chiming voice of a wine glass settling. My maid entered, then.

"Good day, madam. How are your sores today? Are there any?" She saw what I read and gasped, staring at it as though it were a bakemeat, and she was slender with youth and always hungry. "More of that Dweller in the Deep." She had placed my tray with the afternoon's refection and a cup of vermouth on the flat surface that was also an arm which swung in and over my bed, where I laid. Where I had always lain.

Marlela, she, my maid, practiced goodness, and it was notable the attempt she made to seem the one reasonable between us two. "Forsooth, a lady would be hanged or institutionalized, if espied with such a book her lap-warmer. It is thankful we've no longer religion, or I'd worry for you, I would, madam. A psychosis, people would think you had." She was 19 years old, so very dedicated to me, and I was 28 years aged. Marlela began to undo the ties at the side of my thin robe, in order to seek and balm any bedsores I might have. She kept her eyes on the books though.

"Marlela." I stopped her. "I've none. You know this. I will not let this skin rot – this sack of me – any longer." The bed of my chambers was more a machine than a mattress to welcome dreams. Marlela was already pressing buttons to mechanically arrange the bed into a position like a divan, so that I could sit up. I shoved at her hip with the heel of one my hands. "Get away, you gnat! You know I mean to dine with you at the belvedere." I laughed, and she was giggling and falling over herself, like a flowerhead with too many petals.

She was my dearest companion. All others, I only pretended to like.

I sorted out two of the books from the teetering stack upon my bed and gave an easy, underhand toss of them at Marlela. She tried to catch them, but they both clamored quite a ruckus as they met the marble floor. This made her laugh all the more, and she bent to put them in a satchel which she had made herself. I was always prodding her to crochet for me one as well. It was an orange and purple satchel; I told her that I favored the colors green and yellow, but she would reply no more than to say that this she already knew.

Marlela watched me as I heaved the unwieldy mass of myself out from bed and used my own hands to hold my tray and drinking glass, used my own feet to walk to the polished, red cedar table in the room.

"You have the look of Tomorrow in a world of todays." She said it sunnily and with pride. I knew she was happy for me, yet sad as well. "You should hide it," she admitted, as I took the three steps up to the landing which is the platform of the belvedere and came to sit in the wide bench at the table.

A rotunda, like this one attached to my living quarters, is traditionally intended as a viewing area, something which overlooks a greater scene. "In The Grounds," as those of us who live here call it, a *"view"* adopts meaning anew. Being that where I lived, the Alveoli – it's sanctioned name and the name used by those who live above surface – was two miles beneath the sun-stained world, a "view" was nothing more than the caverned expanse that was the Alveoli. Every one of the 32 officials, like myself, could stare out only and across the way at the boxed pigeonholes that were our individual chambers. Built into the walls of the cave, our compartments were of two levels, one atop the other, and arranged in the form of a horseshoe. I lived in the upper level, closer to the curve the formation made.

Bearing likeness to a coliseum or an arena, our chambers were high above and looking down upon a small village in the trench resulting in the structure of our living quarters. This was where our maids and servants slept and prepared our foods or any crafts which we may desire. Necessities came from the village as well: people were brought in to make clothes and bedsheets for us.

Marlela once had a little home there, a mat on the ground of a dome built up in hardened mud and clay. The roofs of the village were all made of glass, so that officials could peer into the lives of their hired hands. Purportedly, it was to ensure no thievery of our goods came to pass at their hands, so they nodded and acquiesced, but there was not one of them unaware that they were our voyeuristic diversion.

We watched them sleep and imagined their dreams. We watched them work and clean, and I can tell you it looks different when they do it for themselves than when they are serving an official. None of us can hear them who live below us, but I know they hum and sing during the completion of chores. When they ate, they laughed with one another and conversed with hand gestures, so different from us who were officials and fed alone. And, since there was nowhere to hide from our gazing eyes, they made love without inhibition. My favorite of them to watch was a unique, polyamorous relationship consisting of three women. Many times, when they made love, one or two of the women would stare back at me as she orgasmed, and the dark-haired one of their relationship would let me watch sometimes as she masturbated.

I once asked Marlela if those living in the villages enjoyed being watched.

"Of course, not!" she scolded me.

Two months after meeting one another, Marlela had given up her mound-like home and now spent every night, asleep on one of the six couches in my apartment. When Marlela had moved in, I'd ceased viewing the three women because it no longer felt decent to do so.

"We must talk," Marlela said. Then, she insisted, "In a *serious* manner."

I leaned over to push out the single chair beside me. It was more dainty and pretty than it was functional, but it carried Marlela's weight, untroubled. "You worry for me, an official to the Government Body."

"No," she said, and sat in the chair that was for her, alone. Marlela had hair that was dark brown like wet earth and hazel eyes which sat against the darkness of her skin. Her mouth was wide, but her smile always small and restrained. She had a little gap between her front teeth, and she spoke in a loud voice only to me. To everyone else, I saw her address them with nothing more than mumbling words. "That isn't why I worry!" She reprimanded me in a strong tone.

I continued: "You worry because I am an official obligated to marry and have children to succeed me, being that only this 'noble and chosen' bloodline may continue in this station, yet I pursue one of my like gender."

"No," she, again, answered. She ate the cubed food from my plate, for it was rare these days for me to eat. I drank my wine. I would have two glasses of water in the evening.

"Because of my recent surgery, then." I lifted my tunic to reveal bandages and a clear, plastic pouch which was adhered to me so that excess fluid could be drained. The gauze wrappings were pinked with seepage from the exertion of leaving my bed. It seemed my body was more truthful than I. In a matter of months, I had shed half the 400 pounds that was the only home I'd ever known, and the stretched skin left was a testament that we can never live in the skin of another, even if that Other was once ourselves. Through surgery – cutting and snipping and bleeding – the excess skin was removed. When pieces of you – old and so familiar – disappear, there is a certain degree of pain that follows. Yet, not one word would I utter how laborious, how tolling it was to begin every day in this different body. Unweighted people, people like Marlela, float out of bed, like scherzando from piano, but me; I feel each my steps in the world, like a tortured artist.

Marlela's face pinched with light-hearted squeamishness when she saw the bag of fluid. "No," she said. She'd stopped eating and looked downcast. I thought it was for wanting the bowl of chocolates usually found in my den, so I rose and retrieved it from the decorative shelves which were built into the walls. It was where she had last left the transparent dish. I set the candies near her. She ate one. "You are wrong, because it is not any one of those you've listed, but them altogether," she confessed to me, then pulled at a buckled strap on one of her wrists. Maids and servants were the only ones In The Grounds who knew the hour, keeping little faces of Time upon their arms. She looked to hers. "And, also because it is my place to tell you: it is time."

It was, *indeed,* Time.

Every week, my heart raced, not from the complaints of my body, but with the elation of fantastical thoughts engineered by my mind. Or, soul – for, I felt it through and through to the largest, pulsing lifelines of myself. And, then, I dashed to the elevating lift – a compartment made by the joining of wood paneling and caged fence. It thrummed obstreperously, but the cables operated without so much a ripple and the motor was faithful. None the other members used it, and if they saw me going to it, they hollered as vehemently as they believed necessary to frighten me that I would be proscribed, exiled from my home, the Alveoli, and the Government Body. Not one of them read the literature I'd read, for none of them understood when I simply yelled in return, "As the Archfiend once was!" and rose above ground.

I emerged into the Face: a white, granite building that drew challenged inspiration from exhibition halls and mausoleums, merging the two designs into an aesthetically-anemic vision. Its most generous compliment ever received was that the ceilings were high; alas, though, they were empty. I hastened my tempo, departing the sheltered corridor that led to the lift, and my footfalls rung in the adjoining gallery which was unable to entertain the eye besides a herringbone floor pattern and towering radius windows. The light came in orange. It seemed sleepy, but alive with little shadows: birds or leaves outside and passing by most likely, winking through the photonic snowfall of it. It was the triumphant truth to the lying wattage in my room of fiercely-white lights, so I paused, and I let my eyes love the sighing of the Sun. Already, the air here was different, as well. It met with my lungs differently for the reason that it lacked indifference, unlike the placid oxygen pumped into the caves of the Alveoli. I let it further my happiness. The skies were near; my body anticipated those zephyr-nymphs. From here, I exited the building to a wide loggia – really, the only place of any beauty – and paused before the gaze of an oval mirror.

I was not beautiful; this didn't bother me. But, a face ordinary should still present well, for sincere expression will not be helmed by the mundane and often dazzles unexpectedly. I ran a hand through my hair, long and dark like nights left to themselves when lovers cannot arrange to meet. It was feathered in layers, and I rested the bulk of my hair over one shoulder, then decided against it and swept it back again. The bridge of my nose was long, my eyebrows undefined, and I was in ownership of a pair of lips formed as if to remain close to one another. Every curve and groove of the sides of them that touched each other was a perfect fit. Yet, I was learning to part them – these twins of shape – and put them to function. The blood of me was "Mexican, Native American." I'd read it in the birth profile, which each government official has filed at the Administrative Department. We are granted the viewing of our own file once, and I only went to look to have something to do for the afternoon. Below my race was listed a history of health issues to afflict my family tree. I hadn't read that part, but I saw one photograph of my mother.

In the glass of the mirror, I continued to scrutinize myself. I had in the past complained to Marlela that I did not reflect the beauty of my mother, but Marlela countered always that I had the eyes of wolves and that made my beauty inhuman. "Let humans have their pulchritude, but keep your beauty animal." My irises' color was titian, so a wolf I was, or some animal wildly-free of this world through death. If I thought of myself in this way, I could believe I once had a mother and that I was her child. She was the human to which I was her animal soul.

The oval mirror was the length of a person, so I could see nearly the whole of my new form, everything besides my feet. Each government official had an array of silk robes in hues and designs unlimitable, but every single one of our tunics depicted an unusual animal in pursuit of a white sphere. No one I asked knew what sort of animal it was on our robes, but one of the servants to the eldest official had once told me the sphere the creature pursued was wisdom and power. Seeing this animal comforted me now. In the daylight, upright as I was and myself beholden in mine own eyes, the pain was made to ebb. My body, that was continually sore for the new exertions I daily exposed it to and now with the surgery still healing, could find peace through the awe I felt in witnessing my own transformation.

Prior to it, the years were many I had spent with each day a manacle of illness and organs threatening surrender under the ballast of my weight. I was 17 years old when I became bedridden. The planes of my existence had come to an end in four, soft white corners where the bedsheets were tucked under the mattress. Being that I could no longer walk here or there, my eyes seemed almost to cease seeing, for there was never anything besides my bed chambers and the same hues of the bedspread atop me. I felt my vision lose clarity in those days. Details skewed, as if every object shook off the lines of which they were composed. My hands and feet seemed to follow after my vision and became muted troglodytes. Without sensation or experience, I entered a silent catatonia. The older members to the Government Body had warned me of this reduction of life – or rather being alive, as I saw it – and that the senses, and properly the emotions that are their ardent bedfellows, would become childhood playmates no longer relevant. But, I could not have imagined that this was what they meant, or I would have fought it all. Even when I cried, and did as each day renewed itself, I felt it not. The tears came out of me. I signed the denizens' permits as was my duty, then I ate and slept – and none of it came through the shroud that was my faculty of perception.

I'd wanted to die the night before when a shrewd, dwarf-like man from the Administration came to me the subsequent morning and told me the time had arrived for me to bear a child. "It is what each the members to the Government Body do. Someone to continue on afterwards. After you are buried," he clarified.

"I am already twice-buried," I said to him. "Once in the Alveoli and twice by this body."

He made a habit of ignoring me from the start. Like someone so scoundrel he cannot even spell the word, he rested near to me a catalogue. Each page was laminated, clasped in a green binder. I was chafed by him, but curious about becoming a mother. There were vague memories I had of my own mother. She had been mad.

I remembered how she always told me that at night, she wandered out of her body – quite awake – and she entered a landscape of stars that burned in place, goliath, and very close to the ground and that when she walked through that domain, she came always to a tree that was not a tree. *"An enormous throat,"* she would tell me, *"rising out of the marl. And, half a jaw there as well; one septic row of bottom teeth – molars and incisors and canines – glinting. Did you know our lower teeth are always upside down? The throat stands, so bitterly frightened by its own half-formation, and it grouses in a stunted, bawling language of rasping, incised moans. When the gullet swallows, the sound it makes is furiously loud, and one star more will waver and extinguish, dead. Dead, my child, as you cannot imagine death. Furthermore, a great tongue whips and hooks at the welkins from this un-tree. It is like a serpent driven out of sanity or writhing in torment, atop that throat, and forsaken of the rest its skull."*

Then, I remembered her being dead. She had been euthanized to "bring her peace." For a number of years, I signed the influx of denizens' petitions in her name, but as I came into my sixteenth year, I signed them in my own name.

I promised myself not to become lunatic when I had my own child, and I opened the binder the stout man had brought me.

That was how I came to know of *her*. I chose her. I turned the pages of the catalogue, and they were all photographs of people. The man at my bedside was a salesman: "They are those above the dirt. They are the Royal Guards stationed with the protection of our government building, The Face, which resides in the Nations." He turned a few pages for me, looking through the binder as if for himself. "These soldiers believe they are given the highest rank possible for their skills and fortitude, but it is for their genetics and, well, yes, their comeliness." He giggled, not so orderly now. "You will not see such beauty or excellence in physique anywhere else. They are like prized beasts, as humans once bred – all sinewy muscle and sweet spots. Delicious. I like to look at the binder when I am alone; I like them all; I – well, anyhow." He drew away from the photographs. "Make your pick. It is a shame you officials are so marvelously large! Or, you'd be able to make love to the one of your choosing. But, regardless, we have frozen eggs or frozen sperm from you each. When you find the one you like, we will sedate your mate and take from them the same materials to bake a little baby in our labs. You may enjoy the outcome." He was ready to make his leave.

Like gazing at a menu, with no more thought than deciding between cubes of sweet fry bread or corn meal tarts for dessert, I said, "Wait. She, I will have." I showed to him the photograph. "'Sasithorn Kingpoyom.'" I said her name, and it seemed to be the last line of a curse, for I was bewitched.

He stared at me. Then, he burst out laughing. "Silly me! Oh, my goodness, how I forget! You, officials, know nothing of the workings of nature." He returned to me. "My dear. You must choose a *man* for your mate."

I was silent. Then: "No," and I was decided.

"You must!" he exclaimed, attempting to seem light-hearted. "We cannot sprout a little baby of you, if you do not."

"Bring her to me. This one."

"But, what about your little baby!"

"Stop saying 'little baby.'" I made a second decision: I hated him. A part of me sensed the violation done to these people – perhaps even, one done to us officials as well - and he was the conductor. "Nothing little ever endures here. There is solely bigness and more-ness in this human enterprise." I handed to him the catalogue.

He was deeply disturbed.

"Sasithorn, you are a dreamer."

I drew away quickly from the mirror and my memories, at the sound of a voice unrecognizable. It came from my right, outside the loggia. Furtiveness caught at me like a reflex, and I hid myself just passed the entrance to the loggia. I peered out upon the open courtyard, where she was due to meet me, wondering at this unfamiliar voice to address my Sasithorn.

She was there.

She was with another.

Sasithorn. A woman with skin the hue of sanded beach shores and hair, impossibly, patina in color. She wore it to her shoulders, but there was also, a long, braided tail that fell down the center of her back, coming from underneath her shorter cut of hair. Her eyes were a blackness which shined, oxymoronic, and unnerving for it. She was beautiful, like a dead language, and just as strange. It was this eldritch disposition that enraptured me, though it was a domineering truth that she was bodily beautiful, like the moment of orgasm or when you first realize that you are in love. I was lost to the image of her and felt my eyes going over the details of her, as if my gaze were a pencil to sketch her in this moment.

The other woman Sasithorn was with laughed, and a hardness drew in between my eyebrows. I turned my attention to this stranger. *What creature is this?* I studied her and the impossibility of her and the inherent threat she presented.

The stature of a god with hair stained as if by clouds, for her head was a startle of pure white. She wore that alabaster crown relatively short and manicured as a gentleman's cut. Every lilting curve and lineation of her countenance was the paragon of feminine and masculine beauty combined. Her smile was the siren's and her eyes the source of infection to turn mere mortals to poets. Those eyes seemed not to have a specific color, always of at least two hues, then melting to emerge as new colors with each slight movement of her head. In horror, I stared at her and her tyrannical height. She was made even more grandiose by a striking tonality of muscular endowment.

My bottom lip had begun to quiver with anger, shock, disbelief, and, strangely, a long-awaited affirmation that Sasithorn was too beautiful for someone of my likes. I felt the smaller muscles in me trembling for being held taut as my body was besieged by inner-alarms wailing. This was not how I wished to introduce to you my adoration, as she cheated me. I looked again to the other woman, and she was, naturally, to blame for her magnificence. I saw that the white-haired woman wore, too, the uniform of a Royal Guard.

I despised her, instantly, for being in the same planetary sphere, the same era of Time as my Sasithorn.

Strong was my intention to march forward and break their interaction, cease them holding in their eyes that of one another. The tall one leaned an elbow upon my beloved's shoulder, told her with soft voice something in her ear. Then, she drew back and sauntered away, and I was still battering my resolve and my cowardice, for my feet would not unhinge me from my place, until their conversation was quite finished.

"Who was she!!" I raged, and hedges and the little pebbled path – all the distance between myself and Sasithorn – fled away. I was before her, that lovely woman I'd now been courting the past year. *"You cheat me! Out in the open, like this. Where you knew I would come for you!"*

She responded very oddly. Sasithorn looked behind herself, as if I must be speaking to another and not her.

I continued, so that I wouldn't crack, like a dam overburdened. *"Tell me who she is!"* I wanted, too, to demand why, except the answer was more than obvious.

"She is Ardyce," Sasithorn answered, bewildered.

"'Ardyce?' Damnable lies and unfaithfulness. You name your lover your 'friend' to me – expecting me gullible! Expecting me to believe it!" How this wrath so resembled sitting with one's back too near to the burning hearth. I was smothered by the heat coming up my spine and neck.

She simply answered, "You believed me before, when I first told you of her." She was calm, and I was suddenly ashamed. She became silent, as she does when she thinks to herself. Sasithorn swayed a little with her gaze on the ground, calculating in her head. "You have now seen her. That is the only difference."

I stared into her eyes of blackness, and my anger within became a candlehead flame, then snuffed out. The smoke to remain was a sudden embarrassment as I felt her thoughts edging too frightfully close to the insecurity I wished to deny was there. I gaped for words. Then, I held my eyes on my feet. *"Sasithorn. Are you leaving me?"* I asked, dejectedly.

She suddenly perked in place, having butterfly-netted a small truth. She ignored my question. "You are," she paused, then went on, surer of herself, "...intimidated by Ardyce's physical bearing."

"Anyone fucking would be!" I snapped, very bladed with her now.

Sasithorn giggled and waved aside my anger as though it was a silly fit. "Oh, come. You are not one to be fooled by a bit of decorative exterior."

I held the silence for long moments, wholly confounded and entirely uncertain if it were she or I who was of unsound mind.

Sasithorn laughed and held at my hand. "Remember, she is the one I told you wears shoes passed the front door to her room?"

"Yes." I answered to see where this would connect.

"And, she leaves her dirty dishes in the sink, *un-rinsed.*"

"Yes. You told me."

She gave an expression as if she'd given me all the obvious answers, ending with an exasperated *"pfffft"* sound. *"Well?"* But, I was mute. "How could I possibly have romantic interest, in that case, my love?"

"Her bust is the size of two my heads," I replied, plainly.

"She has a little boyfriend. This, I told you as well. Besides it all, she was counseling me how it is unwise to tie knots with one belonging to the Government Body. 'Useful,' she said. 'Yet, not, if the heart has anything to do with it.' Then, she laughed, for she would be stripped of her office, too, having taken a servant boy as her inamorato."

It arrived, then, and too much delayed, that I may have been erroneous in my assumptions. How to apologize? I'd been an ass – perhaps, disfigured how she thought of me. "Dear heart," I began, sounding idiot in my own ears.

But, she stopped me and placed my hand over her breasts. "There are these soft, little steps suddenly, across my upper torso – pitters and patters – my lungs ready to giggle." She closed her eyes, as if listening to or in rhythm with music which gently cradled her. She smiled at me. "Yes. I think it is pleasure in me to find that I am so precious to you to draw an episode of impetuosity, *to stir the ravens to a murder*." Her grin went to the very hue of her eyes and their dark abodes flickered with light. "How funny, romance. A birth of beauty from nothingness, from the space which closed and disappeared between two former strangers." She had me by the hand, her smile the quickness of a bird's wing, and she was leading me at the pace of a little frolic to The Archives Hall. I had forgotten the pain of thin knives at me and the way my body was, still, in recovery at the loss of half itself. I followed her happy canter. "Highly unexpected," she continued a moment longer on the same subject. "Every time! Love is a misfit who plays hide and does, too, the seeking. And, I think we are all tickled children at being found, or we are, at least, adults reduced to our cores – you know, the very best of us." She laughed, and I was immersed in an elation that could only be described as Heaven. She winked at me, "Now. To the vaults of history, my beautiful Dayraven." And, in the moments of our time together when she said my name, I felt this peculiar sense of branches extending from me – or I felt feathers along the backs of my arms. It was something I could not sufficiently describe with human-shaped words. She made me feel there was more to myself than just me.

We rippled down the corridors of the byzantine White Face, like blood under the skin to form a bruise at the surface we could not breach. I saw the short man from the Administration, who was, inadvertently, the link to join me with my Sasithorn, and he was caught up in a glower of the likes not human, more similar to how angry food looks when it is dropped and makes a tantrum over pristine floors. I raised a hand in greeting to him. I called out, "The Archfiend finds his mate in sweet Eden! A proposal is accepted; Eve savors the pomegranate! Pandora peers into the pithos!" I saw the wish in his eyes to murder us, but we rounded a corner and he was vanished of sight.

We hurried on towards the central keep, and there, often over-looked, were a flight of stairs, inconspicuous and minimalist in design. We traced the handrails down a few steps to a door simply metal. There was not a knob or handle to it, and it was all one blank face of grayness, except for a keyhole, like a little crack in a wall that will lead to the destruction of a barrier. Officials are given keys to this room, a storage warehouse – or a library, it could be named, if you are the type with rose-colored lens – and the keys were to be passed along to our maids or servants, if we so came upon a permit which deserved research into the past for why it ought to be denied. Officials sought to preserve a percentage of permits that did not meet approval. It was believed this maintained the perception of order and authority. I brought the key from my pocket, and it became the door's handle as I pushed open the bridge into a world forgotten.

The media, the art, the entertainment meant to bring pleasure and discourse, catharsis and intellect to the commons was confiscated, prohibited by the year 2020. The bulk of those relics came here to the White Face.

We went through all of it – the magazines, newspapers, vinyl records, tape cassettes, compact discs, digital video discs, books, comic books, and even the podcasts.

We'd come to the library at the suggestion of Marlela. I'd complained to her, after many months of seeing Sasithorn, that Sasithorn saw nothing of me besides my chambers, and I worried that there wasn't more to me. Marlela had replied that we all found ourselves outside of our little homes and reminded me of a unique key in my possession. We'd gone that very day to discover *this*.

At first, it was our wonderland, miraculous and perplexing at every turn – an exploration that no other seemed to know. Then, it became our shared passion to speculate what was the manifest intention of it all, this accumulation of both fact and fiction. A dissemination of information was one conclusion, and we then set aside all the magazines and newspapers. But, the stories – those we could not determine why there were such an unending horizon of them, all different, yet kin by archetypes, morals, or shared monsters, shared heroes.

That, too, was how we came to know one another, and how a trust evolved, and how we were molded by knowledge of one another and dare I say, by love. It was a sweet denouement to what had been a grievous start.

When we'd first met, Sasithorn and I – that is, when she shook loose of the drugs meant to incapacitate her – she had refused me. She attacked me. This went on for months, but they were months I never tallied. Every week, I asked for her, on Sundays. She was brought in by force, each time. I let her denounce me; she swore and destroyed parts of my room. I watched her from my bed. When she'd used a butter knife to puncture my favorite, mounted paintings, I told her for the first time, "You are beautiful. Your hair is so nice." That was when I hadn't yet many words or thoughts to my avail, but if I could see her, I felt my mental faculties broaden, gradual as it was. She had retorted, *"You dirty, old men shall never have that piece of me to grow beginnings!* No. I know. Your only fantasy is of a replica or a testament to your self-determined government. A child suffocates, like a mind within a comatose body, if that is what awaits them. I cannot submit to that. It will be my choosing when and if I will bring a separate piece of me to this life. *Least of all will I allow* you, *who knows nothing of the tides or seasons by which Metamorphoses claims us, to lay your fingerprints to me, transmute me.*"

She said these words, and I saw many things at once. I peered into a kaleidoscope that fell this way or that and became beauty each time. I muttered to myself, "You are right. We should not be as the Chrises." And, I realized, too, my morbid obesity had obscured the distinctions of my gender. "I am female," I had replied, stupidly. "Therefore, you are not here … for that." Then, I could only stare at her. I added, "I wanted the Truth of you, and you have allowed me to see it. I can ask no more."

After an interval of silence, she found a corner in my chambers to sit. She would speak no more and seemed only to be waiting. She swayed in place, clutching her knees to herself. The guards to oversee our visits eventually came for her and she was gone. I didn't know how to think, what to make of our encounter. All that night, I thought on it. I went to the belvedere to sit and watch. Everyone below looked different to me: the men and the women. There were no children, since each of the male servants brought here is first sterilized, and I looked away with a realization of shame for looking in when I had not been granted their permission. Then, it came to me. I searched for ways to be wrong for my conclusion, but it seemed to equate logic and reality.

When we let someone in, especially by choice and via the corridor of Truth, it transposes us.

She had given me one key, only one. Yet, it shook me to a depth I hadn't known of myself.

"I saw, again, those creatures of the night. At the military dorm, as I was leaving after submitting my monthly report to Headquarters."

I startled from my collection of memories and adjusted focus to the library we sat in. Sasithorn had, rested in her lap, a book detailing Aztec mythology and I held my thumb in place where

I'd been reading of Norse tales. We had been comparing stories found in each of powerful, snake-like gods. "Did you?" I asked Sasithorn, concerned. "They didn't notice you, did they?"

"No," she answered. I wondered how she could not be troubled by what she'd seen. This was a fairly recent development, and any news of it both immersed and troubled me. I tried to imagine being there with her as she viewed the sizeable creatures, who were long and the shape of slugs as she'd described to me. Twice now, Sasithorn had witnessed them, but like before, she was unvexed in her recount. "They were at the same window, like before, simply peering in," she said to me.

"The man's window. The one with the eye of white?" I asked.

"Yes," she replied. "He is a Knight of the Third Rank."

"You should warn him," I urged her.

"They seem harmless though," Sasithorn reasoned. "If I tell him, and he alerts the Generals, they may hunt them out and exterminate them, simply for being animals when animals should no longer exist. Or, they may cage them in the Food Labs." She turned, and the colors of our eyes danced to reflect the other's hue. "Do you wish me to tell him?"

After a second beyond prolonged, I said, "No. You always see into Time in a way I still cannot. Let us not bring ruin to the creatures."

She smiled and was quiet.

The vault of history was lit by two chandeliers of multi-tiered bulbs, and they were substantial in size, fit for ballrooms. The carvings of their splendor wound like roots beneath ground, certainly not elegant, but promising of a fantasy unknown to most the wakeful world. The rest of the dark corners and stray aisles of the library made appearance by the glow of a fanatic's assortment of lamps: they were of every color and proportion, every shape and material possible.

I listened to Sasithorn's words in that great hall with its lights all individual. She sounded musical and like a fairy tale that could speak for itself. She smiled at me, this woman who possessed the might to rank a Royal Guard – even if it was half-staged by the

Administrative branch. Fortitude, pith, and aptness were required to convince the Guards of their earned merit, and therefore, it was not a façade that each of them was honed of those traits. Yet, she of indomitable martial skill, besting the majority of Royal Guards employed to these grounds, had a weakness, something I, alone, knew. More truths. If emerged, this pitiful secret, she would be undone of her employment here and the military as well. All she had labored in effort to build – it would become the dust, the mud we brush away from our feet.

That secret; it was this: Sasithorn could not eat cubed food. It was not just a sickness that resulted, but besides the vomiting, her flesh retaliated in hives of blistering soreness, her airways objected, and if continued, a week would see her bleeding from the inside out. She was not only made weak by the food of our world, but she had bodily been betrayed to coma twice in her life. She had once told me, "It appears as nothingness – the comatose victim – as if we go away and leave all previous function and mechanism of ourselves behind. But, that is the ignorance of those not inhumed. There is a haunting that weaves like a binding made of your own flesh, so it is inescapable. The apparitions which claw at you are yourself; they have no other physical definition, except that they clearly have your very own mouth. How do we know our own mouths? Because the voice is yours as well. And, that mouth that speaks looks as though it is ripping and gnashing, but words are emitting, and they speak to the dungeons of one's body, that freedom can be no more." She told me she hated nothing in the world, but that – to be asphyxiated by her own living vessel: the sea of her blood and the meat of who she was.

The months that followed, I no longer had to ask for her. She arrived on her own accord, sometimes not even on a Sunday, and she gave the other Royal Guards who secured the lift – the only way down into the Alveoli from the White Face – a degree of hardship in order to descend without written orders. We sat together and shared our Truths. She explained to me that the only sustenance she could subsist from was found in District 11. She had to explain it to me; I hadn't known there was a way besides the cubes, so my unintelligible assumption, at first, was that she didn't need food to exist. She thought I was ridiculous. I thought she was a goddess.

District 11 was as far from the White Face as it could possibly be, while still existing within the Tiered Nations. Sasithorn sacrificed every resource to her avail and every hour unaccounted by the military in treks to the hinterlands of our society. I tried to understand this. She had nothing to give of rest to her body, no delights or the pastimes to create memories for herself. All her personal time was spent in trying to survive. And, now, she had halved that time to have a few hours a week with me. I looked at her and realized she was wasting slowly away. I hadn't meant to, but words came of their own will, and I was telling her how she could not continue to do this. Life could not be simply survival. Our bodies, then, have won, and there is nothing our mind and our hearts hate more than that.

She had laughed at my inchoate philosophy. She fingered and traced down the length of strands of my hair closest to my face. She told me that she wanted to believe in my account of life, but the only other option for her was the everlasting solitude of Death, and she loved too many things to yet love Death.

I released the discussion. Some weeks, when we met, she was well and healthy. Other weeks, she was nearly starved out of this world. I had nothing to give her, but water. I held her quietly on the nights she was too weak to speak.

When Sasithorn left me for days on end, it seemed my heart became an army, and when I spoke to Marlela, I terrified her with my crusade. I instructed her, not asking for her opinion or her feelings. She cried sometimes, like a child or a helpless mother, but she brought my orders to the vans which ran errands for Officials and these were the things I requested: shovels and hammers, soil, trellis poles, and more soil. The wealth I had rapidly evaporated. This was because I would come to purchase human greed. I bought, from each and all the Royal Guards, and whoever else maintained the grounds of the White Face, secrecy. Not just that, but brawny labor, in tow. Let them work for the pockets of which I filled. I said to them, "Use the hammers and destroy every inch of the White Face grounds that you can, inside and out of doors, as well. Make a heap of the debris of the Past in one room alone. Then, spread the loam and give to it depth." I left them saying that they could think of goddesses as they laid the earth, but never of gods. Interestingly, this made more sense to the men of the Royal Guards than to the women, who were perplexed with my parting words.

The work went swiftly. I had to hurry to keep up. The seeds were to be the hardest to attain, but when are they not? This task was designated solely to one person of my choosing. I chose myself. Marlela wailed like a wounded, pitiful animal. Officials to the Government Body were strictly forbidden to leave the Alveoli and the White Face. But by then, I had shed the excess poundage of myself and walked with relative ease for considerable distances. This asserted in me a newfound confidence that I should be the one to do this thing, and that I would find success in it.

At night, I crept out and left the Alveoli and the White Face. I went to District 11 in search of seeds. The time it took for me to arrive there was the longest I had known of Time. My feet had never felt so much of the world. For countless hours, the cold of deep darkness walked with me, numbing my fingers and drying my breath at my lips. I thought of the years I'd spent underground. An excitement came over me, causing me to run and run. I ran, until the sun blinked into my eyes. I found I was smiling and gasping and sweating. Still, I walked. I didn't know to rest, but I drank the water I had with me along the way.

Then, I was met by District 11. A small sign just before the gates to it bore only the numerals of it, and someone had graffitied it to turn each number one into two stick figures who were holding hands. I found the sign endearing, but would come to understand that the idea of unity did not apply to outsiders.

Within, I didn't reveal myself, but something about me spoke to my origins. I was beaten by the inhabitants of District 11. A member of the Government Body forbidden to leave the White Face was a member who could not tell any other that she had been beaten by denizens of a shunned district. They robbed me, in addition, and I was lectured on what "you, people" were doing to the human race and our shared, revolving planet. I sat on the ground as they yelled and screamed at me. They ceased when they saw that I had taken from my cloak a pencil and notepad, believing I meant to report them, until they read the written lines. I would add their words to the library in the White Face. I knew, immediately, that I should. Furiously, I was writing down everything they had been vociferating.

They were aghast. And, silent. I looked up. "Go on. Please." They shuffled away from me, told me I should leave. So, I did.

I ached deep into my muscles and on the frightful surface of my skin throughout. I had never before encountered violence. Therefore, I didn't know to hate it and resent it. It felt to me a kind of pleasure, a close cousin to when I exercised to rid myself of excess. I breathed deep, not to alleviate, but to encourage the pain. I rested with it for a little while. Then, I went on, for District 11 was not my only goal. Only a fool would have but one way to get a thing done. I was more than that. I was becoming more than my pain, as well, as I peregrinated on.

I slept in the streets, like one homeless. I ate a little garbage, and one denizen I passed was gracious enough to give me a jug of water to replace my empty one. She comforted me, "You are too fat to die. Same as me. Neither of us would die in the streets, but we would need a bit of water. Drying up is uncomfortable. We'd turn to crumbs with eyes and a voice." I was smiling and didn't realize how offensive or strange I could be after being assaulted and going two days without food or water. I told her, "You are odd. Silly, even. You are the sky with this bounty of rain for me. For that, I thank you. Share a cheering with me, my fellow bulbous one." I drank from the jug, handed it to her, and she drank. She laughed and gave it back to me. I noticed, too, that neither of us were actually overweight; we hardly looked as though we were denizens.

I walked, following the map I had Marlela fetch for me of the Nations. I say, "walked," yet it was more vagabond than that. I was navigating quite well for one new to directions and a map, for one new to independence and self-reliance. My face was in pain; it was not from the beating. How ridiculous must my inexhaustible smile have appeared to those in passing of me, but I couldn't care. I was overtaken, overwhelmed, and redefined by those days and nights on the ways and avenues of our society. I saw that, indubitably, with every footfall I took and every hour that I grew a hundred, distinguished thoughts in me. I felt blinded by over-sight, a beyond-emotion and hyper-awareness. For once, I was a being more than over-weight. I seemed, in those days of staring at manicured front lawns, unused patio furniture, street lamps that were too high to be of use to the blue cards who were the only ones to have need of them by night, and the many gates, the fencing off of everything – a sundry of boundaries, which were equaled only by the cascade of lamps found in the history vault. I stood outside of myself. I saw out of my eyes, but there was also, a sense of seeing my Earth-bound vessel and then, feeling the outer-me: a formless, expansive stratosphere of my consciousness.

I walked by people; they all stared. So, I hailed them with a booming greeting like that of old friends reunited, and they were swift to find somewhere else to be. I had a few who asked if my throne was broken, if I needed one. I told them I had eaten it, and it became me, and that now, I addressed myself as "your high-yet-lowness." I don't know why that was always my answer to that particular question. In those sparse days, I think I found it funny. None of them ever laughed with me though.

As I meandered, the limits of the city edged closer to me. The boulevards had quit, and the homes beyond were not marked at all on the map I carried. I began to pass a different sort of people. They looked sad. Their homes were constructions of tarp and half-splintered crates. Many of them were sick. I had in my valise a calculated amount of medications, fearing I would need them. Perhaps, natural chemicals were more my substance now – serotonin, endorphins, dopamine, and adrenaline – so, I gave to those I met what help I could. They were shocked to momentary speechlessness. Some of them cried and those ones I sat with for a little while and rubbed my feet as we conversed, but not once did any of them wish to speak on their misfortune. I began to think they didn't see it. We shared tales instead and opinions on things like the sun's warmth and what we found most hilarious in people and whether that made us to love or be confused of them. They were strange talks, now that I look back on them as memories. I would have written them down then, if I had realized how crushingly valuable they would become to me.

I believe I was created a true human being in those days. I wonder if I had not had such days, would not I have metamorphosed later? Perhaps, beginnings fetch their endings like favored dance partners.

Soon, I came to the wall which encircled all the Tiered Nations. "The Merlons," as they were known. I stood there, at the obstruction meant to divide people thought to be different breeds of one another, and the barrier was a sour-sweet joke, for it reached to the bottom of my breastbone, and I was peering over it as if it were the counter in a candy store. Immediately, someone spotted me from the other side, just as I had begun to struggle my way over the top of the wall.

"Assistance comes, ma'am. Hold, don't hurry." Embarrassing as it was, he pulled me over the structure with a few grunts and helped me down to the ground to sit. "Where are your things?" he asked after a moment.

"Oh," I responded, and I began to unload the last contents of my small luggage bag, thinking I was to be thieved once more.

He watched me, quizzically, then shrugged. "I estimate my husband and I had more than you do now when we came to start from scratch. You've not much wit, I can tell by your choices." He stood. "I am Lynelis. Your name, ma'am?"

"Dayraven," I replied.

He cracked a smile. "I do enjoy the imagery it yields. Rather romantic. Or, threatening. Perhaps, both."

"Like the Archfiend?" I asked, enthusiastically.

"Who?" He chuckled after a second of not being able to figure me out, then grasped my shoulder. "Follow after. I shall bring you to she who developed these villages, and she will help you determine where to live. From my knowledge, we've at least two empty beds in two, different homes. The Lees' may want you." He was kind. I gathered my things and went with him.

We trekked through mud, and I was expecting him to ask me numerous question, but he didn't. He walked me passed the central vein of the first village, and the homes were little more than caves, human-made, and rutted into the sides of tall, dirt mounds.

Lynelis spoke as we went: "Did you leave the Nations to escape the curse of cancer? All of the denizens eventually develop it." He wasn't watching where he was going, as if he knew all his steps by heart.

I tried to mimic him. "No," I replied. "Not for that reason did I come."

"It would make joyous minstrels' songs to say we deserted the Tiers to be free, to return to natural life, but my truth is that I am terrified of cancer. I believe for many others, it is the same as well. I fear it, cancer, would be like being both alive and dead in the same existence. I wouldn't be able to accept that." He stopped to point towards people a couple dozen feet away. Lynelis motioned at one of the three standing there. "That is Oshin Rysing," Lynelis informed me. "Not like a ruler, but we go to her about anything we need to whine about." I looked, and the woman was quite young. I didn't understand how it could be her to have founded the sole entity to resist the Tiered Nations and the Government Body. Her skin was rich-brown and her hair dark as an abyss and long, and it was shaved upon one side her head. She had a variety of facial piercings, and she was curved with wide hips and thick thighs; the rest of her was narrow, but with soft lines.

Lynelis watched Oshin while she spoke with two of the villagers. He held at one of his arms as though to console himself. "That couple she speaks with now has suffered a horror no parent should have to endure. They lost their young daughter to *something* in the night. The grandfather of her has already departed to find what he can of her murderer."

A cold tremor swept me as I looked to Lynelis. "'Lost to something?' What do you mean?"

"I don't know," he confessed. "Before the grandfather left, I attempted to ask him. He only said, 'a beast of length.' So, I said, 'Of great height, you mean?' But, he shook his head and that evening, his home was barren."

I panicked at the thought of the creatures Sasithorn had seen. "I need to speak to her," I said with need in my tone.

Lynelis gazed at her as the couple walked away. Oshin was left to herself. "You are free to," he told me.

I gathered myself and took a step forward. Then, every hour of the past four days came to take its due. I remained silent, even as my vision distorted. I collapsed to my knees and pitched forward onto my face, my mind thrown to blackness.

The continuity of the timeline falters here. It is strained for me to recall in precise detail the shifts and currents. The paths are beautiful and rich, but much in the way it is to look through the microscope-eye at something. Symmetrical patterns of cellular walls appear to me, when I ask my memory for the recounting of events, and what I can relay is too close in on the subject, so that it is troubling and broken when all I mean to describe is a single leaf or the carapace shell of an insect.

Oshin Rysing of The Merlons gave me the seeds I'd sought.

When I tried to ask her of the death and the beast in her village, she knew no more than what Lynelis had shared with me. I accepted it, confused, then we sat in awkward quiet, until she spoke.

"I will not ask who you are or what you are to do with them. It is enough you are here, searching for them."

I shortened her stock considerably, but could offer nothing in return. "What am I to give you, in gratitude, miss?"

"Change," she said with neutral tone.

I ravaged my pockets. I could not go without an expression of how she had fulfilled my star-flung wishes. I produced a single copper coin from the rags of me and set it before her.

She raised an eyebrow at the small, circular token and picked it up. "A penny-dreadful, then?"

I squinted at that question, for I felt I knew the term and what she spoke of. She was quiet as I recited to her a tale, in return. I told Oshin a little penny-dreadful of how a man with wings fell the greatest fall, and how he had fallen deep into the dirt, and his form became new; he lost his wings. He developed horns and his legs turned caprine.

She told me that the story was absolutely charming.

"There is a Knight I know who would be entranced with this story. I shall share it with him. Thank you," Oshin said to me.

She was wonderful to speak with and I wanted to say more. I thought of how, for Sasithorn, I had come this far. "Someone special to you?" I asked.

Oshin nodded. "He is like no other."

Then, I left those Beyond the Merlons and returned to my place.

The tomato came first. When it was first discovered, it was called a love apple, for it was thought to be an aphrodisiac. I gave this fruit of love to she, who, in loving her had sent me on most worthy enterprise, disorderly conducted. Alas, alas. She was not my passive muse or trophy-like fresco – but, fiery catalyst for me to find another me when I had already self-destructed. I recited this to her as a poem.

That is what happens when Love eats us. Or, we eat of Love. It is one in the same.

I thought on those days when I'd wished for death, when I was yielded to a burden that was not my belief, but the way of the world imposed upon us each – the way of the Body without the cultivated mind. Does Love configure us anew? I am proof of it.

Thus, I made a great show of giving to Sasithorn the one tomato sprouted of the garden, which had now overtaken the White Face. I dressed my chambers for our "dinner date," took from the halls of our trysts love-lilts and set the candles' flames to wish romance into the room with their small, bright faces. I asked her to dress for the occasion. It was, now, long known to her what I'd done, and she and Marlela both feared the day when the other Government Officials would learn how I'd change the Face of us. But, she came to me that night. She came in a green taffeta dress to do the words "stunning" and "exquisite" divine shame.

I see her smile, and she holds me. She tells me that I could have been more traditional. "The courting paramour often gives a bouquet of roses. How you've outdone the history of Romance to give, instead, a garden." She was scared for me. "I thought from your funny stories, *you would know*. Gardens are such beauties that those living there are usually driven out by greater forces." Sasithorn kissed me. "Do away with it, or I will."

We argued over it. I wanted to feed her, nothing more. I told her it was my sole wish in life.

The stalks thickened. The fruit wore their spectrum of hues as they came to maturity, and every room and courtyard, every corner of the White Face burgeoned fresh verdure. The Royal Guards who nurtured it came to love the thriving vegetation as one very dear to them. It became their pleasure to tend to the new occupants and lovingly so. They read from the vaults how to better comfort each plant in all its idiosyncratic needs. For this, I invited them to take their fill. They did. There was an unusual hum of joy in the White Face those days. It spread, like the roots underground.

The family fortune I'd long ago been bequeathed gradually became nothing more than exiguous change. I'd been waiting to purchase a permit to marry Sasithorn, though it was certain it would be denied, but the money had vanished before I could buy it. What's more, I had to tell the Royal Guards I could no longer afford their silent tongues or their backs in labor.

I was nervous.

Sasithorn went with me to confront them with my news. She swore she would protect me and undo any person to step too close to me. I wondered if it would come to that – more violence – or would they quietly descend the one elevator shaft and tell the other members to the Government Body what I'd done and that I'd forced them to act an accomplice.

So, I stood before them. The Royal Guards, as a division within the military, rank from 1 to 13. There are three individuals to each class, notwithstanding the last and highest class of 13, for one individual, alone, is rank 13 all and of herself. It was said the final number in rank was created for her and her ability alone. Therefore, the number of Guards I stood before was 14 in all, being that only classes 8 through 12 were deemed worthy enough to be stationed at the Nation's White Face. The number should have been 15, but there was one who'd declined the prestigious employment. She'd chosen, instead, to act as personal bodyguard to the daughter of the creator of the Chef. More of her, I don't know. Sasithorn had told me it was somehow a love story.

I looked to them each, that day in the garden. There was the aroma of dozens of rooted foods all around us. Sasithorn kept close to me, and it was not long before my explanation was through.

The Guards were silent. They didn't even look to one another. Eventually, there was one who came forward. Sasithorn was quick to intercept her; she was of the 12th class and taller than Sasithorn with powerful arms and broad shoulders. I drew my love back by a jerking pull, and I situated Sasithorn behind myself. I could not bear the thought of pain inflicted upon her.

The Royal Guard of rank 12 came to my face. She withdrew her hand from a pocket, and I winced away with motion to protect Sasithorn as completely as I could.

"Pardon so tardy a payment, ma'am. This is what I owe for the salsa – tomatoes, onions, green bell peppers, chili peppers, garlic, and scallions. From the scorned District, I purchased black pepper and other spices. I made this, an old recipe from my great grandmother, for someone so precious to me that he should know the generations back that this food represents. He is my son I made the salsa for." She placed in my hand paper bills of gratuitous amount.

Another followed after her. He said, "For the many pies I've baked – blackberries, strawberries, and blueberries. At District 11, I bartered for flour, sugar, eggs, and such necessities. The pies were for a Knight who favors the sweet tooth, and he I have married in secret against the restrictions of this post." He gave me almost as much money as the Rank 12.

Still, another Royal Guard continued in place where the last had left off. They handed to me money and their truths to blacken their reputation. We were a collection of humanity, then, so destroying-ly honest with one another.

I hadn't felt my own tears to coat my cheeks, but Sasithorn was hugging me tightly and she was saying, "Shh, shh, my love. *You've changed everything here.*"

That was those days to come. There were players who took their turns and their acts: Sadness, Longing, Hurt, Fascination, Wonder, and Enchantment. And, as the final act, Longing, once more. The story chooses the hero, never has the hero chosen her story. Remember that.

The stout, half-short man of the Administrative affairs was the one to bring the scalpel, and he began to sever most severely. He came to the surface, saw the White Face turned lush-green, and while the other officials were dithering on what was to be done to me, he'd written a proposal, and in that document was my banishment.

The Royal Guards were dismissed their ranks and careers. Sasithorn was imprisoned and Marlela whipped with knotted and barbed leather the day I was dragged from the Alveoli and driven by carriage some long ways. It was out, past The Merlons, and the driver would not cease, until he'd reach the heart of the sanded valleys. The desert filled the horizons at all angles. He shielded himself, especially his face, as he threw me from the vehicle. The steel of his baton tendered to pulpy pain every segment of my body. And, he left me. I had nothing. He drove away.

I believed for many days, even with the gritted cuts and tears covering the soles of my feet, that I would be able to find my way back. I believed that sleep would heal me – short slumbers before continuing on – and that I would overcome this that'd happened to me. I would rescue my love, Marlela, and everyone else, before Death and Torment would make of them their stories.

On my directionless venture, I'd passed the desert weeds of that region many a time and realized later it was them to release the spores that began to corrode my skin to bloody wreckage.

In the final days, I realized that this was not what'd happened to me; this was what I'd become, and the nights were peopled with curious dreams of the sand moving in giant, elongated hills from beneath. I screamed in my sleep, yet the wailings were never my own voice.

There was once a midnight hour illuminated by a full moon, such that my dream made me to think I'd awakened, and I was staring into a face as large and seemingly all-encompassing as a cloud which had descended upon earth, like a ghoulish god of giant-like proportions. The facial distinctions were nebulous. I thought I saw a mouth moving slowly, a tongue which ambulated within as though speech would allow itself to be utilized by so strange a creature. But, the words came by means of a voice not witnessed by the ears. In my mind, this pale thunderhead with her stacked rows of fleshy-pink colored eyes – each roving or searching and straining in omnifarious direction - spoke in gentle cadence to me.

"I am Chinami, the Conqueror Wyrm," she said without speaking.

She told me of legends, of creatures and gods – they were the same – and of pearls hidden within people. I saw a glimpsed memory within myself of Sasithorn telling me about a Knight with one, snow-colored eye, and I told the Conqueror I knew of a hidden pearl, then I began to cry. I asked her what had become of Sasithorn and Marlela, what became of the Royal Guards.

She didn't answer my mourning of them, but said, "That boy is an Orb, indeed, but you have tremendous power as well, my Serpent. Thus, guard yourself against the gods who wish for you and him as a weapon. Or, challenge us. I beg you."

She remained a while longer, while I could do no more than moan in pain, for I was dying of my injuries. Before she left, a girl came forth – hair the color of light – and finally, I told her, "I promise you, Archfiend."

I shed that which I was, and I put those pieces into my mouth. I swallowed myself, because I was certain – by intuition - there was no other honorable means to do away with who we once were.

CHAPTER 21

ONCE HUMAN

The Present:

What arose in place of me many years ago was what is now seen: a feathered beast.

I had survived.

But, not as I imagined survival.

I learned this body. And, in many ways, it was no different from learning the vessel of the government official I'd been after it had undergone the knife of surgery and subsequent shrinking of frame with the mind's expansion. As the Conqueror Queen had named me, I was a Serpent – something separate of both Wyrms and Drakes. This I could discern the more I saw of either species. I was incapable of flight as Drakes are and more reptilian than the fleshy Wyrms. Also unlike Wyrms, I was of one gender and this I found was different from my life as a human. It was unexpected to awaken and find myself male, but I reasoned that the sex of us would, indeed, vary from timeline to timeline.

I learned and continued with my knowledge in this form new to me. I found my memories both as a Serpent and human. It was strange to see the days which I knew and felt were the same, but to be in two separate forms, in two separate environments.

Again and again, I re-lived in my mind the point when my two lives merged into the same existence: that night that I met a goddess. Her words were my shadow, always there and tethered to my side. The human half of me wished for nothing else than to go to Sasithorn and Marlela. It was impossible to breach the domain of humans in my new shape without being seen. What's more, I had doubts how either of them might come to believe my tale of metamorphosis. An inward ranting it became every day within myself whether I should go to them or not, but I knew, as certain as my shadow, if the humans of the Tiered Nations saw me, they would hunt me to my end and perhaps, discover the world of Drakes and Wyrms. It would be war.

And, there was already this war. I had seen it rolling over in its sleep and nearing its wakeful hour, just as the Queen had told me. The impression of her stayed with me. She reminded me of books I had loved, and she seemed to be the same as one who desperately sought to dethrone him of power for the sake of her people, who were so much weaker than gods.

Things grew in me. I became a garden of my own.

Perhaps, one of knowledge.

After those nights in the desert as a wandering human, I sought the ocean, in my body as Serpent, and found her. She, Oshin, knew the Knight I needed to speak to and I loathed myself for thinking I might be able to rescue the world when I could not even save a Face full of people. But, the loathing would not stay quiet within me and it soon became a fever of yearning. I fought to smother it, but it was Love. It was a heart for everyone and everything I had just begun to have in the White Face, and that merciless passion carried over to this life and this form. I felt doubtless that Sasithorn was still alive. Even Marlela. And, it was, again, within my means to salvage happiness for them, possibly peace. I set to work once more. I had been these many years in on my operations, perhaps wishing for but never expecting this day which has now found me.

A Serpent brought to surface a Thai Drake of jade coloration, upon the banks of the River Orb.

She has returned to me, the one who began everything of meaning which my life was given. How to apologize to her for whatever punishment befell her in the Nations which should have belonged to me alone?

I stared at her, and like before, she was more beautiful than a library, than a garden, than a first blossom, and she danced in my eyes, wearing a most gorgeous green, taffeta dress.

I breached the water's surface and carried her ashore. As I turned her upon her side, and she spat up liquid until she could gasp and have air, I noted the commotion brewing at the sight of me, rescuing her, a Drake.

The spectators came, one Drake at a time, and it seemed we intruded upon a rallying of the troops. Sasithorn was, yet, still bereaved her senses, and I felt the curvature of my lives to repeat and mirror each other in strange fashion as I came, again, before a congregation of those I knew not whether there would be harm or acceptance of us. I prepared myself, for I had succumbed to the River, in fact, by a war-infected dragon only hours before.

One Drake, a Ryuu with rippling mane and scales shifting roseate and lilac tones, was approaching with too much purpose, and I coiled in on myself with my beaked mouth on aim for striking, but a Long Drake, cobalt-refulgent, barred his way.

The Ryuu darted angerly from around the Long who was larger than he. "Why have you Sasithorn, the Ngaw – the Protectorate? And, shored from the recesses of the Orb? *Did you mean to drown her? How is that you are here, in the Eye Backs, territory to Drakes?*" He hissed and knocked back the Long, but another Drake had come to obstruct his reach of me. *"Speak, you damned thing! Common is the knowledge, now, that the nightmares no longer pop and startle from the shades. No, terror has acquired words to salt the wounds of violence you and your brethren have carried to our homes."*

He assumed me a Wyrm.

I, then, steadied myself, and by that centering could see that he had suffered an amputation whilst remaining whole; he had lost one of surpassing endearment to him. The blood on his neck and chest were not his, and it was not yet dried.

I spoke to all of them there. "In these transmutations, she and I have only met this day. But, as she was human, Sasithorn was my beloved. The Orb is a strange wonder which revitalized us of our pains, retrieved our past, and, too, laced us, reunited."

There was a crescent shape of them surrounding us; in count, nearly twenty. I kept my head bowed, staring at Sasithorn who was breathing shallowly and looked entranced, as if by a dream.

I let them begin their denial and said nothing for a time.

"Did it say 'human'?" Another, not the Ryuu, asked.

"Once human?" The dissonance fermenting.

"These brutes are fabricators as well! Only demons learn language to lie!"

"How should that be? A life passed, perhaps?"

"Heed him, for this calls to service a reason why the Wyrms seem to come from the wights' domain!"

"Preposterous! Ignorance buys outrageousness, and sometimes, only for the tickle of sensationalism. It has come to deceive us, leak fearful acid into our ears to undo resolve."

"Human, Drake, or Wyrm, we are a people, still, in need of defense! Why dawdle with this nonsense when we are besieged!"

They continued, and there was debate on how or should they imprison me. But, as all of it grew and heightened, a child came from around the legs of the frantic adults. Curiosity made her bold, and respect made her careful. She blinked as she looked from one adult to the next, but because of her smallness, they didn't note her, and her little frame broke the barricade the Drakes had constructed of themselves. She walked into the clearing towards us. A smile touched my face as our gazes met, and I do not know if a smiling, feathered creature the hue of unconsciousness was frightful, but it must not have been – or she was brave – because she smiled in return.

She came to us and stood close to Sasithorn's head. The youth was entirely angelic-white with bits of pink along her joints and the underside of her belly, she was so newly-birthed. I had the impression that those baby-pinks would fade with age. Against the moment and the circumstance, I swooned at her, so adorable and precious was her every step; she was inquisitive in the manner that all children are innocently so. The little, antlered girl nudged my Sasithorn with her muzzle not even the length of my shortest feather. She was short-faced as children-Drake are. Then, over her shoulder, she called, "Uncle Dreyon? Could you bring Father to me?"

And, to step forth was a Firecraw who looked, in all ways, at the prime of his age, yet unduly wizened by sorrow. "Nandenia, you should not run off. How am I to keep eyes on you, your father, and Lynelis all at once?"

At either side of the Firecraw kept close two other males near of his size and age. I recognized the thrice-tiered antlers on one of them to mean his race was belonging to the Tree Crown tribe. He hobbled and looked in all directions too quickly, as if bewildered, or as one does when he is over or under-sensitized. The girl ran to him, her father, and led him in close to us. They went to Sasithorn's face, as she began to wink into the sunbeams and remembered air through a fit of coughing.

Beyond the silver back of he, who the child had called, was a being to sicken my nerves. This one, he shambled, but not for lameness. His breathing rattled from a jaw parted and bumbling close to the earth; untrained, was his gaze. He snapped with his teeth in convulsive tick and drooled. The Drakes were staring at him, as was I. They kept soft their verdicts, but it did not better the disposition of that one ailing of unnatural disease. He was a Pyrolite Drake, and as I stared, his caretaker caught my eye, glaring.

"*Wyrm*," he said, and the manner of him was the anguish of every pit of hatred. "What's this?" His voice rang out to all the others gathered. "Have we, the Drakes, arrived at such humiliation and destitution at the teeth of the dirt-eaters that now we welcome them to our lands, crowd in on them as though they were royalty? Do we let the fear of them cow us to sycophantism?" The suffering one at the Firecraw's side pitched into him before righting himself.

I sought tenderness in my tone. "What've you done to him? He is Unrested."

"He. Is. Unrested!!" declared the Firecraw. "So, he is! Are not we all deprived simple peace? *And, why?"* There was in his eyes the brands of madness. *"Wyrms!! That is why!"* He laughed low, then high and thin, rasping. I noticed he seemed unable to lay eyes on the one so near to him, but that he touched him always, keeping a clawed hand on him or the skin of their shoulders in contact. *"Stare at him, if you'd like – you, Wyrm, and all of thee, us, dragons. It offends him not. He is unaware of so much. When one walks through the clutches of Death, this is how he blunders away from that god. Yes, I played tricks at Death's back. Scornfully, he laughed at me, for this is what I am left with where once stood the lover I'd known all my life! I chose not to part with him when Fate had his name beckoned. And, you and your kith should I blaze ferocious blame upon."* He stepped closer to us, and I saw his throat working strangely. He drew in breath to fill his lungs.

"Drake, please, listen to yourself." I said. I came to position, so that the child, her father, and Sasithorn were behind me. My feathers were bristled, revealing the colors towards the calamus of every, singly leaf of me and those thorn-shaped markings were the outcries of aurora hues; they were ferly in quality, aglow and ember-like. I told him, "Whatever has happened, *you were* you *through it all, even if you could not descry yourself in each decision made – you sanctioned what you did.* Blame not Wyrms or any other."

"Speak no more, you aping atrocity."

The assault of a firebreather can hurl a victim into shock. It is the agony which traumatizes the body that often carries one forth into the grave. Meat, our muscles, cook the same whether dead or alive. Heat which penetrates goes through the layers of us and burns out blood, nerves, the function of our vessels, and if it reaches far enough, we become ash – in our minds, even if the body survives. The Pyrolites emit their flames like an eruption; they awash a broad area with their aim, but the degree of heat is attenuated by the wideness of that reach and its brevity.

Firecraws, however, are capable of murder by a single torching. Their assailment emerges as if first pressurized, then explosively released, and that force is a barreling blast without seeming end; the glare is deep orange – fire at a most unforgiving apex. I had seen much of Drakes, all breeds of them, in my time. I watched them, silently, from afar, and the firebreathers never ceased to unsettle me. Fire is a destruction that cannot be undone.

The Firecraw opened his jaws.

I felt, first, the area just above my right eye catch in pain unimaginable. I had risen to a height that revealed the underside of me and heard the surrounding spectators gasp at the sight of that which I usually intentioned to be kept unknown: I had pectoral muscles, like those structured of a primate, and the delineation of human torso, faint yet undeniable, that receded into the remainder of me which was corvine and colubrine intertwined. Then, I writhed with the pain and cried out, shook loose the burning grasp at me 'til it extinguished. There was a commotion of action too accelerated for me to perceive.

But, the Firecraw had been knocked back, perhaps squarely in the throat for the issuance of his flare came abruptly up and away from the rest of my face, sputtering, instead of that deadly concentration of unending inferno.

I regained myself in time to see Sasithorn drawing back from the blow she'd dealt him, and amazed were all that the Unrested at the Firecraw's side unexpectedly came to keen animation; he'd pinned the silver Drake to the ground. I heard that unfortunate soul and his jarring words to his beloved: *"Dre yon. Cea seee."*

And, now, Sasithorn had turned to me. Her mane and chin hairs playing the gentle winds. Her characteristic swaying stance came in close to me. Our eyes drew direct connection, and I held myself to see if she would know me her familiar, her love out of the Past.

Her eyes became sadness. Then, she looked passed me and said, "Mohonia? And, thee. You are Ardyce's babe." She went to them, as if I did not exist. *"Alive.* It breaks me very goodly to see the two of you before me, safe."

Nandenia informed her, "My father is unable to hear; thus, I try to speak for him as best I can estimate." She walked to the Thai Drake to look into her gaze. "You knew my mother. Will you go to her? *I am afraid for her.*"

Before she could answer, the other Drakes regained themselves from the spectacle and demanded the Ngaw see to the matter first of the Wyrm in their midst.

"Bind the creature. He has about him answers. Answers for all of this!"

"Have him tell us what he knows, Ngaw. The war encroaches upon our lands evermore, but we may an end find if we could only understand."

"It knows nothing. Cast it out!"

Sasithorn rose up tall, over the heads of the Drakes who bickered and prattled. *"Silence."* They continued, hotly in debate of what should be done with me. Her voice then was a miasmic pervasiveness: *"SILENCE."*

They quieted as a whole.

She seemed to have some trouble, some hesitation in facing me. Then, she asked of me, "Do you know, Wyrm, why our two kinds have arrived to war with one another?" There was nothing in her gaze as she conversed with me.

"It is obvious!" a Drake objected. "The Wyrms have come to kill us!"

I withheld my longing for her. She, I would answer. "Wyrms are more than they once were. Thus, the gods came, as they do when people would rather not think for themselves how to accept a newness, a change. The gods urge us retreat from possibilities. To do this, they murder the sprouts of change."

Sasithorn's tone edged a strictness with me. "That is no reason for us to entangle in violence."

I wanted to help, so I said what I could. I went backwards in Time. "From the Wyrms, now empowered with speech to chronicle their history, they told me: The Earth-fallower, who turned the vale grey; she seemed to sicken. The Wyrms wished to go with her, but in her delirium and pain, she had wandered a mark too far and collapsed in Outer Gled Tria where she was found by a Mungkr."

The Thai Drake concluded: "And, she attacked. Rent that Drake to scraps."

"No," I corrected her. "Her mother and other Wyrms with her stayed to keep watch of her, from a little distance – weary for a collection of Wyrms to be found in Drake territory. The Wyrms told me what became of that mother and daughter pair. They saw that the Earth-fallower convulsed in that soil laid to death, and that she entered a Metamorphosis. 'Her bite had now teeth. She moaned with a voice not before enabled.' She became the bone-faced Wyrm, and when the Mungkr arrived, she asked him for help. To that dragon, she was a thing without language, and she asked for mercy, for she was confused and weakened by toil to have changed. And, he must have felt the first witness to a Freak. He made his decision so quick. That he would do away with her before any other could rest eye upon her."

"*No,*" the other dragons murmured. They repeated it, like a chant to ward something away. "*No. No, no.*"

But, Sasithorn had straightened herself. Determination lit itself, small in her posture. "Continue, Wyrm."

So, I did.

"As those Wyrms told me, and this only yesterday, he didn't understand her – how she had become closer to that which he was - and his choice was not to understand. He didn't anticipate it, I suppose, in attempting to erase her. She fought back." I did not look at any of the others there, but Sasithorn as I recited the tale I knew. "When she had defended herself with aid of her dam, other Drakes arrived for investigation, and her mother was terrified of the attack her daughter had just survived, thus she sought to divert and shoulder blame for the Drake's death. She bid her daughter flee, and the mother was foolish. She lashed out at that group of Drakes. That is how the war began. Either halves of that event found its way to either of the two species, and it was a lie to both for never being whole." I looked to the other Drakes, daring to meet their eyes and peer in. Then, I glanced at Sasithorn and braced myself to finish. "Because of this, the Ancient Ones awakened. The cycle was put to wheel. Your god is that darkness-colored Drake. His name is the Scourge Angel. For the Wyrms, you will see her; she is one of whiteness and stacks of red eyes. Her name is the Conqueror Wyrm." Softly, and more just to her – to Sasithorn – I said, "But, I call her the Archfiend."

She glanced at me, and her smile was feather-light.

Carefully, I released the conclusion of my tale. "When they enter our world, as time again and again they have, they search ever to up-end the other. They are the sum of our selves or, perhaps, our origins or both. Yet, it is believed they were once human, as we were, and as we incrementally forfeited what it meant to be human, the essence of Humanity, they became that which we presently see. And, that of them rippled out. Here, we now are. Greater or lesser than human? I know not. But, here to act as humanly possible – yes, that, I think, is the measure of our days. But, not of theirs. The gods are gridlocked in every Past already forsaken. So, they pursue the Legend of the Orb – the one who shall give them the power over the other, and they will swallow that one. It is a sacrifice of such seeming triteness: merely one life to save a species of all others, hand in hand with the destruction of the only other species incorrectly believed to drive the survivors to moribund end. Yet, for all this time, and each and every these cycles, the Angel and the Conqueror have yet to once find this Orb, so neither of them know if this orbed someone is Drake or Wyrm – perhaps, neither. In any instance, the world of us shall have to live in their aftermath, if they succeed in hunting out that one of legend."

I do not know if the Drakes felt me a liar or believed me. But, they granted me audience. By that, I was given hope. So, when the hunch of that charred god arose to blot out the horizon, and I saw his face – not eerie and peaceful as Death is, not harrowing as the demon's grin, nor the majesty of an immortal, but the basal void in the caverns where eyes should have shone out – I raised again my hackles and stood with the Drakes.

They recognized him, their god of vastness and darkness, so much like blindness. He came and fleeing from him were groups of Wyrms, desperately seeking to outrun his crushing claws. He twisted and mangled them to quick demise.

The Drakes with me saw him as he murdered. Some of them were thus stirred to conviction, for five from those who had gathered for my oration shot forth, towards that mountainous giant, and I buckled for a moment in realizing it was to bar his way and do him injury, if they could.

"Wait!" I cried.

But, they were nearly upon him.

An instant more and they would have reached the Scourge Angel. Yet, coming between that black goliath and them was suddenly another, not of his size, although still tremendous in silhouette. That nightmare shadow threw open a wingspan enormous and in protection of he, as he watched, unfeeling. The Drake in service to him caught one of the attackers by the throat and was so swift in dashing the other four to death that we, from the ground, could see only bursts of innards and arcs of blood. She bit down, and the last of them fell away in two pieces from her mouth, the neck with head coming down first, then the heavy body.

Sasithorn came forward as the rest of us reeled in terror. Mohonia had turned his child away from the scene in the sky, and I was benumbed by questions. We watched as the murderous Drake cried out in stentorian heralding of the Scourge Angel, and her three tiers of antlers coruscated in the blinding light. She was pitch-dark in color, as he was. Her antlers were razored and metallic. She bore his eyeless face.

Beside me, Sasithorn was hushed to quiet despair. She wavered, met the ground, and she was trembling as I rushed to her. Her breath that escaped was of one name: *"Ardyce."*

She closed her eyes and bowed her head not to see any more of that which was once her friend so cherished. The sky was breaking apart, coming down in droplets. I drew close to her, and she said, "It is as if it were another garden of yours, but torn down to seeds as was the one you made in the face of white – that mask that became alive only to die. You once turned dirt to fruit, Dayraven. Please, we need you now. I have needed you all this time." She looked me in the eye. "Let us find the one who is the Orb. This one may be the only seed that now truly matters."

I thought how hard it had been for me to first find seeds. I thought of how far I went.

And, I knew she was right.

The rain came heavy. The Drakes around us were staring at it in awe, for never had it rained in this region before.

CHAPTER 22

OTRUNA ~ A WYRM

The Wyrm that Otruna M. Plodd had become was sleeked and oiled with sweat. It flew from his hairless body as he trenched the streets to cracked rubble beneath himself, fleeing from the inexhaustible man who angled for his life.

As he ran, he passed denizens toppled from their thrones and blood spattering into their faces as they gnashed at their own limbs, the meat of who they once were disappearing down their throats. For some, there was a husband or wife, maybe a child or even hired help, at their side, screaming or begging and exerting effort to impede the actions of the denizen undergoing the change. Yet those afflicted, their gazes were frenzied to eye whites, void of sight, and as they feasted, their necks wavered hideously, then stemmed out long. The higher class – they broke their own bones under the moonlight, with newfound strength – and as thick, naked, tattered limbs were plucked, and thus, accumulating over the surface of the Tiered Nations, those bodies Made the Ring. The bodies erupted spines of numerous lumbar, and human skin was decorticated. Beneath the flayed flesh grew dense hide and a form entirely new. Human faces elongated. Teeth of sharpness, creating their own armies, burst forth beneath the eyes of each former-denizen.

The sirens had stopped, but an unending howling had taken its place.

Otruna wished to witness the Rings, as they dawned out of the obsolete vessels of human beings. The neck and spine wrung out, past the limits of fair Nature, then, the half-formed creature – the half-perished human – would curl in towards itself. In the geography of their own mountains of sacrificed flesh, the hewn muscle chilling in the night, and the lakes of blood mapped all around them, the human was entirely lost. Some of them cried, even then. Otruna saw their weeping, the tears from eyes which could no longer be called Humanity.

It was at that moment that they would open their mouths one, last time, and Otruna yearned to laugh. He didn't know why. The very same he had endured, and he had been as these people were: terrified past the realms of sanity. But, he had done it, too. He had opened his mouth for a final bite, and in between his teeth found his feet, the ankle bones of them fused together.

It was then that the transformation would arrive to finality.

A vaporous shroud became concentrated and engulfed the one to change. Otruna saw that the murk was the form and largeness of the Wyrm to be birthed. By gradual measure, a hissing would begin. But, it was not the Wyrm-to-come, for that being seemed submitted to sleep. It was the air to surround the creature, and by and by, it steamed or sometimes crackled, until the veil was expired. There, left to convulsing consciousness, the Wyrm would lay, paralyzed, and Otruna knew the dreams that were not dreams to begin recitation within their minds.

The Past was returned to them each.

A life, parallel to this time yet wholly alien, unfolded to their memories. By expeditious episodes, they saw their youth as a Wyrm and their adult life, as though they had lived always as a Wyrm – for, somewhere, they must have. They did.

Otruna didn't understand much of it. He had seen himself grow to the age he was as a human, but he had been one of these creatures in his memory, and he had not seen likeable memories. He had raped other Wyrms and eaten smaller ones, sometimes raping then eating the same Wyrm. It disgusted the human he once was to think of ever touching one of those foul beasts. But, here he was, a Wyrm, too. He'd climbed up human corpses as a human to find wealth, and the same he would do for himself as this hateful monster he'd become.

Thus, he needed that damned Knight.

The one Otruna intuited was The Orb stalked and chased him, no matter how he twisted down alleys or through gates and front lawns of denizens' properties. Otruna had furrowed through the sun room of one mansion, demolishing chairs and furniture to kindling, crumbling holes in the sides of two walls, and grinding to fine, porcelain dust an unimaginable quantity of tea sets. Still, the Knight gave no quarter. He could not be rid of the man desperate to retrieve the girl whom Otruna had put to belly – that caramel piece had cost him this injurious course through the Tiered Nations.

Still, Otruna devised; he thought he might be able to save himself as well as appease one the gods. Not the one he would have chosen, if he had more time and did not fear the Knight would end him in the next quarter hour. The Wyrm cursed to himself. Reckless had it been for him to pass the girl down his throat, and well should he have guessed the scent of The Orb was about her for the reasons of romantic love. It had been Otruna's initial scheme to subdue and kidnap The Orb, present the one known as "Hadryn" to The Angel – surely, the more powerful of the two gods, but Otruna sensed the Conqueror nearer to himself, and she would have to do. He was not one who understood plans, how to execute them, or even logic very well, but Otruna's assumption was that he would be protected from Death by whichever god he gave The Orb.

Thus, Otruna absconded, and he bled as he did. He was in aggravating pain from his encounters with Hadryn Archidux. A human should not be a feasible opponent for the creature he'd become. But, Otruna's face, where the Knight had nearly succeeded in beheading him, was tattered to clumps of meat by a sword the man had wielded. Thankfully, that weapon he was disarmed of when they'd done their wreaking in the sun room.

I should not be so tormented by a boy, Otruna thought to himself, as he was pursued across the uniform astroturf of some denizen's front yard. *The Orb should be mine! I, alone, am deserving of the glory he shall bring. I will make him a milk candy in my gullet, beside the girl for whom he so earnestly fights.*

Yet, the Wyrm was scared to ingest the Knight. Still, Otruna turned 'round to confront the man, being that the Wyrm could not escape under-earth from his pursuer with such that were his facial wounds. Hadryn's sword, before he'd lost it, had gouged and cut deeply at Otruna's countenance. The Wyrm knew his face would be torn back by the hard soil beneath, if he burrowed, and Otruna would not chance submerging for the risk that he might surface beneath the solid pavement of all the city's many streets.

He breathed raggedly, watching as Hadryn closed the distance between them.

Half of the Wyrm's face from the left side of his lips, back and over his skull, was cleaved away, to the bone. His left eye watered. The vague pupil was directionless, in its frantic movements, through the blood which dripped in clots to the ground. Behind Otruna's head, where his neck would have been if he were still human, a gaping laceration revealed the strata of his meaty layers, and the blood would not cease. He feared it would kill him. He feared his arrogance had named his murderer, but he refused the thought of giving up the girl in his stomach. With stuttering resolve, Otruna waited for the Knight to reach him, and flinched when the man with heterochromatic eyes was upon him.

"Hold, boy!" The Wyrm cried. "Or, I will swallow down pounds and pounds of dirt, as it is trait to my species, *and pinch out any pockets of air still left in my craw to her, your sweetheart.* I will bury her within a monster, and she and I will be one in Death!"

Hadryn held a pipe of metal railing that was, now, his only weapon. "Plodd. I beg thee: exchange her for myself. *I know this is what you wish.*"

The Knight bled on one side his torso, where Otruna had thrown him into broken furniture, and the young man had been impaled. The right thigh of the human was mangled, too, for Otruna had caught him in his jaws, but once, yet not long enough to amputate the limb before Hadryn had hacked and hacked at his neck. The Knight was injured, but stood, not weakened, and the Wyrm was weary of him, just barely stalling his panic before it seeped to the surface.

"Never!" The Wyrm answered the man and cackled to the sky. It agonized Otruna's half-cleft neck, but he made a show of it before the Knight. "I am no fool. I am Otruna M. Plodd. I know. The only mistake enemies ever make with one another is to *trust*. Better to have you chase after me than to gulp you and have you claw me to ribbons from the inside out."

The Wyrm's eyes focused and widened, for the man he fought was uncaring to allow Otruna the courtesy of finishing his words. Hadryn had narrowed the width which separated them by two, bounding leaps, and the Knight drew back the railing in his hands to gain a most damaging arc of force, as he swung at the creature's stupendous head.

The young man was near enough for Otruna to see the exertion of the Knight's body: the veins in his arms, the sweat collecting on his skin, and his gritted teeth. Then, the Wyrm was struck dumb. There was a momentary scalding of pain upon the side of his skull and a red, wrenching burst of liquid from his earhole. Otruna met with oblivion, and he wandered there for almost the count of a full minute. The pain echoed away from him, then ricocheted back to discover him once more, and he tried to scream, as if it might alleviate the searing nerves of the gangrene terror for his life.

But, Otruna only gurgled at the back of his throat. He met with his senses and found the metal pipe lodged vertically in his mouth, extending from roof to beneath his tongue, and there, in his propped jaws, stood the Knight.

For a second, their eyes met, and the man said to the Wyrm, "You have become *this,* Plodd: nothing better or worse than what you were before. Thus, I will set you to death and see you a corpse again."

The Wyrm howled to bitter, dampened eyes, then gagged on the Knight, as Hadryn took a breath to hold and threw himself headlong into the gullet of the creature. Otruna thrashed wildly and attempted to dislodge the pole in his mouth, but it was embedded deep in his flesh, and he could not open his jaws wider than they were already forced. The Wyrm fled again, unknowing how to fight or resist what was now in his own body.

Within the foulness of that beast, Hadryn groped blindly, reaching as far as he could and seeking to maintain a means back out; one of his feet were hooked at the hinge of Otruna's mouth. Around him, the muscles of the Wyrm's esophagus wrung the air from him, as the creature sought to ingest him, and Hadryn defied the loss of mental clarity which besets one with the deprivation of oxygen. With both hands, the Knight cast about in urgency for Oshin to be returned to him.

There came suddenly to his touch the sensation of wet hair, and Hadryn pitched forward another few inches to find a hand. He grasped it and summoned every fiber of his strength to wrest free the engulfed body. Muscles quivering and tearing, Hadryn drew himself up from the Wyrm's depths, and in the space for breath, as air enveloped him, he gasped. His lungs returned to proper function. Panting, the Knight threw his weight back, still holding the other's hand, and that person came out of the thicket of the Wyrm, faced up. Hadryn stared down, his heart sunken.

"No," he murmured and hoisted the remainder of the man, a denizen, out until his feet shown. The Knight peered over his shoulder, for the Wyrm had found his speed, and there was now shrubbery, lawn décor, corners of buildings, and abandoned thrones plowed, breaking at the helm of this runaway beast. The metal bar which propped wide Otruna's jaws began to jar from place, and Hadryn braced it anew with one shoulder. Fresh blood fell from the roof of the Wyrm's mouth, and the beast cried out. Hadryn hand-muffled his ears as best he could against the

furious sound, while still holding at the denizen's unconscious body.

The Wyrm twisted skyward and back, like a hook or a scythe, at the needling distress in his oral orifice. He swung himself about, tilling a young tree as he did, and Hadryn dug his fingers and nails into the beast in order to stitch himself in and not be thrown.

Otruna raged. As the Wyrm dipped low, Hadryn made opportunity to shove the denizen's body out the corner of the creature's mouth, where there were no teeth, and the unresponsive man landed on the stiff astroturf, like an overburdened coin pouch. His eye lids were but barely parted and beyond shown only pupils rolled back. Hadryn did not know if he lived or had long been dead.

With lungs expanded and breath within him sealed once more, the Knight threw himself into the creature's abyss again, and he sought Oshin or sought to force the Wyrm to heave his stomach's contents. Sooner than the first endeavor, Hadryn found human limb again and in the noisome darkness, he recognized it for a forearm, then wrist.

"Oshin!" he cried out, releasing his air. Hadryn began, again, the labor to extract himself, reeling out the arm he held and wishing away both Time and Death, that he was not tardy to salvage the life of the woman who was his epistolary paramour, his disguised suitor, and the one who'd come for him when she knew the chaos to beset the Tiered Nations was nigh.

She could not be dead.

Hadryn willed the thought away.

With thews straining to exhaustion, the Knight emerged again in the cavern of the beast's face, and another pull saw the visage of Oshin delivered to him. With a cry of gratitude, Hadryn crouched to her and cleared her mouth of disgusting mire, which came from within the Wyrm. He pinched off her nasal passage and breathed life into her mouth to resuscitate that warring spirit that ever he had known of her.

"Be awakened, my lady. Or, by Death, I'll marry thee," he swore, and the Knight gave her two breaths more and began to evulse her body from the interior of the Wyrm.

It was sudden that eclipsing darkness inched in all around them. Hadryn turned with swiftness to see that Otruna had chosen pain to overcome then, for the beast was moaning as he bore down on the railing to bring his mouth shut.

"Damn you, Plodd!" And, Hadryn freed the whole of Oshin before rushing to catch the jaws closing them to a blackness beyond nightfall. With his hands, the Knight caught the ceiling of Otruna's mouth, and he demanded his strength anew, as the steel rod went through the bottom of the creature's lower jaw. Hadryn's ankles submerged in blood, and he kept weary eye on Oshin, who was still without movement or reaction.

Hadryn's skin broke to perspiration, and he cried out, using his body and the power of one to confront the jaws of Plodd. The Wyrm fought him, struggling to see his teeth closed upon the Knight.

"Plodd!!" Hadryn demanded. He was brought to his knees, and the Wyrm threw its gargantuan head. Out dropped the railing through the hole coming from the underside of Otruna's bottom jaw. *You mustn't,* whispered the Knight and then, he yelled the name of Oshin Rysing, as she slipped back down the monster's throat. Her eyes were like the denizen's before her: half-open, all white as ghost skin.

The Knight's left arm was twisted, under the siege of the Wyrm's prevailing strength, and Hadryn grunted with the pain which found him. He heard, now, Otruna chuckling in a deep voice.

The creature's mouth came wide open, and with a snapping motion and utilizing its tongue, it lobbed the Knight from himself. Hadryn careened through the air, and with the Fates dogging him, the broad side of his back struck the bole of a tree.

The Knight slumped to the soil, blotched from consciousness, and the Wyrm, still owning Oshin within, kept hard pace in running from the night, which anon, was being washed to a skyline transfused by amber.

CHAPTER 23

SOO-YEON JO ~ KNIGHT, RANK 6

"Hold her."

"She changes."

"Yes, but *hold her.*"

Soo-yeon Jo (Sue-yuhn Joh) came from Parameter Z9, a region as far North as any of them in the military could imagine without falling off the map. Her hair was long and solid black, and it was said that Northerners had a "clipped etiquette," a way of speaking as though the tongue had canker sores. It was too fragmentary for most and could be considered rude or coarse. There were no family names from the North which had attained a Tier as a denizen. Soo-yeon's parents weren't denizens either. They envied the Tiers and spent all their hard-earned income on food to eat as them, looking as denizens to passersby, yet never having the birthright or paperwork to enjoy the mansions, the thrones, or the stipends of denizens. Soo-yeon had attained Knighthood seven years ago, when she was 16-years aged. She had told her parents plainly that she was tired of being fat, and they never spoke to her again.

Soo-yeon had had a relatively uneventful employment as a Knight, Rank 6. She had advanced through the ranks further than she'd ever imagined and exceeded the requirements for Educational Refinement, even completing advanced programs in

Sociology and American Sign Language, but her days of training and routine assignments had left her inept for this living night terror which now rested in her hands. She held the frenzied denizen by one wrist, and with her were two others: a Knight, Rank 5, also from the North whose name was Fox Luciano, and a scientist, Marcus Chen, from the White Face's Department of Health and Scientific Research. The department was a small division. Those employed to it numbered twelve scientists and twenty lab assistants.

Soo-yeon watched Doctor Chen. He was young, most likely a child prodigy before this career. He'd arrived by military transport and seemed, in all ways, like a seasick man. When he was not wavering on flat, solid land or, leaning over, sickening into the grass, she noticed him stealing mouthfuls from a bottle of whiskey that was tucked into the inside of his lab coat.

The Italian Knight, Fox, had been glaring at the scientist the moment Dr. Chen stumbled from the trucks, but Fox kept tight his lips, only imploring Soo-yeon with eyes which lingered upon hers. They said nothing yet to the scientist, for it was known that those of the Department did not tread the public sphere. They lived, and it was said *remained*, in the Research Headquarters: a two-story structure near to, but hid from view of the White Face Government building. In a time, where past resources -- like forests, lakes, prairies, and wetlands -- were now declared "negated environments," the Research scientists developed ersatz food: "edible mimicries," to supplant everything that had been lost to the world. Then, they tested the substitutes, too, to ensure they were not immediately fatal. Finally, every one of their products were sent to market. The Knights knew not if it was this reason the scientists were enlisted to support the military with the outbreak, or because, when the labs dealt not in consumer matters, the doctors were occasioned with the rare cases of unusual bacterial or viral infection.

Soo-yeon doubled her efforts with the denizen, at last binding her wrists together. She was an older woman, in her late 40's, and as she sought to bite at herself, her wig fell away to reveal a balding head. Most likely, she was a cancer patient.

"Her legs, Fox!" Soo-yeon flinched as the other Knight was flung from the denizen's lower-half by unaccounted-for strength. He rose and swept the mud from his cheek, returning to the denizen's knees to pin her at the joints.

"Why has she this force about her?" He asked, gritting his teeth to master his hold of her.

The denizen, dressed in a tight, high-collared robe with all the proper accessories, turned and thrashed beneath their hands. She had been chosen at random, when the military caravan had arrived, from a field of writhing bodies. Soo-yeon and Fox had moved as one to her partly-eaten body. She looked, still, more human than those closest to her. The research scientist had followed, after a moment of gazing upon the streets, which were mottled with denizens abloom to the horror of metamorphosis.

The denizen was beginning to seize.

"Dr. Chen!" Fox broke to panic, then attempted to swallow it, though his voice shook. "Hurry. The sedative." He was trying not to come in contact with the older woman's blood, but her thighs were mostly consumed.

"Yes. Immediately." Dr. Chen reached for his shoulder bag and rooted through his vials and syringes, unprepared, despite the briefing they'd received a half hour earlier. Soo-yeon and Fox glanced at one another as they struggled with the denizen and her accumulating strength. She had begun to scream. The scientist, feeling their tension, spoke to persuade a sense of normalcy. "It is not for pain she screams. The nerves cease transmitting as they are overtaken by the new growth. Imagine if the nerves didn't. Didn't shut down. Imagine if they had to endure that pain." Dr. Chen fanned himself with his clipboard, swallowing several times. "They would not get very far. And, that's not what the transformation wishes. No, the transformation serves itself well. No pain. Not much blood. The cruors prevent a bleeding out. Beyond that – Well. We know almost nothing else of the autosarcophagy process or the resulting transmutation." He was rambling. In his mind, he was alone in his lab. "None of us know how the extraordinary mass of the new body forms. Where does it come from? The tests reveal nothing, only that this sedative," he plunged the syringe into the denizen's body. "It will not affect the subject in the least—" Dr. Chen wildly flung his arms over his head to shield himself, as the shot of a bullet minutely echoed in the air. He lowered his arms after a moment, blinking and staring.

The older woman laid still. The bullet had gone through her right eye. Her face was all that remained of her humanity. The bridgeline of her nose was still so perfectly defined and matched, in conspicuous beauty, to her dark lips and her one, hazel eye. A pristine, human face, so utterly recognizable, in a body of grooved segments: pockmarked, elongated, and with a sickening elasticity.

The hollow left by the absence of her screaming became to them each a vanished sibling or lover, parents or irreplaceable friend. Then, that feeling transmogrified, and it was, individually, themselves who had been spirited away to a dusk beyond the horizon. The silence pulsed in their veins.

"Fox." Soo-yeon stood, reluctantly letting go of the denizen. *"Fox."* She said it more clearly.

The Knight Luciano had turned on his boot heel, handgun set squarely in his grasp, and he went to another citizen.

"Fox!" Soo-yeon cried out, but it didn't stop him from discharging another round. There were two dead denizens now. She hurried after him, but he took only a couple of steps and, turning in place like a dial, the weapon erupted thrice more in his hands. He had ceased the movement of terror in those afflicted. Five people rested, forever in coldness, with no more movement than their locks of hair, stirring in the halcyon breeze, like lit candle-heads flickering just before they were blown out.

Dr. Chen made an incredulous, snorting sound. He was wiping his hands on his pants, though they weren't dirty. "I never," he began. He was muttering to himself. "I never wanted to see what I did. I just wanted to do what I do."

Fox was breathing hard, but he continued down a line, as if being pulled by a cord. He adjusted the handgun in his grip after reloading.

Soo-yeon drove herself to a sprint. Within seconds, she had passed Fox to kneel upon the ground. She spread her arms, as a shield. Fox leaned into his brisk walk after her with a certain, detained anger. He leveled an aim at his fellow Knight, for she had made herself a fleshed barricade to the next life he sought to take. The denizen lying on the ground behind her had a complete, annelid body. Its age and gender as a human was indeterminable. It had, still, the vague delineation of a human visage, but that face was stretching, contorting, and growing a maw of fangs.

"Remove yourself, Knight Jo," Fox said.

Her refusal was silent, at first. A rigidity overcame her body, and her jaw was clenched firmly with determination. "I will not," she answered him, even as she imagined the trajectory of the bullet, impossibly solid for how little it was, scoring through her frame and, possibly, even into the denizen, whom she meant to protect.

Fox exploded, "You want to save those things! They aren't even human anymore!" He tried to move around her, but she kept within the aim of the mouth of the gun.

"But, they're people, Fox," Soo-yeon told him.

"No, they aren't!" His canines showed, as he yelled. "Humans have heads, a torso, limbs – hands and fingers, Jo! Look at them. They're fucking demons!" His Northern cadence and patois came to the fore.

She tensed, not knowing if she saw or imagined his finger tightening on the tongue of the firearm, but she continued speaking to him. "Demons are people, too. *'Demon'* is just a word for people who others, with weaponry, don't understand." She realized that she had beliefs, yet, until this day, had never sculpted them into words.

"You don't understand what a person is!" he cried.

"You don't!" Her resolve met his anger. They were quiet a few seconds, and she glanced back to check on the denizen. It had completed its transformation, and seemed to be resting from the ordeal, breathing heavily. "Fox." Soo-yeon met his eyes. "You want to sign their death warrants?" She pressured his muted expression. *"Do you?* Cause of death: a fearful soldier, with ammunition, who didn't understand anything."

"Shut up, Jo." He glared at her with the awfulness of Truth weighing on his tongue; then, he said it: "I want to shoot you, because I have this gun."

"I know," she answered. "You should probably put it down."

"Never."

"Don't you understand, yet, Fox? We aren't under attack."

"You know nothing!" It angered him to have to debate. "Why do you think we were authorized these guns!"

"Fine!" she volleyed back at him. "You want to play their judge, Fox? Everything for these people are resting on such small things: your trigger finger, a bullet, your sapience. Think about that. *They've changed.* And, all of these small things could end them before they've just begun – *before we've just begun.* To figure out if we can help them."

"You're crazy! They should die," he whined at her.

"We don't know enough about them to put them to death."

He tried: "Something may be spreading. We could end it, maybe, if we killed them."

"But, maybe not." She knew he knew that answer.

He shook his head to himself, then raised the gun to her forehead. "Get out of the way, Jo. It's almost fully formed!"

"They aren't hurting anyone!" She was enraged now and trembling.

"They're killing themselves!"

She glared at him. "Even if *you* believe that, *we don't murder suicidals.* Suicidals are people who were hurt by the world, by life, or living." She didn't know any longer, in this instant, if she was, too, a suicidal person. "They're worth saving."

A moment of utter nothingness occurred, then a sudden throbbing, like the functions of the heart, reverberated with increasing magnitude through the whole of Earth. Beneath their feet, the loam shifted deeper than they could see, yet they felt it.

"What the hell is that?" Fox looked about them, wildly.

Then, a sixth bullet rang the air – the air that was churning with a preternatural force, like pinpoints of static everywhere, and the morning sky wore her funeral shrouds. Dark clouds bore down, close to the lands where humans tread.

Soo-yeon turned to look behind herself, for there came the sound of gasping and gagging from beyond her shoulder. She gazed back.

The denizen, or the Wyrm, but it was to her both, shuddered and bled out a hole in its throat. It had a voice and, choking, it said, "I remember. Everything. *Everything*. The. Conqueror. And. The Angel King." Then, it relaxed into the dirt and moved no more. It died peacefully, accepting Death.

Fox stared at Dr. Chen, not realizing the scientists were issued their own firearms. The doctor stood, looking over the corpse he had made. Fox saw Soo-yeon stand, out of his peripheral view. In one, fluid breath, her body became like a bow with the string drawn taut, fist on the ready. Then, she was upon Dr. Chen and released her blow. A crack, like lightning within flesh, echoed. Dr. Chen's frame made one end of a parenthetical mark, as he flew backwards in an arc, feet leaving the ground. Soo-yeon was above him, beating him, when his body returned to the soil.

"Soo-yeon!" Fox ran over and grabbed her, but she dead-weighted in his arms long enough for him to lose his hold of her, then she pivoted and dealt him a blazing uppercut. All the air drew out of him, then he was staggering and blinking to find his vision again. He saw the other Knight, after a moment, and tried to back away, but she swung one fist, then the other with true marksmanship.

Fox landed roughly on his rear end, impressed that she did not have a dominant fist, but could utilize punches equally with both hands. He looked up at her, since she had paused. "I'm sorry," he said. He wiped at his bleeding nose, thinking how the Wyrm had spoken. "I heard his voice. Entirely human."

She stood over him, saying nothing and breathing raggedly as one does to hold in tears they don't wish to shed. She was infuriated and crushed. He'd never known before how much she hated to see anyone die. Then, a military truck came sliding to an idle behind her. From the driver's window, a Royal Guard called to them: "Jo! Luciano! Get in."

Soo-yeon let out a hard breath, blinking her eyes with hurt and sorrow creasing her features, then she offered Fox a hand, and Fox took it to stand. They ran towards the vehicle. "What's happening?" Soo-yeon asked the Royal Guard.

"A unit traced a lead to District 11. Something about two or three denizens seeing a young girl with one of those worm-monsters stealing large quantities of food. We arrived at the house described, broke down the door, and the first Royal Guard to enter *turns*. She fell to her knees in the door frame, tearing away her skin. She pitched backwards, and her limbs grew – There were scales. Every time she thrashed on the ground, she became more massive. Then, the wings. Then, she flew away." The Royal Guard had opened the truck's door as he was speaking, and he was trembling and climbing down from the vehicle. "Go on. I can't." He wanted to sit, so he did. "Go," he said, again.

Fox glanced at Soo-yeon. He was not ready to get into the truck, but she patted his back and was already lifting herself into the driver's seat. The Knight Luciano darted his eyes behind them to place the scientist. Dr. Chen sat, dazed, where they had left him. There were bodies all around him and the early morning sky had gathered clouds, like mourners to a grave. The shadows they created fell over the denizens, the Wyrms, as if to bury those who were dead since no one else would.

"What about him? He knows something," Fox said.

"He knows nothing more than his own guilt." Soo-yeon nodded at the passenger side to Fox. "Hurry."

He went to the other side of the vehicle and came to sit beside her. "Why do we have to do this, Soo-yeon?"

She was in her own thoughts, or she was answering him. "You're a murderer," she said quietly.

Fox looked to her, feeling burdened by the names he hadn't known before he shot them. He rubbed his hands over his face, unable to speak. The walls of the truck around them felt like a closed casket, unresponsive in the very same manner.

Soo-yeon put the vessel to motion. "Don't do it ever again. I hate seeing one of us destroy, where we should be helping. These people have no one else, but us."

Fox sighed, leaning back into his seat. "But, we are part of those who need saving as well, Jo. *Look at the world. Look at everyone!* You heard the Guard: one of our own turned, too." Then, earnestly, he implored, "We don't have to go there."

Soo-yeon kept her eyes ahead. "You know we do. It's our duty." She knew she shouldn't say it, but it emerged, almost without her consent: "Aren't you curious? You read the only intel we have on the Wyrms – their new forms. They remember things: their lives as Wyrms somehow, like they've lived two lives at once. Human to Wyrm. Two running timelines. And, why do they mention 'The Conqueror?'" They were beginning to catch up to the caravan of military trucks.

"This girl, the one stealing food for them, has something to do with 'The Conqueror,' I'll bet," she said.

The ground shuddered again, like an enormous horn blaring and not being heard, but felt.

"Watch it, Jo!" Fox screamed too late. A fraction of suddenness later, the vehicle was side-swiped; it was tipped and wave-washed onto its passenger side. The truck fell heavily, making Soo-yeon cry out, as she braced herself.

One of the headlights flickered out, and from their canted angle, they saw a sweat-gleaming Wyrm of ill proportion rush by with an unconscious human in its mouth.

"Archidux," Soo-yeon said to herself. She yelled next: "Come on, Fox! Get out!" She undid her seatbelt, falling atop him.

Fox wasn't moving. "Did you see that? They're starting to eat people."

"It wasn't eating him." Soo-yeon was yanking on his seatbelt, but it wasn't releasing. "That was Hadryn Archidux in the Wyrm's mouth. He's a Knight, like us. We have to find out what the Wyrm is going to do with him." She didn't understand the words to come from herself, but once they were freed from within her, the rest of her followed. Soo-yeon felt as though an alternate version of herself had taken command. She pulled hard at the belt clasp again, then looked over her shoulder.

They were still in view of the abducting Wyrm, who had capsized their truck, for he had slowed as the skies lost the light and became suspended gray foam, like sea-froth.

In synchronized motion, every Wyrm Soo-yeon could see in their vicinity swiveled their heads in the same direction. Upon an unearthly cue, they began all at once and in the same second to click or scissor their teeth, creating an orchestra, like the whine of insects at night. Continuing was that heart-hammer in the soil.

Soo-yeon finally freed the hold of Fox's seatbelt, and she climbed up and out of the driver's side door, running towards the Wyrm, who had Hadryn Archidux. She couldn't help but notice that the kidnapping Wyrm and each the other Wyrms she passed were facing in the same direction their military cavalcade was headed: District 11.

"Soo-yeon, wait!"

She heard Fox struggling within the fallen truck, until she was out of ear-reach, then she realized a gentle, pulsating vein-work woven through the charred clouds. It looked like tamed lightning, fading and brightening with the regularity of one's breath during blissful dreaming.

Soo-yeon had stopped a dozen feet from the Wyrm who held Hadryn, standing at the backside of the creature. She could see the other Knight's face, and she told herself that he didn't look dead; he was only unconscious.

Around her, sound had slipped away, like a god succumbed to mid-morning nap, when gods have never slept before this day. Soo-yeon covered and uncovered her ears, but there wasn't any difference in her sense of hearing.

Above them all, emerged a greatness from the blackened clouds. As if coming to shore, a beautiful, terrible monster made entry into the world, and her eyes were many: each of them pink, like the newborn's skin of little mammals, and she, the monster, was entirely the unbroken hue of angels' wings. Pristine white, like first snowfall, she came, and those eyes were mounted as if upon two ice shelves extending up and coming together to make the front of her face. Her head was roughly a triangular shape, if the shape rested upside down. Below the array of eyes was a mouth relatively small in contrast to her demanding frame. The teeth of her, though, were thick cones of sharpened ivory and, as she drifted forward, her jaws rested slack and partly open. It seemed, perhaps, her teeth were very heavy.

Stouter than most Wyrms, her body was mostly that stately head, then tapered as a gradual sloped hill to her tail, which rested half-curved beneath her back end. Most extraordinary of the white titan was that she hovered, like mist, in the air.

Just barely residing above the earth, this mistress thunderhead sported appendages running the length of her sides: they were each of two joints and three segments with formidable, dagger-like hooves at the ends, and the limbs brief for the matter of her size. They hung, relaxed, as she eased out over the land by eldritch lack of visible effort.

Below the great Conqueror Wyrm – for no other could she be – residing in her immense shadow, ran the drove of her kith. Smaller Wyrms fled under her aegis, careful to steer within the boundaries created by her umbra, and they, with their queen, came forth from the skyline which led out from the 11th District.

Near to herself, Soo-yeon was grasping clips of sound, as if the scene, with all of them in it, had come up from a deep sandtrap to the hearing senses once more.

"Jo, what's happening!" Someone of her rank demanded of her, having seen her come running. The assumption was that Soo-yeon understood more than any of the other military personnel, and she didn't.

The Knight Jo stared, with all wonder and attention, at the xenomorphic goddess. "I see the girl within," she said, not loud enough to be heard, but she pointed to the center of the Conqueror, and there, ghost-glitched the image of a frail, young woman: albino, wearing a tattered robe – she who was Chinami Ishida.

The other Knight, who Soo-yeon gestured to looked, seemed to see nothing of what Soo-yeon saw, for his eyes settled not, going from the matriarch Wyrm to the nigh-approaching horde of her lesser kin. Frantic cries seeded the wind-churned scene, and machinery of deadly intention was unleashed, snapping the air, as if there were invisible branches everywhere, betwixt every individual, and now those limbs were breaking with violence. The ordnance of the human race came alive in the skies, targeting the Wyrms.

The goddess-thunderhead absorbed all cruelty: the bluster from the semi-automatic rifles, the torrent from the Gatling gun, and the paroxysms of three hand grenades. If the ambition was for her own injury, this she permitted, but for those who locked aim upon any her brethren, she would dip and maneuver herself to shield them. One of her appendages was blown off and fell to the ground, in a sprout of blood.

The swarm of them neared, and now Soo-yeon remembered the Wyrm with his captive, for that Wyrm hastened forward, ducking and sneaking by the haphazard bullets fired. With determination, he was suddenly before the queen and the lesser Wyrms, where he deposited the body from his maw. Hadryn Archidux landed face-down. The procession of them came to a halt.

In stentorian voice, unnerving the humans to witness it, the presenting Wyrm cried forth: "My Conqueror! I, Otruna Plodd, have brought to you a great gift! Here lies the Orb for your consumption. By trade fair, I demand you protect me from the Drakes we are to war with!"

The Knights and Royal Guards to the human realm were spectators from their armored vehicles with weapons braced and momentarily-silenced in their hands. Plodd caught the Knight by his clothes in his teeth and flung the young man closer to the assembly of Wyrms.

The Conqueror, she afloat and bloodied by fusillade, stared down at the Wyrm Plodd. In the waiting quiet, she loured down to him, and her two dozen eyes, incarnadine gems affixed upon the serac of her visage, bore into the meager form of Otruna Plodd. There was naught of perceptible movement from the empress Wyrm, yet her voice came to reckoning, like a sudden flock of ravens to fill the sky as murder.

"Never shall an Orb be taken by force. It will damn our way and tear out the tongue of Life's discourse."

Hadryn's hand groped in the air, reaching blindly, as he began to return to his senses. He struggled to his hands and knees, and Soo-yeon ran forward to retrieve him. As she came upon the other Knight, kneeling to him, Soo-yeon froze as the color all around her abruptly took on a dark tint. She looked up instinctively for answer and found herself the sudden concentration of the unnatural deity who had just spoken. Soo-yeon trembled in the shadow of the creature known as The Conqueror, who drew low to the ground to peer at her, and the Knight Jo let out a halting cry from between clenched teeth as the pale being came nearer.

The great Wyrm in the sky stared at her as though they knew each other, and Soo-yeon was speechless and terrified, until she saw again the image of a young woman, suspended as though she lived within the window pane that was the etiolated goddess.

"Who are you?" Soo-yeon mouthed the words, as if she asked herself the question.

The woman's hands moved, and Soo-yeon couldn't understand that she knew what the woman had answered. Instead, a memory awakened to her and she saw herself singing in sign language at an overgrown park in the 11th District. Confused by why she should remember this now, Soo-yeon found herself taking a step closer to The Conqueror.

"I'll kill you, Plodd."

The Knight Jo whirled around at the voice, watching as Hadryn Archidux struggled to stand. Soo-yeon glanced back once at the goddess monster, but the young woman had vanished from sight, and then, Hadryn was lunging, in fury, at the beast who had taken him. His half-numb body betrayed him though and he fell forward, but the 6th ranked Knight caught him, dragging him away. She didn't know if the abducting Wyrm would turn on them to do harm, but staring at that injured beast, it appeared dumbstruck and the new focus of she who ruled over their kind. The white queen leaned in on the Wyrm who had demanded her protection and sneered at him with her teeth bared.

Plodd shrunk, as if overtaken by involution, and the blanched Wyrm in the sky breathed in towards him. She was prodigious in bearing, dwarfing him as a gull to a pismire. As she caught up the scent of him, she hissed low and ending in guttural tone. She exhaled, deadly serene.

"Human-killer," she marked him, and the Conqueror, with that, resumed their exodus from the Tiered Nation. Yet, now, that sentencing clung, in breaths, surrounding Plodd, as the throng of Wyrms repeated his malediction.

"Human-killer."

"Human-killer."

"Human-killer."

And, they rent him, turn by turn, as they followed after their mistress, lacerating him hatefully. Plodd wailed. He was shredded where he stood, and he tried to ward them off, but it came to no avail. He fell, in strips, towards pain, then torture, and finally arriving to Death.

"Oshin!"

Soo-yeon nearly had Hadryn at a distance, safe from the procession of Wyrms, but he found his footing and broke away from her to run into the migration of tightly-packed flesh.

Not knowing why, Soo-yeon ran after him. She saw him make his way to the Wyrm, who had offered him as sacrifice, and that Wyrm was decimated and a havoc of what he had once been. Plodd's head was rolled over, resting upon one of his eyes, and the tatters of his body and organs were spilled in every direction. He wept as he died, and Hadryn pushed through the hulking clumps of him, screaming that same name.

"Oshin!!" He was nearly deranged by consuming terror, but at last, he came to the body of a woman and held her and did all he could to redeem her her life.

CHAPTER 24

MAKING THE RING

The mid-morn came to some stillness, like silt to return to the riverbed after the thrashing of a catch. They picked their way through the streets in a world they no longer knew. Nature had stormed reason and quaked reality so that there was a flooding of terror and trembling faults to everything of understanding. A moaning lapsed the quiet as well as a skittering of people who were trying to escape themselves. Occasionally, there were thunderclaps of action and terrified wailings, but the hum of quiet in between was insistent, as if it would find its own peace with no other help from anyone.

Hadryn and Soo-yeon wordlessly watched everything. They saw through the windows of people's houses the silhouettes which grew out long. In one bedroom, a man furiously tore bedsheets from sleeping quarters, and Soo-yeon tried not to stare, but couldn't turn from it. She lost sight of the man for a moment, then he appeared in an adjoining room where his wife and daughter were. He trussed them in the bedding he'd gathered, and they were sobbing and yelling to him. He went to the ground in a violent fit, and Hadryn called to Soo-yeon to continue on. The Knight of Rank 6 looked back only once and saw a large, red Wyrm slithering from a window where the family had been. She tried to keep her head down after that, not knowing if the father had saved the wife and daughter from turning and knowing

295

that it would rend her sleepful hours at night. She wanted to ask the Knight Archidux if they shouldn't be helping everyone they could. Soo-yeon caught up to him, but before speaking, she saw his face and the shock and horror resting there was also tired-looking. He didn't look a Knight, and she realized she didn't feel as one either.

They walked. A woman came from direction of a shopping plaza, crossing before them, and when she had found a lamp post sturdy enough, one she could trust, she dismounted her throne and stood against it. With the chains she'd managed to procure, she draped herself in links and links of it, like heavy arms to hold her from herself. The last of the burdensome twine she made to encircle her neck. When she saw them walking by, she paused, and they did, too, not knowing if they ought to assist the lady or tell her to cease. Her eyes were sickened by bloodshot. Her remaining free limb, she bounded along her throat and somehow maneuvered her hand to clasp closed the padlock she had under her chin.

Soo-yeon could no more keep silent. With hurt for everyone they'd seen, the Knight Jo said weakly to the woman, "You'll starve."

The denizen's eyes misted, and she broke into a smile made savage for knowing the dignity she had lost. "Do you know, I love my husband? I never knew before today. Never thought much—or at all! About love, that is. He Made the Ring. He said, 'I never declined a dish. I ate everything, even if it did not look particularly appetizing. I ate it.' He said, 'I love you, Nanita.' Then, he Made the Ring." She laughed through an expression tight with sadness. "Now, I don't want to change because a foreign hope in me feels that if I can remain human, I might find a way to save him, turn him back. Back to Alex." She became dazed with thoughts, then without looking to them, she spoke. "Leave here. Promise me to be human."

Hadryn started to go to her, but her words stopped him.

"Please. One promise?"

With difficulty, Hadryn answered. "Yes, ma'am."

Soo-yeon was shaking her head and resisted him, but Hadryn led her away. She whispered, "She'll die. At least, the other way, she'll live."

"She has decided herself," he replied solemnly.

Soo-yeon stared at the other woman, Oshin, who rested upon the Knight Archidux's back. They carried forward, down more streets, tracing from avenue name to avenue name. Hadryn always glanced at her, if she fell more than two steps behind. He seemed worried for her.

They saw a denizen sitting at an open window upon the upper level of his mansion and, pliers in hand, he wrenched teeth from his mouth and threw the tiny, white pebbles out, like hail to pitter and patter against the roofing of the first story below him. When he saw them walking by, he cheered with his mouth a gaping hole of blood and, using the metal instrument, he toasted them. "It works!" he cried victoriously. But, he didn't see that his face was stretching, protruding outwards. "It works!" he called out again, his voice clicking at the end.

Alas, there is a grace and leniency to every disease and virus, every outbreak of war or witchhunt, and every famine and wildfire, for if one could travel far enough, salvation might be found in distance alone. But, this.

"How to escape one's self?" Soo-yeon asked the silence between herself and Hadryn.

He said nothing.

Soo-yeon stopped. "Perhaps, I want to be alone when I change," she speculated.

Hadryn turned around to her, adjusting Oshin's weight upon his back. He said, "No one ever truly wishes to be alone when they are scared." Gently, he added, "Will you come along?"

She did.

Outside the Archidux estate, the Wyrms were still screaming as they shed the human species, like caterpillar molt.

Hadryn stood in his mother's room, staring down at Oshin Rysing, who laid upon the bed. Pink light, frosted by the earliness of the day, came in through the sheer silk of Cyssiline's bedroom curtains. Hadryn's mother was frantic over him returned to her.

"What's happened to her?" Cyssiline asked her son as she touched Oshin's face and her hair which was matted in a thick film. Cyssiline had made Soo-yeon's acquaintance moments ago, and it was her tick now to hold one of Soo-yeon's hands for comfort off and on. The Knight of 6th Rank rubbed the back of the mother's hand, whenever the older woman grasped her. "You ran off and we were so afraid—My son, you are harmed!" She saw his leg was bloodied and his weight a burden to it.

Hadryn replied to his parent, "She was ingested, whole, by a creature and, I fought with it. But, now, she will not wake no matter how I try to rouse her up." His voice strained all the while to relate what had happened to them. Cyssiline shed silent tears, wiping at her face, as her boy spoke. She cleaned and dressed his wounds as best she could, unwilling to wake Isia for guidance, for he had fallen to fever and had just drifted on to sleep. Then, though the two Knights were weary, the three of them began with renewed effort to awaken the slumbering woman. Pungent smells did not animate her, nor shaking and calling to her. Like sand stacked too tall, she returned to the soft mattress, terribly slack, when they sat her up in bed. They doused her face and neck with chilled water, but Oshin would not return to herself. Even when it was agreed that they should bathe her to rid her of the mire from the Wyrm, her breathing remained regular and deep with her closed eyelids gently trembling under the habit of dreaming, but there was no other reaction by her. Hadryn and Soo-yeon submerged her body in warm waters. They freshened her skin and hair as Cyssiline departed to figure out a way to feed them all.

She knew nothing of how to operate The Chef[3], and in the rooms where their loyal help had once slept were only claw marks upon the floors and walls. There were dark streaks as well everywhere, and Cyssiline told herself it was mud that had been tracked in. In the many rooms of the house, there was only a dreadful vacancy. Jonren had disappeared as well.

"Good riddance, you ninnyhammer," she said to his deserted chambers, then a grieving cry the size of a coin escaped her as she cupped her mouth, for she hoped he was not scared, wherever he was. His bed was disheveled, the sheets laced with something Cyssiline knew was not mud, and the largest window of the room stood open. She wished for him not to suffer, then she left and went back downstairs. She stared at the enormous machine which had always produced their food and it was a thing of silence and stillness, like a chapel which has forgotten its god. She arrived again to the former rooms of their hired help. She hadn't realized, until now that she had been walking this entire time. They weren't that many steps she had taken, but vastly more than she could ever remember walking in her adult life. Her ankles hurt, or they pulsed with blood. She couldn't place the sensation and was going to sit on the bed of the room she was in when she saw an unusual chest in a corner of the room. It wasn't wood. She kneeled beside it, tapping it. It was plastic and cold to the touch. Carefully, Cyssiline worked the lid loose.

They had now food, but ate little. They debated what should be done and what could be done, as the sun was rubbed out of the sky. The collection of two melons, grapes, bread, cheese and a jar of pickled vegetables which Cyssiline had recovered from the plastic chest sat on a tabletop beside them. The Knight Archidux retrieved from the back room with the hearth the food Oshin had brought from Beyond the Merlons and this enlarged their stock.

Hadryn went to where Oshin rested every quarter of the hour to search for signs of consciousness, but he was disappointed each time. He was pinned to her bedside, yet yearned to venture out.

"Thaddius and LeShawn have each other, my dear. I think they are safe and well," Cyssiline said to her son.

"They would be here by now, if they were, Mother." Hadryn softly replied. "It is a walk of two hours there to Thaddius' home. I will be back before another day awakens."

Soo-yeon was staring at Oshin. "What if she turns while you are away?"

"My boy, you said that beast was after *you* for whatever reason." Cyssiline's voice was shrill with fear. "Other monsters may be as well. You mustn't go!"

The Knight Archidux was quiet.

"I'll go. Tell me where she and her wife live." Soo-yeon stood.

"You'll not go alone, my dear!" Cyssiline cried.

Hadryn, then, spoke without looking to them and wrung his hands until they pinked with blood under the skin. "Though Thaddius is my sworn sister, she is not my little sister. I must trust in the strength she has always shown me." He lowered his head to his hands for a moment before turning to them. "The Wyrms seem drawn to the realms beyond the city. The last of them Make the Ring. We can wait a day more for them to be clear of the Nations and for Oshin to be revived. Then, I leave, for after finding Thaddius and LeShawn, I will search for the one Oshin wished to contact. He knows something of all this. He may be the only one who does."

Thus, they waited another day and a night, listening to the sounds of chaos as humankind was threshed by transformation.

Hadryn begged Oshin to awaken, making her promises and vows, but Oshin remained in soporose atrament, and Hadryn reviled himself. Many a time, Cyssiline lent him soft words of how she would be much safer, kept from all possible harm, by staying here, and Hadryn knew his parent was right.

As the second evening bloomed with the dark, they realized there no more wailings or trilling they could discern. Isia had awakened, and he and Cyssiline stood close to each other as they watched the Knights prepare to depart the estate. Suddenly, Cyssiline broke into a wreckage of tears, covering her face, and her son dropped the pack he had been filling to go to her.

He trained his tone for lightness to assuage her fears. "Too soon will you find me in this same room, as though I never left. I promise you, Mother."

He long-held her with her nodding through tears only a mother can know, then he left for the bed where Oshin slumbered, and Cyssiline went to Soo-yeon to cling and cry against her, too.

Hadryn was loathe to leave Oshin. He leaned against her bedside, and his eyes were not for any but her somnolent countenance for some time. He spoke to her, telling her many things in a hushed voice.

Isia made sworn oaths to guard the women both. Hadryn told his mother he would return for her; he would let no harm come to her, and she, for a final time, told him she loved him. Then, he went to Oshin a final time, and in her presence, he took the velvet box from hiding, which Oshin had given to him as "Mr. Ro," and Hadryn put the ring on.

Then, he and Soo-yeon left.

CHAPTER 25

THE HIGHER COUNSEL

I spent the crepuscular hour watching two Drakes – youthful adults, new to maturity – make love under the radiant largess of the impending Moon. The male of the pair was a Firecraw: a dark, ashen color, and his lemen, a Mungkr female with body of pavonine hues. They soared the empyrean and, in their play and coquetry, made the strokes of elegant calligraphy with their silhouettes.

When they alighted the terra mater, they held close their heads with eyes swooned to half-mast. They spoke of the war of the Drakes and Wyrms and swore they would never partake, never choose a side. They had never known a Wyrm an enemy, or a Drake, for that matter either. But, their parents would expect them to hate the Wyrms, promise allegiance to Drakes and protect their younger siblings or elderly relatives.

They had their own ideas though, and they were subscribed to fables: the legends of clandestine islands away from this continent – somewhere, hopefully, not too far. They acknowledged that they may fly forever and never find earth for their feet, that they may drown in the seas, if their exhaustion could not be alleviated. Full of romance, they laughed at this. They chose it, still, over their forebearers' world.

Then, darkness curtsied over the vale, and the Firecraw mounted the Mungkr's lower body. She of adder-like agility and length coiled over his shoulders and around his burly neck, 'til they pleasure-fulfilled together.

I stared, lovingly-lost of myself, at the Moon, who I'd witness her waning shapes over the past couple of nights and wondered why no one challenged her for changing.

I turned away from the amatory youths to find Mei Xian, embarrassed at having caught me watching them. I was, too, ashamed and fumbled a meager string of abstruse words about needing to see Time love-framed, as this couple had so crafted the twilight, after our many excursions and forays with Death through Drake territory. I apologized for my voyeurism, but when I met her eyes, her gaze upon me was softness.

We stood across from one another, our injuries worse than when we'd, together, escaped the Scourge Angel.

"Eryx," Mei Xian said, so I went with her, trailing after her steps as she chose a thicket of tall shrubs to bed down in. Our first night of sleep, I had dug a burrow for us, but since losing a number of my teeth along the right side of my face, we have had to settle for the open lands. She was wheezing, the pain clawing at her breaths, and I felt sorrowful and responsible for everything to have happened to us, but I didn't know either how to stop any of this. This war.

She rested upon the ground, curving her body to shape of a crescent moon, and I laid along her backside, embracing her as well I could to keep us warm and ensuring not to touch the parts of her gashed by talons of another Drake. The wounds seeped the discharge of infection, and I fretted silently for her.

"Did those sweethearts fetch a yearning in you for love, Eryx?" Her voice was soft, so that we would not be heard by any possible others.

I felt tested to answer her. Most probable, she asked out of undecorated curiosity, or as a passing thought into exhaustive sleep. I waited for her to close her eyes to dreaming, but she glanced back at me, instead, expectant. I said, "I have never, but

I wonder if have you. Has the Heaven Drake seen Wyrms become one of passion, where once there were but two?"

My question was to her unforeseen. "I have not," she replied. "Only Drakes."

"Certainly. Foolish me." She was warm against me and beautiful enough to fill my eyes full of memories. Thereby, did she reconstruct everything I knew of nights. I asked of her, "And, neither then – of course – have you witnessed Drakes in union with Wyrms? Nay, impossible, for both houses would rage and never-abating would come those storms."

She lifted her head, so I could see more of her face. "War is ever-present. It's Love that's special. Let Houses do as they will, for it should not be forgotten: the house is a structure for the individual to grow from childhood, but we, eventually, venture outside our familial walls."

Her eyes met mine, until I broke the entrancement. I said, "Indeed, as those young paramours decided, thus upon their wings they fled. A negation of this war and over the seas, by their destinies, were they led."

Mei Xian turned around, so that we were face to face. The cold crept over me, like submersion, faster than I anticipated. "There is nothing out there," she said. "You heard them say that they sought 'the islands,' those which don't exist?" I nodded, staring at her. "They will drown," she concluded. "There will be no perch for them."

"Say that not." I shook my head.

"A due for ignorance, neutrality, and self-absorption," Mei Xian rejoined. She would not be mollified. The profile of a cavalier temper overtook the Drake I'd come to know. "Juveniles. I suppose they said that they hated everyone."

"Nay, not so; they hate no one: not Wyrm or Drake." I tried to counter her. "Wish them their dreams to truth, for it was their lives, their love, their happiness at stake."

She stared at me, and her mane was a slow cadence in the evening breeze. "One belongs to their times, Eryx. To dismiss it without concern is to negate one's own existence, for we are the moments which comprise us. So, it is for us all." She upturned her snout somewhat. "If they hate not Wyrms, then they should have stayed and fought for Wyrms."

I was flabbergasted. "How could you say such a thing? To Wyrms, they owe nothing."

"You think that those who enjoy more power, an elevated social standing, owe the trodden and the abused *nothing*? How much more lands do the Drakes inhabit than Wyrms, though your kind is greater in population. *Tell me,*" she demanded. "From Gled Tria, crossing the River Orb to where we now stand -- and still a day's journey 'til the inlet leading to the Higher Counsel – how many Wyrms have we seen destroyed by the fire, teeth, and claws of Drakes?"

I had pretended not to look, pretended not to count. With her, I wanted to seem that I was not afraid of what I'd seen. But, I answered her: "Twenty-nine we did see die. And, we passed, too, a heap of Wyrm carcasses as gallimaufry."

The look on her face was grim. She asked, then, "And, the count of Drake deaths we witnessed?"

"None," I gave reply. "But, nearly one." I gazed at her and her injuries, feeling my own. Her backside bore teeth marks and gashes. My tail was nearly severed in two, and I bled from a side wound, for she had recklessly confronted a Pyrolite much larger than us both, who was one moment away from killing a Wyrm-child. We had fought and won the child's life to return the boy to his sire. The Pyrolite had forfeited the battle only for belatedly realizing Mei Xian as Shield to the Tianlong.

The Heaven Drake was, still, upon her argument. "Thus, we see there is an advantage to the dragons. That Angel king, too, commands them and will see to the obliteration of all Wyrms." Mei Xian laid down her banners, and with them, her body returned to mine for repose. "If one should belong to the class of the oppressors, yet be not one, then I should think all goodness within and consciousness would impetrate that individual to design her or himself as armament in the hands of the thralls."

I asked her, "Was it all along your strategy? To go to the Higher Counsel and raise an army?"

"Perhaps, more so, after meeting you."

She showed to me her many faces; how could I not love them all? She had revealed to me, as well, the discourse she would present to the other Drakes when we reached the Higher Counsel. I trusted her that she would win them over, as she had me, and in that found sleep.

The morning to arrive granted us safe passage, and Mei Xian and I were stunned to see naught of Death. It seemed the war had been pushed beyond an invisible barrier, and we came, without event, to the first of many temples in decline. The high square roof of it was not whole in any one place. It was cracked all around, like a Time-honored porcelain doll. The structure stood as little more than weed-garlanded rubble with a crooked roof and unsure pillars. The walls had fallen through at random points to make the mouth of caves, like the entrances to a medley of small animal dens.

Delicately, we went through the entrance, where gates should have been, and I, never having tread human structures as a Wyrm, stared at everything not meant to be of note. I circled the open floor that expanded after entry to the building and gazed upon the pores of rocks or cracked stones, which were the floors of the temple now lost to history. Moss, dried of its color, cast the ruins in a sepia tone, and motes of gilded reflection hung upon the air, as if Time had shattered a giant hourglass to suspended animation.

Mei Xian and I looked to each other, confused tourists, and knew the other wondered, too, what had become of the Higher Counsel, being that no one was here. I felt the dread, whispering from a distance, like stifled breezes made small by how far they'd come to reach a person, and I shook it away. Mei Xian didn't appear concerned, only curious.

She came with me, passing through a collapsed wall, and we stood now on a hillock outside the temple to look out on the

River Orb. In the rays of the morning, the water shimmered, seemingly up to the sky. How close it was! From where we stood, we could see the firth, which joined the River we all drank of, to the magnificence of greater waters. Out of the depths of awe, I laughed at it, for it was the sea, and I had never imagined seeing the marine kingdom. It was its very own realm, impossibly expansive, and a twin smaragdine welkin laid to land by goddesses, I fantasized. I was carried off by the vision of it, so much so that my eyes dampened to their own briny waters, as if in reverence to that sight.

Mei Xian was shocked at my emotions. "Have you never seen the ocean, Eryx?"

"Never," I replied, unable to say more. She gazed at me with her cinnabar eyes and began to speak when we both noticed a figure coming up the talus. "How?" I asked Mei Xian, bewildered.

The creature's diminutive size and slow, steady pace told my eyes what it was, but I could not believe it. It seemed impossible for a human to be so far from the Tiered Nations, beyond even the sanded regions, which were my home. She, the human, neared, and I could see she wore strange habiliment: a hood covered her head and was of one piece with the cloak to cover the rest of her. It was made of a course fabric with careless stitching and the same could be said for the pants she wore. Her clothes were of demure colors, except for a pair of fuzzy, aquamarine slippers on her feet.

"Most peculiar," Mei Xian said softly, for my ears alone. "Not many Drakes, except the Aegis and Shields of each tribe, know where to find the Higher Counsel. I assumed it impossible for humans to know of this place. Perhaps, she is lost."

I surveyed the landscape, wondering from whence she came and saw, this time, temples like the one we came from, but they were on the other side of the River Orb. A wide bridge with low, carved railings spanned the narrowest flow of the river before it ran out to the ocean.

The woman, so oddly-attired, began to run towards us, and Mei Xian eased out in front of me, becoming rigid.

"Is that a weapon she carries?" the Heaven Drake asked, beginning to coil.

"It is a woven basket; you needn't fear," I said. "I smell apples, peaches, and pears."

"Nearly too late!" The woman called out to me and Mei Xian. I saw that her hair was long and blonde, streaming out from her hood and obscuring one half her face. She had reached us more quickly than I estimated. "You should be just in time though, I think." She was smiling, and I saw that she was young and fair-skinned. She came right up to me, and one moment, her hand was in the basket, then in my mouth as she thrust an apple past my lips. I was dumbfounded that she had fed me. She shook off her arm that came back, heavy with my saliva, and leaned back to peer upwards at Mei Xian. "Empty belly?" And, she threw a pear straight up for the Long to presumably catch, since Mei Xian's mouth was not within the woman's reach.

The pear flew up, then fell for many seconds, until it struck the ground and split open, as we, unmoving, could only watch her. She was running, again, in a great hurry.

Delayed, I mumbled, "Thank you," for I ate what was given me, and it was quite delectable. To my embarrassment, she circled back around, retrieved the pear from the ground and stuck it in my mouth.

"Waste not!" she declared, before returning to her course. This time, I did not thank her. She said, "A little more hustle! Quickly, follow me!" She ran, nearly out of sight.

Mei Xian was only standing there, staring after the human. I nudged her, and we exchanged glances before moving to catch up with the woman. I whispered to the golden Drake, "I believe she is leading us to the Counsel of Drakes." Mei Xian returned, "Or, she is a lure for a human army that lies in wait for us." I returned: "We've no other option with which to partake." Mei Xian was frowning as she muttered, "Or, we could simply eat her." I soured my face at that, hoping she was joking. On we went though, keeping a few paces behind her, and if she heard us conversing, she gave no indication.

From over her shoulder, the affable human spoke with us. "You two must be from over the bridge. The Counsel did its best to let everyone know that today would be the last day to decide. So, we are glad to see you. If you're scared, I understand. Everyone is. But, for the future are we more terrified. In that, are we given a curious strength." She seemed to become faster, and I was mindful of keeping her within sight. She was still talking: "A strength, I suppose, all parents have for the sake of their children." Her steps seemed too fast for a mere human, and I wondered if my ears were made unfaithful by the questions in my head. She brought her hands up to push through the outgrowth of tall shrubs. "Watch your step!" And, then, she was vanished, as if she had fallen through the marl.

Mei Xian and I halted, then I pried through the lattice of tiny, branched arms to discover a dank mouth, which invited entry, descending along a sloped path into the earth. Mei Xian peered over my head, and when I next gazed at her, I realized we were committed to revealing the same answers, so I began to edge towards the lip of the hole, but she stopped me. The Long went first, and I watched her aureate form, with that variegated mane, slip away into a bramble of darkness.

We went down, departed from all realms, whether Wyrm's or Drake's, that we had known, and we crept in the dark, as the mind does towards sleep. In fact, I believe I might have closed my eyes for a mere blink, but one of some duration, listening to Mei Xian in front of me as her talons or tail brushed the soil. The hue of slumber extended, even as I opened my eyes, and I wanted to ask Mei Xian for answers she wouldn't have about where we were going, or I wanted to stop for a moment to think about everything. I wondered if we had been separated from reality, or if we would be mauled or burned, once we reached any sort of illumination.

I was near to speaking out to her whom I followed, perhaps to ensure it was still her and not another, for the sounds she made seemed to me muted. Yet, it was then that I heard something behind myself and froze. It came, rustling and belonging of some distance from me, but that did little to settle my nerves. I increased the speed of my crawling, feeling the dirt slide against me and the small nips of sharp stones, with the expectation of running into the Heaven Drake, but she was absent, both by touch and sound.

"Mei Xian?" I tried, but the susurration behind me came closer. The sound changed to longer drawls, but my mind was now at a run, and it kept me from understanding what I heard.

"Mei Xian!" I threw myself onward and fell through a gleaming of light, most abruptly. I squinted in the glare of firelight, and Mei Xian was swarming me, bright with concern.

"Eryx, what happened? Are you hurt?"

"No," I said, gathering myself up and pulling away from the chasm we had journeyed. I looked around, and the underworld with which we were met was a midnight city leveled of any obstruction and sprawling through etched and carved rock and minerals. Possessing of its own vault of heaven, the ceiling of the nether kingdom extended so far up that the fire pits and torches lit here could not find its limit, and it was a widespread, inked night above.

I wondered if I were dreaming because this was far from what I imagined for the Drakes' Counsel.

Mei Xian stood at my side. The wonderment of the cave system was only secondary to the inhabitants bustling before us. By marching queues or rows of them, they filed from place to place, greatly rushed, and there were strays seeking the order to which they belonged. Calls for this clan or that emerged in brief, sharp repetition with members to their respective families tarrying not to fulfill their post.

"Pardon."

I moved aside at the sound of someone's voice behind me, and a great, white Wyrm slid from the blackness which we had traversed only moments ago. He came around me, between me and the golden Long, and I was astonished by both his height and the hard plates that grew in sectional, shelled pieces down his body. Upon his head and upper-fourth of his body, the natural armor was even thicker and formed tusk-like protrusions. He stared at me for several seconds, then smiled and left to join a group of other Wyrms. I was fascinated to see that they all bore similar bony or chitinous armament and were his likeness, too, in pale color.

"Why the hell was he staring?" Mei Xian muttered at my side. Her tone was of irritation and a snobbery which accompanies jealously, if I had noticed, but I was overwhelmed by the commotion which surrounded us.

"What do you make of this mysterious township? It seems Drakes and Wyrms coexist in curious partnership," I observed.

It was a demesne divorced of the surface terrain, for here, the two species that were submerged in bitter enmity above-ground walked these caverns side by side, expressing loyal camaraderie and, though I could scarcely believe it, one or two instances of obvious romantic bonds.

"It is a people in preparation for war," the Shield to the Tianlong answered me.

I looked with her perspective now and saw that the coveys to gather were of individuals displaying kindred fortes and tantamount strengths. The ivory, armored Wyrms had formed a larger unit with Tree Crown Drakes, who each had an unusual excess of chalcedony to sheath parts of their bodies in glinting chainmail. Another congregation I saw was of Wyrms who spewed crackling electricity. "Death Wyrms," a passerby said of them, and the crimson Wyrms' mouths opened at the sides: they had left and right jaws, not upper and lower rows of teeth. To the right of them were a collection of Mungkr and Long, who were known to bring the rains, gliding through the falling water like any sea-born creature. With them were Wyrms with curious dorsal fins, semi-translucent skin, and faces vaguely fish-like.

Everywhere I looked, I saw the intention of the coterie brought together. There were firebreathers in rough play and jesting with eyeless Wyrms – either species with the capacity to pierce the veil of darkness with vision most unique. And, I turned to see at the rear of the caves, Wyrms and two Drakes of staggering size.

They were majestic giants, speaking intimately with one another: a garnet-colored Tree Crown female, two Earth-fallower Wyrms, a Wyrm entirely black and smallest of the massive beings, and lastly, a gargantuan Dilong of sapphire hue. He had been the one doing the most talking in that group of titans.

That Drake, the Dilong, was now gazing at us with such intensity that he leaned from his place towards where we stood and had ceased all conversation with the others gathered at his side. I panicked, certain that we were intruders to a secret guild that would do away with any to reveal them. I glanced to all corners, seeking to find the human who had led us here, in effort to explain the circumstance, but she may well have never existed, for there was not a trace of her. My eyes turned to Mei Xian, and the Heaven Drake stood proudly, looking the other Long in the eyes.

The Dilong's voice struck as lightning: "Shield to the Tianlong of the Eye Backs! You have come! Here!" He laughed, deep within and then, rumbling forth. The inhabitants of that underworld all lent their ear, for his voice was such power that none had escaped his announcement. He continued, "And, this day, the most opportune." He nodded at me. "With a little sweetheart, too, I see."

I was abashed.

She went forth to him, surveying the bands of Wyrms and Drakes. She was every measure of complete sangfroid as she spoke to the other Long. "This army." She looked around once more. "You mean to defend the Wyrms, don't you? To keep them from the wrath of the Scourge Angel and all those who obey him."

The Dilong was grinning to hold in another burst of laughter. At his side, the black Wyrm nudged him and told him to stop. She scolded him in a low voice. "Tell her," she said.

"An army to defend Wyrms?" He was smirking.

Mei Xian's countenance flickered with anger. "Surely, you do not expect these Wyrms to fight for *Drakes,* do you?"

He chuckled heartily, again. "Mei Xian," he said, calming. "It is good you are here. But, I see it is by chance. Not because word has spread so far."

"Why have you amassed this force of Wyrms and Drakes, Daofeng? And, what's become of the Higher Counsel? The Mungkr, the Pyrolite, Firecraw, the Shenlong and Tianlong – where are they?"

I remained silent, intrigued by the trove of knowledge to be illumined within the holds of this buried city. Not only did I recognize how very far the evolution of Wyrms had come by view of the uncommon breeds to accumulate here, but I learned, too, of Mei Xian's world – the life of Drakes. I waited, alongside her, for Daofeng's answer, realizing the Higher Counsel of Drakes must have, originally, been comprised of one breed each of dragons.

Daofeng stepped closer to Mei Xian and sat before her to be nearer her height. He grinned, seemingly pleased by all as it came to pass. "Them?" he said. "Those Drakes you will find in the blood-gorged fields. They will be out there, ripping out the throats of Wyrms."

Mei Xian was stern and reserved. "It was wrong of me to come here, thinking you would help those Wyrms who so desperately need us. Hide away with your chosen dozens, Daofeng. When you all have survived what the rest of us have made our duty to endure, you will find you have gained nothing. A generation of peace, at most. But, the children of our children will be susceptible to the Past. If *we* have hid from it without learning from it, without fighting for better, we will see the same war in our grandchildren's eyes."

The Dilong stared at her, casting the buried realm to silence. "'War in children's eyes?' Children have never seen war where we imagine it, Mei Xian. Choosing this side or that side? Enemies or allies?" He began to chortle. "Good or Evil? Winner or loser? Fleeing or hiding? No. None of that." Then, his voice boomed in sudden anger. *"None of it!"* Mei Xian cowered for a moment, then the Dilong smiled once more. "Join us, Mei Xian. We number fifty, and with you and your darling, we become fifty-two. By that, will the game become the Players, and the Players will be no more." He looked, now, serene, even amicable.

"What is your intention?" Mei Xian drew back from him. His eyes were glinting, unseeing of her.

He answered slowly, *"We will kill the Gods."*

I stared at that unusual Drake, stunned. At once, I saw the encompassment of his vision, and with it, Mei Xian's perspective as well. My thoughts darkened their voices to me. I heard them, but faintly, as I felt myself a Wyrm and a human, simultaneously.

Mei Xian was unwilling to comprehend him. "Kill the Angel? And, the Conqueror? You are better aged than I, Daofeng, thus I needn't tell you that their monstrous puissance is *Time*. They are ageless and arise in every era."

He waved a finger at her with a long claw sheening in the fireglow. "I know a little, little secret though, Heaven Drake, and that is: *we are, too*. Again, and again, we come to being. A Soul is like a *wheel*. A soul is a cycle."

"Fantasy, then? Let us play along: say you murder the gods. In their place will emerge new gods. Unending, continues the suffering of the commons."

He was enthused to verbally explore possibilities and theories with her. "Yet, we suffer the same beneath the Gods. Just as Wyrms suffer beneath Drakes for believing their place is a tier lower than ours. Gods belong to their times and must always perish. The people fight them, even if they don't realize it. Then, the yoke of predetermined fate cracks and falls away. Mei Xian. We, Drakes, know the history of humankind. Answer this: how have humans become so perfectly efficient at killing one another?"

"Experience," she answered without qualm. "Practice." A tiny fragment of her wished to see the thread of this discourse to its knotted end.

"And, it is such that we shall gain in killing Gods, if we can now begin this new thought. In time, we, the people, will be so enlightened of how to murder gods that we will have only to kill the very small god within us all. He will be hushed to peace and, nevermore, shall we know war."

I listened to their philosophical debate, deeply enamored of both for their opined views, yet also, distracted from the absurdity of the discussion by movement of a shadow, which no other appeared to take heed. I looked and saw the young woman from before. She, most pointedly, waited for our eyes to meet, then she took to a quick gait, departing the assembly of Drakes and Wyrms.

It seemed, to me, impossible not to trail after her, again. I left reluctantly, catching the last of Mei Xian's and Daofeng's argument.

Daofeng was continuing, his words risen upon the audacity of which he proposed: "Do you know how I know this, Mei Xian? There is a girl, living here with us. She is called a Dreamer, and she knows our future, our past. She told me of our history set to repetition, yet still varied by minor degrees: that Wyrms have always acquired speech, but not teeth before our age. Each cycle, each generation has some slight deviation. But, Wyrms have historically perished. She told us, in this world, every time we seem to fail as humans, we become either Wyrms or Drakes. Then, the Gods awaken. Like a curse, until we can choose and withstand the most arduous path – to protect *everyone* and everyone to come. And, we shall, Heaven Drake. These times are most serendipitous, for we have discovered that which will distinguish this era from all others!" His laughter knocked the halls I threaded through.

"Listen to yourself prattle on, Daofeng. How can you be so ignorant to believe you have everything figured out?" Mei Xian demanded of him.

He was too impassioned to share with her. "This clock we were born to has with it an extra pair of hands. *A Serpent, Mei Xian, and an Orb.* I have spoken with the Serpent. He embarks on his own methods, and with his efforts and those of us gathered here, we'll brace against this gravitational pull. We'll see this planet brought to new orbit."

She rebuked him, "You underestimate the gods. They will take who they can, including those oddities born to this time.

Gods will exist so long as there are humans. It is highly likely the gods are the accumulation of humankind's most callow and fundamental emotions: fear and hate. Therefore, will they always exist."

Their words were whispers to me now, even with my Wyrm's acute sense of hearing, for I was many lengths away from them with layers of rock between us. I strained to hear them, even as I watched the human shrink in my view, as our distance from one another gaped. The dispute behind me gained pace.

"Therefore, *must they die*. How is it we agree, yet disagree?" Daofeng challenged Mei Xian.

"You wish to sacrifice these lives to forces indomitable, like that of the sun and moon, all for a madman's vainglorious delusions! By strategy, we could save hundreds of lives!"

"And, only these lives here and now, Mei Xian! Consider what will remain after this war. *Understand me*. I tell you, no one who is free will follow or obey the gods, and if there are no longer gods, why then, everyone is free." The Dilong's words came up short, for there was quaking upon the roof of the midnight city.

I paused, and so did the woman ahead of me.

"They've arrived," Daofeng said. "Perhaps, hunting *gold*, my dear Heaven Drake." She balked at this likeliness, but he addressed the others within the caverns. "Tree Crowns and Armored Wyrms. Welcome the Scourge Angel's liegemen. All others, out the East and back tunnels to reinforce them."

"Wait!" Mei Xian cried out.

"Wait!" I yelled, at the same moment, to the hooded woman. She had sprung to action and disappeared down a ramp composed all of stone. I quickened myself to track her. Well did this serve me, for she ran through byzantine corridors and descended a flight of stairs.

By the next rounded corner, I stood alone in a great hall, well-lit by phosphorous rocks, and the hall opened on both sides to the mouths of large dwellings. I stared, wondering if these were the beds of those in allegiance to Daofeng's dreams. I tried to imagine Drakes and Wyrms sharing the same breath of dreams as they slumbered. Did they dream of the new world the Dilong promised them? Something to end the hierarchies that apparently originated in the Tiered Nations, in human thought?

Alone, a sorrow eased into my pulse, something I could not ignore. Daofeng's people made their burden the future, valiantly giving themselves for something they couldn't see. I tarried in place, knowing I was less than their valor, for I preferred the things which I could see, and what I saw were those who were still alive. I crawled down the hall a bit farther yet stopped where I saw the woven basket of fruit the woman had been carrying when Mei Xian and I first met her, resting upon the ground. I crept closer. All I could think on was that she had shared her food without fear of us. A yellow pear remained in the curverture of the basket, looking perfectly healthy as though its vigor came from it being shared. But, I knew that was my imagination.

A swelling overhead of hard and ruthless noises.

I listened, and even so far removed from the surface, the hearing afforded a Wyrm allowed me knowledge of the savage ferment to vex the lands beneath the open skies. There is, within the very marl, an energy which tightens, locks rigid, when grisly intentions affront the environs. I looked up, then back the way I'd entered, knowing Mei Xian would be searching for me.

"The war is upon us. The Angel is here. And, the Serpent with the Orb nearby."

The voice came from my right side, and I turned to see the woman had reappeared. She walked towards me with her blonde hair surrounding her face, the hood still over her head.

"Will they truly be enough to avert the ancient, tidal forces? Or will the seas of pain leave us to familiar fates and our stubborn curses?" I felt obligated to ask, believing that's why she'd brought me here.

"Who knows?" she rejoined. "But, perhaps, the answer is no concern to you." I went rigid, yet she continued speaking. "Because, for you, the wager is not worth your life. Or that bright lady's who stirs in you the rays of love."

I wouldn't look at her. In the quiet of that stately hall, and in the timid warmth of it and its shining glow, I saw by our silhouettes that she stood close to me.

I thought I could explain myself. "Being a Wyrm, I have this lowly thought. Yet, I know it is worthier to die and have fought."

"Why?" she suddenly challenged me, and my gaze was swept to her. "Dying for something you don't even believe in? That is more cowardly and detestable than abandonment of war." She smiled at me, and I liked it and didn't at the same time. "Are you, too, tricked by all of this? This is not a war, my friend."

I began to form all my questions at once, but, my words were clipped before they had emerged.

The woman's face I could now see. She looked at me squarely, and I saw her left eye was brown. However, across from the eye where should have been her right eye, were two eyes stacked, one atop the other, and those eyes were a bright green. I recoiled from her, unsure.

"You may call me a Dreamer," she told me. "If I can, without lies, call you one as well."

The earth was jarred, again, and detritus from the ceiling fell to the ground.

"Eryx!"

I recognized Mei Xian's voice, and looked at the human. I turned away from her and fled back down the hall, through the entrance I'd come.

CHAPTER 26

___

LAST OF THEIR SPECIES

Hadryn gazed upon the ring to encircle his finger. Oshin had had it cut and polished of a material he'd never seen before. The band was a pale amber color and mottled by luminous patches of soft argentine, like the shifting of lights one sees through their eyelashes before the eyes are entirely open.

Hadryn stared longer, then closed his eyes. The negative silhouette made by the glimmer-memory of the ring imprinted itself upon the darkness left to Hadryn's vision. And, that, too, was beautiful, just as the wedding ring was.

He shifted in place where he laid. It was the lounge room of the Franquios House, and he drew the Royal Guard, who rested in his arms, closer. She braced against his chest, pulling away, but Hadryn kept firm his hold.

"Let go of me, stupid," Thaddius said. She resisted him a bit longer, then broke to stifled sobs, and finally, after several minutes, Thaddius escaped consciousness into sleep. Her head rested against Hadryn's chest.

The Knight, Rank 3, opened his eyes when he felt his friend breathing deeply. Across from the wide, velvet Chesterfield sofa where he and Thaddius laid was a camelback settee. Both pieces of furniture were a royal purple with pink accent pillows, which

319

the other Knight who laid on the settee threw from the couch to make a little more room for herself.

The lounge that was their refuge was a protruding corner of the mansion, possibly sidelined from memory by shame or regret. It was likely, too, that in the daylight, it would receive an overbearing amount of sun. In the room were boxes without lids, and those boxes cradled picture frames of Pelena before she'd taken the throne: slim, young, and practicing ballet. The white drapes to line the windows were pinned and sewn to the sides, a pristine presentation, or an unwillingness to ever shut out the sky.

There was a great deal of dust in the room, as well. They'd all coughed at it and agreed a bit of housekeeping with an open window would create an easier night for them all.

Hadryn watched Soo-yeon, across from himself. "Thank you for coming with me to find Thaddius," he said.

"We should remain together," Soo-yeon replied. She nodded at the Royal Guard. "She's been through Hell. I'm worried."

"She'll be alright," Hadryn answered. Soo-yeon didn't have to say it for the other Knight to know she was concerned the Royal Guard might Make the Ring. "I think we'll all be alright." He knew how unconvincing he sounded, but it was difficult for Hadryn not to say it.

Soo-yeon thought to herself for a moment, then she rose and went to the door of the room and gently closed it. "The smell," she explained.

"I should move the body," Hadryn offered. He rose to one elbow, unsure of how to move around his best friend, who slept in front of him.

"Don't bother." Soo-yeon waved aside his intention. "She'll sleep better with you there. Besides, I don't think we could move it, even with the two of us."

Hadryn remained silent, because it was true.

They'd come to the estate by the peak of night, when the trough of darkness was deepest, to find the residence, for all appearances, seemingly abandoned. Hadryn used the key Thaddius had given him upon her marriage to LeShawn. At

Hadryn's back, he shouldered a leather knapsack, filled with water canteens and foods from the collection they had garnered at the Archidux House. They had taken a few items, but left Cyssiline, Isia, and Oshin with most of the food.

As Hadryn and Soo-yeon entered the mansion they gave the rooms brightness by turning on the lights. They filled the eyes of the house with a luster that spilled from those tall window panes onto the flowerbeds outside and decorative walkway paths that circumambulated the two-story structure. In the soil and surrounding gravel of the flowerbeds, they failed to notice the sunken impressions of great claws so near to the glass panes.

Within, Hadryn and Soo-yeon had discovered, room by room, devastation. The contents of oak cabinet displays were gutted from their shelves and strewn about, mostly broke to pieces on the floor, and couches were slashed wide to reveal the white innards of their cushioned stuffing. Portraits were torn from the walls and thrown across the rooms. There were photos of LeShawn in every room, usually found atop the only furniture not overturned or damaged in some way.

It was obvious the destruction was not the work of a Wyrm. Soo-yeon had seen the panic gathering in Hadryn's face, and the Knight with eyes of different hues began to run through the house, calling for Thaddius Merlone. He bolted through the dead mansion, no longer mindful of the darkness, and Soo-yeon had to run after him, turning on as many lights as she could. They'd ascended a carpeted ramp and arrived at the main hall of the house on the second level. It was there Hadryn tripped forward. Soo-yeon had pulled him to his feet by one arm and tried the light switch closest to them, but the wiring must have shorted, for they remained in the feeble luminance coming from the foyer at ground level and from a light towards the end of the expansive hall, emitting from one open door, which Hadryn knew to be Thaddius and LeShawn's bedroom.

"Thad, come here," Hadryn had coaxed the eclipsed corridor. It was then that Soo-yeon saw an indistinct human form, leaning against a wall.

They waited for reaction, and in those sparse moments, there came to them an odor, like forgotten meat. The figure pried itself from the wall and stepped forward.

Soo-yeon became nervous. "How do you know that's Merlone, Hadryn?"

The shadow was racing at them, footsteps sounding.

"Get back, Soo-yeon!" Hadryn cried and pushed the Korean woman down, behind himself, somehow catching the attacker by the forearms. It was thankful for Soo-yeon that he did, because she saw the steel blade reflect a modicum of light in all that surrounding tenebrosity.

Hadryn fell away from her, disappearing into the nightfall shade, and joints bumped the floor; limbs scraped along hardness.

"Returned of the dead, are you! I knew you'd rejoin, a sick revenant! So, I waited. Now, die. Again!"

"Thaddius, it's me! Hadryn!"

"Bring back my wife, you hateful sow!"

"*Release it.* The knife, Thad. Drop it, my friend. *Please.*"

"Hadryn?"

"It's me. I'm here."

Soo-yeon's heart was hammering. She waited, staring into the impossible dark.

Weeping edged the evening hour, small at first, then grief-tolling. Soo-yeon wiped at her eyes, not realizing the emotions her body had squeezed from her. There was a low noise, like the mildness of fabric unfolding, then a fainting quiet.

"Soo-yeon?" Hadryn's voice seemed a mile out. "Trace along the wall, please. Be careful. Go to Thaddius and LeShawn's room. There are candles there."

She nodded to herself, willing motion to come to her. Soo-yeon went and found the candles, thankfully out in the open on a dresser, and noticed the bedroom was the only room left untouched. The gory bed and a wide trail of smeared blood, like a red, pulpy carpet, running out to the balcony were the only signs of disturbing event. Soo-yeon gave orange, dancing heads to two three-wick candle columns with a booklet of matches from her own robe and carried one waxed tower in either hand. With her modest torches, she stepped into the main artery of the upper story to cast sight on the scene no longer claimed by the hue of raven wings.

Soo-yeon walked, looking all around herself. She saw points of impact on the ceiling first, the crumbling of plaster and shed paint, then matching wallops on both walls of the corridor, some accented with dark, red streaks. She went on another couple of steps, then instinctively paused. Soo-yeon looked down. Under her left boot was a lock of curled, blonde hair.

She dropped one of the candles, and the fire light blinked away, then recovered itself as a side-stepping flare, igniting along the thin layer of carpet meant more for décor than comfort.

"Shit." Soo-yeon stamped at the growing flames.

"What happened, Soo-yeon?" Hadryn asked from somewhere down the hallway.

"I got it." Soo-yeon extinguished the threat beneath her boot. "But, there's a corpse," she told Hadryn.

"We're coming. Stay there."

Soo-yeon worked to re-light the candle she'd retrieved from the ground. All three wicks caught aglow, and she lifted the candle to cast farther the beacon for the two approaching. When Hadryn emerged from the dark with Thaddius, he and Soo-yeon froze, staring at the Royal Guard's body, naked and blood-spattered beneath Hadryn's long robe which was now draped over her shoulders. Thaddius' gaze was bereaved of understanding and reality; she muttered to herself, but it was nothing Hadryn or Soo-yeon could define as coherent sentences.

"Is she hurt?" Soo-yeon asked.

"Not at all. Physically, at least," Hadryn answered.

"Where's her wife?"

Hadryn paused and said in a low voice. "I'm scared to ask her." He motioned for one of the candles. "Show me where the body lies."

Soo-yeon gave to him light to see by. "Take fifteen steps. In that direction."

Hadryn hesitated. "Could you take Thaddius to the bedroom? We'll clean her of that gore, then ask her what happened."

"Yeah," Soo-yeon said, in her Northern tongue: a clipped word without any other layer.

"Thank you." Hadryn gave her his sincerity, knowing the other Knight didn't have to be here, but chose this. He took his steps, following the hair that rested on the floor. The tresses wound and curled, directionless without the governance of the lady to which they belonged, yet faithful enough to remain with her even unto death. The face of the corpse was turned away, so Hadryn knelt, placing the candle down, and touched the head. He tilted the woman's visage, revealing Pelena Franquios.

Her age seemed advanced, perhaps, by horror, for the wrinkles and folds of her face were beyond that of a 40-year old woman. Her mouth gaped, full of sharp fangs, and her upper body was bare; it was elongated with the skin and fat of her breasts stretched down to where her hips should have been. Yet, beneath the wide girth of her belly, Pelena was a woman no more. A gray mollusk-like body extended into the dark. Everywhere upon her, there was gashed and flayed skin. Her human torso reflected the same wounds, and the mark of the blade could be found in Pelena's neck, her mouth slit open, and through one eye, as Hadryn came to find, moving aside some hair from her face. Oddly, there wasn't very much blood on the cadaver.

Hadryn drew a silk handkerchief from his pocket and draped it over the woman's face. He took the candle in hand once more and walked the length of the creature's body. The swollen, gray bulk, saturated in a thick mucus, grew enormous at the middle of it, then thinned gradually to a tail found broken through the banister of the ramp. The Wyrm was the length of the great hall.

The Knight crouched on the landing to overlook the foyer, suddenly overcome by nausea and sweat. Fatigue made his limbs feel thrice as heavy. He wondered if some part of himself had seen too much and began to reject it, or if, ironically, he was just hungry, his body deprived too long of necessary energy. He looked to his own limbs, wondering if there was the urge to put his own skin in his mouth, and he waited with held breath. But, nothing terrible arose to his urges. His body ached quietly, patient for water and food. Hadryn covered his face with relief.

The Knight breathed deeply. He tilted his head, staring out the tall windows at the front of the house that ran from first level to nearly the roof. He had felt he saw a shadow pass towards the upper arches of the windows. But, there was nothing, no matter how he stared. He saw only the murky outline of his own reflection, so small in the immense panes and barely identifiable. The sole feature that gave him knowledge that it was himself he stared at was his right eye, unnervingly conspicuous by its white iris that appeared almost shining. Hadryn covered his right eye with one hand, and he was erased to other shapes of the night, then he lowered his hand, and he was returned by pinpoint of that star-glow from his face.

An eruption of noise broke his pensiveness abruptly, and it came from the bedroom: the sound of furniture being deconstructed to its lesser pieces. Then, Thaddius' voice, terrifying in its pitch of renunciation of sound mind.

"LeShawn left me! She is gone! She is dead! Hostage! LeShawn ran away! Murdered by a beast! Abducted by a monster! Gone!"

Then, Soo-yeon's strained voice, reaching out: "Hadryn! Assistance! Now!"

The Knight of lesser Rank, Hadryn, stared down at his best friend, who slept so deeply it was as though she'd lost a battle with exhaustion and slumber. He wasn't sure how long she would be succumbed.

An hour earlier, he had run to Thaddius' bedroom to find Soo-yeon fighting to restrain the Royal Guard from shattering everything in her view, as if Thaddius could no longer look upon wholeness for the loss she felt within. With her lunatic rantings unending of the many tragedies which had befallen LeShawn, Hadryn and Soo-yeon forcibly extracted Thaddius from the bed chambers. It was agreed that finding a room rarely used, one that would not elicit memories or thoughts of LeShawn, would be best, and they'd been lucky to discover this lounge towards the back of the mansion. It had a bathroom, so they'd washed and dressed the Royal Guard, who fell to a spell of muteness. They were unable to persuade Thaddius of eat or drink in that state.

Soo-yeon stayed with the Royal Guard, while Hadryn left to search the mansion. He called lightly for LeShawn and searched every room twice over for her or any detail which might reveal what had become of her. Hadryn found nothing. He returned to the lounge room and it was agreed that they and Soo-yeon would benefit from sleep as well.

Soo-yeon stretched on her couch, then grimaced as her stomach growled noisily and for long seconds.

Hadryn waved her attention and motioned to his leather backpack on the floor near her. He'd secured a portion of the food Oshin had given him in the rucksack. "You are welcome to it, Soo-yeon."

"Thank you," she said gratefully, picking up the sack to rummage through it. "We should ration it, right?" Then, she thought to herself. "Where are we headed in the morning?"

Hadryn looked out the only window in the room. It faced him, behind the sofa Soo-yeon rested upon. There was a clutter of chairs in one corner of the room, and when he wasn't staring at it directly, it looked like one of the creatures everyone had become in his peripheral view. "Beyond the Merlons," Hadryn stated, but he became quiet soon after. "I'm sure we'll find he who Oshin knows out there."

Soo-yeon nodded. "We'll die in the sands. People say there are weeds there which bleed the lives from humans." She already had her mouth full with sesame bread and a pecan tart, alternating bites between the two foods. "But, still, we'll go."

"We'll cover ourselves from head to toe." He watched the Korean woman eat hungrily. "You don't have to come, Soo-yeon. You have no reason to go with us."

"I have no reason to stay here," she said simply. "Merlone isn't staying either. She'll hunt whatever it was she saw here."

"It was LeShawn," Hadryn said softly.

"I know." Soo-yeon was nodding again. "She turned. All the denizens are now the worms."

The Knight with heterochromatic eyes wore strained features. "I can't imagine what Thaddius had to see. To see LeShawn—" His words would not come. "Now, LeShawn is out there, lost."

Soo-yeon attempted some comfort or logic. "The Wyrms seem to know their purpose and where to go." She knew her effort was inadequate or misplaced. It made her go inside herself, and she admitted, "I want to understand why this is happening. This *shouldn't* be happening. Perhaps, humans are being punished."

"By who?" Hadryn asked, genuinely confused.

Soo-yeon felt she'd had done more thinking this day than in the entirety of her life. "Our creator?" she guessed. "Karma?" But, both answers felt wrong to her.

Hadryn tried: "Oshin was told that this has before occurred, that it happens always."

The other Knight was struck at how absurd that sounded. "But, we would have known if *this* was in our Past, Hadryn!"

"*Shhh,*" he firmly reprimanded her. Hadryn shrugged. "There is a dependency on us recording what happened for those, later, to know of it. There is a dependency on us *remembering.*"

She shook her head. "Who told her this?"

"A Wyrm, I'm guessing. She said his name is 'Dayraven.' He is the one we'll be looking for."

The Korean yawned. She chose to think of other things. "I suppose we could restock here. There's plenty of food." Lazily, she looked through the rest of Hadryn's rucksack. "But, we shouldn't eat cubes," she reminded herself. "We'll *crawl*, then. Who do you think would make an uglier Wyrm: me or you?"

Hadryn laughed, curbing it slightly to keep Thaddius from waking.

Soo-yeon heard the rattle of a tin in the backpack and withdrew it from the enclosure. She opened it to look inside. "Are you going to eat these little rocks, too?"

"They are seeds, Soo-yeon. Or, nuts. I'm not sure which they are, but they are edible."

She tried one, then the judgment of its lack of flavor passed through her facial expression. "No thanks." She tossed the tin to Hadryn with some bread.

⸺∘∘◦▣◦∘∘⸺

The Knight ate and met with sleep. In his sleep, the hours went by with the flight of minutes. He felt Thaddius trying to tug herself free of his grasp, but he worried she would be overtaken by a fit of rage and destruction, again, or run off, as was Soo-yeon's prediction. He held her as enervation was the other contestant to yank at him in the opposite direction. Time seemed to increase its pace, and Hadryn felt more and more the lassitude that had come to claim him. He didn't think, before, that it was possible to become more exhausted in one's sleep. But, Plodd's face, and the Wyrm of him charging Hadryn, filled his dreams. He saw Oshin blink away, as if someone had turned the light out in the room.

"Thaddius, stop…" Between his dreams, he fought to keep his best friend near, for having lost Oshin. Hadryn was aware that, for a miniscule second, his arms went limp around Thaddius. Then, he dreamed of emptiness that nearly panicked him to wakefulness. Yet, in another moment, Thaddius had returned, and he put his arms back around her.

However, the scent beside him was not that of Thaddius.

Hadryn's eyes sprang open. Oshin smiled down at him. Her hair brushed his cheeks. He went to say her name, to embrace her, but her eyes slowly closed. He waited, confused. She opened her eyes again, and when she did, a dozen more eyes opened as well, all over her forehead. Hadryn cried out. Then, he saw the white queen Wyrm to whom Plodd had offered him, and she floated in the sky.

"Hadryn?" Soo-yeon exclaimed from the window where she and Thaddius stood, and the Knight Archidux was truly wakened from sleep this time. He panted, sitting up and looking around. "Are you okay?" Soo-yeon asked him. "I had dreams, too," she admitted.

The Royal Guard had been inspecting Soo-yeon's wrists and ankles for bite marks or injury, any sign that the Korean woman may be upon her turn to Make the Ring. Hadryn left the couch and went to them, whereupon Thaddius wasted no moment in examining him, too.

"It seemed to me that Oshin was here," Hadryn answered the Knight Jo. He looked to his best friend and embraced her. "I am thankful to find you, Thad. You must eat."

"I've eaten," the Royal Guard stated. She was stiff in Hadryn's arms. "*She ate, too.* Then, she was gone."

"Tell me what happened," Hadryn begged her. "You can tell me, Thad. Whatever it was, we'll get her back."

Soo-yeon watched them from the corner of her eye, feeling as though she imposed. She went through their rucksacks for a few items, then left for the bathroom to refill their water canteens at the sink.

Thaddius stared at the ground, and, to Hadryn, there were too many pieces of her missing. The Royal Guard shook her head after a moment and said, "We have to leave. Immediately. Follow me." And, she hurried from the room before Hadryn could stop her.

"Thad!" Hadryn called after his best friend. "Soo-yeon? Are you ready?" Frantically, the Knight of Third Rank threw the food items that had been left out into their packs.

"You should first find weapons. Those things won't go down easy." A voice answered them from the hallway leading to the room they occupied.

The Korean woman leaned her head out of the bathroom to roll her eyes. "Oh, unlucky us."

Fox Luciano eased his head passed the door that Thaddius had left ajar. "Why didn't you wait for me, Jo?" He spotted her easily in the room, then came in.

Soo-yeon was honest with him: "My assumption was you'd torn off your own manhood, ate it, and had become a giant d---."

"Dammit, Jo, why do you have to talk like that to your ex-boyfriend?"

"Rather liberal use of the word, don't you think?"

"Hey, you're the one who pretended not to even know me our entire military career together."

"I guess you *cheating* made me 'forgetful.'"

"Well, didn't you enjoy your payback, slugging me in the face, out there in the field?"

Hadryn had paused and was listening to something beyond the room. Quickly, he moved past Fox and Soo-yeon and said to them, "The vehicle port is opening. Pelena owned a carriage."

The thrum of an ignition catching could be heard, and Hadryn was gone, running down the hall.

"Thaddius," Soo-yeon determined. "Come on."

Fox stared after them. "Why am I even chasing her around?" he questioned no one, in particular. But, he followed, and the two of them wove through the house, after Hadryn.

At last, Hadryn threw wide a door, and morning had climbed into the sky to make everything more real and vibrant of color.

Hadryn watched his best friend. Thaddius' color had returned to its deep, rich tones with rest and sustenance, but there were, still, her eyes which didn't seem to Hadryn to reflect the light they once did. The Royal Guard had the carriage's engine idling and the back doors of it standing open to load oxygen tanks into the empty cargo space. Attached to each tank was a respirator mask to cover the nose and mouth. Denizens often purchased the canisters to assist when they felt short of breath, wheezing or futilely sucking at air that would not come to their lungs. Pelena had quite the abundant stock, and Thaddius took them all from a mounted storage locker which now bore a broken-arm padlock.

Hadryn peered in through the driver's side to see that all the vents of the vehicle had been sealed with masking tape. It appeared to him a reasonable scheme to shut out the particles that would be emitted from the baleful weeds of the desert region and the oxygen for them to breath as air diminished in the cabin of the carriage. "We're going with you, Thad," he said to the Royal Guard.

The African woman positioned the last of the oxygen within, having rendered them fixed by use of the many straps and chains in the transport car. She finally came around towards the front of the vehicle, where Hadryn stood. "Yes, but I'll drive," she said to him, then pointed to the cache of military rifles and handguns tucked into a center compartment between the seats at the front of the carriage. "The rest of you slept in. But, not I this morning. I found these firearms laying about and plucked them, like morning flowers." With the guns, Hadryn could see the foot-long knife Thaddius had wielded the night before. "We'll fell it, that flying beast, with whatever it takes," she said.

Hadryn glanced back once at Soo-yeon, and the Korean woman shrugged helplessly. "Do they fly now, Thad?" Hadryn asked the Royal Guard.

Thaddius looked at him as though he may be crazed. "The flying ones fly, Hadryn, and the crawling ones crawl!"

The Knight held her at the shoulders to calm her. "I understand." He nodded towards the box-like vehicle with its low tires. "Are you sure this will get us through the desert?"

Thaddius was, again, her soldier-self. "The military trucks are all open beds in the back, so it will have to be this carriage. If we become mired in the sands, some of us will need to push it out."

Fox scoffed disdainfully. "This plan is full of holes, same as we will be, if we step foot outside this van with all those weeds around." He grabbed at Soo-yeon's wrist. "You can't be considering going along with these lunatics. Why even go out there? Nothing's there."

Thaddius marched to the other male and held a pocket knife to Fox's throat, seemingly unaware of how small it was. "Who the hell are you? And, have you been eating yourself?"

Hadryn shifted himself to intervene, wondering when Thaddius had so developed an affinity for blades. "Thaddius."

The Royal Guard would not be tempered, and her knuckles stood out, blanched, by her hold on the weapon. "Show me your wrists and ankles," she instructed the Italian male.

"No," Fox said, then he sneered. "I don't even know why I'm following you fucking crazy women around." He glanced at Hadryn, as he spoke.

Thaddius' eyes widened with anger. In a clean downward stroke, she plunged the knife into Fox's left thigh. The dark-haired Knight howled in pain and fell to one knee.

"Dammit, Merlone!" Soo-yeon went to Fox, shocked by the Royal Guard's actions.

"What the hell is wrong with you!" Fox cried.

Thaddius glared at him. "Don't call someone with a knife 'crazy.' It's almost giving them permission. And, this is a *mixed* playground, asshole. Two boys, two ladies. You're just the ugly boy. Don't forget that." Hadryn had plucked the small blade from her hand, distressed. Thaddius knelt, shoving back Fox's sleeves and pant legs. She said, "He'll turn. Look."

Hadryn was preoccupied with finding a first aid kit in the small garage, but he looked over one shoulder at the other Knight.

Soo-yeon, too, was staring, transfixed by the tears along one of Fox's forearms, near the wrist, and a longer gash on his wounded leg, beginning towards the ankle. "Fox," she said, softly.

"It must've happened when the truck flipped over from that Wyrm," he told her.

"Soo-yeon," Hadryn called. He tossed her the first aid kit he'd found.

The Korean woman thanked him, and she was silent as she opened the lid and set to treating Fox's wounds.

"That's not what these wounds are," the Italian man said, but Soo-yeon wasn't answering him. "No way I'm changing into one of those things. I'd rather die," he proclaimed. At that, she shot him a look, and he hushed.

Thaddius had taken a photo of LeShawn from her inner breast pocket and placed it upon the dash of the car. The photo was from the day of their marriage ceremony. "I'm unloading him, if he turns," Thaddius told the others. "Leaving in sixty seconds."

"How can you be so heartless, Merlone?" Soo-yeon finally spoke. "The four of us could be the last humans."

Thaddius was already climbing into the driver's side of the carriage. "I'm not going to be eaten nor will I watch someone destroy himself. It's horrible. Watching someone destroy themselves." The driver's side door creaked, then slammed shut.

"Like I'd go with some insane freak out for her death fulfillment," Fox muttered. "Don't go, Soo-yeon." He met her eyes.

Hadryn took the passenger seat, looking back at the other Knights. "It's your choice, Soo-yeon. Do not feel it is your obligation."

The Knight Jo hesitated, looking from the van, then out to the climbing morning to overtake the sky. She admitted to Fox, "I just have to know. I could stay here and be safe, but then, I'd never know more of what happened when the world became monsters. I don't even know why I have to know." She gave Fox half a smile, squeezed his hand, and climbed into the cargo hold of the van. "The city's dead," she tried once more to persuade him, as Thaddius drove the car out of the port. "Are we circling back for Oshin and your mother, Hadryn?" Soo-yeon asked.

Hadryn paused, silently thinking. "I want nothing more," he admitted. "But, the city is probably safest, now that those turned have already fled the Nations."

Fox left the garage, walking slowly. He watched the carriage descend the driveway and take to the street. Soo-yeon stood in the back, staring at him. He turned away and walked the opposite direction of the departing vehicle, and the fumes it trailed came near to his ankles, then dissipated. Fox gazed down at the bandages on his wrist. "I am an asshole," he said, under his breath. He looked over his shoulder.

Soo-yeon was still waiting for him. With a tilt of her chin to gesture to the interior of the van, she invited him a final time.

"Shit," Fox said to himself. He stopped walking, then turned around, running after the carriage. Above the vehicle, a tattered lacing of light shot forth, from the direction of the Archidux estate, then it relented to nothingness.

C H A P T E R   27

———————

THE BACKS OF ONE'S EYES

Sasithorn stood in the falling rain.

It dampened the chitin and the skins of the trunk atop her head. Her chin hairs collected the weight of it, like plant stems leaning with over-watering. The rain wandered over every inch of her jade scales in tiny rills, cupping the translucent bleeding of the skies in the grooves of the golden encirclement found a third the way down her body. Yet, even that was not as it once was. The gold band, which had shattered in her battle with the first Wyrm she and Ardyce had encountered, had grown back with lavish elaboration, resembling a wide armlet, like those worn of ancient times. In a series of stacked flameheads, the gilded armor created the form of a bird in flight.

Sasithorn shuddered in the frigidness brought by the rains that should have never to came down.

There was he, who stood close at her side, and she said to him. "The Eye Backs have fallen. I fear what we will see, and that we will not be able to understand what stands before our eyes." For as it was known to all Drakes: *the backs of one's eyes are unerringly near to sight, yet behind perception and a link to the mind's light.* Thus, were The Eye Backs given their name, and if they truly were the binding from sight to the center of one's knowledge, they would be doomed. Sasithorn hoped for the myth of it to be false. She

335

looked, directly up with her head back, towards the heavens, and she saw every individual tear droplet in its rushed descent to Earth.

"Come away. It is not safe here," the creature near her said, and he said it because they stood at the heart of war.

But, Sasithorn felt isolated from herself. Her ears performed as they should, accepting the dense, splintering sounds of the bones which broke, the screaming, and the sound of falling blood, much more burdensome than that of falling rain. And, her eyes were their own entities, simply staring and absorbing the tones of reds made by encroaching Death.

She observed. Spectator. Bystander.

The Wyrms had arrived to The Eye Backs, and Sasithorn knew, without seeing it, that the crawling ones were, too, in The Nocturnes, Wymira, and Gled Tria, for they far outnumbered every tribe of dragons, and indeed, the entire population of all Drakes summated.

The shrill cries of a Wyrm made her turn attention upon it, and she saw as the Wyrm was hoisted to the lambent welkin by two Long Drakes and rived, muscle from bones. Another Wyrm had dashed the brains of a Ryuu upon a merciless boulder and ate of the Drake's dying. She wondered why they all believed that they must kill one another to survive. It was the words of their gods, but gods by their nature speak ever and only in tongues of hierarchies. There were no other means to ensure they'd remain at the zenith of everyone's beliefs. How was it no one else, in the eyes of one another, saw this?

She wished for it to end. She wished to tell them these simple things. But, War was not one for words. It thrived, in the desolate silence between those pitted in opposition to one the other.

Similarly, was Sasithorn divested of language and rejected to an obtuse pain. Within herself began an etiolating consumption that originated at the former break along her spine and pulsated out.

Sasithorn realized it was fear.

She stared at the darkened form, the Scourge Angel, mountainous and distanced from the goring of the species in contention. The being of him rose up and stood, a black thorn in the underbelly of the heavens. Where the rains fell into the burning runnels to separate his plates of armored hide, steam seethed and hissed in ominous eructation. With his eyes of hollowed Death, and the sparse gestures of a king not to be much bothered, he ordered the Drakes who looked to him to kill and violently so.

Sasithorn saw, also, she who was of unyielding loyalty to him, and that Drake knew to gauge the tremors of the soil. Then, she struck. Sasithorn sickened to witness the Aegis of the Tree Crowns, mighty Ardyce, as she tore Wyrm after Wyrm from the earth – a murderous weeding of the land. With her claws and teeth through their bodies, the mounds of their viscera grew to nauseating heights. She was their officer of damnation, and as her badge, she bore the skull of mickle Iryskython – the Earth-fallower who had left her mark in the form of a gaping rictus upon the face of Gled Tria. The skull hung from its eye sockets at Ardyce's left side, hooked by the spires of chalcedony to grow as armor on her shoulders.

Then, that Tree Crown, once pearl-white and now the color of shadow puppets – once donning noble antlers, yet now diademed in steel – had fulfilled her awful mandate and, affirming a cue given by the Angel god, suddenly and with magnificent force took to her flights, on errand to complete the next of his bidding.

Desperately, Sasithorn locked eyes with Dayraven, her love returned. *"I must go after her,"* she told him.

Behind them, the fire-breathing Drakes they'd met earlier struggled to pin Mohonia's wings to his side and keep him grounded. Nandenia, Ardyce's and Mohonia's only surviving child, was trembling at the sight of her dame and the ensuing commotion.

"Stay," croaked the Unrested Pyrolite, holding Mohonia close. "Good … father. Stay. We go." Lynelis weighed heavily into the Tree Crown male, and their eyes met.

"Like Hell, we're going, Lynelis!" The Pyrolite's lover, Dreyon, burst forth. "Never. Not with you like this."

The undead Drake drew to anger: *"We go!"*

Dreyon gaped at him, incredulous. "*Stop.* Or, I shall knock you out cold, my love. It is impossible."

Sasithorn went to Mohonia to soothe him. He was staring at the skies, where last they'd seen of Ardyce. "Keep with your babe, Mohonia. I swear I will return her to you," she promised the young father.

Lynelis staggered closer to Dreyon. His breath was a tattered sail catching wind. "She saved ... my life."

"And, we saved her Vow and their child! *No, Lynelis.* We are cleared of debt," Dreyon said.

"'*Debt?*'" Lynelis wheezed. "She ... is ... a part of me." There was now pain in his gaze.

Mohonia had sat upon his haunches to relieve the burden on his amputated limb. He held Nandenia to himself, and he told her he believed, with all certainty, her mother would be rejoined to their family.

"Quickly," Sasithorn said, as she weaved passed the others. "We've lost considerable ground on her." She paused before Dayraven. "I'm sorry. Goodbye." There wasn't more she could say. Their reunion would have to wait or chance another revolution in time. She snaked away from him, her head bowed.

With a darting peck, Dayraven seized the end of the Mungkr's tail in his mouth; he yanked.

"Ow!" Sasithorn cried, more offended than hurt. She looked back at him, as he came to her side.

"It is so awkward for you to pretend you do not want me to accompany you," he said. He found the eyes of the two firebreathers. "I hope there are no objections, gentlemen."

"None," Lynelis replied.

"Quit speaking for us," Dreyon grumbled, though he adored it of his Vow. He and Lynelis extended their wings and took to the skies in perfect synchronization, flying above the Mungkr and her beau. "You will practice the utmost caution," Dreyon instructed the Pyrolite Drake.

The Unrested flew well enough, even with having to labor a bit more to maintain controlled direction. "We retrieve her. Bring

Ardyce. Home." Lynelis drew wearied breath. "We do not. Take sides. In this war."

Dreyon was quiet at that. He huffed and felt his throat warm with fire, for the snares of enmity towards Wyrms had latched Dreyon, being that he could not pardon the Wyrm who had stolen Lynelis' vitality. He'd heard the feathered creature's tale of misunderstanding betwixt the Wyrm and Mungkr in Gled Tria that had led to Lynelis' release to un-death, but it did not find acceptance in his heart.

Below them, Sasithorn curved through the air, keeping close to the ground to travel near to Dayraven, who could not fly, yet overtook the lands at wind-rushed pace. They departed the Eye Backs, leaving behind the icy rain and the fierce battles there. By side glances, she took measure of him and heard his words repeating in her head of how every Wyrm and Drake were once human.

Sasithorn could remember, then, the sunlit garden Dayraven had bloomed for her, the library with its many lamps and many books that were the days they spent in courtship of each other, and she could remember first meeting her, Dayraven the government official who'd requested her, and the titian eyes which Sasithorn had both lost and discovered herself within them.

As they skimmed the distance together, in beastly vessels of incomparable capacity, Sasithorn was amazed that she felt, too, her human body – the joints and pumping of her legs at full run. Somehow, she felt the flare of her hair against her momentum and the human smile on her lips because, she realized, she was happy to run with Dayraven. They never had as humans together. With Dayraven brought back to her, she believed they could retrieve Ardyce from the blackness which clutched her.

They crossed the River Orb as a singular velocity, taking direction from the firebreathers' vantage point, which steered them towards Ardyce, and Sasithorn was awed to see Dayraven skimming along the water's surface, such was his unstoppable speed. She watched him, as his plumage showed its colors in the bursts of winds.

He shifted his eyes to visually apprehend her staring at him, and he smiled. "Will you not speak to me as one you once loved?" he asked.

Sasithorn twirled upside down, still gazing at him, and then, righted herself. "Why are you now male?" she wondered aloud.

He gaped, momentarily interrupting his stride with a sudden fan of water-spray, which threatened to plunge him into the depths of the river. "This is your question?" He faltered once more. Sasithorn thought upon it, then nodded. "This?" he said, puzzled. "Do you not see what we are, Sasithorn?"

"We are creatures out of a most bizarre dream," she answered.

Dayraven laughed. He didn't know why she looked the same to him, despite the fantastical bodies they currently inhabited. He felt, too, it wise not to tell her yet that he was not a Wyrm as she and the other Drakes had assumed.

In front of them, the waters glittered and shrank, like a jewel being tucked away into a vanity drawer, as they neared the opposite side of the River Orb. Dayraven took to the banks without falter, and Sasithorn glanced above to see the flying firebreathers veer Northwards, their bodies undulating between the flashing silver color of the Firecraw, then the ashen hue of the Pyrolite with every stroke of their wings. They were a cadence of harmony together.

Sasithorn led Dayraven to follow the bend of their direction. The pit of her stomach dropped, as she realized they were headed for the esoteric realm of the Higher Counsel. It quaked her nerves, the muscles of her body knitting tightly. The Scourge Angel knew of the Higher Counsel, where they resided, and had sent Ardyce and the minions under her charge here for a reason.

The sun was now on its knees, throwing forth streaks of pink inflammation into the broad skies as though to tinge every white cloud with that aching color, like eyes that have spent a night crying. It was then that they saw Ardyce.

But, Ardyce emerged from a thicket of dusk-released fog in yet another form unrecognizable to Sasithorn's eyes. She was not murdering Wyrms, as the Mungkr had expected to find her.

Instead, the black Tree Crown hung unnaturally from her neck, like an old robe upon a dresser hook. Her skeletal visage had relinquished to original form; there were, again, her eyes visible, and they were barely open. Sasithorn realized the Great Aegis could be returned to herself, in seeing this. There was that hope, though fleeting, for, as Sasithorn stared at her friend, she saw next that which had arrested and now held Ardyce.

A cerulean Dilong – a more mammoth Drake, Sasithorn had never seen before – had cinched his jaws around the Tree Crown's throat; his coiling body circled the muscular frame of Ardyce's limp figure. And, he mounted the firmament with that taxing ponderosity, hefting her several spans up and continuing towards the nimbus clouds.

Sasithorn bolted forward, just as the Dilong bellowed a cry to dwarf all other senses. It was a bugle to claim attention, in particular, Sasithorn knew, the force whom had arrived with Ardyce as their commander. He demanded they watch her die, an oath to their lives as well – that her fate was theirs to come.

Daofeng, Dilong of the Higher Counsel, reached a pinnacle in the sky, and his scales of azure coloration shimmered in the dying light with his movement to disengage of his unconscious enemy. He would let her immense tonnage pulverize the spirit from her.

"Ardyce!" Sasithorn shrieked wildly, but she was too late, too far away, and the Tree Crown was released. Ardyce fell through the skies towards the insuperable solidity of Earth.

"We must go."

"Why?" Eryx found herself repeating the words of the Dreamer to the Tianlong.

Mei Xian gave pause at the Wyrm abruptly without rhyme to her words. "To take part. Wyrms are dying, and the Scourge approaches. You know this, Eryx."

The beige Wyrm was quiet and unsure. Purposely, she rid herself of meter to convey what she wished to the Drake. "They've chose, and to each their beliefs." Things were arriving too quickly to Eryx. She glanced to one side to see that the blonde woman had followed her, and the shadow of her words left the Wyrm. Her voice was nearly indistinct. "This is not war."

"What?" The heaven Drake could not be sure what she'd heard from the Wyrm. "Eryx."

"Might some of us choose life?" Eryx asked.

Mei Xian stared at her. She looked around at the cave which surrounded them, seeing everything for the first time. The Drake was suddenly overwhelmed by the actuality of what they would see when they came above ground. She questioned the Wyrm who was dear to her, "At the cost of ignoring everyone who battles, bleeds, perhaps dies to give their face to the world which we all belong? How can we do that, Eryx?"

"We will do it, if Life is our belief." The Wyrm said this without faltering, suddenly so certain of herself that Mei Xian could not respond.

It was then they heard the roaring of the Dilong.

The heaven Drake hesitated for a moment. "Eryx. I must go." And then, she was rushing back down the hall.

The Wyrm watched her go. Then, she went too for knowing that her decision was Love. To Eryx's surprise, the human strained to reflect her in speed, and Eryx paused to let her catch up.

"Your name?" Eryx asked.

"Naehska," she answered.

"Climb upon me, Naehska. Hurry."

She did, and they wove the intricate cave system at the Dreamer's guidance, then they were arrived to see Daofeng coiled in the sky and what appeared to be an eerie replica of the Angel god plummeting to the ground.

CHAPTER 28

THE RINGS WE WEAR

(5 hours earlier.)

"Thaddius, slow down. Put your seatbelt on." Hadryn clasped the metal tongue into the seatbelt slot for his best friend.

The carriage bumped over a sidewalk curb, then accelerated through the city streets, passing the estates and expensive flats once belonging to the denizens. The Tiered Nations were empty but maintained a steady breath in the form of a rippling, gentle breeze, and the day shone with a high sun, ripe with vitality. Through the windows of the van, the four people traveling felt a massaging warmth, and when Soo-yeon asked for Thaddius and Hadryn to roll down the windows, the effect was undeniable.

They had been driving for nearly two hours, and there was peace. The Tiered Nations revealed her unknown face, and the city seemed washed, as if by a warm cloth that was this afternoon's basking brightness. Even Thaddius' anger and tug-of-war with sanity had been buried under a countenance which appeared tranquil with the reminiscence of fonder times.

"LeShawn and I always stole away in this machine for long drives along the Northern perimeter, where no one knew us,"

Thaddius said. "We would sing – it was so ugly. Then, she would tell me the most absurd jokes and anecdotes. We laughed so much."

Hadryn was nodding with a smile. "Her laugh."

Immediately, Thaddius snorted and chuckled. *"Her laugh. Beautifully annoying."*

Soo-yeon still worried over any mentioning of the Royal Guard's wife. "Do you want me to drive, Merlone?" she offered.

Completely dominant of her better senses, Thaddius simply waved aside Soo-yeon's words. "No, finish your breakfast. I've eaten already. I'm fine."

Hadryn took from the backpack the last pecan tart and turned around in his seat. "Soo-yeon, do you want the last one?"

Soo-yeon declined, admitting she had had two the night before and finished an apple. No one spoke whether the food should be held in reserve. Hadryn looked to each of them. He wondered if they, too, felt their human-ness and the undeniable need of anything living to eat, despite all they'd seen. There was a rigidity to each the humans left to discover what had become of humans, but a calculated levity on their faces.

Fox filled his mouth with the rest of the milkbread he'd been given and, chewing, he leaned back his head to groan with pleasure. "This food is amazing," he said with his mouth full. "Where did you get this, Archidux? It's better than cumming."

Soo-yeon giggled and made like she was going to kick at Fox's groin, but he closed his legs and caught her at the heel to wink at her.

Even Thaddius laughed heartily. "Nothing is better than cumming. Especially, after the fourth time. Everything after that: humans know, then, of divinity without having to die."

"Right," Fox reluctantly agreed, perplexed. "'Especially, after the fourth time'...." Fox swallowed his food and drank some water. The vehicle raced through the quiet streets. Fox patted the back of the driver's seat. "I have to shit. Pull over, Merlone."

Soo-yeon scowled and swatted at the other Knight. "You're so gross, Fox!" She worried what the others thought of her, since it was her decision to bring Fox along. "Why do you sound so excited about it?" She wondered why she ever dated him.

"I haven't shat in a week," Fox answered her. "Merlone, come on."

"It's the cubed food," Hadryn said. "It stops one up. Thad."

Thaddius was instantly angry. "We don't have time for this!"

"Thaddius," Hadryn attempted once more to persuade the Royal Guard. "We are only human with our human needs. We need to let people go to the bathroom."

The carriage slowed and came to a halt near a high-rise building of apartment flats. Fox opened the back doors and hopped out of the van to enter the lobby.

Soo-yeon followed at a smooth jog. "Pee!" she said, alerting Hadryn as he stared after her, and the Knight Archidux nodded in response. Soo-yeon and Fox disappeared past the main entrance, and Hadryn removed himself from the vehicle, walking around the front of it where Thaddius was already leaning against the nose of the van. Hadryn came to stand in front of her, pretending nonchalance.

The skies spoke first between them, rumbling a throaty cry of thunder, and streaks of light came again, as if originating from the direction they'd left.

"It's as though these rain clouds and spears of light follow us," Hadryn said. He stared upwards for several seconds, admiring the unusual sky.

Thaddius said nothing in return.

Hadryn needed to see her face, as he asked, "Do you want to tell me what's become of LeShawn, Thad?" He readied himself for a paroxysm.

The African woman had her gaze pinned to the sky. She drew in a long breath, then allowed it slow departure of her lungs. "I've thought about all this," she said, "And, I'm glad you do not have to marry that odd, little, stout man."

Hadryn smiled. "That was Oshin in disguise."

Thaddius grinned widely. "No."

"It was," Hadryn insisted.

"I should have known she'd come for you. I didn't believe her letter, proclaiming she'd ended it with you." Thaddius sighed. "Look at you two, masquerading as the other sex to get to one another: you, first, as a woman, then she as a man. Hilarious."

The Knight saw that it was true. He ventured: "Maybe as proof to one another that gender may not matter?"

Thaddius thought to herself. "I agree. Love is probably bigger than that."

Hadryn fell silent. He was careful as he questioned his friend. "How big, then, Thad?"

The Royal Guard jerked her stare away from the sky. She crossed her arms, feeling herself, once again, on the balcony of her and LeShawn's bedroom chambers. She turned and slammed a fist down on the hood of the carriage, gnashing her teeth. "Get the others. We leave, now." Her fist left an imprint upon the metal, as she left to board the van again.

"Thaddius," Hadryn called after her, but her name hung in the air, alone, as though it had not an owner, so the Knight hurriedly turned with intention of finding the others. He nearly ran into Soo-yeon.

"What's wrong?" she asked him. "And, why has the weather been so strange since we left?" But, she questioned the last part more to herself.

The horn on the vehicle blared, and the carriage had begun to roll forward. Hadryn was distracted, watching Fox dash into the back of it. "We need to go," Hadryn said to her.

Soo-yeon was thinking to herself: "We didn't talk about what we'd do if one of us changed and we should talk about it."

Hadryn gazed at her a moment, then took her by one hand. "Let's go."

And, they slipped into the van before Thaddius had gathered much speed. Inside, Fox had found a few crates from the apartment complex to use as seats in the open transport bay of the carriage. Soo-yeon sat on one of them, and Fox was staring rather obviously at the back of the Royal Guard's head. He looked to Soo-yeon with questions in his eyes, but she only lowered her eyes.

Hadryn clamped the van shut at the rear, then the passenger's side as he got in. He glanced at the side windows to measure their whereabouts. The Knight Archidux stared for a moment at the heavens, for a row of clouds, unusually dark, seemed to trail after them in an arc from out the depths of the Tiered Nations. He turned away from the odd formation to speak to his friend. "We're nearing the wall, Thad. How are we supposed to get through it?"

The interior of the van rattled, as the machinery came to increased power. They were cascading through the deserted streets, Thaddius barely eyeing the road. She was glancing upwards, leaning over the steering column. "There's something in the sky," the Royal Guard observed. She took a tight turn, making the two in the back scramble for a hold at the straps and chains being used to lodge the oxygen cylinders in place.

"Easy, Merlone!" Fox warned the driver.

"Hadryn, look. In the sky!" Thaddius commanded, pointing.

The Knight Archidux leaned forward and turned his face up to see an indiscernible figure, little more than an irregular dot, in the faraway heavens and framed by the dark clouds which kept after them. Then, it was obscured by the roof of the carriage. "What was it, Thad?" Hadryn asked.

"Where did she go! Where!!" Thaddius cried shrilly, suddenly engulfed in wild desperation. She tried to peer further out the windshield, then looked out the back window for further vantage.

Hadryn was now steering the carriage. "Dammit, Thaddius! Strike the brakes!"

And, the roadway directly in front of them buckled under the sound of frightening impact. Up came whole slabs of pavement and a miasma of dirt and dust. In the smokescreen of that debris stood a grendelian giant, unwavering.

Thaddius threw both her feet down on the brake pedal, just as Hadryn cranked the steering wheel hard and to the right. The van skittered for traction, and a whine of protest came, piercing, from the tires. Soo-yeon screamed, and the vehicle felt as though it would dump them, but it swung and struck the creature in the street in such a way that managed to keep them upright. The colossus was not affected in the least.

The carriage settled back into its axles with a final creak. Thaddius' eyes would not leave the window at her left-hand side, where scarlet, scaled haunches filled the frame. There was the sound of the beast's breath, somewhere over the roof of the van, and the ripple of life beneath the skin they could see of it. The nearness of that enormous being rid the voices of each the four human beings.

It was only Soo-yeon who gasped audibly, as the creature stepped away from the vehicle. Fluid were the extension and contractions of its muscles, like a predator species. However, the mien and carriage of the creature was noble, like that of a well-bred steed. It walked a stride away from the wheeled machine, then turned and lowered its head with its wings swan-flapped forward, issuing a soft, reptilian cry. There were hollows where the eyes should have been and running the crest of the beast was a torch-like mane, the flames gliding and snapping, like a dancer's skirt – so lively that, with every movement of the animal, the tresses courted a burst of ember sparks into the air. Its four limbs were heavy with power and the barrel of its body: strong, trim without waste. Behind the beast, a long tail whipped with nervous patience, for the creature seemed to be staring deeply at Thaddius, and it clicked gently in its throat at the Royal Guard.

Thaddius snatched blindly at the weapon closest to her, a handgun, and threw open the door to separate her from the beast. The others in the carriage were paralyzed by shock, as Thaddius took three steps towards the winged being.

The handgun erupted, shaking the silence and the blood in everyone's body.

A short spume of dust rose five feet in front of the creature, where the bullet became embedded, and the dragon reacted not; she gave only a melodious trill and bobbed her head once in Thaddius' direction.

The Royal Guard was perspiring, her teeth clenched, as if to bar everything which stood before her, so that she would not have to digest any of it. Thaddius cramped over in the street, pressing the top of the gun to her forehead; her hands shook. Finally, the grieving woman stood tall, with outstretched arm, and the firearm grasped so beseechingly in her hand that Thaddius felt she would lose her fingerprints to absorb the stippling of the grip.

"Where is my wife, you nightmare beast! What have you done with her!" Thaddius yelled aloud, then to herself were the words: *"Come back to me, LeShawn."* The Royal Guard cried out and lay her finger to the trigger once more.

"Thaddius!" Hadryn pleaded with her, calling from the open window.

Behind them, the Tiered Nations, with every home pitted of its humanity, echoed the gunfire which pigeon-fluttered throughout the vacant rooms and halls.

Thaddius stared ahead of herself to see what she had done.

The front locks of the dragon's fiery mane snuffed out for the blink of an eye, as the shot tore through it, then returned as blazing inferno – the crimson Pyrolite came to anger.

Hadryn had crawled over the car seats to reach his friend, for the creature's throat was working to some function, and the air around them had bloomed to an uncomfortable heat. The Knight extended his hand, when the beast lowered her head to be of level with the Royal Guard's body, and Hadryn grasped nothingness, as he missed the collar of Thaddius' robe.

The dragon parted her jaws.

A gust of air struck Thaddius firmly, expelled from the creature's lungs and enough to land Thaddius on her rear. The Pyrolite gave a final, dismayed huff. With a shriek, the Drake pivoted away from them and ran down the street. Hadryn pulled the bewildered Royal Guard into the vehicle's safety.

Stowing the handgun back into the center compartment and groping for the carriage's steering column, Thaddius was dazed, yet had the van redirected and tearing down the road in a matter of seconds.

"After her," the Royal Guard said. The hand of the speedometer plucked by in increments of ten, and they trailed very near to the dragon's hovering tail, as the beast looked back at them once in her maddened dash towards the wall that ran the perimeter of the city.

"What the hell is that?" Soo-yeon erupted from the back. "You've seen that before, Merlone?"

"She is a flying one. I *told* you," Thaddius insisted. "Hold tight."

"Don't do it, Merlone!" Fox demanded. But, they and the winged creature were headed directly for The Merlons. "Stop! She's trying to kill us!"

The vehicle accelerated, just as the Drake did. With wings spread, the Pyrolite charged the barrier and emitted a deep bleating of differing tones. Upon that cry, she laid to waste the already-crumbling brick and mortar of the wall. Her chest went through the low barricade with loudness, and the agitation of her tail behind her swept larger pieces away.

The van found freedom from the Tiered Nations, careening passed the demolished rubble.

Soo-yeon clung to the back of Hadryn's seat. Strands of her dark hair were matted to her face with sweat. "She helped us!" the Korean woman gasped.

"She merely sought escape from our pursuit of her," Thaddius corrected Soo-yeon. The Royal Guard's focus was driving, and she banked an acute right to chase down the running dragon, who kept within sight of The Merlons, following it out, westerly. "I will have her," Thaddius muttered to herself, leaning into the gas pedal. "Same as before."

Now that the Drake, and the carriage, too, were no longer confined to the predetermined paths of the city and its ruling of asphalt, they acquired a sort of heathen liberation. Masterless, as one is when they divorce of the society and home they were born from, the creature and her human hunters gale-swept the terrain, coarse as it was.

Hadryn held at the interior of the vehicle and slowly turned askance his gaze to look to his best friend. "Thaddius. Is she?"

"She is the murderer of my love!" the Royal Guard swore. "I vow, here – *now* – to occupy my life, henceforth, in the capture and killing of that love-red monster."

"You don't mean that, Thad," Hadryn said.

"And, now she bestrides the wind!" Thaddius exclaimed. "But, the vaults of Heaven will not rescue you, beast."

The Pyrolite stretched open the sails of her wings, and one or two sweeps of those extra limbs drew her up into the clouds' domain. She flew well overhead of the carriage, yet remained in clear sight of it, leading it for many miles.

"Where the hell are we going?" Fox asked. "Was this the plan?"

"I think we should trust the creature," Soo-yeon replied. "It isn't a Wyrm, so did humans become one of two species? Or, did these winged ones already exist?"

"They're probably what infected humans," Fox rejoined. "Maybe this thing is just leading us into a trap."

"Look." Hadryn pointed ahead of them, and the shimmering was nothing more than playful light, then the marl peeled back, and to them was revealed a turquoise palace. Small, white-headed waves trotted towards the shore, then laid out wide to hug the sandy planes. The smell of salt, more stringent than they knew of seasoning found at their dinner tables, perfumed the air, and the Drake above them shifted direction to glide South, following the winding coastline.

Hadryn cracked his window, needing air. "We're bypassing the desert this way."

Thaddius tore away the masking tape from the vehicle's vents. "She plots something," the Royal Guard mumbled.

"Pull over, Merlone. We need to think this out," Fox said, his tone with a note of pleading.

"We will lose her, if we do that – if we lessen in speed even a little!" Thaddius yelled at him, hot with trembling nerves.

"What about finding that one who knows Oshin?" Soo-yeon quietly asked of Hadryn.

"We will, still. This has come first, so it is first," Hadryn replied.

Then, they continued in silence for a stretch of time. Thaddius drove, muttering to herself and glancing upwards to ensure the creature was still with them. The others had fallen to a muted quiet.

Hadryn nodded off in the passenger's seat, then woke with a jolt, as the vehicle came to a stop. He straightened in his seat, looking all around, and the sun was in the act of reaching for the night, like dancing partners trading off. "Where are we?" he asked.

"She's descended," Thaddius whispered. The Royal Guard snatched a rifle and departed the carriage. The dragon was not in sight.

After hours of hearing the hum of the engine and the tread of the tires, to have it suddenly cut off left an oppressive stillness. Solely the sky and the sea to their right seemed to have life and be of the present. Everything else, like Hadryn's thoughts, were slow and loping, like memories. Without warning, he remembered a night where Thaddius and LeShawn had taught him to dance; he saw them laughing, but there wasn't sound in his reverie, only the present-now of his heart beating.

"She isn't going to shoot her, is she?" Soo-yeon's voice was pricked with fear, and Hadryn returned to himself.

"Thad, don't!" he called, exiting the van.

The back doors came open, just as the Royal Guard disappeared over the rise of a hill. Hadryn, Soo-yeon, and Fox left the enclosure of the carriage.

Hadryn ran. Thaddius had disappeared over the small rounding top of a mound in their path, and Hadryn took it next, but Soo-yeon and Fox stopped at the summit, staring, for indeed, the crimson dragon had landed. Her wings were folded at her back, and her head was down, close to the ground. She seemed larger than the first time they'd encountered her, but it may just be that she was awe-inspiring.

"What is that she's found?" Soo-yeon tried to peer through the veil of arriving-dusk.

"An animal carcass?" Fox guessed.

They could see little more than a white shape in the grass, as the creature nudged at it with her muzzle. The dragon pushed against it, and it moved. Looking to them and squawking, the Drake's mane grew, like fingers of lava towards the sky. By the light she shed, the patch of grassland around her was illumined.

"She's eating a human," Thaddius claimed and rushed forward with the rifle aimed. "Back away, creature!"

Upon sight of the weapon, the towering beast snapped at it with her jaws, and her flights unfurled, like the banners of an alien nation.

Fox fell over on his rear the moment the Drake's wings lightning-cracked the air, though he was still a couple dozen feet from the beast, and he drew a rapier from a leather sheath tied at his waist. "I don't think we should get any closer to it." He regained his feet, putting a hand out. "Careful, Soo-yeon."

But, the Korean Knight went around his outstretched hand. She watched her footing on the descent and neared as close to the animal as Hadryn now was. "Do you think she'll let me take the girl?" she asked the Knight of Third Rank, and, there on the dirt, rested a naked woman with disheveled hair to veil her face. Her hair was entirely white and her skin just as pale.

Hadryn glanced at Soo-yeon, answering her with a slight nod, then he walked to his best friend to rest a hand on the barrel of the rifle, lowering it. "She wanted us to find her. Go ahead, Soo-yeon." Thaddius was staring into the pits of the Drake's eyes. Hadryn rested a hand on the Royal Guard's shoulder, and he attempted to pierce her thoughts: all turmoil and threatening to overwhelm her. Hadryn could see it in her eyes. He said to her, "You will always love LeShawn, Thaddius. What could possibly change this fact?"

"Shut up," Thaddius warned.

Soo-yeon was kneeling in front of them, cradling the human form on the ground. Now, the clouds which were their followers from the Tiered Nations swelled and adopted a lightly scarlet hue. They towered over the pale woman they'd found, and Soo-yeon winced as she stared up at the foreboding heaven's before speaking to the rest of them gathered there: "She's alive." She wiped mud from the unconscious woman's face, and Soo-yeon remembered the exodus of Wyrms from the Tiered Nations, the goddess-creature to evacuate them to salvation, and the image she had seen of the girl in the midst of that savior's gargantuan form. "I've seen her before," Soo-yeon continued. "She's badly injured." Puncture wounds, bright red with exposed muscle which still trickled blood, marked the upper-left side of her abdomen, and three fingers of one hand had been blown off. "Gunshot wounds," Soo-yeon said. "We have to help her."

"Doesn't look like a 'her,'" Fox called from his safe distance, away from the dragon, but he had dared to come a bit closer. He nodded at the naked genitals of the woman, for she bore the traits of both genders.

Soo-yeon doffed the robe of her military uniform. Beneath it, she wore linen trousers and a silk *dudou* – an ancient-style halter top with string ties in the back – to cover her frontside. The silk robe she put over the albino woman's bare frame. Soo-yeon took her in her arms and gathered her legs beneath herself to lift the smaller woman. "I'm taking her back to the carriage. There has to be a first aid kit there."

"Speak with her, Thad," Hadryn said, trying to guide his friend, for he disliked the thread and knots of tension growing betwixt the creature and the Royal Guard, as they measured one another subconsciously mirroring each other in bodily intention.

Haltingly, Thaddius declared: "I did not come to speak with a beast." And, she brought the rifle to her shoulder to steady an aim on the Drake.

At this, the Pyrolite cried out and knocked both Thaddius and Hadryn to the ground, her head swinging upwards.

Soo-yeon turned with the woman still in her arms and yelled, "Help them, Fox!" But, the other Knight was petrified by the instinct to preserve his own life.

Hadryn threw out his arms to protect the Royal Guard, for the dragon came at her with teeth glinting, and though the Knight cast aside the creature's muzzle once, then twice, the Drake succeeded in catching hold at the long-ness of Thaddius' robe. The red dragon pulled, then with a toss of her head, she catapulted Thaddius to the embrace of the darkening empyrean. Thaddius was screaming.

Hadryn shot to his feet. "Thaddius!!" He searched the skies for her and found her figure falling rapidly towards death. *"Thad! Thad!"* Alarm surging in all his limbs, Hadryn aligned himself as best he could to mitigate the impact of her fall. It was then the Pyrolite gathered momentum beneath her flights and soared to swipe the Royal Guard into one of her clawed hands.

And, she flew away. Thaddius' rifle dropped to the ground and knocked a clean shot into the air. Following that was nothing more than the quiet evening, staring and unseeing of all that had taken place. The winged creature disappeared with the Royal Guard.

"Thaddius," Hadryn said to himself. He began to walk forward, the way the dragon had gone, but Soo-yeon was at his side to stop him.

"Get in the van." Her gaze held his. She had one arm under the albino woman's weight to support her who had awakened and clung to the Korean Knight, her arms around Soo-yeon's neck. "We'll follow them in the carriage," Soo-yeon said to Hadryn. "She wouldn't hurt Merlone." Hadryn nodded, and they returned to the vehicle, setting the headlights aglow. Not needing them, they discarded the oxygen tanks, and continued the way they'd been headed.

They drove and soon came within view of a collection of neglected temples. Farther in the distance, across a bridge spanning a river, a terrible conflagration the size of a volcano erupted in the evening-hued hour, and the force of its burning came without end.

CHAPTER 29

WAR

Ardyce didn't feel herself falling, only a gradation of thoughts that what was about to take place was happening much too quickly, and that this tempo had come to claim her because there was one who meant to extinguish her soul.

And, Rage then arrived, crowned in the iron diadem of Hatred.

The Great Aegis saw her vision sink away, as though disappearing down a deep well, and every fiber of muscle that was strung in her to comprise her being ached as sered wood, the likes of which venerable trees experience just before the ends of their reign and they have no more of living. This was how Ardyce may have died, with Peace threatening for her the bliss of Forever Breathlessness.

But, the Great Aegis opened her shadow eyes, and she screamed the cries of blood-wrath. With that, her skin cracked, like a mirror struck in disdain by the beholder, to reveal beneath her thickened scales grim-fire which burns as white flames. Its heat exceeded the temperature of any fire of Earth. Lesser gods of old had been known to barter their immortality for the tyranny which is grim-fire – for some, the seduction of unchallenged power outweighed the need for eternity.

Now, the Tree Crown who should not have possessed the element of Fire released from her jaws the slaying of incineration. The sheer power of the expulsion subsided her descent, and she righted herself to advantage her wings for flight.

Beneath the conical downpour of her besotted revenge, none were shown mercy. Those directly beneath the Tree Crown received the initial blast, and the essence of them was instantly reduced to embers. Then, might they all have died, except that the firebreathers gave resistance.

In that crowded vale, housing both Wyrms and Drakes, with War acting as a mirror cursed by Truth to reveal to each individual the self who lived within, something else was discovered. It was something ancient, much older than Hatred. It was Hatred's opposite.

For upon the next fraction of the same moment which the grim-fire came, the character of those belonging to the umbra nation manifested. The people of The Nocturnes drew to action, as if of one mind. Firecraws and Pyrolites sped towards the hellfire vortex to stand against that ravenous eruption, and they extended their flights to net the blazing that would kill any other species. By quick succession, they formed a ring to contain the destruction and endured, second by second, the white inferno lashing at their bodies and wings.

Daofeng, who hovered far above the Tree Crown he had meant to kill, cried out. *"No!!"*

Then, came their screaming, for grim-fire is not a flame belonging to either house of the Firecraws or Pyrolites. Naturally, they are immune to the fires of this world, but grim-fire is an element owned by none but the timeless Scourge Angel.

Wave after wave came. Those with the visages of skulls held – to the last Drake of them. Not one fell, even as her or his vessel was burned away by layers. Torturous was their end which saved everyone else of that sward.

Ardyce finally landed, and the white fire ceased, leaving sudden blindness, in the eyes of those surviving, from the abrupt absence of that glaring heat. By sound alone, the Drakes and

Wyrms left alive heard as each Firecraw or Pyrolite fell to the earth to become charred soil in a realm not their home, but a land which would harbor their yielded souls forever.

That was how every adult firebreather perished, save but two – one a Pyrolite, the other a Firecraw.

When Sasithorn had gone to her friend, who was falling through the welkin, she had not understood what it meant when she saw Ardyce's integument become patched and laced with white fire. But, Dreyon and Lynelis knew, and they had charged her to shield and protect her, tumbling out of reach of the blast zone. They had meant well, but Sasithorn had watched as Dayraven below them was engulfed in the fiery torrent.

She fell in a heap, with Dreyon and Lynelis, to the ground. They gathered themselves slowly, turning towards the event, and all others, as well, were but lingering, or just arriving to the remains of the sacrificial firebreathers. They were delayed to comprehension, as they stared at blackened bones.

The Tree Crown - with her head pronged in sharpened steel, with her darkness-body seething from fissures the color of star collapse, with her breath the damnation of grim-fire – she stood in the clearing of death she'd created, stately. She appeared unaffected or unknowing of her sanguinary actions.

As it was that Paradox had come, too, to this day, uninvited, so was it answered by seeming irony: a Wyrm, those unfamiliar to spoken words, uttered brokenly, "Why? Whatsoever would possess them to do this?" And, it was he who began proper grieving, for he came forward to the bodies from his grouping of other Wyrms. Behind these Wyrms were naught of Drakes, same at other sections of the perimeter The Nocturnes' residents had created, thus it was abundantly clear their declaration was that *all* were intended to be rescued. The Wyrm who had spoken stood close to the piled bones of his protector and bowed his head. He touched his forehead to the skull of the deceased Firecraw and closed his eyes.

The Drakes all stared at this; there were other-worldly thoughts and feelings in their breasts. Other Wyrms were asking of each other, "Why?" and there was no answer. It was nonsensical that this had taken place in the middle of a war.

"Dayraven?" Sasithorn asked herself, and without consent, a searching of hope, and the bitter feelings of a widow began. She strained to see through the haze of smoke, which tarried like wandering phantoms. Scenes previously lost to her stepped forward, as if from around a corner, and Memory of her life as a human was revealed. She remembered losing Dayraven the first time. She made wishes and pleas within herself, the very same as she had when she was human and Dayraven had been banished from the Tiered Nations.

As a woman, a Royal Guard, she had not been answered. She had gone to public execution for her crimes, never knowing what became of Dayraven. Her last thought, as a human being, was a wish for Dayraven to live, to survive. The last image she saw was Ardyce, bent over upon the floor to weep for her. Then, Sasithorn had died or believed she had.

Sasithorn eased forward, through the patchwork smoke, in her Mungkr body, saying in a soft voice: "Go on, you fanatic of the Archfiend. Resist. Change everything. Once, again." And, the wetness that is sorrow fell from her eyes, because those of the umbra nation were no more, and therefore, Dayraven could not either be.

She shut her eyes against the last of that thought. But, opened them when a voice came, filling the air and overwhelming the evening, which stood, quivering.

"Continue," said the Tree Crown to those left of the Scourge Angel's army. They numbered some 200 Drakes, much more than Daofeng's now-diminished band of fifty-odd Wyrms and Drakes.

But, no one moved, feeling the ghosts of those firebreathers left in a ring of bones.

Ardyce walked forward. With her bladed coronet sweeping low to the ground, she minced the Wyrm nearest to her reach, and the Wyrm was he who had given his respects to the dead Firecraw. He was murdered quickly, emitting only an inarticulate sound of pain. *"Continue,"* Ardyce ordered them. "The Dilong's followers first, then the Wyrms. It is *his* command."

The populace of that pasture drew back a couple of paces, still very much stunned, except for the great, azure Dilong, who was now returned to earth. He spoke to the Tree Crown, though his gaze would not leave the dead. "We, all of us here, are not charmed by the Reaper, therefore, we do not wish for the death of our sisters and brothers, whether they fly or crawl. It is unnatural to desire this. The children of The Nocturnes acted upon our deepest instinct: something of the heart, not the debating mind. In the rarest, most urgent moment, they chose, unanimously. Might we honor them with a shred of bravery to equal theirs?"

The moon crowned the night. By increments, there was a taproot growing to connect every vein of thought, and sixty-six Drakes defected from the court of Ardyce and the Scourge Angel. They went and stood at the shoulders of Daofeng's Wyrms and Drakes.

Ardyce glowered at them. *"Kill them all,"* she said.

Daofeng was solemn and staid of resolve, as he said, "Kill the Tree Crown."

His people, on the ready, meteor-struck the vale, in operation by strategy and a dauntless conviction. They were swift and clean, opening up bodies to bid vital organs descend to the loam. Ten of Ardyce's charges were fallen within seconds, as the first unit of Daofeng's army, the Longs and Mungkrs, went looping and spiraling through the air, manes of color dancing. They dispatched a row of Ryuu, who guarded the black Tree Crown's flank, by physical prowess, alone: with jaws and talons, or by suffocated lungs or broken bones. The Mungkrs wove their snaking bodies around the smaller Ryuu Drakes and flexed their strength or bent their enemies' bodies to angles unforgiving.

With that opening made, the Longs belonging to Daofeng's allegiance drove to engage that dark General. The wish of Daofeng was to end Ardyce speedily, so that the spirit of her warriors would wane to peaceable surrender. The Longs came on their waterways, the waves churning beneath them and trailing out behind their whirling figures, just as the rains have always heeded the behest of the Chinese Drakes. In the swell of the waters, hidden, rode the Water Wyrms as concealed assassins.

Another subsection of Ryuu soldiers came, then, to replace those cut down, but Daofeng's Murgkrs held the defense, clashing mightily with them.

By pincer technique, as much for distraction, as to stall efforts to reinforce the new wave of Ryuu, the large, pale Armored Wyrms attacked Ardyce's opposite flank of warriors. There, they gridlocked with the handful of Tree Crown Drakes in service to Ardyce.

It was a brawl of brutish spectacle, this contention between Armored Wyrms and Tree Crown Drakes. The Drakes' preferred method quickly became a reliance on their branched headpieces, aiming for the soft joints between sections of carapace-growth on the Wyrms, or for the eyes of them, or through the roofs of their opened mouths. In return, the plated Wyrms utilized their brawn, their size and weight, to club the Tree Crowns most ferociously, swinging their heavy heads and tails. It was a gruesome sight to see the pale Wyrms gouged and the antlered Drakes fustigated unto death.

Sasithorn saw that Ardyce was absorbed by the confrontation of Armored Wyrms and Tree Crowns. Whether it was because she still regarded the Tree Crowns her own kind and felt herself still their Great Aegis, or because the pale Wyrms had drawn near to her person, beating back the ones with antlers who were fewer in numbers, the attention of the darkness-Tree Crown was held. Ardyce crushed underfoot the Armored Wyrms she could, the crepitating of their shells making a most chilling earful within the pandemonium of the glen. She did not see, at her other side, Daofeng's Longs, upon their streams of rain waters extracted from the skies, closing in.

Sasithorn charged through the dell that was sickening with bloody welts, as either side labored to end the other, and she was a streak of jade coloration past them all to intervene just as the Water Wyrms were powerfully disgorged from the riding waves. With her tail and the newness of her broad and dense encirclement, she struck aside two of the Wyrms as they launched, airborne, towards Ardyce. Their circular mouths opened frightfully wide.

The assault, though, was well-coordinated, for three of the finned Wyrms whipped beyond Sasithorn to find different marks upon the Tree Crown's massive frame, latching onto her with hooked teeth: two at her throat and one at her belly, points where the toughness of her hide did not extend.

At first, the black Tree Crown did not notice the Water Wyrms, much smaller than her, adhered to her skin, then she released a cry, as the Wyrms vomited corrosive acid, which served to reduce the Wyrm's victims to slush inside, so that they may slurp the innards turned to puree. Again, Ardyce roared. Her skin where they were attached was melted away, and next, the Wyrms bored into heavy muscle. The head of the Wyrm at Ardyce's belly disappeared into her body.

Sasithorn drove her teeth into the Wyrm's back to halt its invasion into the Tree Crown's stomach. She sought to coil herself around its length, but the Longs who had come with those Water Wyrms stopped her, pulling and clawing at her. As she fought them, the darkened Tree Crown thrashed with the searing pain beneath her integument.

I will not lose you, my friend, Sasithorn swore inwardly, and she looked up to see her silent plea attended to by Lynelis and Dreyon, who combined their efforts to tear away one of the Water Wyrms from Ardyce's throat. The pair of them were soon knocked away by Ardyce's wild attempts to dislodge the last Wyrm at her neck. That Wyrm had already driven half its body into the cavity it created in the Tree Crown's throat, and Ardyce threw back her head as the grim-fire sputtered in her maw, unable to come forth.

Deftly, Sasithorn shrunk away from the Great Aegis, aware before the Longs who attacked her that Ardyce was reaching with one of her clawed hands to scrape the Water Wyrm from herself. In doing so, the mighty she-Drake rent the Wyrm and Longs to pieces. A talon of Ardyce's clipped Sasithorn, scratching along the gold ornament wrapped around her being, then the threat of her bladed hand had passed, and the Mungkr removed what remained of the Wyrm from Ardyce's wound. A steaming stream of blood and liquified muscle erupted from the burrow left in the Tree Crown's underside.

Sasithorn hastened herself, flying upwards to overcome Ardyce's height and reach the Great Aegis' neck. The jade-colored Drake chanced a glance at Daofeng, who monitored the field of strife with his titan-like counsel. She knew he was weighing the outcomes, withholding, for now, those at his side to reserve their size and strength for their original ambition of murdering the Scourge Angel.

Sasithorn caught the eye of the Dilong, and he addressed her. "Why do you fight for her, Ngaw of the Mungkr tribe? She will never, again, be herself."

Sasithorn dodged one of Ardyce's frantic wings and clenched her teeth to stay on course. She ignored the Dilong, as the last Water Wyrm crept into the side of Ardyce's gullet, and the Tree Crown began to spit up crimson essence from her mouth. She was choking.

The Mungkr flew passed where the Wyrm had made entry into the blackened Drake to come to level with the gaping pits of the Tree Crown's eyes. She swam in Ardyce's vision, demanding her attention.

"Keep still, friend," Sasithorn instructed the Great Aegis. "I will now hurt you, yet you trust me. You always have." The gargantuan Drake gurgled blood, but said nothing. She stared at the Mungkr. "Ardyce," Sasithorn demanded.

Sasithorn? The questioning was delayed and telepathic, but it was undoubtedly Ardyce's voice. Sasithorn realized Ardyce may no longer have use of her vocal chords, due to the Wyrm's offense.

At the same time, the Mungkr almost had to swallow a delirious laugh of relief, feeling as though her friend was not so far lost as others had assumed. "I will help you," she said to the Tree Crown, and left her gaze to go to the breach in Ardyce's neck, which was widening as the Wyrm thrashed inside.

Sasithorn paused a moment for true aim, then she thrust her head into the aperture of flayed skin and destroyed meat.

Ardyce did not remain still.

The Tree Crown gagged on pain and blood, stooping forward. Sasithorn was larger than the Water Wyrm, and the gilded helm on her head felt like a sizeable rock being driven into Ardyce's burning injury. The Great Aegis fought to keep upright.

Sasithorn's face and head were awash in the blood of her friend. She could not see or breathe. It came to her, then, how dangerous this surgery may prove, and of the same instant, she reached with her teeth and caught hold a mouthful of Wyrm.

Yanking backwards, the Mungkr heaved with all her power to unearth the Wyrm from flesh. She and the parasite came free of gore, and Sasithorn heard the high-pitched ululation of the Wyrm, as it fell, being incapable of flight.

Ardyce staggered, bearing her weight upon one wing bent to the ground for support, and Sasithorn felt they might be able to go home to Outer Gled Tria and Gled Tria together. But, Sasithorn was suddenly ensnared. That circular mouth of the Water Wyrm caught at her before the Wyrm had completely fallen away, and with its added weight, she could not right herself for flight. Then, the acid came, haunting at her nerves. Sasithorn was beaten back from consciousness by that torment, so immeasurable as it was. She felt her stomach thrown to all directions at once with panic. She felt the skies rushing away from her. She felt the greed of gravity and the promise of her skull and body dashed to fragments.

Then, she felt softness. It was light as feathers, and there were arms to enfold her.

She hadn't thought Death would be so seductive. It made her think of the many nights she'd spent tucked away in Dayraven's embrace, when they wore human forms. It had been luxurious, and this moment was not so far off from that.

Sasithorn opened her eyes.

She was lowered to the ground. Then, she saw Dayraven, and he was ever more fantastical each time she was reunited of the same person. He was plumed in his night-colored feathers, his snout more like a beak, and his asp-like body adorned in sleek, pebbled skin, but there was a strangeness to him. From his upper-half, where the feathers covered him, two appendages had emerged. They were black in hue to reflect the rest of his body.

Sasithorn watched as he went to the Wyrm who was still hooked to her frame. He took hold of the Wyrm by its mouth and forced the jaws past their limit to break open its hold of Sasithorn. The Wyrm screamed and fell away, and Dayraven returned near to her face, tucking his hands and arms back into his plumage to conceal them, again.

Sasithorn was staring at him, for the limbs were unmistakably enormous human-like arms and hands. She blinked. "You are a most queer dream," she said. Then, she realized: "You are alive, Dayraven!"

He coiled around her to cradle her. "I am impressed as well. It seems the elements do hamper Serpents, but there is not a halting, altogether, of life."

"A Serpent?" she asked, much confused. Then, she said, "Of course. How could you be a Wyrm or a Drake?" And, there was adoration in her eyes.

He was staring back at her. "We haven't much time, my lady in taffeta. I need you to make a most dire decision, and that is to abandon your precious friend. Please, I beg you. She cares not if you die at her side, and I will not have that Sasithorn."

She parted herself of him. "The last I knew, you were not choosing my friendships," she stated.

"*Sasithorn*," he entreated her.

"Serpent." Daofeng's voice came across the clearing. Beside him stood the black Wyrm of his self-made Counsel. "Leave the Mungkr. Allow those who have elected Death to fulfill their fates. Your destiny is more urgent than this."

Sasithorn looked from the Dilong to Dayraven.

Dayraven pleaded, "Leave Ardyce to this hamlet, where she will be or not be, as she chooses."

The Mungkr of jade and gold ornamentation was staring at the hunched figure of her friend. By the moon's light, Sasithorn watched as a red and heated cataract poured from Ardyce's neck; there was nothing the Tree Crown could do to end the bleeding out. She said to the Serpent, "You have that which you know and understand; I have mine. Do what you must, as will I. I will follow my wish and that is but to protect those I love. Follow yours."

Dayraven lowered his gaze from her, drawing closer to her. "Make your choice. I will make mine," Dayraven said to her who he had read poetry with late into the star-filled hours.

Sasithorn stared at him, then blinked, looking sad. She weaved away from him, peering back once.

Dayraven felt Sasithorn's words in his chest. He wanted to go to her. He resisted. Before she had departed the range of hearing, he said, "I should have married you before I died as a human."

There were, now, Earth-fallowers and Death Wyrms closing in on Ardyce.

The Mungkr was silent, then honest with him of the things which took place after Dayraven had been ostracized. "I married you, even though you had died. The petition was signed by half of the government officials, who would afterwards renounce their royal offices. They, like me, were sentenced to death by the remainder of the officials. Curiously though, I remember each of them dying happily."

She flickered away.

She left Dayraven feeling the Past and the weight of the Present.

At a distance, Mei Xian and Eryx had climbed up through the veinwork of the nether city and stood with Naehska to see War without the mask of words and ideals. It was more hideous than they could ever fathom.

CHAPTER 30

A LITTLE LIFE

"Back away!"

The crimson Pyrolite watched as a rock sailed past her right side.

Thaddius held part of a tree limb, waving it. The Drake tried to catch the branch in her mouth, but the Royal Guard was quick to pull it from her reach. Thaddius glanced to her sides to see she was alone with the creature, and her heart thudded blood which suddenly seemed too thick for her veins. She blinked away the rearing of a migraine and knew she could halt its advance, if she could only keep the fantastical alien from her view. Thaddius peered over her shoulder at what must have been a temple in previous times, but was now mostly moss shaped into rectangular puzzle pieces, which just barely fit together. She wondered if she should run to the structure to take cover from the dragon, least it breathe fire or attempt, again, to fly off with her.

"Thaddius," said the creature.

The African woman's breathing came hard, creating fleeting bursts of mist at her mouth in the night air. She did not turn to face the winged animal. "Do not use the voice of my wife, beast," Thaddius warned.

"You know me." The words tapered to a soft trill, yet no longer strange was the cadence or the gentle roundness of that utterance. Even in her sleep, Thaddius would know that voice if it whispered to her from miles away.

The Royal Guard threw down the tree branch angrily. "I know nothing of what you are! Or, why you've done this!"

"I didn't choose this, Thaddius! But, it happened!"

"You are *not* LeShawn!" Thaddius cried out, into the darkness. "LeShawn could never be a thing as you are!"

The Pyrolite's burning mane was the only answer to the silence which extended between them. Then, the Drake said, "You would erase me to yourself? Desert me? Break your vows to me?"

Thaddius fell to her knees, grieving. *"LeShawn is dead."*

"Yes," the creature agreed. "Murdered by the words of her wife, driven to extinction by denial of the only one she trusted."

"Stop speaking!"

"And, disappear?" LeShawn asked.

"I did not say that," Thaddius answered, at war with herself. The threatening migraine bit at her, kneaded her grief to a cutting tone in her reply.

The Drake stared at her wife, who was brought to the ground, unable to stand in her new presence. By careful steps, she went to the human slowly. The winds danced, invisible yet tangible, in the night air. LeShawn stretched her neck to touch her muzzle to the Royal Guard's back.

"Accept me," LeShawn coaxed.

But, Thaddius was only shaking her head, as tears ran down her cheeks.

"If I had been maimed and disfigured, lost a limb, or if I had shifted my visible gender, as Hadryn did, still, I believe, you would continue to love me." LeShawn stared at her wife. "When the doctors diagnosed me, you were there, rooted at my side. You accepted that I had cancer, listened to every miserable word as they described my medication, my treatments – my early death to come. Still, you didn't leave me for it."

Thaddius gaped, clawing for her thoughts. "Cancer is foreseeable in our society. We know it exists."

LeShawn paused, as those words seeped too deeply within. "You would rather I had died from the cancer than become this."

Thaddius was wretched. "How can you say such a horrid thing! *No.* Never would I wish for that." Her words broke from within, chipping like eggshells whose time was due.

"Then, accept that I have changed." The Drake moved closer to the human. "I do not feel it – *the cancer* – in this body, Thaddius. *I am free of it.* This is my second chance for life. It is unpleasant-looking, but do we choose Life only when it is pretty?" She touched the Royal Guard again, as the African woman turned to face her.

But, Thaddius would not look at her. *"I cannot, LeShawn.* You changed … too much."

LeShawn refused her words in her heart, and she told Thaddius, truthfully, "We so often do not get to choose how – in what way – our loved ones will change."

Thaddius had drawn a knife from her boot, the very same she'd used to quiet Pelena unto death. The blade gleamed, like another set of eyes; the only gaze that could look LeShawn in the face. It glinted in the Drake's eyes as Thaddius spoke. *"Forgive me, my wife,"* the Royal Guard said, crying, and she brought the blade to her own throat. *"I can't, so it is Death I must choose, instead, rather than live a deceiver to the vows I've promised you."* Thaddius began to draw the sharpness across herself.

"Stop!!" LeShawn screamed, but blood had come forth. "If you do!" she cried, "You have ended me as well, for I will not be without you, Thad!"

The Royal Guard's hold of the knife quivered. She said, "Tell me why you brought me here."

The dragon paused. She was completely still and quiet for a moment. Then, she gave her answer. "You hadn't changed in the Tiered Nations. Outside of it – here – I thought, perhaps, you would."

"You wish for me to become a monster?" There was accusation in her tone. "How absurd. How revolting. Do you think I will shed this skin to something beautiful, as you are? *I will be a crawling one, LeShawn. You know this."*

The Pyrolite stared at her with her bottomless gaze. "And, I will love you, even still."

"No!" Thaddius yelled, against this thought. She gripped the handle of the blade longingly, terrified at the possibility she would become a creature of the soil.

"You're right," LeShawn said quickly. "Why did this happen to us? It *is* revolting. *It is horror, my love; you are absolutely correct.* But, look." She turned her gaze out, beyond the lopsided temples and the river which ran out to the sea. There, in a far-reaching dell, were hordes of creatures – abnormal to reality or logic. They were in full abuse of vitality; they had to them speed and strength. Their presence took up more space than there was capacity in this world. They were like every dangerous thought come to life to vie for belief and validation in the eyes of a formerly-sane society. "Everyone," LeShawn continued, "has changed. So, the *world* has changed, Thaddius."

The Royal Guard made her claim: "This isn't the world I want."

"I understand," LeShawn said.

"I cannot change."

"I accept this. And, you." The Drake nudged the knife towards the human's throat. She brought a claw to her breast, and LeShawn slid open the skin and muscle which protected her heart. She was ready, now, to reach into herself and pull the life out.

Thaddius watched the blood flow from the incision made. It landed at the Royal Guard's feet.

"Before we do this," LeShawn spoke to her wife. "Tell me, Thaddius Merlone. Say it. You owe me that much."

"Say what?" Thaddius asked, bewildered. Her heart was racing, preparing for their end.

"Say that you could not love me as I am."

The African woman blinked back her tears, full of hatred. She despised where she now stood: a life she'd labored so hard for and invested everything of herself in was gone in less than a day. She wished for more hatred from herself, but in her thoughts were a memory, and she saw herself placing a ring on LeShawn's finger. *"I can't,"* she repeated.

The knife Thaddius held fell to the ground.

"I can't ... say that." Thaddius finished her words.

Then, the Royal Guard tipped forward, losing sight for blackness, losing breath. The migraine came as oblivion, instead, and when Thaddius awoke, she was no longer as she once knew herself. She had lost everything to gain everything.

The head lamps of the van tilted upwards to trace the ends of the sky, as it came up over the rise of another slope, then the vehicle trekked its way down, away from the view of the coastline. It hit a firmly-packed ridge, shimmied over it, like an uncertain toddler, and scraped underside before finally leaving the rudimentary path, which paralleled the shoreline. In the sky, the string of clouds which seemed to pursue them had all turned blood-red. Hadryn drove the carriage into the grasslands, sinking and rising with their uncertain ship over uneven ground. Lightning flashed briefly all around them.

"His driving is awful," Fox commented. "Why isn't she talking?" He gestured to the albino woman. "Make her say something, Soo-yeon." The Knight of Fifth Rank was agitated. He hadn't liked seeing Thaddius, one of them – a human – snatched away by a winged nightmare. "Ask her something." He nodded, but didn't look at the woman they'd found. "She creeps me out."

Soo-yeon kicked Fox in the shin. She reached over to the passenger seat and touched the woman's arm. The woman stirred awake, still holding at the bandages wrapped around her torso with her good hand. Her blood was coming through the wraps, staining a red sun across the midsection of her frame.

"What's your name?" Soo-yeon asked her.

Chinami read Soo-yeon's lips, then spelled her name with one hand.

"A mute?" Fox observed. "Oh, that isn't spooky either. Just like this weather." He glanced out a window of the vehicle.

The Knight Jo reached over and tried to slap Fox for his sarcasm, but he dodged her hand. "Her name is 'Chinami,'" Soo-yeon told the rest of them.

"Could you ask her what happened to her?" Hadryn kept his eyes ahead, just barely able to see by the light of the van. He tried to keep his head clear, but fear over what had become of Thaddius was catching, like wildfire, and threatening to burn everything down. He looked to the pale-haired woman beside himself. "Are you alright? I'm sorry the ride is so jolting." Her eyes reading his lips were a half-transparent pink, like the burst blood vessels, and her pupils, a smoky cinnabar hue.

Chinami signed to Hadryn, as Soo-yeon watched.

"She thanked us for helping her."

Fox cut in. "I feel that we don't have time for pleasantries, personally. I mean, we found her out in the middle of nowhere, passed out and bleeding." He was ranting now. "We're the last humans we know of, and we're chasing monsters, because apparently, that's what people do when the world has turned into beasts. Like some kind of self-invoked punishment. But, we're innocent; we don't have to do this." He sighed. "And, Hadryn, how do you even know where you're going?"

"I saw LeShawn go this way," he answered simply. "Besides, *they* are *us*. The 'monsters.' You've seen that, Fox."

Soo-yeon had been signing with Chinami, as the others carried on. She felt sorry for the young woman, who struggled, at times, with her hand that was missing three fingers. Soo-yeon said to the others, "I'm not getting very much from her. I don't think she's up to speaking. She's only said that she became sleepy. She went to sleep."

Chinami was staring at Soo-yeon, gazing at her as though she were a memory. Chinami spoke with her hands to the Knight Jo: *You're the singer. I saw your song.*

Soo-yeon stared at the younger woman, confused. She brought to mind her habit of going to the 11th District to practice sign language, the same memory when she'd first seen this girl as creature queen. *Were you there?* Soo-yeon signed to the ivory-haired woman, and Chinami nodded.

Fox was indignant. "So, now we're naming the creatures!" he yelled at Hadryn.

"I'm sure the winged one is Thaddius' wife. Why else would she take her?" The Knight Archidux chanced a brief look over his shoulder at Fox. "You're free to get out, Luciano. Walk home to your empty house, probably go mad before you Make the Ring and become a Wyrm. But, some of us are tied to those 'monsters.' I can't leave Thaddius. I can't leave Oshin, alone in herself. She was following what we thought were 'deaths' for a reason."

There was nothing Fox could say to this. He looked out a window, silently. The carriage hit a large rock, then rolled over it, gaining momentum for a few seconds.

"Wait, Hadryn. Stop," Soo-yeon said, speaking softly from the back of the carriage, but Hadryn had already slowed the vehicle, and they stared at what was before them.

In a clearing, like a stage partly-wreathed in trees and hillocks, stood two titans of outlandish configuration. They were a likeness to the one who'd taken Thaddius: the shape of dragons. One stood, staring at the other from across the distance of the sward, and the other appeared impaired by damaging affliction. At their feet, wrestled their myrmidon in treacherous deadlock: they were every imagination of winged or crawling motion, mighty and baleful, and their tenacity came as delivering fantastical destruction. The humans watching could not determine allegiances, or those of the same side or opposite, but a war it seemed by all accounts. They saw that some most certainly perished, before their eyes, and every being was of decision and action all their own. It was not the indolent, self-gratifying Tiered Nations which had feasted away, mind-numbingly, upon one's own health and longevity. Here, every being was much too awake to, any longer, eat away themselves; they were each imbued with Life, even if the risk was possibly Death. As animated as an individual rain droplet, they each came together to create a storm of the new world of monsters.

"'I lied to them,'" Soo-yeon translated.

The young woman of pale hue had risen in her seat, clearly anxious and despairing. Soo-yeon stared at her and saw in her eyes how she was not as they were. She was beyond human, and though frail as she was, there was a certain magnificence in her bearing and radiating from her semi-pellucid skin and eyes. Soo-yeon became afraid for her.

The sky had darkened, and the clouds heralded in the night and its secrets.

Chinami kept signing, almost speaking to herself, but Soo-yeon was translating her, as all eyes watched the pair of them.

"'I lied to them, as any god would. I thought it would help them to survive. If, they fought back. If, they killed the ... Drakes? (I think she means the flying creatures.) Then, they wouldn't all die. I thought. I was wrong. Always wrong. I couldn't save them. I can't. I must, though.'" Suddenly, the girl turned, and Chinami yanked, in earnest, at the passenger door, then figured out how to open it.

"Wait!" Soo-yeon grabbed her by the arm. She had to release her to sign to her. "How did you lie to them? The worms?" She thought of the many creatures following a goddess who had stacked rows of eyes. Then, she said, "Don't go. It's too dangerous."

Chinami paused to stare at Soo-yeon, as if they were the only ones there. She stared for so long that Soo-yeon felt the same for a moment. Then, Soo-yeon blinked away from her blush-colored gaze.

"She's crazy," Fox announced.

Chinami's eyes darted to the rest of them of that van, then wandered away to return to Soo-yeon. She answered the Korean woman. Soo-yeon spoke the words Chinami signed. "'I told them that if they ate Drakes, they would become one.'"

Fox laughed loudly. "That is disgusting and ridiculous." He watched the scene before them, feeling nauseated with terror. "What are we looking at?" They were close enough to see gruesome details of the creatures' encounters. "Why are they fighting?"

"Human nature?" Hadryn guessed, allowing the paradox to stand, for they were monsters pulled from their human parallels.

Chinami read their lips by turns, shifting in her seat to view either speaker. Her eyes rested for several seconds on Soo-yeon, then Hadryn in knowing she had crossed paths with them each once before. She shook her head at Hadryn's estimation, and her hands moved slowly; the focus of her gaze dimmed. Soo-yeon read aloud the words Chinami made. "'It has never been human nature. It is the influence of the gods which possess Earth's children to purge blood. I think ... gods are dirtied by immortality." Chinami glanced at each of them, envious. "'A little life is purity.'" The strange girl touched Hadryn's shoulder, so that he met her gaze. She traced her fingertips from his right temple to his cheek, staring at his eye of niveous brilliance. The color, and the ring it was, filled her vision. She felt a separate sphere rising overhead to outdo the Sun upon day, and at night, to house with glowing, celestial cinders. Thus, the Conqueror knew and recognized the Knight from before when Plodd had presented him to her.

In the rafters of the heavens, the clouds spoke with thunder, and Hadryn, Fox, and Soo-yeon glanced at the shifting of the night.

Chinami's voice issued forth, the shape of her words lacking form, and yet her voice was a specific, indescribable comfort as well as androgynous in tone. She said to Hadryn who looked to her, "Go home, boy with an eye of pearl. Live a little life."

Hadryn stared at her, confused, then his gaze was drawn to the thunderheads which floated. They were tinted red, and he didn't know why. Chinami's voice was softer this time: "You can still have that with her. She approaches. Somehow, she rises. Within me, too, I feel it. No, *because* of me. But, she will not Be the Ring, unless you go first. Resist it and you both may remain human." She smiled at him, and she spoke the truth to him.

"Whatever human may be." In his mind, Hadryn thought he asked her what she meant, but he never heard his own words.

Then, Chinami's eyes were on the field of battles. She traced individuals with her gaze, then she leapt from the van, landing barefoot in the grass.

"Chinami, don't!" Soo-yeon threw open the back doors of the carriage.

"Just let her go, Soo-yeon," Fox said. "What do we care? We don't even know who she is."

Soo-yeon looked at the other Knight, wondering for a second if she was overreacting. "But, she's hurt." She ran after the younger woman.

"Don't lie!" Fox yelled, irritated. "You think she's cute!"

Soo-yeon caught up to Chinami, standing in front of her. "I don't understand," she told the albino woman. "What are you going to do?"

The shorter woman was touching her bandages, again. For several seconds, it seemed she hesitated to sign what she did next: *You care.*

The Knight stumbled over herself, then she admitted. "I do. I don't want you to be hurt any worse than you already are."

Chinami's gestures read, *But, we are strangers.* She was unsure of herself, in talking with the other woman. Chinami realized she hadn't spoken to anyone human, besides her family members.

Soo-yeon replied, "The world is ending, so we are more than that." She risked a faint smile. "We're survivors." Then, she insisted. "Please, tell me. What are you going to do?"

The pale-haired woman answered, *I will kill … that one.* She pointed to Ardyce, who was beginning to regain herself. *She and her people have come for my Wyrms. I need to protect them. I am … the goddess.* Chinami confessed to her.

The Knight took her by the shoulders and pleaded with her. *"No. You don't have to be. You're a woman. Human. You don't have to do this. It's impossible, Chinami."*

In the van, Hadryn wasn't staring at Soo-yeon and Chinami as Fox was. Even the Japanese woman's words to him had been forgotten in this instant. He was looking elsewhere, abruptly rigid, and then, he threw open the driver's side door. "I see them." Hadryn left the carriage and was running across the open grassland before Fox could look over at his empty seat. Hadryn had spotted the crimson dragon by her fire-lit mane and she was no more than a quarter league away. He ran for her, for standing beside her was a figure he swore he knew.

"Shit," Fox cursed, watching the other Knight leave. He grabbed a high-powered rifle and left the carriage, running as well. He came near to where Soo-yeon and Chinami had paused. "Soo-yeon, come on!" And, he sprinted after Hadryn, assuming the Knight Jo was certain to trail after him.

Soo-yeon watched as Hadryn and Fox ran in closer towards the warring giants, nearly coming to the bridge which crossed the river and was the last to divide humans from preternatural entities, like a thin, brain synapse. The two of them veered right though, without traversing the bridge, and Soo-yeon could see the largeness of a Drake standing in the vicinity of time-razed structures, once belonging to humans. The temples were crumpled, like a furrowed brow.

Soo-yeon turned away from them. She saw that the albino woman had walked several feet away from her, and a franticness as well as an eerie tranquility pervaded Soo-yeon's being. Her need for asking questions, an attachment to the world she once knew, fell away, like the last particle of sand in an hour glass shattered by antiquity. She had followed Hadryn and Thaddius out of the Tiered Nations to know and knowing had found her in this teeming nightscape. Here, the creature of every person was drawn out, whether beautiful or dreadful, and each of all, in this lustrous phantasmagoria, had come to their own decision. Across the river, there were no more questions, only a deadly fight for Truth to be answered.

Soo-yeon stared at Chinami: the woman, the queen, and The Conqueror. Behind her, the multitude of clouds with their crimson tones had become one enormous mass, semi-transpicuous. Chinami knelt in the grass, trembling and holding herself. She had removed the robe Soo-yeon had given her to wear. When she lifted her face, there were a dozen of her pink eyes, blinking out from her forehead. They shimmered within thin films of moisture and roved as though untamed, each in their own individual manner. The earth beneath them shivered, as if from the cold of the night and the winds swirled upwards, as if to escape the earth's tribulation. Chinami's hair veiled her face in those dancing winds of chaos. Soo-yeon cried out to her, and all elements of perception and understanding accelerated for an eye-blink's worth of time, then everything slowed, and finally paused. In the space of one gentle sigh, perhaps it was Chinami's, a behemoth figure emerged, concealing or submerging the pale-skinned woman.

The Conqueror Wyrm hovered in the sky, breathing in broken gasps, and one of her appendages leaned into a window of the vehicle, which she and Soo-yeon had been standing near to. The pane of glass collapsed to shards without Chinami's intention. Then, the snow-white goddess spurted blood from her side and mouth. Her injuries were, still, direful. The form of The Conqueror dissipated, like a candlewick suddenly denied its warmth and luminance, and Chinami remained, hunched on the ground and crying out in vain anger. She clenched her jaw, then screamed a scream she couldn't hear, thinking of the Wyrms who were undoubtedly dying, just barely beyond her reach. She looked out, along the ground, to watch as walking feet approached her. Chinami lifted her face to the Korean woman, who now held a machine gun at her side.

Chinami signed to Soo-yeon because Soo-yeon was there, and the albino woman didn't want to feel alone. *I've become too human,* she said to Soo-yeon.

Soo-yeon spoke with both her hands and her voice: "If you are human, you are under my guard, for I am a Knight, and that is my duty." The black-haired woman loaded a clip into the firearm. From across the River Orb, she noticed Chinami had alerted the attention of one of the larger Drakes upon transforming into the queen, and the look in the creature's eyes unnerved Soo-yeon.

Her heart raced, and she braced herself as the dragon rushed towards them.

The red cloud above them crackled with threads of electrical current and Soo-yeon glanced back as it became a dark crimson color. Then, it vanished like an apparition caught in daylight. A dark figure slipped from the folds of the sky where the scarlet cloud had been and spilled to the ground.

Soo-yeon staggered and gaped at where the hovering cloud once was and the unmoving figure, sprawled on the soil. "Hey!" The Knight Jo called out, but there was no response. She couldn't see the face of the person, only ink-black hair. "Hadryn!" she screamed for the other Knight, but he was too far away.

CHAPTER 31

A WORLD OF MONSTERS

Daofeng crushed a Mungkr belonging to Ardyce's forces in his palm and threw aside the remains. He signaled for the last two of the Water Wyrms to his army to come to him and when they did, he asked for them to seek out the Angel of Scourge and report back the location of the god. "We haven't time for this," Daofeng muttered to himself as the finned Wyrms left, availing the River Orb for quicker transport. They slipped into the waters like lost thoughts, and the Dilong returned his attention to the acrid war he wished would end. Each battle was like a muscle contracted, trembling with power, until the spill of blood or innards forced the sinews of life slack. He stilled himself for wanting to rush into the mesh of it, knowing who his strength was in reservation for – and there were two of them.

Bitterness stewed in the Dilong's gaze, watching the raven-feathered Serpent. He caught view of Eryx and Mei Xian at the periphery of the events. "It does not rest well in your bellies to see a cemetery be born, does it? Have you changed your minds of the actions to which you will pledge yourself? I do not blame you. War is not for the sweet." He moved away from them, farther into the depths of ferocity.

Eryx turned to Mei Xian. There was sadness in her eyes. "I cannot fight in this."

Mei Xian was in shock of the terrible things which her eyes told her. She didn't think she could witness anymore of death; it had filled her throat with a dryness like sand meant to bury her. "We can't leave our own world," she said to the Wyrm.

The human with them stepped forward, then turned to them. "Or can you? Come with me. We needn't look on this."

The Tianlong watched the Serpent Daofeng had marked. He was a fitting, fantastical raven beast in a story she suddenly felt she knew nothing about. Then, Mei Xian did the only thing to make her detest herself. She rounded around to give her back to that horror progressing in its torment, and she saved herself the pain of it. She went after the Dreamer and Eryx went with her. The Tianlong thought to herself, *Why is there that which we must do and that of what we* will *do? Answer me this, Serpent.*

Dayraven sped towards an angle left unprotected of the black Tree Crown. From Daofeng's council of leviathans came the red Tree Crown to clash with Ardyce, creating a width of vulnerability where Ardyce could not possibly defend herself, as she quarreled with the other Tree Crown, who was also part-Pyrolite.

Shyandra, the Great Aegis named the scarlet Drake, remembering her of the Past. *Have you come, again, to attempt ownership of my title?* Ardyce frothed at the mouth, unable to emit words, given the Water Wyrms' assault, and she was, too, at a faltering consciousness after being poisoned during a brief confrontation with the black Wyrm who kept close to Daofeng's side. That Wyrm, slug-like in appearance, could produce a number of toxins from both her skin and as projectile-liquid from her mouth. She'd cast Ardyce to severe disorientation, then retreated hastily, and piece by piece, Daofeng's warriors sought to hale Ardyce to her doom.

Thus, Dayraven made for the dark Tree Crown's point of weakness. Above him, Sasithorn somehow managed to shield Ardyce from the jaws of two Earth-fallowers. She utilized the hard growths on her head and encircling her body to strike what teeth she could from the enormous Wyrms' mouths. Bloodied and tattered where the Earth-fallowers had caught at her with their dagger-like mouths, or smote her with the rigidity of their half-bone faces, Sasithorn was crumbling with exhaustion. She saw Dayraven aiming, like an arrow, for the Great Aegis' lower body, and inwardly, she pleaded with him, *Don't do this, Dayraven.* Wheeling around, and leaving herself exposed to the Wyrms, Sasithorn drew close to her friend's face. "Ardyce!" Sasithorn beseeched her. *"Return to us now!* Mohonia and your newborn daughter await you. There is nothing worth the price of never seeing them, again! Disencumber your heart of hatred and of the Angel of Scourge!"

The Great Aegis turned her gaping maw on Sasithorn, her neck a graceful arc and muscular and rushing with the power of a hundred waterfalls. By a mere foot, those jaws careened past Sasithorn and slammed into the neck of the Earth-fallower who nearly had the Mungkr in its teeth. There was a thunderous and wet, cracking sound as Ardyce's bite went all the way through. The Earth-fallower's head descended from its body, and pumping blood leaped in a confluence of streams from the frayed stump of its neck.

At the same moment, Sasithorn witnessed Dayraven's ambition. Those unusual arms had reappeared from the depths of his plumage, and with his fists, he struck aside the faces of the Death Wyrms who'd come for Ardyce. Soon joining, at either side of him, were Dreyon and Lynelis, as the Death Wyrms sent their crackling galvanism in bright, crooked limbs at them from out their maws.

Sasithorn swam in a sea of blankness for a moment, the blood-loss coming for its due, and every breath she bargained for, her body answered with searing pain and a wish for numbness. Sasithorn closed her eyes.

The jade Mungkr fainted, rolling down the length of Ardyce's stalwart neck to the Tree Crown's shoulder. With a small movement of her wing and tilting slightly of her frame, Ardyce guided the smaller Drake's limp body to a protective groove she'd created by bending her wing just so. *Rest friend,* said the black

Tree Crown, poisoned, slashed, and abraded by acid, as she was. Ardyce fought, with one wing folded to hold Sasithorn.

Meanwhile, Daofeng's engrossment was no longer Ardyce. Across the river, he knew what he had spotted, though it was only there an instant, then gone. A massive, land-perched cloud, or rather, a goddess who resembled the phenomenon.

"Daofeng?" The black Wyrm at his side asked.

"She is here," he replied, before gathering himself into the winds. "The time has come to kill the first god." And, then, he crossed the River Orb with a swelling speed.

"You're alive!" Hadryn held Thaddius strongly, clapping her back with mist stealing to the corners of his eyes. "I was worried you'd Made the Ring or done something rash." The Knight's words were clipped, as his hair fizzed from being brushed by fire, and his cheek burned for a second. He extinguished the tiny, climbing flame along his hair strands with his fingertips and pulled back to look at his best friend. "Thad?"

The Royal Guard was silent, and Hadryn couldn't look into her eyes, for they were no longer there, only a darkness remaining of a skull's empty eye sockets. Upon Thaddius' back, emerging from between her shoulder blades, were wings. They were abysmal-black in hue, and the flames atop her head were colors of reds and golds.

"Are you alright, Thaddius?" Hadryn touched her hair, then pulled back his hand quickly. "Ow." He did the same thing, again. "Ow."

"Idiot!" Thaddius roared. "They are actual flames! What are you thinking!"

Hadryn laughed and said easily, "Genius."

The Firecraw-human that Thaddius had become was humbled to silence before asking, "You are not frightened, my friend?" Her hair of fire licked at the breezes which went by.

Hadryn reached behind himself to make Fox lower the rifle he had aimed at the Royal Guard. "Only terrified that I'd never see you, again. Or, that you'd say something foolish to LeShawn, and she would desire to leave you." He grinned at her.

"She said plenty of asinine things," the Pyrolite Drake told Hadryn, and Thaddius was disheartened a moment, so LeShawn added: "And, one or two very sweet things."

"I've changed," the Royal Guard concluded.

Hadryn nodded at this. "You wear it very well, Thaddius."

Thaddius drew a weighted breath, then sighed. "Already, I miss who I was. I never thought – *could have imagined* – *this* for myself. I am hideous, Hadryn." Thaddius was struggling with herself, and LeShawn attempted to comfort her wife.

Hadryn said, "You are, but in a lovely, most beautiful way." His words brought a crinkled smile from her. The Knight told his best friend, honestly: "Don't hate what you've become. You've survived it because Life could not give you up." Then, he returned Thaddius' small smile. "Besides, all of life cannot be as beautiful as your wife."

The red dragon stood, gazing at Thaddius serenely. Her fire-locks of hair dazzled briefly in a gust of offshore breeze.

Thaddius, too, was staring back at the Drake. "True. By comparison, everything will be less beautiful than she." The Royal Gurad looked to the Knight of Third Rank and said, "Enough with your unending philosophy, Hadryn." She sighed as though it was a burden to her lungs. There was no repose from the churning of events, and Thaddius knew she had to keep time with it. She feared how much was at stake. To her best friend, she said, "We have found my wife and myself, re-imagined, as well. We must find you your answers now and your love's way back to you."

But, Fox was staring at Thaddius. Fear and disgust edged his features. "How the hell did this happen to you, Merlone? What the hell are you even!"

"You're using up a lot of air, Luciano," Thaddius growled, irritated.

"Look, this isn't normal. None of it is! So, I'm asking questions!" Fox defended himself.

"Still, we know nothing!" Thaddius' voice was louder than his. "We know nothing, and it will all go on as it will, whether we're versed in this upheaval or not! We can stand here and talk, until the sun burns out of the sky, or we can do something with what little we know."

Hadryn was in shock, staring at his best friend. LeShawn gazed at the Royal Guard, as well. They stood there, in the timeless stillness of one moment, thinking of everything at once, but in the end, Thaddius was correct.

LeShawn said softly to Hadryn: "She and I had a heart-to-heart about many things."

"You're the most arrogant shit I know, Merlone!" Fox yelled at her, finally speaking again.

"That's only because you don't know yourself very well, now, do you, Luciano!"

"And, dammit, you're right!" Fox cried.

"I am!" Thaddius insisted.

"I hate that," Fox muttered. "And, all of this." Then, he was resigned. It seemed the night would continue with its freakish nature. The four of them stood there, unwilling to leave one another. Fox asked, "What do we do?"

The vermillion Drake spoke to them as she looked to the battle in the distance. "We know more than we think. It is clear that those, across the river, are in a fight for their lives. We are now a close reflection of their shapes same; our world will become theirs as the last of us turn. The victor will likely determine the future of whatever will stand when this time is no more, and, I think, this is our only chance to influence what will become. So, then, there is one undecorated, uncomplicated question we must ask ourselves: what do we want for this world?"

Fox wished the beast wasn't talking, but she was, sending shivers down his spine. He was first to answer. "For things to be as they were."

"Really?" Thaddius raised an eyebrow at him, as the others made their own faces at his answer. Her tone was strict with him.

"No." He thought on it. Fox remembered life in the Tiered Nations: so quiet, that people died without knowing it. He said, "It was awful. Everyone around me— They were dying. The denizens. You could see it in their faces. Dead people eating. Cancer. Disease. I think, only the pills kept most of them alive."

Hadryn was quiet, kneading the words which he'd been told. "The woman we found mentioned gods."

"Maybe if they die, everyone can return to being human? Maybe we wouldn't turn." Fox sounded as though he were trying to persuade them or himself.

"'Whatever human may be,'" Hadryn muttered.

"Better than that!" Fox gestured angrily across the waters.

"'Better?'" Hadryn said. "Or different?'"

LeShawn answered gently, "*This*," and she meant herself, "is no longer 'different' to me." The Pyrolite looked again at the murder in the vale. She watched as a Drake suddenly lost his limb, the shattered bone coming forth at his outcry of pain, and half a Wyrm's face was blazed away by fire. LeShawn said to them, "It is my feeling that humanity is more important than being human."

"Are you serious right now?" Fox stared at her.

A storm of bullets rattled suddenly, like a metallic flapping of wings when a cluster of birds are frightened up into the skies.

They looked back to the direction of the carriage, and there, Soo-yeon stood, firing a machine gun into the open jaws of a titan of azure coloration and beyond any conceivable proportion a human mind could imagine. Behind Soo-yeon, Chinami crouched on the ground, as if preparing for impact.

"What the bloody hell!" Thaddius cried out, and the grouping of them ran towards Soo-yeon and Chinami, except for Fox.

The Knight Luciano watched as the Korean woman stood, armed against a beast which seemed to expand, like the reach of the heavens. Fox was gaping, resisting to believe that another of the monsters had come to pierce their human sphere and do them harm.

To himself, he said, "She'll die." Because it would be impossible, if she didn't.

CHAPTER 32

THE UNRESTED

Dayraven wished for the world to run out of time. If there was nothing more to spend of it, every heart-helmed vessel could find repose and do something of healing. Time made everything desperate. He thought of the power of that, as the strength began to stale in his muscles, impeding action and even his breathing, it seemed.

Dayraven's stare found Sasithorn, and she, at last, was safe, though he knew it would be momentary. Tucked into a groove of Ardyce's wing, she seemed to sleep, and he wished for her dreams to hold her from further battle, until he could retrieve her. But, the Tree Crown, her keeper, had realized for herself the deepest abyss of ferity and so, the siege of her would continue with no foreseeable respite. Another wave of Daofeng's followers drove in towards Ardyce, and Dayraven's wounds were gates to his every desired action. He was forced to cease and pant for his will, or at least, for air.

He had endured quite a beating from the Death Wyrms. Though as a Serpent, it seemed he was of an order more tolerable of abuse and with a certain limit of indestructibility, though not pardoned any measure of pain or that of fatigue either.

The electrocution that was the weaponry of the Death Wyrms did not stun him or banish him to the stillness of death, as he saw was the fate of other Drakes to encounter them. Yet, he had felt as though his nerves had split and weakened with each their strokes of lightning to hit their marks of him. They were acutely formidable, acting in ferocious concordance to avail their traits of crackling element, latching with serrated teeth, and their muscular bodies. They had learned to throw the lower halves of themselves, clouting bones to splinters. There was, too, their numbers to consider: three dozen of them, and Dayraven could see Dreyon and, in particular, Lynelis flagging under the barrage of Death Wyrms.

The Unrested Drake was addled, wasteful in his efforts and futile with his attacks. Such was this that became of one to exist of both the Living and the Dead. All movement, even his own, happened too quickly for him, and though he did not feel much of the wounds he bore, there appeared in him a rage and sense of helpless despair, deep within, which threatened to distend and fragment the shell of his being. Lynelis' eyes continually shifted, coming to the foreground, then sinking back to darkened pits. They repeated this, as though his vision could tell naught of whether it was day or night.

"You are weakened, Lynelis! Fall back!" Dreyon could not reach him, though he tried.

Lynelis knew the voice. He'd had emotions, once, for that voice. But, emotions felt small and thin to him now. He had to concentrate on his defense, or the Death Wyrms would have him. Yet, when he looked about, he saw nothing of them. Then, from the side of him: the sound of lightning bursting in his ears, and his frame was seized by torment. He fought to remain himself – what he knew of Lynelis, the Pyrolite Drake.

"Lynelis, no!"

But, Lynelis detached of who he was and knew but pain and wrath. He howled, until his throat filled from deep within, and the Death Wyrms halted, for in the Unrested's maw whipped thick filaments, like ghost-hair rippling, of obsidian-dark smoke. Next, the black flames came rolling out and struck two of the red Death Wyrms. They were awash in the asphyxiating brume, and when it evanesced, relenting their shuddering forms, the breath those Wyrms drew next and released were the last as members to the kingdom of Life. Death accepted what He could of them. The two Death Wyrms staggered and, in alarm, all others on the field yielded to them a distance, as they watched what had become of them.

Lynelis fell to a stupor, and Dreyon could finally reach him in those moments of suspended breath and action. He struggled to remove Lynelis from the scene of battle, looking once at Ardyce, who still tangled with the vermillion Tree Crown, and Dreyon felt that she was not worth his Vow, that she had never been worth Lynelis. "Fight your own battles, you demon's paw," Dreyon muttered, and his only concern became his lover. Though Firecraws were typically of larger stature than Pyrolites, Dreyon was small for a Firecraw, and he was burdened by his wounds and Lynelis' dead weight.

They drew away from the spectacle of the affected Death Wyrms, who lurched and contorted, and from their jaws trailed a gelatinous scum which fouled the air. They emitted rasping trills and long groans, enough that one of the Longs from Ardyce's numbers came forward to behead the ghoulish and ominous episode, at once.

It was then that one of the Death Wyrms struck, like a spear thrown and without warning, sinking its teeth into the approaching Long Drake. The other infected Death Wyrm expectorated its scintillating electricity upon another healthy Death Wyrm, who should not have been affected by its own element. Yet, the healthy Wyrm writhed, as though in the clutches of Death. The Long, too, who had been bitten, fell to the same manner.

"It is shadow-fire that Unrested Drake wields," one of the dragons said. Of whose ranks the Drake belonged was unknown. She said, "*Flee*, for if the disease overwhelms your blood, the soul is pitched beyond the holds of Nature to forever wander oblivion, amassing miserable company."

Yet, it was hard to believe, to comprehend she who had spoken, and the hesitation of those nearest the newly-undead lasted a second too long. Four more Wyrms and Drakes were bitten or electrocuted by shadow-fire, then six more. A contagion now swept through the house of war, dominating in its tally of victims.

Dayraven saw Dreyon struggling with Lynelis, and he began to move towards them, feeling that they deserved none of this, that he could protect them.

But, the Serpent was abruptly entwined in a hard locking of muscles. He looked and saw that it was the black Wyrm, most loyal to Daofeng.

"Release me," Dayraven warned her. She didn't have eyes, but there were indentations on her head that looked as if a human skull were trying to press through the crown of her outer shell. What she lacked in features, her abundance was teeth, and Dayraven saw the heavy, long fangs as the rind of her peeled back to reveal an enormous maw.

She cut into his speech with knives in her tone, *"Be now the Serpent's curl.* You know what you must do. Find that Orbed one to grant us the power of the Serpent With Pearl! *The World Serpent destroys to create anew!"* She spat as she spoke, and with her poisons it was dangerous that she did.

Dayraven's feathers burned under the saliva of hers that landed on his coat. He strived to shake her off and twist free. His arms were pinned though by the coil of her body, and when she squeezed, the breath left him.

"Loving attachment is not a luxury of this world!" She was furious with him or crazed. *"Did we not relinquish that as humans? It didn't matter enough to us then, now into freakish forms we've been hurled! You've a path which illumines! You are the only promise for less of Death. And, in this world of titans, last should these people see is that goliath."*

Dayraven strained for air. *"I am my own decisions, same as all others here!"* he said.

But, she wasn't listening, preoccupied with the pestilence ravaging the living and, acting in Daofeng's place, the black Wyrm issued a command to those fighting.

"Destroy the Unrested!" Her voice echoed across the lands, down to its roots and the roots in all those there. She told them, "The brain must be annihilated for animation to cease!"

Dayraven didn't know how she knew this, if it was a desperate conjecture of hers, but his eyes went to Sasithorn, still nestled in a crook of Ardyce's wing, then to Dreyon and Lynelis. The Wyrms and Drakes had heard her, and the momentum of war found a new trajectory. The extermination of the Unrested began.

Dreyon was fending off an Armored Wyrm and a Ryuu at once, but the design of their wrath and determination was beyond his control, and the pale Wyrm crept behind Dreyon's back to the Unrested Pyrolite, who was still dazed and motionless. With his hard-plated head, the Wyrm battered Lynelis' skull to sickly pieces, leaving a crater of gore where a face had once been. Then, the Armored Wyrm and Ryuu vanished to repeat their actions on another affected by Unrest.

And, Dreyon remained, made singular, and he stared at the corpse. He could not even touch Lynelis. He stared, instead, and Dayraven broke inside to imagine what Dreyon, in his heart, saw.

Soo-yeon had witnessed the obstruction of what she knew of the boundless skies and of space. A prodigious, cerulean beast had turned towards her and the other woman near herself, rearing up into the welkin and locking his gaze upon Chinami from across the River Orb. By the blood-tint in the creature's eyes, Soo-yeon feared what was to come, but to do nothing was against the code which imbued her. She had run to the carriage, and from it, extracted a machine gun and – how Thaddius had acquired them, she could not fathom – four hand grenades as well.

Now, she stood before the beast, firing the machine gun into his approach, and Chinami was cowering behind her and doing her best to crawl to the silent person who had appeared from the red cloud.

The dragon fled upon the winds towards them. A great beard bannered from the framing of his maw, and the Drake's eyes were a maelstrom of both fevered darkness and terrorizing light. Soo-yeon felt her body wishing to disintegrate into a panic attack, but she willed it away. She saw the creature's teeth stretch from the gumline and align with herself. The bullets she fired rocked the deadly instrument in her hands, and though her aim proved true, Soo-yeon could see that the inundation of bullets made only a small, bloody wheal on the monster's tongue. She cemented her nerves and made a target of one of the dragon's eyes, instead. Her trigger finger slipped in sleek sweat along the tongue of the weapon, and she forced herself to intake one, steady breath. From her peripheral view, she could see Hadryn and the others running towards them, but besides LeShawn, and possibly Thaddius in her new form, she wondered if they would be able to damage or stall the huge creature. Her mind darted from one thought to another.

Soo-yeon felt the rushing of Time that was the threat of death, and it stole over her senses for a moment, her body seeking to mute her as an only means to protect itself.

Yet, she held her gaze on the dragon's eye and blinked away the perspiration to roll into her own. She exhaled and without hurry. Soo-yeon fired one shot.

It missed the beast, and the weapon she held was depleted of ammunition. Soo-yeon stared at it, then sent it clattering to the ground. She ran to Chinami who had reached the other woman on the ground and as a human bundle with arms wrapped around as much as they could hold, they rolled out of reach of the Drake.

His jaws came down a mere arm's-length from them, hallowing out a trench in the earth. He pulled back, letting grit and soil fall from his mouth, and Soo-yeon stared at the pit he had carved. It seemed the measure of a dining hall, and she imagined all the people that could fit in such a space.

Though it was, perhaps, impractical and ridiculous, Soo-yeon signed to Chinami, *We have to run.* There was no other choice left for them. But, the woman with pink eyes was shaking uncontrollably with the terror wild in her eyes.

"No," Chinami gasped. When she spoke with her hands, the Knight could just barely decipher what she said, but it was this: *You shouldn't have to do this. I need to fight. You're only a human.* The albino woman stood, after that, and her knees and her stance were feeble with fear. Winds clouted them, then clouds, which seemed to expel from a flayed dimension, hung in the form of a queen over Chinami. The pale goddess came forth, her many eyes blinking and her small mouth with those heavy teeth hung, slackened.

Soo-yeon scrambled over to the unconscious body and shook the brown-skinned woman. "Hey! Please, wake up!" She patted the woman's face, then checked for a pulse along her neck. "Oshin!" she cried to the woman who should not be here.

The great Wyrm reared back, then bludgeoned the Drake with the frame of her enormous head. He reeled, and she sped for him to find the underside of him, just below his throat. In her teeth and with the first set of her pincher-like limbs, she held him, but he wrenched free, bleeding. Then, Daofeng lunged at her, ran his claws through her. He would not relinquish an opportunity to do away with her.

"Chinami!" Soo-yeon screamed.

Crimson brutality painted the chest of the thunderhead queen, and the pale Wyrm collapsed all the way backwards, until she was, again, a human vessel, lying supine in the loam.

Soo-yeon rushed to her. Chinami's front was tattered flesh, and she looked impossibly delicate to Soo-yeon. The albino woman was so terrified that tears had come to her eyes, and she whispered to Soo-yeon, "I don't want to die. I'm afraid." Then, she swallowed laboriously and signed, *Please go.*

The Korean woman clenched her teeth and her eyes narrowed. Any fear she'd had was sieved out upon seeing that face, so frightened and in all its youth. Thus, Soo-yeon took a grenade from the pocket of her pants and spun around to face the enormous creature. She plucked the pin from the bomb and let out a cry, straining her arm to its limit. Then, the grenade was slung through the air. Yet, it came up short by several feet, missing its mark, and all the while, the dragon was charging them.

But, fortune came to them, for Thaddius, in her first flight, arrived to the explosive just before it began its descent to earth, and with a light touch, she hurled the grenade the rest of its way. It lodged in the Drake's right eye and detonated.

The Dilong threw back his head, bellowing, as his eye turned to liquid and dripped from his face. Soo-yeon panted with adrenaline and helped Chinami to her feet. Her instinct was to grab Oshin and escape, though she knew not where they could possibly be safe.

"You are wrong to protect her," the creature spoke to them. "She must die. She and that other, you've doubtless heard of him, perpetuate this war. Every timeline reborn to this world, they pit Drakes against Wyrms." His voice was austere and filled the sky, like the new dawn which was inching into their vision. Daofeng's eye bled, as he continued, "You are human, forever tardy to an understanding of the seasons. You do your best to survive them every year, every lifetime. You are not at fault that your wisdom is as small as you are. Or, that you are as small as your wisdom. I tell you, though, walking ones, that *I will kill the gods.* I will *eat* the gods. Thereby will their essence be obliterated, absorbed by my body, and I will drown myself in the heart of the sea. I promise you this. You don't know what you would be doing for us all, if you would only give up the girl."

Soo-yeon kept Chinami and Oshin behind herself, and she made her voice strong to be heard by the titan who stood before her. "She is human, no longer a goddess. You've no reason to take her life. But, if you attempt it, we will answer your challenge, and the rays of this new morn will mark the victor: either Drake or these 'small humans.'"

The beast drew up tall, obstructing the aurora-light from entering the day, as his shadow fell upon them. His tone was grave. "It is your choice, if you wish *to die.*" With one hand, he crushed their vehicle to jagged metal, showing them he knew where their surplus of weaponry rested. Then, came his next onset, and Soo-yeon and Chinami had turned from him to scream at and plead with Oshin whose eyelids had begun to crack open like an eggshell to show the life inside. With desperation as their strength, Soo-yeon and Chinami heaved Oshin to her feet, and still not quite yet a part of this world, Oshin willed herself to motion.

Underfoot, the earth swelled, as they ran. They skittered and pitched down a hillside, as it was being formed, for the ridge was where the beast's snout had missed them and drove into the land. Soo-yeon cursed to herself; she had stumbled and rolled away from the pale-haired woman, and the Drake was coming for Chinami, again. Oshin was a few feet from her, staring at the ground in a daze. She didn't look right. There was a wounded pigment beneath her skin the color of her scarlet birthmark.

Soo-yeon screamed though the Japanese woman couldn't hear her. "Get up, Chinami!" But, the younger woman was wheezing and holding at the gashes upon her chest, only sitting there, as the dragon came in behind her. The Korean Knight tried to stand, but her ankle twinged. She had fallen poorly upon it, and it threw her balance now.

"Chinami!" Soo-yeon cried, again, and the land pulped, like wet paper, beneath the speed of the Dilong's onslaught. The sense that is horror crept up Soo-yeon's throat, as she instinctively thought of what would become of the deaf woman in mere seconds. The Knight threw herself forwards, unable to do more, and by that, she felt a second energy and the warmth that came with it. Soo-yeon's arm was flung over a shoulder. She was hoisted to her feet, enabling her to run as best she could, and Soo-yeon looked to see Oshin at her side. Their eyes met. She'd never known this woman, but Oshin's gaze lingered on her like stone for elongated moments, and Soo-yeon, in staring back, knew there was even less to understand of this world. The fear remained, tyrannical to the scene, but there was more that was growing beneath. The Knight Jo saw another eye within Oshin's before the dark-skinned woman had looked away, and Soo-yeon thought of how she shouldn't be here and the sky which delivered the other woman. Then, Soo-yeon was hauled forward by Oshin's strength, and they gained ground together.

"Oshin! You're here!" It was Hadryn's voice, nearly crushed with emotion, with relief and gratitude. *"How?"* he started to ask, but there wasn't time for that. He was running towards them, against their direction, with Chinami on his back. He'd managed to get to her before them. Without instruction, Oshin switched their course to mirror Hadryn, and the Knight Archidux came up alongside them. *"Are you alright?"* he begged of Oshin, but she wouldn't answer him. Her stare had drifted to one corner of her eyes and remained there, even as she ran in perfect time with them. *"Is she alright, Soo-yeon?"* Hadryn caught her eye, desperate for an answer.

Soo-yeon felt herself pulled along. Frantic nerves were jostling her every action and judgment. "Get us out of here alive, Hadryn," she requested of him.

That silenced him. He concentrated on his path, on holding Chinami.

"We head in, towards the creature," Hadryn explained to them, gathering some of himself, but still using every other moment to peer at Oshin by his side. "He is too large to turn easily upon himself. The danger will be in being crushed by his movements, so keep a keen eye. But, the farther out we go from him, much easier will it be for him to strike us down." He wanted to hold Oshin; Soo-yeon saw it in his every movement, but she appeared to be with them only in body. She ran on, as focused as a fired bullet, yet silent to them.

Soo-yeon nodded in agreement to Hadryn's plan though it terrified her. She took a second to stare at Chinami, and the younger woman met her eyes.

"I think her ankle is sprained," Oshin finally told Hadryn of Soo-yeon. They each stared at her for speaking, and now it was their voices muted.

"Oshin—" Hadryn needed to speak to her. It seemed impossible for him to release this need, even with a Drake hanging over them.

Behind them, LeShawn had taken to flight, and she hovered near to Daofeng's face, as the Dilong pursued them, bending in towards himself to reach them. LeShawn opened her jaws at his one, remaining eye, and she erupted a jet of flames.

"*Shit,*" Hadryn said, as they dodged one of the azure giant's claws, which ran by them like the Reaper's scythe, glinting. "I can carry her," the Knight of Third Rank answered Oshin. Now, she looked to him, and something in her semi-aware regard of him brought him a measure of comfort.

"I'll take the girl," Oshin agreed with him.

"No!" Soo-yeon resisted the other woman. "I'll be fine. It doesn't hurt—" But, Oshin had shoved Soo-yeon aside.

The Dilong worked to preserve what was left of his sight. He maneuvered around LeShawn's fury of fire, then he screamed and swiped his talons at the Pyrolite to maim her. LeShawn was nimble though, avoiding the harm Daofeng would do her, and the beast's hand descended on a downward arc upon the humans below him.

CHAPTER 33

FOX LUCIANO ~ KNIGHT, RANK 5

Fox Luciano remained where the others had left him, and he lowered to his knees, watching.

A chill met his frame, coming from the sea that was at his back, as if the scud had carried this far inland to touch him. The cold alighted his robe, but was more insistent where it brushed his neck and face. He swallowed the cool air with his heavy breathing, and Fox yearned for hushed thoughts, for his heart to diminish, so it wouldn't pound out of his chest.

But, the mind is indulgent, acting on reflex and on whims. Memories came to him on a low hum, like music playing in an unknown room. The images arrived bleary, until he submitted his focus to them, then he saw Soo-yeon. She was arguing with him, or eating the food he had prepared for her, or walking, then running and saying she could outdo him in speed. She combed her long hair. She was bathing. She sneezed, making a ridiculous face, and he heard himself laughing.

Then, he saw her dead. Her vibrancy had completely dissolved. She rested in the dirt, as motionless as stone. He knew that was not his memory. He knew it was his imagination.

In death, she still appeared beautiful to him.

But, he hated it.

398

He loved, instead, her beauty, as she was yelling at him, or when she was rushing off to a training exercise, or when she drank a cold beer with him.

"She'll die. She'll die," he said to himself, again. "She's nothing to me. Nothing."

Fox looked outwards, away from the inside of himself. He watched the monster, its scales shimmering, like fireworks during the New Year, if fireworks could ripple with direction, and the mane and beard of the creature was darting with its every action. Those hairs on the monster were pale blue, like seeing the veins underneath your skin, Fox thought to himself.

His eyes traveled to Soo-yeon. He saw that the other woman beside her – maybe Hadryn had said her name was "Oshin" – had pushed Soo-yeon away from herself, as the clawed hand of the dragon came down upon them. Soo-yeon would have been impaled, if not for Oshin's deed, and, instead, a single talon went through one of Oshin's thighs. She screamed, and Soo-yeon and Hadryn ran to her aid.

Fox stared at Soo-yeon.

She was fighting so hard.

She would die any second.

He covered his eyes with his forearms, so he wouldn't have to see it. "I don't care, if you die. Go ahead and die, Soo-yeon. I should have shot you through the head when the denizens first began to turn, saved you the pain of having to die out here."

He thought about eating.

"'I won't even cry, when you die someday,'" he repeated the words she'd said to him when he confessed to her accusations of cheating on her. She hadn't reacted as he had expected. She hadn't cried, or yelled at him, or walked away. She'd only said those words and told *him* to walk away from her. So, he had. He had left her in that shopping complex of which he no longer remembered the name of, or where exactly it was located. There had been voiceless music playing somewhere from a boutique. He'd left without looking back at her.

"Then, die," Fox said.

With his teeth, he bit into the flesh on his forearm. It blazed with pain, and he cried out around the meat in his mouth. It was a divided and meshing experience to feel food in his mouth – for, he realized how very alive he was, and in that, that he was food – as well as feeling the torment of being consumed. He swallowed, struggling to resist vomiting. The blood fled down his forearm, hot and thick, but he went to his other arm and put his teeth to it. He ignored it, if there was any taste to himself.

"Why, goddammit!" The pain was unbearable.

He remembered Dr. Chen. The scientist, in his thoughts, was going on about how, when denizens Made the Ring, the blood didn't flow, and the pain was numbed to nothingness.

"Why!" His voice screeched in his ears, but Fox continued biting, tearing, chewing, and swallowing.

His blood was everywhere. The front of his robe was so warm with it.

"Change, you piece of shit." He spoke to himself. "You said you would change after she left you. *You need to do this. You're a fucking bastard. For once, don't be afraid to change!"*

Fox gulped one, last mouthful. His eyes rolled back in his head, and he collapsed from blood loss.

Inside himself, again, Fox was disappointed, but there was warmth everywhere, and he thought about the day he was born, since this would be the day he died. There weren't any images this time, but he felt suddenly strong and that he was giving his muscles a good stretch, even muscles that he didn't have, and he stretched for a long time, breathing into it.

When Fox opened his eyes, it seemed Soo-yeon was staring at him, even from across the distance between them. Rapidly, though, he could see her in more and more detail.

I won't let you die, he told her, in his thoughts.

CHAPTER 34

PRECIOUS BURDEN

Dayraven witnessed the massacre of the Unrested. It was true that those infected would not relinquish a hunger for the Living, until the brain was terminated, and only then, could they finally join with Death and belong, once more, to the intentions of Nature.

But, he wished he hadn't had to witness it. There were comrades who had to do away with each other – friendships and a few lovers, who met with inconceivable ends.

Dayraven flailed to be free of the black Wyrm, but her might exceeded his, and Dayraven stared at Sasithorn who was still unconscious and perched precariously upon the midnight-colored Tree Crown.

"Let go of me, Wyrm!" Dayraven's voice thundered, but she latched all the more firmly to him.

"Leave these battles not meant for you! Save your strength and prove your promise true. Kill the Scourge. Let the world be purged!" The black Wyrm was nearly chanting as though it might throw Dayraven to a trance where he would obey her, but he bludgeoned her with the end of his tail, furious to find freedom from her.

Ardyce's power was abating in her combat with the crimson Tree Crown. Without Dayraven, Dreyon, or Lynelis to act as a palisade of defense for her, Daofeng's ranks came with renewed vigor. Armored Wyrms, an Earth-fallower, and what was left of the Death Wyrms labored to fell her. Ardyce fought them all, but every second, she gave blood, and every motion of hers seemed to result in more of her muscles torn open. She would, soon, be no more.

I wish for you to die, Great Aegis.

The thought came of its own. It slowed Dayraven almost to stillness. There was shame in it, in realizing that the only vision he wished to create as reality was to weave in close to Ardyce, as she warred, and sneak away with Sasithorn in his arms. He wanted to leave the black Tree Crown, alone to her fate. She would die with no one to care for her, and that was his desire.

Dayraven had thought he'd known himself before this day, that he had known this self much better than his self as a human being. He had gathered knowledge; he had made decisions. He believed he was prepared for this day.

But, he hadn't thought Sasithorn would return to him.

Dayraven's mind fled between Ardyce, who had Sasithorn, and the creation of the World Serpent. Finally, those oscillating thoughts started to make thread, tying themselves together, and Dayraven released the idea of his false-self.

"I am not your weapon! You will not tell me who to fight!" He injured the black Wyrm, for he felt a sudden weakness to her frame.

"Not who to fight, but who you are fighting for!"

He heard her words more with memory than a sense of hearing. She was picking and choosing who should live; was he not doing the same?

Dayraven gave attention to Ardyce, once more. He understood everything a little better now.

The Serpent rushed through the field, closing in on Ardyce, just as she fell upon one side, nearly spilling Sasithorn to the ground. Dayraven reached her, and his serrated beak delivered a fatal blow, as he ripped the belly out of the Earth-fallower, whose intention was the softness of the Great Aegis' gullet. Entrails matted the grass beneath them, and Dayraven fought for Ardyce, realizing the cruelty of his thoughts in wanting to reject someone who so desperately needed caring for.

Ardyce's vision reduced to a halo of black light. She felt a precious weight escaping her grasp and righted herself, scrapping for strength and her footing.

Is that you, Nandenia?

But, she remembered she hadn't yet had the chance to hold her daughter, so this couldn't be her. Still, Ardyce kept the weight close, because she could hear a faint heartbeat coming from it.

The Tree Crown blinked several times. Her vision was from the bottom of an endless cavity, and she heard her own breathing, which sounded more of choking than lungs of air. Surrounding her was hatred, either her own or that of many others; she couldn't rightly define it. Then, images emerged to her, and she saw before her an unusual creation.

It was a monstrous raven with the body of a cobra, and its wings were, instead, arms, as primates do have. It was hideous. It had come for her, and Ardyce happened upon a word, in her throat-like abyss.

Serpent, she said to it. It danced in front of her with mocking speed and the agility of a rain droplet tumbling through the thicket of a forest's canopy. Its back was to her, then it turned to her and mouthed words, as though it knew speech. She choked once more, forgetting she was without verbal speech as well. Even then, she said to it, *Even you, an Impossibility, have come for my life.* She confronted it: *All of you here, to bleed me to bones. But, since you are not of this world, I will cleanse it of you. Aroint thee, Serpent!*

Why this hatred, she couldn't say. It had come for her and seemed to be eternity, as though she knew nothing else. She remembered wondering the same of the Wyrm they'd first encountered in Gled Tria. Now, that question was for herself, and she still could not answer it. But, she fed it. She couldn't understand why.

With her crown of blades, Ardyce swept her head to fill the bizarre animal with sharpness through every inch of him. She struck the weight with one of her tiers of metallic antlers and a damning hardness. Ardyce lifted his body up to hang upon her coronet of pike heads. The Serpent, she would have.

But, he remained in his place.

His eyes were filled with tears, staring at her.

She blinked, and Eternity cried out within her, as if struck by the clockwork hands of Time, and Ardyce arrived to the present, returning to herself.

Ardyce looked to her wing, which had nestled the weight with the faint heartbeat, and her wing was empty.

No, she said.

The Serpent was reaching upwards with his hands, as if beseeching the gods.

Ardyce's head felt heavy. Down her face and neck ran the incarnadine tears of Life.

"*Sasithorn,*" the Serpent whispered. He was in pain.

No, Ardyce repeated.

The jade Mungkr's body rested along one side of Ardyce's neck, and the Tree Crown stared out into the void of the entire world and this day.

"*I beg you, give her to me,*" the black-feathered Serpent said to her.

Ardyce's jaws parted, as if to answer him, but nothing came forth. She stood in that clearing with the terrible burden of what she had done.

"My friend," Sasithorn breathed.

Ardyce's eyes widened. Still though, she couldn't move. Instead, the steel running through the Ngaw's body did. Like daylight emerging from the blackness of night, the metal transformed to that of bark. It was a slow, ripping transformation that happened speedily, a conundrum to perception. Wooden antlers now stood, once more, upon Ardyce's head, and then, they shriveled, like natural death, and broke, completely withered by age.

With that, Sasithorn descended into Dayraven's arms. Her body was ribbons of blood and jade. When Ardyce rested her gaze upon her friend, her eyes stung, and she closed them tightly for a moment. When she opened them, they were no longer the hollows of a skull, but her eyes of oil-spill likeness.

Sasithorn, I didn't mean to, Ardyce fought to explain.

The Thai Drake's eyes of onyx grew dim. It seemed she couldn't even turn her head to look to either Ardyce or Dayraven. "I know," she told the sky. "I cherish you both. Immensely. … How happy … ." But, Sasithorn was unable to finish her words before Death arrived for her.

She was gone before either Dayraven or Ardyce was ready.

The Serpent hunched over Sasithorn's body and cried bitterly, the creature of him shattered and the human, equally destroyed, for they both had so loved The Lady of Green Taffeta. Dayraven cursed every day to come.

The Tree Crown was, however, utterly still. Silent. Steadied. *Begone with her,* she said, after several minutes, to Dayraven.

He held her protectively. "I can't leave you," he rejoined. "She would never forgive me."

Ardyce fixed upon him her stare. *You believe her a lingering haunt? A specter to speak to you at night? She is erased. She is nothingness now.* Dayraven glared at her. *Leave,* she repeated. *But, bring her. Away from my eyes.*

"She died for you," Dayraven said, with shaking voice.

No, Ardyce stated. *She died for* you. *I murdered her.*

Dayraven emitted a convulsive cry, then he gathered the Mungkr into his arms and fled away with her.

The Great Aegis turned to those still left upon the footing of War, and she said to them, in each of their listening minds, *I permit you the destruction of what I've become.*

CHAPTER 35

THE ARCH-BRIDGE

The center of Hadryn's palms peeled open wide, nearly to the bone, and his blood smeared over the beast's talon, as he struggled to remove that ivory spear from Oshin's thigh.

"Oshin, hold on!" Hadryn said, and the Filipino woman was; she was gritting her teeth and bearing the pain.

Soo-yeon arrived to Hadryn's side, and from her pocket, she handed him a grenade. The Knight Archidux peered up into the blue empyrean, where the creature's head hung, so far away. Powerfully, Hadryn launched the explosive with its pin pulled, and it was a feat that the detonation colored one of the Drake's shoulders the hues of a miniature sun.

Yet, the detonation affected the dragon not, though it had met the creature's vessel. Blood sprayed from the wound. Hadryn looked up, again, to realize the eye of the Dilong hovered behind the veil of a cloud, like a star too close to earth, to gaze down upon them. He was staring at Oshin, who he'd hooked in his grasp, and when Oshin cried out, the birthmark running along her neck blazed deep red, like a banner of warfare.

"What's this?" the Drake questioned. "What a curious collection you all are. Some still human and others with Rings abnormally made, but *what are you, girl?* Tell me, and I will not pluck this limb from your figure—"

But, Thaddius with her wife had swept in on agile wings, and with a rifle in her hands, the Royal Guard opened fire upon the back of Daofeng's skull. LeShawn threw strokes of fire to Thaddius' fusillade of bullets.

Daofeng rang the heavens, as a howling roar stormed from his maw that was all teeth and a crater-like cavity of darkness. Below him, Oshin screamed as well, for the claw sunk into her muscle another inch.

"Oshin!" Hadryn cried and availed all the force he could wrought from his arms, shoulders, and back to cleave away at the joint of the Drake's finger with his short, gauntlet rapier.

"Hadryn, what do we do?" Soo-yeon was panicking. "I think she's passing out."

The shuddering strain in Oshin's body and the arch of her back relaxed; her head fell to one side. Hadryn stared down at her with hammering heart, feeling that she should never have come for him. He yelled out, burying the blade into the beast's finger.

Chinami came to them, then, still bracing a forearm over her clotting wounds, and stared down at Oshin, whose skin was now lit with tracings of her marking over the whole of her body. There was fear in Chinami's eyes.

Suddenly, the unconscious woman awakened, and Oshin cried out once more, leaning away from herself. In her throat were two voices, screaming. One voice was not human, almost trilling. The albino goddess reached down with her free hand and pulled at Oshin as Hadryn wrapped his arms around the amputated finger, lifting it, and threw it aside to free her.

The Dilong cried out, at the same time snapping his fangs at Thaddius who wielded the rifle. Finally, he brought his claws away from the group of them on the ground beneath him, and Daofeng roared at LeShawn as she burst fire from her jaws at him. His scream snuffed out the flames of her shot.

"I have you, Oshin." Hadryn bent for her figure and had her in his embrace before more words could be said. He carried her, fleet-footed, as the blue Drake bellowed once more in pure fury.

The four humans upon the terra firma needed no other goading. They began to run.

But, their movement attracted the eye of the Drake, and suddenly, Soo-yeon's voice pierced their frantic nerves. "Look out!" she cried. Yet, the creature's hands were already overshadowing them, then the dragon closed one fist around Hadryn and Oshin, and his other grasp claimed Soo-yeon and Chinami.

Enormous clods of loam came with them, as he grated the glebe to have them, and they were lucky for it. It was these sections of earth to slowly crumble first in Daofeng's fists, and it brought them precious few moments.

"Release them!" Thaddius demanded of the Drake, but she was depleted of bullets for her firearm and had thrown the useless weapon to the ground. Instead, she and LeShawn eructed forceful waves of scalding fire upon the Dilong, and though they could not hope to badly burn the gigantic beast, they made their target his eye and the point of damage they'd pared at the back of his head. It was their only hope that the distraction would be enough to keep the creature from triturating their friends in his grip.

"What do we do?" LeShawn pleaded with the Royal Guard when she came near to her, for they could see no way to compel the Drake to surrender the humans he held.

Thaddius just barely escaped a fang of the beast, and she admitted, "I do not yet know, LeShawn."

Fragrant water pattered along, separate from the warring world.

The bridge to span the River Orb was old and made of stone. The width of it was convenient to the Wyrms, permitting two or three to traverse side by side, if they so wished, and it was utilized for such: to marry the populations on either side of the bridge of those belonging to Daofeng's created society. The bridge arched in the middle, allowing the waters to pass beneath it, through a wide carving the shape of a dome. The reflection of the bridge upon the face of the River Orb created a perfect, symmetrical circle where the archway was, and Dayraven stared down at it, as he came to the center of the bridge.

He had left Ardyce, condemned her, and was unable to forgive her. The knowledge of that was set in his tensed shoulders. Perhaps, he knew it was wrong, but he couldn't think of her any longer.

The stones he stood upon were cold, but the look of the bridge was so serene that it lent a sort of warmth to the eye, and Dayraven was drawn to it. He held Sasithorn in his plumage to keep the corpse of her warm, and he spoke to the spherical opening, which the waters pranced through, rippling the ottelia flowers that bloomed at the surface of the river. He told the perfect circle that he knew its secrets: half of it was solidity and weight – immovable – and the other half only a shimmering illusion: pervious with the swell of action behind its façade.

"You think we don't know, that we don't understand," he said to it. "Well, we do." He could cry no more, so the tears remained within his being, besotting his mind with grief.

Dayraven finished crossing the bridge, and he lingered an eye over one shoulder where Ardyce still stood. She was utterly without movement, and he could help her no more, as her enemies drew in upon her. "Forgive me, Sasithorn," he said, and looked away, passing plum blossoms – the likes of which grew at the banks of the River Orb, here, but nowhere else along the winding flow – and the pink flowers shook at him with the capering of a gentle breeze.

The Serpent was lured to the diminished temples with a yearning to worship his lady who had been stolen from him. He trekked through a layer of mist, which was gradually deepening, and he paused abruptly at seeing the motion of something pale, misshapen and convulsing upon the ground. The tail of it whipped and wrenched with pain, and Dayraven saw the eyes of it before hurrying along, undesiring for an encounter when he carried the body of his love.

Dayraven made it to one of the temples and began to deconstruct it, separating the heavy pillars of rock. He spoke with Sasithorn all the while, gibbering foolishness about their past together – a display she would have teased him for, had she been there. He recited to her poetry, as well, building a tall pedestal to rest her face of beauty upon. Around her, he assembled an encasement for her body, so that she may be protected, even as she stared out onto the world, however it would soon become. He wished to give her that: the truth of what would happen, and a different sort of poem came to him then, as he toiled to complete her raised grave.

The gentle scents of the stones and the moss they wore moved him. He gave to Sasithorn this poem and, too, to the others deceased and the remainder of them to live through these last days of heinous contention, this recounting of what they each endured, attired in words both beautiful and terrible.

Whispering to himself, Dayraven's voice traced through the broken mist:

"Lo! 'tis a gala night
   Within the lonesome latter years!
An angel throng, bewinged, bedight
   In veils, and drowned in tears,
Sit in a theatre, to see
   A play of hopes and fears,
While the orchestra breathes fitfully
   The music of the spheres.

Mimes, in the form of God on high,
   Mutter and mumble low,
And hither and thither fly—
   Mere puppets they, who come and go
At bidding of vast formless things

That shift the scenery to and fro,
Flapping from out their Condor wings
    Invisible Wo!

That motley drama—oh, be sure
    It shall not be forgot!
With its Phantom chased for evermore
    By a crowd that seize it not,
Through a circle that ever returneth in
    To the self-same spot,
And much of Madness, and more of Sin,
    And Horror the soul of the plot.

But see, amid the mimic rout,
    A crawling shape intrude!
A blood-red thing that writhes from out
    The scenic solitude!
It writhes!—it writhes!—with mortal pangs
    The mimes become its food,
And seraphs sob at vermin fangs
    In human gore imbued.

Out—out are the lights—out all!
    And, over each quivering form,
The curtain, a funeral pall,
    Comes down with the rush of a storm,
While the angels, all pallid and wan,
    Uprising, unveiling, affirm
That the play is the tragedy, "Man,"
    And its hero, the—"

Dayraven turned quickly at a sound and saw that the creature from before was lingering at a distance, watching him. He set, for Sasithorn, the final stone of her tomb, and then Dayraven faced the thing that was little more than a silhouette in the rising day. "What do you want?" he asked it.

The articulation from it had an animal echo, and the creature was not entirely Wyrm or human. It said, "Did you love her?"

Dayraven stared at it, then he laughed, as tears ran down his face. "'Love' is not a word expansive enough to explain what she was to me. Even that word – as beautiful as it is – lacks vows and a sort of blooming, were I to use it in reference to her."

The animal was stillness, breathing slowly and deeply. "Not well-learned am I, but I think I know your word—and, feel it, too." It hesitated, then asked, "And, even that was not enough to save her?"

Dayraven had for it an answer, but his teeth only clenched, and he was overwhelmed. The Serpent turned to Sasithorn, whose face shown through the wall of rock, and Dayraven bowed his head, as his mourning came anew. He was anguish and ruing, and the pale being watched him, then left as though it was suddenly snipped from existence, disappearing into the fog.

CHAPTER 36

LAST ARMOR

Fox fled from the feathered creature. If he could stop the titanic monster from killing Soo-yeon, then he was certain he would know nothing of regret. It was as though he could finally see himself in the clearest of mirrors. Yet, the incongruity of this was that he no longer knew how he looked.

The Knight Luciano knew he had Made the Ring, for swiftness had before never been his gift, but now, if he leaned into his muscles, the speed by which he overtook the dale nearly cast to shock his human heart. He felt, too, that the creature he had happened upon was not overpowering in size.

Was he a smaller one, then? He wondered to himself, thinking of Dayraven. But, he could not imagine, before The Ring, ever using any concepts of "smallness" to describe the creatures with which he and others had crossed paths. *In fact, I seemed to unnerve him,* Fox noted.

But, his chances to more fully understand the transformation he'd forced upon himself expired, as the cerulean Drake came to his view. The blood of the Knight Luciano surged at what he found, for in the monster's grasp, Soo-yeon was about to be crushed.

Fox called out to her.

Hadryn and Oshin utilized their heights, with arms extended up, to brace against Daofeng's shrinking fist. Soo-yeon did the same, but Chinami was too short to support her efforts. The Korean woman cried out in despair for feeling that her spine or the bones of her arms would splinter at any moment.

Then, an eerie utterance, with bestial undertones found her: "Soo-yeon! I will free you!"

She sought to look from between the closing fingers of the Dilong's grasp, but abruptly, she and Chinami were falling, still within the fist of the Drake. Blood fled down with them. Soo-yeon caught Chinami to cushion the smaller woman's body, as they met with impact, rolling somewhat in the hewn limb. The fall they'd endured was not bodily threatening, but the wind was knocked from her, and it took Soo-yeon a second to gather herself. The Dilong was howling with irate torment, and he sounded far away from where this hand of his now rested.

Soo-yeon sought to regain herself, and she rose to one elbow. Chinami was struggling to part the dead fingers enough for them to escape, and that was when Soo-yeon saw the marauding figure: a giant, human torso – the hue of colorless wax – atop the body of a Wyrm, and every segment of it encased in a dense chitin to resemble the armor of ancient Knights. There was a helm over his head, and upon the forearms of the creature grew sharp, serrated bone, formed into curves, like crescent blades, and it was this the animal had used to shear Daofeng's arms from his body.

The Dilong's second hand crashed into the grassland, and Hadryn pushed open the clamped fingers to allow Oshin freedom. The Knight Archidux came for Soo-yeon and Chinami next, but the Korean woman's eyes were fixed upon the Wyrm-human who fought the massive, azure dragon.

"Is it Fox?" Soo-yeon asked softly, almost to herself.

Then, Hadryn was there to answer her, helping the women loose from the taloned fist. He replied to her, "It can be no other." But, his gaze was on Oshin who was still climbing to her feet. The strawberry mark of hers, there since birth, was spreading like a strange infection. He wanted to go to her.

"He said he would never change, never be one of them because they were 'monsters.' That's what he'd named them," Soo-yeon was saying, and then, her speech closed up, as the Armored Wyrm was delivered a shattering blow by the swinging of the Dilong's head.

Soo-yeon saw him fall to the ground before dodging Daofeng's body, which aimed to crush him under sheer weight. Where the Knighted Wyrm had been struck, one of his plates bore a crack across the width of it. Still, he fought, and Soo-yeon stared at this.

In the past, when they were dating, she'd wished for Fox to change. They hadn't fit together well. He could be arrogant and was prone to the pleasures of distraction, instead of being present, usually engaged with network gaming or shows on the feed. She'd found it was difficult to be herself with the way he went about things. Not that she'd altered or veiled her personality for the sake of being with him, but she refrained from that which brought her joy, since he simply didn't respond or was uninterested. There was a selfishness to him that wasn't out of the intentions of doing more for himself, but there because he didn't know any other way to be. Thus, she teased him and nagged him a little to change, and he had, on isolated occasions, bared to her his inner feelings and insecurities: he'd wished himself to change, as well, to be a little more considerate of others, to be more connected to her. He had sometimes said that he would change, and other times, said that he didn't know how.

But, this.

Now that he'd become different than what she knew of him, Soo-yeon was terrified.

"Fox, stop it!" she cried out to him. But, he wasn't listening to her, or he couldn't hear her, for he had surpassed his own expectations.

The Knighted Wyrm inflicted deep arcs of lacerations upon the Dilong's frame. Thaddius and LeShawn were given opportunity, then, to renew their efforts at attacking the vulnerable areas upon Daofeng's head. They charred away the skin and muscle at the back of his head to reach his skull, but the Dilong was still viciously-quick, despite his blood-loss, and his jaws closed on one of LeShawn's wings, mangling it.

"Soo-yeon! Hand me the explosives!" Hadryn called to her and orienting herself from the daze that had taken her, Soo-yeon passed off the two grenades to him, as he charged the body of the creature.

"Hadryn, it has LeShawn! It's hurting her!" Thaddius was beginning to panic, circling the blue Dilong, and her voice reached the Knight of Third Rank, even aerial, as she was.

"I'm working on it, Thad!" Hadryn yelled to be heard, then he needed the attention of the Knighted Wyrm. "Fox, can you help me?" He'd come within paces of the Wyrm-human and stared at the transformation which was Fox Luciano. The pale Wyrm stood nearly ten-feet tall, Hadryn estimated. The creature Fox had become turned to Hadryn and nodded at him. Fox's eyes went to the grenades which Hadryn held. They faced the Dilong, at the same moment, having seen each other's plan.

The Armored Wyrm went forward with swiftness to cut deeply into the gut of the Drake. He felt powerful for once, and it wasn't just his body. Though his actions were the most brutal and barbaric he had seen of himself or anyone he knew, he didn't feel a violence within himself. There was something of serenity for finally realizing a piece of who he was. Fox drew open the belly of the dragon, and it was there that Hadryn deposited, as far in as he could, the unpinned grenades.

"Now, we fall back, Archidux!" Fox gathered the Knight with heterochromatic eyes and flung them away from the Drake. The Knighted Wyrm shielded Hadryn with his armor of bone, as the explosion ripped through Daofeng, sheeting the vale with his blood and innards. The Drake released LeShawn's wing, and Thaddius escorted her wife carefully to the ground.

Fox looked to Hadryn to comment of their success, for the azure dragon bled washes of pain and was stalled for it, but the Knight Archidux was staring down at the Knighted Wyrm's body. Fox's armor was heavily damaged, split to puzzle pieces in many areas.

"This isn't good, Fox," Hadryn said. "You need to get off the battlefield." He fished with his gaze for Oshin, and saw her holding herself, trembling as if from cold, and limping towards him. "Oshin, stay there!" Hadryn begged her.

The Knight Luciano wiped at the blood around his mouth, but more trickled from the corner of his lips. "Archidux," he said. Then: "Hadryn. I have no right asking for favors. I know. But, could you protect Soo-yeon for me? I know none of you here know it, except I think that little one is catching on," he motioned a pointing thumb at Chinami, who, oddly, was staring at them. "But, Soo-yeon is a *damn, good woman*. All I want is for her to live."

Hadryn was about to give reply, but, instead, the voice of the Drake they fought seethed into the air, haunting, for it had relinquished its sublimity and vim. Daofeng sounded old, like a hoary animal in a winter trap. "You have braved well these times, humans," he said. "And, she may garb the face of you, but she is not one your own, thus I beseech you, give me the Conqueror Queen."

With that, Daofeng's gaze strapped to the albino woman, and he rushed Chinami, jaws gaping.

Fox pushed Hadryn back. It was the instinct of the Knight Archidux to run to the women, though he'd never reach them before the Drake, and the Knight Luciano said, "Consider my request."

"I will," Hadryn answered, and the Armored Wyrm was gone. He pierced the distance between themselves and Soo-yeon, who was with Chinami. Furrows in the marl were all that was left of him who had just been at Hadryn's side. Hadryn watched him leave, then he sprinted to Oshin, and it was then that he could finally embrace her. They spoke in panicked whispers against each other's necks, and all of her answers to him were that she didn't know, so he held her since that was more important. They didn't part until their hearts claimed the same pace.

Fox had seen Hadryn arrive to Oshin before he was out of sight of him. He envied them.

Fox attempted to measure the next, few seconds. He could see, as if through another eye of his mind, that he would be short the pair of seconds it would take for him to turn and brace in front of Soo-yeon and Chinami in order to catch the mouth of the creature in his hands. There were only moments enough to—

"No!!" Soo-yeon's scream came in the same, eternal instant that Fox had stretched his hardened body in front of the charging Drake, and those teeth collided with him, crushing him at all angles. Hadryn and Oshin, still grasping each other looked up.

There was a sound, like a brick structure toppling, as the Dilong clenched the Knighted Wyrm in his sneer, and Fox's armor gave in sections, fracturing to shards. Blood was forced up Fox's esophagus, and he spat it to wheeze for air. He laid in the jaws of Daofeng. He could see Soo-yeon staring at him, shocked to damaging heartache. She moaned weakly for him.

"I've changed my mind," Soo-yeon said to the Knight Luciano. She had a hand over her mouth, as if to keep her soul from leaping out, and her eyes glistened with restrained tears. "Be as you were, Fox," she continued. "Be, instead, selfish and a coward. Run from here." The Knighted Wyrm trembled from nerves overwrought. Soo-yeon grew angry and clenched her fists. "You owe me *something*, you cheating bastard! Run from here!" she demanded of him.

Fox gazed at her from out the shadows of the helm of bone to encase his head and huffed a light laugh. "You always think so highly of me, Jo." Then, his smile faded, as Daofeng leaned in more pressure upon his body. Fox said to Soo-yeon, "You were a good woman to me. I've never forgotten that." And, the Knighted Wyrm gripped the jaws of the beast who held him. He pried himself free of the dragon's teeth. Securing handfuls of the Dilong's beard, he climbed towards the back of the azure creature's skull. The Dilong wrenched his head from side to side to be rid of the Armored Wyrm, but Fox held his place.

"Luciano!" Thaddius yelled for the Knighted Wyrm. She and LeShawn flew towards Fox, desperate to rescue him.

But, Fox had reached the wound on Daofeng's head that the firebreathers had made. He looked once, down at Soo-yeon. He wasn't much familiar with her crying face, but found he loved how she looked in every emotion. Chinami was holding her, as she cried out to him, but he couldn't make out her words. Then, Hadryn and Oshin were at their side, and Oshin was stern, even rough, as she forced Soo-yeon to turn away from what she would see. They struggled, but the darker-skinned woman prevailed. Soo-yeon was left screaming into Oshin's chest, and Fox had never felt more grateful to anyone than that woman he'd never known who took Soo-yeon's eyes from him.

With the sharpened endpoints of the crescent-formed blades upon his forearms raised high, Fox rallied the remainder of his power, and began to cudgel the weakened point at the dragon's skull mightily.

Daofeng's skull suddenly split.

The Dilong heard it and lashed the heavens with cries that were the chaos of fear. He darted and plunged recklessly, in effort, to throw the Wyrm, but Fox held and revived his assault when he could.

Chinami stared at the back of Soo-yeon's head as Oshin clung to her. She sought to feel everything they felt, but it hurt too much.

The pale goddess left them at a run. Hadryn chased after her, calling to her. Then, every gray cloud in the sky flashed, as if lightning bloomed within them, and Chinami's pale hair whirl-winded upwards a moment. Next, the Conqueror Wyrm emerged, immense and semi-pellucid. The daggered appendages of that queen hung beneath her, and the alabaster head lolled to one side, then righted with consciousness. Her profusion of eyes flashed opened for what she had seen of Fox and Soo-yeon: an indiscernible experience which tied them together and was outside her sphere of understanding. But, she could act on what she'd seen. She could give them something, she believed, for Chinami felt human.

The mouth of the Conqueror Wyrm slammed into Daofeng's body. The goddess fought to hold him, straining with his strength, and she kept him from rolling the back of his head in the loam to kill Fox under his weight.

The Dilong was maddened and distressed, dragging forward the Conqueror, and it seemed his intention was the River Orb. Chinami bit into him harder, feeling that he would drown the Knighted Wyrm, if she, at all, lessened her resistance as the Dilong made it to the waters. The Conqueror anchored herself, as best she could, thrusting her appendages into the dense marl. The dragon thrashed in her jaws, uprooting two of her conical teeth and washing her mouth in blood, yet, still, she refused to release him.

Chinami's voice wakened the new morning, as though minions of light found their way to the greater sun and coaxed forth that reigning star. Even Daofeng's last, remaining eye saw the yellowed rays tip the sky to sunflower hues.

She did not need her mouth to speak. The goddess' words rippled the air on their own: "Leave, Knighted Wyrm. Be with Soo-yeon."

Now, the Dilong remembered himself and turned back on the Conqueror, stretching his jaws to their utmost limit. He came down upon her ghost-white head, and the Drake's eyes rolled back in his head, as he swallowed again and again. Again. In this way, he began to ingest the Conqueror Queen.

Fox hastened his labor at the base of Daofeng's skull, battering away with just one of his forearm bones, for the other crescent-shaped weapon had splintered, then shattered under the hardship of his attack. It fell away, like a boulder and its chipped pieces went down the cliffside of the Drake's immense figure. The absence of the bone weaponry left Fox's arm felling raw, but every part of his new body was, too, calling for attention, and he could answer none of it with due repose or care. Fox was closer to the albino goddess now, as the dragon attempted to end her by burying her alive within himself, and the Knighted Wyrm made a confession to the Conqueror: "I can't be with her. In the past, I did something to her which is unforgivable."

Chinami's many eyes widened, and so, too, did Daofeng's as Fox threw aside the section of skull he had chiseled from the Drake.

The Dilong regurgitated what he had of the goddess-queen, and he roared, pitching himself backwards with tremendous force. As he fell back, he saw the black feathered Serpent for a moment.

Chinami heaved against the cerulean Drake with the entirety of her weight, hoping to save the Knighted Wyrm. But, Daofeng's skin and muscle ripped in her mouth, and his entrails splashed blood into the multitude of her eyes.

Fox heard, or perhaps, he felt, an inner earthquake – the shifting of tectonic plates and the destruction of a planetary sphere. He winced because there was pain. The fortress that was his body was no more. The armor of him was demolished, and he was cold, fragments of stone floating all around him. He realized he was underwater. With what remained to him, he took another handful of brain, excising it from the chambers of Daofeng's head, and the creature went silent and surrendered to inanimation. Fox let go. He joined the Drake in stillness a second later, as his heavy body found the silted bottom of the River Orb.

At the surface, Dayraven hurried to the water's edge.

The current was impeded by the magnificent size of the azure Dilong's carcass, and how naïve or uncaring was the sunlight to play a flitting glimmer over the dead Drake's sapphire scales. The Serpent inched closer, but he could not see more of the Dilong's visage, for Daofeng had sent the back of his skull through the midpoint of the stone bridge, crushing it to rubble, and Death had left him with a face mostly-drowned.

Soo-yeon made it to the river as well, and on its banks, she sat beside Chinami, who was, again, of human form, and Soo-yeon cried weakly against her.

Morning, now, would have no more of sleepiness and crept into every groove of pain and sheened the fallen blood that was everywhere.

CHAPTER 37

THE DEEPEST MIRROR

Ardyce had accepted her death. She didn't wonder how it would unfold, or if she would have to suffer. She didn't consider what, if anything, would follow after the final pulsations of her heart.

She thought of Dayraven, clutching an armful of someone she once knew – that little bit of jade she saw before she would never see it again. She thought of the eggshell pieces strewn in the dirt, like a scorned love letter mangled to shreds, and how they were what remained of two sons she was meant to have. Ardyce saw, too, in her memories, the darkened shapes Mohonia's brothers had made as they left this world, then she remembered each of the Wyrms and Drakes she had rent, pulped, and burned. Their deaths overlapped, like dream sequences imbricating one over the other.

She wondered why she had followed a path of blood and hatred, when her life prior had been predominated by love. And, care, she remembered, too. Then, she recalled admiration and respect for the station she had held as Great Aegis.

I was wrong, Ardyce said for her own ears, and, perhaps, for those Drakes and Wyrms who surrounded her and would be the ones to eliminate the last of her ruminations.

I would not have given chase to this murderous hunt, if I knew it would end in me tearing you from the skies, my friend, Ardyce told the

Mungkr in her thoughts, for there was nowhere else the Ngaw now existed, except in memories. *I am sorry, Sasithorn.*

A rustling came from those who had formed a ring to surround her, and Ardyce raised her gaze to see them chary of her, inching back, as their eyes ran over her. They stared for several moments, agitation in their muscles.

Then, they turned away.

Singly, or by pairs, they abandoned the conclusion of her demise and submitted her to the quiet of the day. Ardyce watched them, for she felt unmistaken that there was a new shadow in their eyes, another silhouette of misfortune.

Soon, she was alone.

Death had wandered away from her, and her fury had deserted her to chilled hands which clutched at her insides. Ardyce felt raw within and worn. Every thought of Sasithorn that came to her was a reenactment of her demise and in finer and finer detail. It was as though Ardyce had no other memories of her.

She wished for her own death. She told herself she would have been happy to follow her friend to the silence which emerges after the pain of Life departs.

Ardyce screamed, down against the marl. Only the loose stones could withstand her anguish.

Her body shook, and she felt herself grotesque with injury. She wondered what any of them had gained since the tides of bloodshed. Whether coerced by individual rage, as she was, impelled by one's ethics, or as defense of the self and others, Ardyce felt they had paid. There would be voids which would forever eat of them.

The Tree Crown raised her head, searching for the sight of another Drake and faintly wishing for some reason why this history should be theirs. There weren't any Drakes left, only a Wyrm who had been staring at her. She knew she'd seen concern in its eyes before it quickly slinked away upon being noticed. Ardyce gathered herself. She followed the Wyrm and with it, the other creatures, for there were strings of them, all weaving in the same direction. The Wyrms and Drakes who went wore defeat in their bones, and their postures were of fatigue, as the ideals of war and death putrefied and became the burdens of the Reaper.

The vale they crossed imprinted a mural of their collected tracks, and when Ardyce looked out in the distance to one side of her, she saw the treeline of a forest. The wooden sentries seemed to be looking back at her. Their twisting and irregular limbs imposed and intertwined with their neighbors, creating the scribblings of one deranged against the brightness of the heavens. Ardyce wondered why they were all disrobed of their frondescence. They reminded her of home and the Up-Ended Trees. She realized it had been too long since she'd thought of home.

Beneath her and the group she trekked with, the blades of grass were vibrant, like newborns, promising things which only daylight can promise, and the hour went easy and loping, as though to comfort them who were left with the illusion of time slowing, after the immediacy of war.

The dell led out towards the river, and with the advantage of her height, Ardyce saw, before many others, the soul-less vessel of the great Dilong. She realized it was he who drew them. The blue Drake rested in the waters, partially-arrayed in the eddying flow, and his eye was a void, full with the glare of the Sun. His maw laid wide, as if with hunger, but there was only the Orb to fill it, and the waters were blushed by his extracted organs.

The corpse did not resemble what Ardyce knew of Daofeng. His body conformed to the boulder-like outcropping which endured of the demolished bridge, partially draped over it, and from afar to her, he looked like little more than a discarded banner trapped in a sewer grate.

Who could possibly fell him? She, and his followers, wondered the same, impossible thought. They gathered at the banks, some of them bowing their heads in respect, but Ardyce stood and noticed two women upon the opposite land. One of them was of hue entirely white. Ardyce stared at her, and their gazes met. There was blood at the young woman's mouth. She nursed bitter wounds, which stood, glaring, against her alabaster skin.

"Please, Great Aegis of the Tree Crown nation. Could you help us? He ordered your life be taken, so it is wrong for us to ask, but Daofeng was loved by us." A crimson Death Wyrm requested this of Ardyce in meek voice and flinched when the Tree Crown's eyes settled upon her.

Ardyce quelled her vexation at being addressed by a Wyrm and softened her thoughts, as she gave attention, instead, to the Serpent with corvine plumage, who had crossed what he could of the ruined bridge and stood near to the face of the deceased titan.

The Tree Crown looked back to the Death Wyrm, then went to the other end of the bridge. There was empathy welling in her heart, as she watched those accumulating at the river to bow their heads to he torn from vitality. She realized she did not hate the azure dragon for wishing to kill someone she too felt was deserving of death: herself. If he and his people had triumphed, Ardyce knew Sasithorn would still be alive. She said to them all, *I shall bury him for you.*

The Serpent lifted his eyes at her telepathic voice and startled at the sight of her. Ardyce thought it was for seeing her alive when she should have been dead. Bewildered, he questioned, "Ardyce?"

She studied him, perplexed by him questioning her identity. *Of course, it's me,* she replied, then stopped. The Tree Crown recalled the Wyrms and Drakes who had bestowed her with similar expressions. She went to the edge of the river and peered in.

Ardyce was a Tree Crown Drake: 95 tons of tattered muscle, with eyes like glossed, prismatic light; they had an oil-spill likeness. Chalcedony grew near the aperture of her eyes and upon her shoulders and haunches, as well. Adorning her head stood but two tiers of antlers where there should have been three, and still, of those two remaining, they were steel and gleaming their cinereous color. However, there was a transformation to her being which ceased her breath for moments on end.

"You are pearl-white, Tree Crown," Dayraven said to her.

It was true. She no longer mirrored the hue of the Scourge Angel. Ardyce was dazed by that reflection of herself. She was altered, yet felt more belonging to her name, her title, and her very existence. Her skin became her chosen raiment, and her eyes gave her, not the vision of the world, but *her* vision within the world.

Recovered of her merit, Ardyce performed as were her wishes that the Great Aegis should. She treaded into the River Orb, and though it was a formidable task, she retrieved the body of Daofeng and ascended the firmament with it. In the pinnacle hour of the Reigning Star, she held the Dilong in the sky and allowed the believers of Daofeng to mourn him, casting their farewells to the wide empyrean. Then, she flew to the brilliance of the sea, and she deposited the corpse in a sapphire tomb.

Daofeng disappeared into the Kingdom of the Deepest Mirror. The waves were greedy for him, then they hid him, so Ardyce returned to earthly footing, and she wandered for a few minutes. She passed those facing the sea, and they made obeisance to her, brimming with gratitude and grief. Humbly, she acknowledged them, then she shied away from the scene, yearning to venture home to Mohonia and Nandenia.

But, if she went to them, she knew she would have to await the conclusion of their times with her Vow and daughter, unable to do else for their survival, and Ardyce was certain that, once gods awakened, they did not placidly return to dreaming slumber.

Ardyce turned away from home, though it strained against her every desire. She went, instead, in search of Dayraven, and when she found the Serpent, a rifle was pointed at his skull.

"You lied to me to get to Hadryn."

"I didn't lie to you. I had information you wished to know."

"Giving me bits and pieces, knowing all the while that it didn't matter if I solved the unexplainable 'murder' in my village. People were going to change no matter what." Oshin appeared familiar with the weight of the rifle, bracing the butt of it against the inside of her shoulder. "And, you knew that, too."

The Serpent gazed at her, ignoring the end of the rifle directed at him. "If I had told you what would become of people, how could you believe it? It was better to let you discover it, in its entirety."

"You could have told me what you were!" she retorted angrily. Hadryn stood beside her and touched her shoulder, but she wouldn't lower the gun.

"Enough of this," the Knight Archidux coaxed. "Let me look at your wound. You shouldn't be standing on it."

Thaddius and LeShawn kept to one side of them, tending to each other's injuries, but listening intently to the argument betwixt human and creature. The Serpent also noted Chinami and Soo-yeon near the waters of Orb, arms encircled to protect one another from the mind wandering alone through the trauma of the hours spent.

"Again, how to explain what I am?" the Serpent asked. "It was better you saw for yourself what else existed in this sphere."

Oshin yelled at Dayraven, "*You could have told me what Hadryn is! That monsters would come for him and offer him as a prize to reckless, self-serving gods!*" She breathed to steady her voice. "You are all concealed truths for your own personal aim!" The Filipino woman's finger weighed heavily on the trigger of the rifle she held to the Serpent's face. She said to him, "If I shot you for every time you lied to me, you would look the giant asshole you are, you fucking beast!"

Dayraven's feathers were slightly bristled.

Hadryn was there to restrain Oshin. He guided her hands to lower the firearm. He said, "Let him speak to us. We've come all this way to find him."

"*No*," she said sharply and gritted her teeth. The terror in her eyes was half-fettered. "We will hear nothing of what he has to say." She took Hadryn by the hand to lead him away, but he reeled her back to himself and held her.

Hadryn kissed Oshin's knuckles of the hand which held his. "You fear what he will offer me, though it may be the truth. I don't know what I am. I don't know what it means to be an 'Orb.'"

Oshin didn't choose her words. They chose themselves, bursting from her. *"He thinks you are something meant to be eaten, in a world where people should only be eating themselves!"* Then, her words caged themselves for seeing his expression, unflinching, and she didn't know how much he'd considered or ruminated on when she'd been unconscious. Fleetingly, Oshin wished they had letters between them to read of each other's thoughts, for he was unknown to her in that moment with the look in his eyes both determined and serene.

Behind them, the plumed Serpent gently said, "It is because he already ate who he was."

A rock struck the hardness of Dayraven's beak, but inflicted little pain. Hadryn had to stop Oshin from bending to pick up a larger stone.

Oshin turned to the Knight. "How can he offer you 'truth,' Hadryn? A martyr's fantasy, more like it. He will play to the nobility in you." Her eyes squinted with tears she didn't wish him to see. She struck lightly at Hadryn's chest, in frustration. "Play upon the goodness that is you, Hadryn. Your stupid, knightly oaths and principles." She pulled urgently at his robe in the direction opposite of the waiting Serpent. "Come. We will find our own answers."

Dayraven watched them, then spoke. "I apologize to you, Oshin. There was no other way for me to reach Hadryn. If I could have gone into the Tiered Nations, myself, I would have to seek him out."

The Serpent's apology and confession were kindling for her fury. "So, then, you used the woman who loves him as a tie to him! *You knew I would say your name, then you would have a bridge to his ear and thoughts, that he and I would follow that archway to you.*" She glared at him. "You, then, could wait for us to come to you." Hadryn caught her in his arms before she could have at Dayraven, and he had to lift her from her feet somewhat to nullify her traction, for she was powerful for her size and determined.

Thaddius was nearby and now attempted to take part and ease the tension, as she finished bandaging LeShawn's torn wing. "You are as guilty as they come, Dayraven. I've learned to never trifle with the heart of a woman." Hadryn was having a difficult time containing the Filipino woman. "She is a proper storm, Hadryn."

"Do not rally her, Thaddius," Hadryn said.

LeShawn spoke next, saying that which her wife could not. "Oshin." The other woman had ceased struggling, so the Pyrolite knew Oshin saw the truth before she spoke it. "If Hadryn is an Orb, this would be our route, no matter the direction we came to it."

"Please," Dayraven begged to reason with them. "Hadryn. May I ask you the question for which I sought you?"

"I will beat you, if you speak, Dayraven!" Oshin pounced towards the enormous creature, again, but Hadryn bolted her in place. She yelled at the Serpent, "You have no right!"

The congregation of them there hushed after a moment, and there was a rawness to the air. For each of them, the love of those most dear to them ached far worse than any of their wounds.

Hadryn steadied her and brought her a couple of paces away. He stared down into her eyes and touched her face. He let her count her breaths, even though she wasn't counting, to calm and find a trace of patience. The Knight of Third Rank was quiet briefly, then he admitted, "I did not think you would so care for me, like this."

Oshin sighed dramatically, much exasperated, and turned away from him. "You are always so sappy, even in your letters."

Hadryn spun her back around and kissed her forehead. "Can you trust me? We need answers for you as well: how you came to arrive here and why your birthmark is spreading." He touched her skin with its red tint, but she ignored his concern for her.

"Dayraven is not as any of those we saw in battle – neither dragon nor worm. He is something else. What did you tell me of her: Chinami?" Oshin pointed to the river bank where the cream-colored woman sat, rocking Soo-yeon.

"She is the Conqueror," Hadryn answered her.

"And, she would not accept your power, your life. You want me to trust Dayraven who obviously yearns for these things?"

The Knight touched her hair. "I want you to trust me." Hadryn kissed her mouth.

She was stubborn but tempered by his affections. "I already do." Oshin reluctantly went with Hadryn back to the Serpent.

Behind Dayraven, a fitting length away to be unintrusive, yet also within earshot, Ardyce sat patiently. She watched them, intrigued.

Hadryn stood across from Dayraven. He said, "Ask me the question."

And, the Serpent looked at each of them, before he began. He confirmed what they knew of the ever-lasting cycles their world endured – that freakish transformations would arise in every age; violence and war repeated ceaselessly. He told them that the gods always awakened when the humans, through metamorphosis, were no more, for then, the Angel and the Conqueror would bid their respective kin to take up arms against one another. This was how the gods believed their own would survive. Neither was willing to wager trust in each other to deny war, least it cost them their species. When that happened, Death claimed dominion of the days and nights, until no one remained but the gods, and it was said that the coal-black god and pale goddess fought, until the world burned anew, returning them to slumber. Then, the cycle was reborn. The suffering would pass to the subsequent generation.

He told them that it was Daofeng's belief that both gods should die, that the world of our children should be godless and free – that the gods' deaths would break the chain of repetition. But, Dayraven was learning, he admitted. When he said this, he turned to stare after Chinami who was signing with Soo-yeon. Soo-yeon was nodding often, and her tears had dried. She'd dressed Chinami's flayed skin with wraps made from torn pieces of the clothes the Knight wore.

"I haven't learned enough, but I don't know when it will ever be enough. I search for truth, and I've come to consider the Conqueror may die as a god should. Not through violence, but absorbed by a human heart. A god submitted to the love of a human." Dayraven told them. "And, that leaves the Scourge to this world."

There was the eventide refrain of a breeze lightly treading and the branches with their leaves which bestrode it and the river like the footsteps of many children hurrying off to some adventure. All of it was as kindly and subdued as mental chatter. In that space of quiet, Soo-yeon and Chinami joined the group, and even Ardyce edged closer. The woman of pale skin stared at Oshin, noticing that the Filipino woman's hands were now tinged red to match her scarlet marking.

They sat inland from the river, but still within view of it, for Soo-yeon felt not yet ready to part from Fox's grave. A copse of trees mostly shielded them from the cooling breeze of late afternoon, and LeShawn had easily made for them a pitted fire, which they encircled for further warmth. Oshin had, earlier, spotted near the fallen bridge, ripe plums collecting on the trees which grew there. She and Hadryn had climbed the trees and picked enough of the fruit for them all to stave off the pangs of hunger.

They were, now, finishing the last of the plums – even, Ardyce had been given her share by Chinami who had ventured near her, and the Tree Crown laid out behind the group at the fire.

LeShawn asked them, "If there is only one god, then their opposition will be lost, and they won't destroy all in their quarrel. Is that right?"

Chinami lifted her hands and signed as Soo-yeon gave them her words. "'My Wyrms will all die though. He'll kill them. They were people. So, we sacrifice those people to him, if we do nothing.'"

"Daofeng's people will take care of him," Thaddius tried.

Everyone startled badly as Ardyce's telepathy touched them. She had to repeat herself twice after they'd recovered from the shock. Inwardly, she sighed a little at human limitations. *They've lost Daofeng, and the Scourge's army which I conducted and myself laid waste to their small numbers. It isn't viable for them to pursue him.*

Dayraven was collecting himself, and they all noticed him straightening in place to say that which they didn't wish to hear.

"As a Serpent, and you an Orb, Hadryn. Together, I know we would be powerful enough to create the World Serpent: a being capable of bringing an end to the Angel. And, end him, we should, if for no other reason than to save what lives remain." Dayraven finally asked of Hadryn: "So, will you help me rid the world of the Angel, Hadryn?"

Oshin glared at the Serpent. "I knew it. You are asking for him to die. He'll be no more, once he's given you this 'orb power,' is that not true?"

Hadryn tried to calm her, least Oshin's anger for the Serpent take over once more. Dayraven was opposite them, coiled in around himself, and Soo-yeon and Chinami had made themselves warm in his layers of black feathers. The robe Chinami had earlier discarded to assume the figure of the Conqueror Wyrm had been retrieved from the grasslands, and the Japanese woman looked even tinier in it, yet content and comfortable with warmth. Beside Hadryn and Oshin sat Thaddius with LeShawn.

Ardyce rested against cousins to the trees she had seen earlier, and she was comforted by those wooden sentries, as Tree Crowns commonly are soothed by the presence of trees. Ardyce's injuries pendulated her in and out of a hazy sleep. She had not yet spoken much with this unlikely collection of souls, but enough for them to know she wished to accompany Dayraven in his pursuit of the Angel's destruction. Ardyce found herself comfortable in their presence, an affection gaining for them. Oshin and Chinami had done what they could for her by clay-packing her open wounds, and LeShawn had cauterized the boring in her throat to cease the last trickling out of her blood. The Tree Crown waited on their debate and dreamt of her home, hearing voices in her sleep – perhaps, coming from the group of them or from memories.

Dayraven was staring at Oshin, who had once trusted him, and his desire was to answer as honestly as he could. "We will be joined as composition of the same creature, Oshin, both still alive. But, we may die, battling the Scourge Angel, or the World Serpent may perish or vanish after the work of it is done. These are my speculations, but it is impossible to attach certainty to them when the World Serpent has not before been forged."

"That's understandable," Hadryn assured Dayraven, but Oshin flashed him a disapproving look.

"I don't like it," Thaddius concluded. "What other options do we have?"

Dayraven glanced up towards the heavens, looking away from the two women who had nestled in his plumage, and he saw the first few stars emerging. "We wait to see what becomes of our world, and as we wait, Chinami and the rest of the Wyrms may be hunted out of existence. If the Angel realizes the presence of a Serpent and an Orb, I don't think he'll leave us to peace either." The Serpent drew in a breath. "Or, we can attack him as we are."

Ardyce's voice crawled to them, drowsy-sounding. *I will fight alongside you all,* she said in their minds. Readily, she volunteered herself, for this company was an unexpected warmth to her. With her eyes closed, she felt as if Mohonia's siblings had returned to her.

"She's in no condition for more of war," LeShawn stated. "Did you know she is newly a mother and has not yet had an hour with her daughter? She told me this. I think we should escort Ardyce home, then-- ... then, recruit another army, or something, to kill this Scrooge Angel."

"'Scourge,' darling," Thaddius gently corrected her wife with a smile.

It was then that Chinami stood. She began to sign to them, but after several seconds, their faces remained blank and questioning. She realized Soo-yeon was not translating for her, and in fact, kept her head turned away so as not to see Chinami's hands.

"Soo-yeon," Oshin called to her. Her next words were tender of tone to the Korean woman because she knew Soo-yeon still had not dried her eyes over the loss of Fox. "Come now, don't be a brat. Tell us what she's saying."

"No," Soo-yeon answered.

Chinami knelt in front of the Knight of Sixth Rank and touched her face. The albino woman lifted her hands for speech, but Soo-yeon caught them in her own, turning her face to look into Chinami's eyes.

"Running off to battle him on your own? You're wrong. You're wrong, if you think I'll allow losing you as well."

Chinami stared at her, then she wanted to free her hands to reply to the Korean woman, but Soo-yeon would not release her. They tethered one another's gaze, but the pale-haired woman was the first to lower her eyes, and it was to look at Soo-yeon's lips, as she leaned forward to kiss the Knight.

Chinami didn't hear as a murmur of approval rippled through their shared company.

The Japanese woman pulled back, and Soo-yeon was flushed in the cheeks. The smaller woman stood, again, and stared out at the others who hid their smirking. Chinami cleared her throat. Her speech emitted haltingly with the accent of one unaccustomed to using her voice. "It has always been my place to combat the Scourge. No other should. I will go. It is difficult for me to ascend to the Conqueror Wyrm. But, I think I can. I am very fond of you all here. I think that will help me. Now. I must talk with Soo-yeon. Excuse us." She took Soo-yeon by the hand, leading her away.

"That was sweet," Hadryn remarked, watching them leave. "But, we aren't agreeing to it, are we?"

"Not a chance," LeShawn replied. Then, she observed of Chinami: "She looks like she's fourteen."

Thaddius countered, "She's Asian. She could be fourteen, she could be immortal. We'll never know."

"As for you," Hadryn continued, turning to Oshin, "there are things we, too, must discuss." He stood with her.

"Put me down, Hadryn!"

Oshin and the Knight of differing eye colors passed Ardyce, who still slept, and they disappeared into a grove of trees.

CHAPTER 38

OF MOONS WITH NIGHTS

Chinami walked under the clearness of the moon that had wandered into the sky. She felt Soo-yeon's footsteps behind herself, and Chinami questioned her feelings to see whether any of this had a sense of familiarity. She felt it didn't. If she'd fought the Angel for all of time, why was she terrified of the thought of him? Abruptly, she thought on Oshin and her unusual, red birthmark, but could make nothing of it though she felt it was somehow how Oshin had come to be at their sides. Chinami brooded to herself.

Soo-yeon stopped Chinami to turn her around. She said to the goddess of Wyrms, "You didn't have to risk yourself for him. But, thank you."

Chinami asked with her hands, *Were you in love with him?*

"No. But, I cared for him." Soo-yeon used sign for her next words: *I care about you, too, so I don't want you to fight that thing.*

If you were me, Chinami gestured to the taller woman, *how could you let everyone die without trying to protect them? I don't think you could do that.*

Soo-yeon was without words, until a despondent breath of laughter, which wasn't laughter, escaped her, and the wetness came back to her eyes. She was shaking her head. She signed, *What do you want from me, then?* "You want me to permit it? Do

435

you want me to send you off with a smile and a kiss? Do you want me to watch you die? To cry over you?" She was bitter over the reason Fox had fought to his death. She realized that seeing cowards become heroes was awful.

Chinami stared at the dark-haired woman, piercing an unknown stratum within herself in seeking to understand the human in her gaze. The pale goddess felt of herself that she was both human, like Soo-yeon, and then, entirely not-human. Un-human. But, that her burgeoning emotions for the Korean woman had rendered her identity malleable. Chinami watched the gamut of feelings flickering in the Knight's eyes. Soo-yeon was transparent to her: she could see the arrayed interior of her, but Chinami didn't know exactly what she was seeing or how to absorb it. Humans seemed, to her, predisposed to their emotions. Chinami felt it made Soo-yeon pretty.

I want, Chinami said to Soo-yeon, *to join with you this moment, as humans would. Do you accept me?*

Soo-yeon wore, again, rose petals in her cheeks. She stumbled over her words. "Ch-Chinami. We haven't known each other-- ... for very long."

The albino woman was quiet, analyzing this. Then, she said with her hands, *So, there is a time element for humans.* She thought of another question. *Is it meaningless to love someone for one day?*

The Knight became pensive. She signed, *I haven't thought of that before. It's strange to think of love as being meaningless though.*

Interesting, Chinami observed. She waited a moment before saying, *You have rejected me, and I understand. We can return to the others, if you'd like.* Being human was difficult, she thought to herself.

"I haven't rejected you, Chinami," Soo-yeon rushed her words. *No. I accept you,* she said with her hands, feeling honest and suddenly seeing of her life that her only experience of genuineness was the autumn morning she was knighted in ceremony with a dozen others. That time and these turbulent days with this unearthly woman were a reality beyond her current understanding. She saw how to look at her life for the first time.

You do? The Japanese woman asked her. Chinami wore moonlight in her hair as she stepped closer to Soo-yeon with a little, questioning smile.

Yes, the Knight replied. She saw those pink eyes in detail now, and the albinism, and the frame so slight, yet carrying within it an impossible legacy, power, and albatross. Soo-yeon touched her. She held the pale queen at the waist, as Chinami came to her, and the Knight leaned down. Soo-yeon kissed Chinami, and from that shared breath, she felt the immediacy of their existence and discovered that Chinami felt more an articulation of Nature than she'd ever known before. The Knight both wondered how it came to pass and regretted that the Tiered Nations, and those of it, had lived as little more than half-mobile stomachs. They'd all wasted their lives when life could have been more of this.

Soo-yeon separated of their warmth to look into Chinami's eyes. She didn't know for how long they'd kissed, but she had the sense of time elapsing.

The Conqueror's soft breaths were quick and crowding each other. Chinami remembered to speak: *Did we join?* Chinami felt a gentle pang, which she couldn't comprehend, but that was embarrassment. She continued with her hands: *I was not sure if we needed to say specific words, or perform a particular action. Or, if there was something we needed to give to one another.*

But, Soo-yeon was undoing the strings tied at her backside, and the dudou fell away from her breasts. She worked loose the sash which held her pants, then stepped out of the garment with Chinami watching her. The pale goddess' eyes widened, as she stared at Soo-yeon.

Soo-yeon signed to Chinami, *To join, you'll need to come within me.* And, she held her hand out to Chinami.

"Oshin, wait."

But, Hadryn's senses were smearing together under a delicious warmth, and a chord within his body was being stretched taut by a demanding need, which Oshin strummed of that chord each time her tongue fell over his and the swollen softness of her lips found his mouth. It felt to him a little like when the need to run overcame him, and the urging began at the center of his chest, and as he began to answer it, his body rose to heat and the force of his own strength came through all his limbs. Except, this time, there was a responsive tempo and cadence to both further his desire and drown him. He felt Oshin holding his face, then her hands slipping down to open the front of his robe. His chest met with the cool of the night, and he froze.

"Wait." Hadryn pulled back to redo the clasps of his military uniform.

Beneath him, Oshin sat up. "Why?" She searched his eyes, confused and afraid, as if she, too, worried over rejection. But, Hadryn felt that was impossible.

He shrugged to diminish the possibility of this moment and quell the terror which the thought of this conversation had induced for nine years. Because he had to be truthful with Oshin, he said, "Underneath their robe," he touched it lightly, "there is nothing left that is female, Oshin. Or, rather, there is very little."

She was quiet, still attempting to sort him out. "You penned to me every step and stage of your transition."

"But, you saw none of it," he replied gently.

They were silent for several seconds, each feeling cautious for what would be said next, except that Oshin abruptly blurted out: "This is why you never came to me."

Hadryn always knew she would confront him directly, once she knew, but it didn't lend him any more ease or grace in the actual moment. He picked through his words and tried to sound in possession of himself. "My thought was that it may be easier to accept when one doesn't have to see it."

She judged him. "You thought we would meet, and I would turn and leave after seeing you without breasts."

"It's more than that, Oshin. Much more."

She had spoken from a shock of hurt, but recovered quickly and admitted, "You're right. It is. I'm sorry for saying that."

Hadryn sat with her, afraid and uncertain of where their next words would take them. But, they were overdue, and it was his fault for that. "You told me that, since you were little, you knew you preferred girls. Women."

"I did say that," she agreed.

"And, while we wrote to each other, you've been attracted to others, haven't you?"

"Naturally." She was forward and honest with him. "And, content to let those attractions walk by. I never needed them for anything."

"But, were they all women?" Hadryn asked.

"Yes." She would not lie to him.

He lowered his gaze and resented the questions he needed answered. "Never once was it a man?"

"No," Oshin confirmed it.

In his imaginings, this had gone better. And, it had gone much worse. Thus, Hadryn continued on, questioning her. "Tell me, then, how this – right now – makes sense to you, who are a lesbian."

She stared at him, though he wouldn't return it, and Oshin said, "I never proclaimed to be a lesbian, and lesbian or not, I simply fell in love." With sincerity, she told him. "I'm just a person who fell in love, Hadryn."

He lifted his eyes to her. He touched her face. "But, what will you love when I am down to my skin, Oshin? You can't know that."

"There is a simple enough way to find out," she returned. Oshin saw the Knight's posture go rigid. "I will be honest with you, as I've always been. We can conclude your fears here, this moment." He made no movement, said no word. "Go on," she encouraged him. "If you wear my ring, there will be no secrets kept from each other." She stared at him, already seeing more of him. In one of his letters, he'd mentioned, with casual detachment, Oshin felt, that some had been unwilling to see him as anything more than freakish and unnatural: his father, foremost, most denizens, and 'certain sorts' of the military. But, when she asked more of his feelings over this treatment, he had dropped the issue and not returned to it. She'd always felt the only thing unnatural of him was his strength in not letting others whittle his conviction of self.

Oshin stood and gestured for the Knight to rise as well. He followed her motion, and his stature was over half a head taller than hers.

Hadryn said to her, "I have always loved you, Oshin. From female to male, that has never changed for me."

She touched the clasps of his robe, again. "But, you have loved your fear more than me."

He would profess it to her, though he didn't wish to admit it, even to himself. "Guilty," he said.

She went on, "And, that changes this day." Oshin worked slowly to disrobe him. Under her fingers – bending, pressing, parting – his uniform loosened, until it resided on the ground, no longer the shape of him.

The woman who had formed life Beyond the Merlons gazed upon every plane of the Knight Archidux and of his details both handsome and sweet. Oshin touched her fingerprints to him, tracing the scarred skin just under his pectoral muscles, and tips of her fingers went through the light hairs of his body. He was lean and strong, under her touch, and a bit underweight. Oshin looked into one of his eyes, at the coalescence of violet and cerulean, then to the other eye of unblemished white. She caressed the ring to encircle his left finger.

Hadryn closed his left hand, afraid for a moment that she would remove it from him. His heart ferreted in the cage of his chest, for he felt she would surely leave.

"Never go without this," Oshin said, "for it is the shape of forever which I have promised you. And, as you can see, its form is unchanging – neither twisting, cracking, or breaking, even though you are completely bare to me." She placed a palm upon his chest to feel the racing of his heart's meter. "You are beautiful, Hadryn." Oshin rose to her tiptoes and kissed him.

Hadryn returned that kiss and each of her kisses of the night. And, now, his body caught up with his heart in knowing the entrancement which is love. He found himself of singular mind and in it was her pleasure which led to the peaking of his own. When she clutched or clung to him, he moved deeper into their rhythm to extract his name from her lips. Having never heard his name said this way – of this tone and embodied with such emotion – he felt it create another identity of himself.

"Hadryn," Oshin cried out, as she came, again. He returned to her face, moving back up her panting figure, and he kissed her forehead, as she gradually calmed her breath. Hadryn embraced her and, loving the silk of her black hair, ran his fingers through her long locks, until she fell asleep against him for several minutes.

He looked at the moon, criss-crossed by branching shoots of the tree to overhang them. Then, he gazed at her skin and worried still that the strawberry mark once on her neck had elongated to mask over half her body. But, she seemed unconcerned with it and said that it didn't hurt. Oshin had passed it off as an "odd reaction" to her arrival here.

"Tell me, now, if you will be the one to reject me," Oshin softly said, against Hadryn's chest, and he departed of his thoughts.

He stared down at her, much confused. "'Reject you?' How could I ever, Oshin?"

She lifted her head to meet his eyes. "If tomorrow you leave me for Dayraven's idiot plan, then, you have rejected me. I'll be without you."

Tomorrow came too quickly for him, then, though it wasn't yet here. He stared at her, feeling she was trapped beyond his reach, even as he could feel the pulse of her body pressed to his. "I should have gone to you after our tenth letter, or fifth ... or third. I should have been with you all this time, Oshin."

"Then, stay with me, if that is how you feel," she pleaded with him. *"Stay with me, Hadryn."* With two fingers, she reached between their bodies, and Oshin entered him once more.

Hadryn struggled with this: so much of wanting her and wanting them. He knew he needed to tell her. *"Oshin. That -- ...*

Every way I look at it, *what he proposes is the right thing to do.* A part of me hates it, because it has nothing to do with loving you. Oshin, I'm sorry."

But, she was already making love to him. "I've only just met you while loving you," she told him.

"Forgive me," he asked of her, losing himself. "Do you wish for the ring back?"

"My only wish," she confessed, "is a million more days together." She bit at his lower lip, for he had penetrated her in return.

He knew, now, that her wish was his own, since the moment she stood before him, as herself. Perhaps, there was nothing he'd ever wished for more. "A million more dinners together," he agreed with her.

She held at him. "A million more nights. Like this one."

"And, a million more possibilities."

Then, they were as the night and the moon, enveloping each other, reigning one over the other in turns, and finally, belonging to one another, until dawn came to separate them.

CHAPTER 39

THE LAST CONTENDERS

When Ardyce woke, she realized nearly half her strength had found her in the middle of the night, like a migratory bird arriving to its destination a bit tardy. Still, it was good to be reclaimed by her own power.

"I am the Great Aegis," she mumbled to herself, and the sounds she uttered were like stones dragging over one another. It seemed her voice had returned, as well, while she slumbered, but it was of battered form and worse off than her body, of which she could feel more and more.

The sun was somewhere above her, warming the chill out of the air, and Ardyce felt trees nearby, but they were not the Up-Ended Trees she had known all her life.

She attempted to open her eyes, but her vision was stalling under a blurred cloak, and she thought she saw Dayraven coming to her with more plums to eat. But, it wasn't the Serpent. It was Hadryn, kneeling to place the fruit near her, then checking of her wounds.

"Go on, lovebird," she told him, knowing Hadryn and Oshin shared the bond of new lovers. "Cast off," she said and flicked him lightly with her tail, as he began to clean and redress one of her wounds. "I am well enough for a fight. Just a few sands more of sleep," Ardyce muttered and gave up trying to shoo him away, as the drowsiness refused, just yet, to entirely leave her.

443

He replied to her, but she only heard his voice and couldn't define his words, for the sun had lulled her to a state just past dozing, but not of dreaming. Her senses pattered just outside her consciousness, making her sleep uncomfortable, yet still, her body welcomed it. She felt Hadryn finish with her wounds, and then, he sat against her, eating his share of the plums. On instinct, she bent a wing over his lap to keep him warm, the same wings she had used to keep Mohonia and his brothers shrouded in warmth at night.

Hadryn's appetite was hearty, and when he was sated, Ardyce heard words from him, one by one, and ignored them, until they finally threaded together to make sense to her.

"Ardyce. What would you do to protect your love? And others whom you love?"

It was Hadryn's voice, but Mohonia's face asking it of her, and beside her Vow was sweet Nandenia, laughing. In odd, canted angles, waxing and waning over each other, she saw snippets of the violence she had both wrought and endured.

Ardyce murmured, "I would cheat Death, boy. Even if it meant I'd have to create and re-create myself to do it." After a while, he stood and ran his hands over a part of her face. She was light with him, uncaring, as she said in the tone which is sleep-talking, "Do not pet me. I am not your pet."

Then, he chuckled and left, and she had more of sleep. It seemed to Ardyce that dreaming began, then, for she walked to the circle of humans, embodied of human form herself: impossibly tall, white-haired, dressed as a Royal Guard, and she listened to them speak.

Dayraven said, "We'll need to find him first."

To which, LeShawn replied, "He is enormous. If we take to the skies, we'll make short work of it."

Soo-yeon was translating for Chinami. "Chinami knows where to find the Angel. 'He is tearing down the trees which sprout from the heavens and bloom into the soil of Earth.'"

"'Tearing down trees?'" Thaddius questioned. "Why would he do that?"

Soo-yeon watched Chinami. "'The trees encourage growth, affecting those who live near to them.'"

Ardyce knew they couldn't hear her voice, as she said to this, "No."

"'Like, evolution. Adaptation,'" Soo-yeon continued for Chinami.

Ardyce saw her kin, those sleeping Tree Crowns nestled against the boles of trees. She saw their antlers emerging and wings forming upon their backs.

Chinami's words came through Soo-yeon: "'The territory of the Wyrms are near to those trees, and the Scourge Angel believes the trees are how Wyrms developed speech and teeth. He would eliminate that possibility for any survivors and future generations of Wyrms.'"

"*No!* That is my home!" Ardyce yelled, and it was soundless. She turned from them and walked out to a clearing, searching for the feeling of flights at her back.

"Ardyce!" Her name was now clear and sharp; she was torn from sleep. Oshin had called to her, and Ardyce was, once more, a Drake, filling the grassy dell with the greatness of her ponderosity. "Where are you going?" Oshin asked her, concerned.

"It is my home she speaks of," Ardyce said, again, and this time she was heard. "Mohonia. And, Nandenia. I have to go to them!" Her wings arched, then spread, prepared to meet the welkin.

"Take us, Ardyce," Thaddius said. "We've only so many pairs of wings, and we need to cross the sanded region."

"I beg you, hurry," she answered, and within seconds, those who had never known the firmament, besides in looking up at it, had mounts and winds against their faces, which tasted different, as they breathed them into their lungs, than when they stood upon the ground.

Ardyce sped towards Outer Gled Tria, and it was not long before the desert kingdom sprawled beneath them. The gamboge of the sands extended suddenly in all directions, and there were natural ridges, short and smooth, upon the otherwise gilded and planate surface. Then, there was that which was against Nature.

The images below them augmented in horror by surging intervals, and upon LeShawn's back where sat the albino goddess, Soo-yeon, and Thaddius, who hadn't been able to keep pace with the Drakes, Chinami cried out in grief. Ardyce carried the remainder of their party.

Ardyce glanced at the one known as the Conqueror Wyrm, and she had crumbled on LeShawn's back to see the gutting of her home and ravaging of her people. The eviscerated carcasses of every race of Wyrm made rubbish heaps beside deep furrows in the land, and the sanded region was no longer an arid dwelling, but saw new lakes formed by the pooling of a people reduced to the blood of themselves. Ardyce saw eyes and faces, this which she hadn't seen when the hue of her had been tar, and she found in many visages terror that had not submitted to sleep, even in Death.

Well the Great Aegis knew this may have been her own handiwork, if she had made it as far as the desertlands. But, this was not her doing. It was, undoubtedly, the work of the Scourge Angel and his flock.

"At first, I thought it an unfair fate that the hope of this world should fall upon our shoulders alone," Thaddius called out to the others to be heard. "But, we were never alone in this."

Hadryn stared at her from Ardyce's back. "We are simply the last of the contenders."

The Drakes, Ardyce and LeShawn, drew their wings to a slant upon the winds and swept in towards Outer Gled Tria, home of the Tree Crown Drakes.

Dayraven looked to Hadryn, and he asked the Orb, "Have you made your decision?"

C H A P T E R   4 0

THE MOTHER RETURNED

Nandenia had had nightmares for a sennight. On the backs of all hours were hefted the wailings of Death, of brutish torment. Because her father could hear none of it, she was isolated in the terrible keening to come from the land of the Wyrms. He held her though, as she cried, and he forced himself to go without sleep for days so that he could sing to her telepathically and drown out the sound of a nation dying.

When Nandenia was admitted into the halls of slumber though, she saw her mother as a monster, or her mother dying and trilling as a Wyrm before succumbing to a perished silence.

So, she slept always with her skin to the trunk of an Up-Ended Tree, and the presence of these Ever-Standing Ones gave to her a sense of being protected and florets of courage. She felt her antlers attain one, careful inch of height upon her crown and the limbs at her back formed their first joints. They were undeniably human-like arms, instead of the wings of a Drake, but because her father said nothing of them, Nandenia, too, remained hushed to acknowledge them.

The hours they were both awake, Nandenia knew it was her duty to keep herself and her father hidden. She listened all the while for other Drakes, but it seemed they had become the last. She feared it. She wished even for a Wyrm to come along. The

447

night before, Nandenia had nearly thought her wish granted, for her father had wakened her, having felt a shivering of the land. Nandenia imagined it was the sensation one above ground would feel at a Wyrm burrowing through the earth, but she became fully awake when Mohonia questioned her.

Is there sound with this tremoring of Outer Gled Tria? he asked her.

And, she heard it, then.

Bursting wood. Splintering frames.

Trees torn from their lives and crying out, in their own manner, as the Wyrms once did from the sanded regions.

Nandenia hated it. It had continued the length of the night and well into the morning. Mohonia had held her to himself to deny her running off to confront the coal-black titan, who was the destroyer of the Up-Ended Trees. They could see the back of that god with his hide charred and split, the fires beneath the integument of him. He was quite a way off, but his vastness made him to seem closer.

Please, father, we must do something! Nandenia beseeched her parent.

We mustn't, Nandenia! We are to wait for your mother! Mohonia stared into his daughter's eyes, afraid of her and afraid for her that her desire was to make herself known to a god who seemed to perform solely for Death.

The she-Drake refrained at first, but her words found their way from out her world to this reality upon the tears which came to her eyes, and she said what she felt to her father. *Most likely, she is already dead, father.* She saw how heavily those words hurt him, but she could not find a way to be silenced. *Or, she is a terrible beast, just as that monster is who topples the majesty of Outer Gled Tria.* Nandenia looked towards the sound of the trees being ripped away from their lands. *Perhaps, that monster is she whom we await. I'm sorry,* she said to her parent. *I must know.*

Nandenia dashed from Mohonia's sight, and she was faster and nimbler than he knew of her. He cried out for her, but within the close knitting of the forest of Up-Ended Trees, his wings were useless, and he was made to hobble after her, still healing from the loss of one his limbs. In his heart, he begged for Ardyce and felt worthless for it.

The child-Drake knew this forest like the feeling of her own body. She went quickly, to gain upon that sound of the trees dying. A league she traveled in that forest. With barely a thought, she wound and twisted past the mickle widths of the trees' trunks, until she came to an awful void where there should have been another mile more of weald.

Nandenia froze as her clawed hand first came to contact with the pillaged marl. She saw the decimated wildwood piled as knolls of timber as far out as she could see and smelled of their opened vessels and of the damp soil turned over to the air. The hunched back of the enormous murderer and marauder was to her, and the head of that beast was down, deep in the heart of the land. Nandenia discovered her first throes of fury.

"Tell me who you are!" she demanded, as another tree was demolished in the giant's jaws. But, he remained ignorant of her, by choice, or for not hearing her. Before Nandenia knew it of herself, her ire had moved her teeth, and the pearl-white child-Drake went to the tail of the creature. He was the size of all darkness, even beyond the night, and his scent was the burning of a world. It came through his cracked skin. But, she was angry with him and at his tail: there, she sank her fury into the beast, hurting her teeth and burning her mouth on his tough skin where, beneath, ran coruscating blades of fire. Nandenia wrested out a mouthful of him, and he bled.

The Scourge Angel paused. He lifted his head, which seemed the size of a blackened sun, and the forest partly fell to shadow. He turned slowly to face Nandenia, peering down at her.

She spat out the flesh of him she'd taken, and it seemed his bottomless eyes widened, but only slightly.

"Who are you?" Nandenia required of him. She searched his face to see if there was any part of him she might know. "Do you know me?" she asked, and her fear made her voice softer than she intended. She was afraid but looked to see if her mother was within this deranged beast.

The Scourge Angel stared at her.

"A child," he said, as though he'd never seen one before. *"Nandenia!"*

A voice, somehow orotund, yet rasping at the end, as if from sickness or a hiatus of use, filled the skies with her name. Nandenia watched as a Tree Crown Drake of tremendous bearing anchored the land and swept her up in one wing to put distance between her and the Angel of Scourge.

The Great Aegis faced the coal-dark god, growling. *"Keep distance of my child, or I will lie you out by your bones piecemeal."* The injury at Ardyce's neck had begun to bleed, again.

Nandenia stared at the other Tree Crown, who was of an unbroken alabaster hue. She was perfect with her oil-spill eyes. She was not a monster, and she had returned to them, as promised. Nandenia breathed, just as she saw her father arrive to the clearing.

"Return to your father, sweet Nandenia," Ardyce asked of her child, and Nandenia did as she was told.

"She is beautiful," Nandenia whispered of her mother to herself. She rejoined Mohonia, watching as a Pyrolite Drake came to Ardyce's side.

The Scourge Angel stared at them, unimpressed and unmoved. "Why are you here?" He seemed not to notice the Great Aegis' transformation. "No matter. Kill the Wyrms." Dayraven had slid from Ardyce's winged transport with Hadryn and Oshin within the plumage of his backside. The Angel caught sight of him. "Begin with that one. Kill the Wyrms—" Then, the pits that were his eyes settled upon Dayraven, and the god knew, as he drew a sharp intake of air. *"Serpent."*

Dayraven announced solemnly to the Drake of massive proportions, "We've come to end you, Angel of Old. There is no other way."

Hadryn held Oshin's hand whilst they sat astride the feathered Serpent, and the Knight Archidux stared at the god before them. The integument of that god was treacherous terrain: clearly rock, but also of a halting elasticity that could be thought of to move somewhat like skin with sharpened ridges running down his back and jagged pockmarks. Thorned spires accreted upon every inch of him. The skin of him appeared to be the only chainmail worthy to contain what laid beneath it, and Hadryn thought the Angel was surely a being comprised entirely of fire. In the rifts of the sable-hued rock which the god wore, Hadryn stared at the white flames licking outwards and throwing the snap of ember sparks in the air. He had never seen fire so white. The pulsing grooves left retina-imprint upon his vision, even when he looked away. But, Hadryn returned his gaze to the god, and the rest of them, too, were staring up at the black Drake. His eye-less stare held upon them, and those two caverns, unending in their darkness, were like tears in the fabric of reality. Perhaps, they led to the oblivion of space.

Hadryn cast eye along their party: four humans, two Drakes, and one Serpent – against an immortal – and Hadryn did not know how they could possibly survive, except that here they stood and not elsewhere. If one's mettle could ever woo Fate, they would see it now or else not.

The Scourge Angel, above them, said nothing, scrutinizing the feathered creature, as if he had a glass eye upon Dayraven. He said finally, "You are wrong to come here, Serpent. This realm is landlocked. Of sorts. Outside the flow and ebb of Time. Curse-locked, I tell you." The company to gather was silent, unable to decipher him. The Angel, then, repeated himself, "No matter. Kill the Wyrms." He huffed, and a bit of steam released from the fissures running over his body, for he had noticed another oddity in attendance to this event. "You've brought the pale queen, I see." He shifted his gaze to her, who was still atop LeShawn's back with Soo-yeon and Thaddius near to her. "Why this pitiable form, Conqueror? Lost, are you? Alas, you will need to die, even if you can no longer ascend as the Conquering Wyrm."

Chinami and Soo-yeon's eyes widened, for it was implausible that he should know. The albino woman had spent the morning in vain efforts to attain her godly shape, but however she struggled, she could be no more than human.

"Perhaps, because you love of one, you have become it," the darkness-god answered her thoughts. "But, that human frivolity is every element of suffering. So, I will rid you of that. And, rid what Wyrms are left their queen." The maw of the Scourge Angel parted, and from the depths of him came a clicking repetition, which increased in tempo rather sharply.

Ardyce knew this sound.

She looked at her child and wanted not for her daughter to witness Death before her eyes.

And, Ardyce wanted not to be reminded of what she'd done.

But, the grim-fire danced as ghastly light at the back of the Scourge Angel's throat, and Ardyce saw herself in him. As though a pane of glass had chipped from the dome of the heavens and fell before her as a mirror to look within, Ardyce saw the reflection of herself: a terrible and hateful reaper who had burned out the souls of so many firebreathers.

This was her adversary. This, that was the stage of her previous self; indeed, that self of only just yesterday.

In her past, she had been weak, someone unable to make her own choices, and the duty of Great Aegis had befallen her. Then, she had been tried and lost those most precious to her. From that sorrow, she'd made a most damnable decision, becoming a likeness to the Angel of Scourge. Hence, it was her place to kill her former self and grow from the death of it, again. Ardyce, now, knew herself.

The Great Aegis had intervened before she could understand the actions of her own body, and though she knew the severity of her throat injury and that she was no longer the hue of abysmal darkness – though she knew she had lost the weaponry of grim-fire, Ardyce opened her jaws.

Grim-fire did not come forth for her.

But, she had done this to shield those she considered her friends. She wondered if it had been sheer ignorance which led them to believe they could defeat the Angel. Or, if it had been desperation with no other choice. In any case, she hadn't meant to die in front of her daughter and her Vow.

"Mother!!"

The grim-fire came towards Ardyce, erupting from the Scourge Angel.

She heard the humans she'd come with cry out for her, in time with Nandenia, and even LeShawn released a high, whining call of reptilian voice. They were cries for her to retreat. They were afraid for her.

The waves were all assault and of a whiteness like being held in the mouth of a star. It was a thing beyond burning. It came for Ardyce, and she knew the terror and anguish she'd bestowed upon the Firecraws and Pyrolites, as she'd slaughtered them in that glen. She rued the hatred she'd allowed in herself, yet accompanying this eye-blink moment, she felt, too, their bravery, for Ardyce opened her flights, just as those of The Nocturnes had.

Nandenia's eyes filled with the image of her mother, the greatest Drake she knew. She saw the Tree Crown of pearl opulence twist and rear upwards to meet the blast of the Angel who was a titan, even to the Great Aegis of such domineering carriage. The jaws of her mother had opened, and with it, her second tier of horns – for, the first had been lost, and Nandenia knew not how – caught the gleam of the Sun most glaringly. The curve of those horns, like that of a ram's, seemed to ignite with that alien light from worlds away, and then, both witchcraft and miracle, together, befell the hour, as Ardyce of the Tree Crowns countered the Angel of Scourge.

The grim-fire met with an opposing force, and there was an audible backlash, like a sonic implosion, as the two powers collided in the sky betwixt Ardyce and the god. The force to resist the grim-fire was helio-burn, a fire marshaled by the greatest of stars. It was wild, untamed, and other-worldly. No Drake should have possessed it. It whipped and undulated, tentacle-like, from Ardyce's maw, and it was the colors of lava, if lava were turned to pure light. Arcing arms billowed from the heart of it, and as it swelled with radiance, so, too, did the Sun in the heavens seem to widen and feed the inferno of it to have found the being upon Earth.

The helios-burn and grim-fire blazed one another to a stalemate, then extinguished with ribbons of steam from both the mouths of Ardyce and the dark god.

"What are you?" The Scourge Angel hissed. He regarded the Tree Crown with agitated contempt. Ardyce's breathing was still uneven at the power to have found her so unexpectedly. But, she was catching up to herself. "Not of Nature. No," the god continued, eyeing her. "You are worse, she-Drake. Nature's intention. A climbing, shifting, morphing thing, you are. You are vile, like a roach, which refuses to die." His voice was now rising to a crescendo. "You are beautiful, *like a roach which refuses to die!* Therefore, will I *taste* your death. I will find your limit, Tree Crown. *You will be remembered, for revolutions of Time, as the delectable tartlet you were!"* The Angel's mouth filled with the skies, and his teeth hung upon the air for a moment before he descended towards the Great Aegis.

"Move away, Ardyce!" Thaddius yelled, and Ardyce heeded the words of the Royal Guard in time with her and her wife, who flew up from under the mouth of the coal-dark Drake. In LeShawn's grip, with Thaddius to support it, was a sizeable portion of tree trunk from one of the Up-Ended Trees the Angel had laid to waste. The piece of it was lengthy and jagged, creating a burdensome, yet formidable javelin in their hands. Wings gunning, the firebreathers braced themselves for the impact of the god's descent, and when it came, they held strong their position and the wooden lance. The makeshift spear gouged the titan through the roof of his mouth. Thaddius and LeShawn cried out at the exertion brought upon their wings. All the muscles in their backs were taxed and burning with strain. The tree pike continued through the Scourge Angel's mouth, finally ceasing when a foot of it breached the other side of his face and came up just beneath one of his gaping eye sockets.

The god paused with the splinter in his view, and LeShawn and Thaddius fell away, retreating to a safe distance. The Angel closed his mouth on the wood protrusion, breaking it with a flick of his tongue. He swallowed the splinters of bark, realizing now: "So, you've come for my life. Why didn't you say so? We could have spoken of that, rather than let me gibber on so." He huffed or sighed.

Above them, the clouds arrived like rows of soldiers to blot out the brightness of the day, and Ardyce's curved horns returned to the grayness of steel. The Knight Archidux glanced at the empyrean, so quick to change its raiment to darkness, and thunder came, haunting the distant horizons. In the midst of it, the Angel stood, as if patiently waiting.

Oshin clung to Hadryn's back, and she whispered into his ear, "Please, don't do this. I can't lose you." She was panting a little, and her voice sounded odd.

"I swear it to you, I will return to you from the World Serpent made." Hadryn looked back at her as her grip on him tightened. He whirled around to her suddenly. *"Oshin? Your face."* The redness of her birthmark covered her face. She was in a sweat yet shivering. *"Oshin, what's happening!"* He cried out to her, but she slumped against him, and Hadryn raised his face to the skies. He searched in one direction, then to another and found it. That eldritch cloud of the same hue as her skin had returned. It was pulsating strings of light, just as before.

"No matter what, wait for my next letter," Oshin whispered. "By the pen, we will find each other again."

Hadryn feared she was still under influence of the coma she'd suffer – a concussion maybe, or the trauma of Plodd when he'd imprisoned her in his belly. Hadryn shook her as the direction of her gaze became nebulous. In soft voice, he vowed to her, "We will do this impossible thing: end a war and gift to the Reaper a god. Then, no more. A quiet life. Simple. As humans should."

Dayraven broke in on their words. *"We can wait no longer, Hadryn. We must now converge."*

"I don't know how," Hadryn cried out, above the approaching thunder.

"You do!" Dayraven returned.

"I can't leave her like this," Hadryn said, holding Oshin to himself.

Against what they knew of Nature, the clouds blackened and lowered in on them with the appearance of stone.

Ardyce looked all around them, then said to Chinami and Soo-yeon, whom Thaddius and LeShawn had had to leave upon the ground during their attack on the Angel, "It is dangerous to be at the feet of titans. Hie yourselves to my back." Ardyce knelt to let the two women climb their way upwards to her back. She attuned her senses finely to track where the tiny figures were, and she told them to hold at her and not let go.

Soo-yeon braced herself and Chinami against an outgrowth of chalcedony near the base of the Tree Crown's wings. The Knight Jo peered up, just as the rains came down. "Is he doing this, Ardyce?" She asked with fear in her voice. Thunder shook out of the clouds, as if being unearthed from them.

Ardyce could not answer Soo-yeon. The Tree Crown watched the black god. He was as motionless as a statue, then he nodded to her, answering the question she hadn't yet asked, even as the rains washed over them. Puddles and the sop of mud became the ground the Drakes and Serpent stood upon.

"Back away," Dayraven said to their company, and they acquired a couple of lengths from the Drake with skeletal eyes, keeping him in their view without looking away.

"I think you know," the Scourge Angel said to them. His voice was low and deep, and his next words tremored through their bodies with the feeling that it hallowed out the marrow from their bones. He spoke: "I cannot be drowned, for the rains and their waterways bow to me when I call upon them." From behind him, a deluge rose up, not cascading outwards and not yet tilling the loam with furious waves, but held at the ready, like a swollen, riled beast leaning into the ends of its reins. It was a waterfall falling into itself, indeterminable whether the angry currents fed or fought one another.

Ardyce backed away. "Everyone, behind me. Nandenia! Bring your father here, child." Nandenia came with Mohonia to crouch behind the enormous Tree Crown. Joining them were LeShawn, Thaddius, and Dayraven with the two humans astride him.

Hadryn watched from around Dayraven's plumage, as grim-fire, again, scintillated in the Scourge Angel's throat.

The Knight Archidux knew that there had been eons past where gods sat on high to direct legions of people – royalty and the peasants alike – to the fields of war. And, now, he and Dayraven could end that and re-write history. Yet, he hesitated with a distorted feeling within himself, like the hollow along the spine of a book when pages of it have been ripped away. There were things Time needed, in order to finish a tale. He looked to Oshin and knew there were things which needed Time.

"I can no more be buried," the god was telling them, "than can mountains be entombed. I will not burn, for grim-fire is like the blood within me. There is no element that can undo me. Do you understand, Warrior in White?" He addressed Ardyce.

The Great Aegis looked to the skies, extending her flights. She considered the sanctuary of the firmament, but lightning netted the vaulted dome, cracking in their ears.

"Do you!!" the Scourge Angel cried out to the alabaster Tree Crown.

Strokes of lightning fell all around them, walls of lightning, and the group of them huddled together to avoid death by electricity. LeShawn balked in fear, as a bolt flashed too near to her face. She broke their formation, but Ardyce guided her back to place with one of her wings.

Hadryn watched all of this, which surrounded him – so near to him. He struggled with who he should be and who he was. He looked to Ardyce who had so selflessly came to the fore to be their shield. He panicked, inwardly, at her steady eyes, ignorant of how he could be anything like her or Dayraven.

The Great Aegis was staring at the god. She knew now that though the Angel vaguely resembled a Firecraw Drake, and well may he have been one in lives past, the charcoal-hued giant was no longer a Firecraw, or any other race of Drake.

He was an immortal, and his might was that of each the breeds of dragons. Like the Longs and Mungkrs, he could summon the weather's ire and augment it to become a din of the heavens or manipulate any body of water to be his causeway and loyal follower. Just as the firebreathers could, he wielded rushing flames, and his vision did not falter, even in the pitch of night. Ardyce stared silently at the creature to witness as black chalcedony grew out of his face in irregular horns and atop his shoulders to double the armory of his thickened skin, and in that, she saw the likeness of him to her breed of Tree Crown Drakes.

But, the deluge toppled, then, as if coming down, brick by brick. Whatever restraint had so tamed it was gone, and it split whole trees, as it dismantled from a churning, wall-like structure to a rabid herd of stampeding leviathans.

Ardyce pivoted to encase the others in her wings and shield them with her body. She held at them, and the waves layered upon them, as though to bury them alive. They were swept deeper into the forest by the frenzied waters, and the Up-Ended Trees were their shipwrecked mates, creating a maelstrom of roughly-hewn spears. Ardyce clenched her teeth against sudden pain, for another wave had collapsed against her and riddled one of her legs and much of her lower back with wooden shards, now firmly embedded in her body.

"Ardyce!" Mohonia called to the white she-Drake, though he could not hear himself. He could see from around her, and her blood was joining with the flood, then became it. He drew up close to her and said, his voice chiming in her thoughts and briefly stilling the madness to surround them, *Leave with Nandenia, my Vow. You needn't protect everyone. It is simply our time to die. That fate has nothing to do with you.*

The trees screamed in bark-breaking moans as the fingers of them, their roots, were torn away from the grips of earth, who'd known them through every season and every year.

The mother Tree Crown swallowed thickly, as another surging of wood impaled her, but the other Drake, humans, and Serpent were kept safe in the fortress she'd made of her body. *But, it does,* she told Mohonia. *Because, I am the Great Aegis. I will never, again, abandon who I am.*

Lightning and the rains found their peaks, as the Angel of Scourge stared at Ardyce being swept away from him. He could see the male Tree Crown drawn up against her and knew they must be exchanging words. *Lovers,* he thought to himself, *entwined in their Vows.* He, then, shattered sight with the illumination of lightning, so dense that it seemed a second sun for a moment. He bellowed incoherently, and next, the skies became the sea. The rains curled in upon themselves, like threatening fists. The Scourge Angel said, only loud enough, at first, that the speaker should hear, "Die. Or, do Death. Over and Over. Cease, all, I bid you: cease." Then, his words stretched out over all else. "'No matter.' 'Kill the Wyrms.' Kill their Queen. Then, the Trees. Die, or do death." He repeated this, in that voice half-hushed by age, and his chanting breath became a chittering to fill the void of chaos.

"Make him stop!" Soo-yeon cried out and covered her ears against his mirrored words. Chinami put her hands over Soo-yeon's, yet even the goddess, in her deafness, could feel the Angel's chant, like a pressure swelling beneath her skin.

"*Die,*" said he of Scourge.

The assault of the immortal had come too abruptly with more force and destruction than they could fathom. The cries of a child rang as a low chiming against the mobbing of the storm.

"*Mother!*" Nandenia was trying to squirm free of her father's hold. She was sobbing, hysterical. "*Mother, Mother!*"

"'*Or. Do Death,*'" the blackened titan continued.

Far off, Ardyce heard the mantra of an old man in his old ways. She heard her child, too, and scrapped for hold of her strength. She had still to murder this god. She told herself she believed she could do it, but with each of the Angel's words, she felt a step behind. She lost sight of her daughter, her Vow, and her companions, even as she held them to herself.

She's dying, Hadryn suddenly thought to himself. *We'll all die.* He turned to gaze upon Oshin, knowing he must cheat Death to save her. Finally, his voice came forth, against the sleeting of rain and furious winds. "Dayraven. We will create the World Serpent. *Now.*"

"No!" Oshin cried out. Then, her head snapped back and her teeth emerged. The lightning overhead burst in a divided second of illumination. Thereby, did Ardyce witness what occurred. And, Dayraven, Thaddius, LeShawn, Soo-yeon, Chinami, and Ardyce's family saw what happened.

She bit him.

Oshin's teeth delved into Hadryn's skin, and his blood swelled up around her mouth that was upon him.

"You mustn't! Oshin!" Chinami wanted to go to her who had wounded her love, but Soo-yeon was too terrified to let her go.

"Kill—" said the beast-like god. Then, he stopped speaking as a scarlet-colored cloud loamed before him, gaining solidity. He noticed now the woman staring at him with blood in her mouth.

"'Kill the Wyrms!'" screamed the Scourge Angel. "'Kill their *Queen!*'"

Oshin released Hadryn, and he fell back, holding at his shoulder which bled from between his fingers. *"Oshin!"* he yelled for her, reaching.

Crimson-bright arcs fled from the center of the cloud, entangling upwards into a cylindrical column to spear the heavens, and from the column bloomed scores of lesser arcs, smaller and creeping in every direction, like roots. Indeed, the manifestation created to image of an Up-Ended Tree but briefly before Oshin stood and stepped into it. Then, it was clipped from existence and eyes which seemed the size of twin moons hung aglow in the skies all red as though bloodied.

"But, cease!!" cried the Angel of Scourge.

The flashflood of sound to batter their ears was suddenly drowned, like someone absolutely alone who pauses in walking and their footfalls leave a path of silence. There was a veil of voiceless, vermillion light, then Singular Darkness arrived for them all, blacker than nothingness.

The Scourge Angel opened his eyes. Very wide. He blinked.

CHAPTER 41

GOD OR CREATOR

At first, he felt blind – that the pits of his eyes had always been his inability to see. Then, his memory rushed in, as if to save him from Fear. Yet, what he saw must have been the reason for his racing breath and the knotting of his muscles.

The Angel of Scourge was given clarity too late.

He saw, as he'd never seen before.

Ardyce had been pierced through by the very trees of her realm. She was bleeding, unmoving, and the Scourge Angel demanded the heavens to quiet for her corpse-like respite.

He blinked, again.

Outer Gled Tria cradled itself in the gentle swaying of one with broken mind. The limbs of fallen trees heaved, as if with final breaths, in the last of the fading winds. He saw the power of himself leave the scene before him, and the Scourge Angel watched as the waters peeled back, like a desquamating wound attempting to heal, and revealed to him the Orb he had failed to recognize.

Hadryn stood on what was left of the earth, screaming skyward. His voice dragging in his throat. *"Oshin, no! You don't have to do this! Come back to me!"*

An Orb, the Angel thought to himself. *Kill—No. Eat.*

His thoughts bandied unintelligibly on how to proceed. Then, he, the Scourge Angel, charged the man with one eye made of white ring.

The dark Angel had never felt himself torn away from his own footing, so he could not understand it now as he was thrown into the ground. He felt his own weight in a manner he'd never known before. Then, one side of his face was clubbed in, and a flare of fire raged for a moment from the wound and next, extinguished.

The darkened god rested in the marl for several seconds, then he howled with pain, clutching his face as he righted himself.

"Oshin!!" Hadryn cried, but Dayraven recovered from shock in time to catch the Knight Archidux in his arms and carry him away from what would unfold.

The Scourge Angel stood, staring at the successor to the Conqueror Wyrm. The new queen was breathing in even meter, watching him.

She was scarlet-hued without the multitude of eyes as the pale Conqueror had had. Her two eyes were embedded along either side of her face, and this new Wyrm appeared to have integument composed of a dense keratin, grown in ridges and horn-like points, to encase the entirety of her body. Six arms extended from the upper portion of the long body, and this queen did not serenely hover in the air as Chinami had, but snaked and crawled upon the ground, sometimes using its human-like arms to clutch at the loam in its movement.

The Angel was silent, gazing at this abomination. *"I fear no one,"* he told her.

The mouth of the Wyrm dropped open several feet. When the god of Scourge thought it would stop, still it elongated further. A staccato laughter emerged from the gaping maw. This queen was of a form vast in size, much larger than her predecessor.

"Dare you?" raged the darkness god, that god of fire.

The Conqueror Wyrm raised up tall, and they clashed. The queen had emerged by blood of the Orb, and perhaps, she was made more powerful by it as well. She withstood the grim-fire which washed over her, and her volley was crackling electricity which leaped into the fissures of his skin. The king of Drakes cried out, but he was not badly injured and quick to regain himself. So, they took to the swords of themselves, unsheathing their teeth to one another, and the winds grew to fury as they captured mouthfuls of each other. In bitter error, the Conqueror was deprived one of her arms. The Angel ripped it from its socket, and she screamed in agony.

Hadryn fought free of Dayraven. *"Now!"* he yelled in terror. *"We have to save her!"*

The Wyrm encircled the Angel of Scourge with the length of her body. She clasped her remaining pairs of hands together and clubbed away at his hardened body as he flayed her skin with teeth and claws to be rid of her grip. Clumps of charred rock flew away from the god's body as Oshin chipped through the heavy armor of him, burning and bloodying herself.

Dayraven looked away from the battle of gods. He yanked Hadryn to stand in front of himself. *"Concentrate, Hadryn."* The Serpent wished to believe in himself, that they could fight against fate.

The Scourge Angel's flights came forth as curtains of blackness to edge light out of the day, and the god mounted the empyrean, taking Oshin with himself.

"No! Oshin!" Hadryn wanted to run to her, but Dayraven kept him near, manacling him in place.

"You must give up being human, Hadryn!" the Serpent demanded.

The Conqueror had loosened her hold of the Angel. Before she could free herself of him, he dived back down to the earth, and he crushed the lower fourth of her long body under his weight. The Wyrm mewled with pain and shock. She lashed out, unfocused by the torment of her ruined lower half, and her fist was strong, dangerous. Her hard knuckles erupted through five of the largest fangs along one side of the Angel's face. Splintered ivory shards shattered out of his jaws. For that, he bit into her with the other half of his mouth; his teeth caught, then went through another of her arms. She writhed and found his throat in her own bite. They held each other, and the blood of gods wet the ground.

Hadryn stared at her. His gaze went to Ardyce, who was dying of her wounds and the others that were all that was left of a life he once knew – they were huddled around the Tree Crown Drake. They sought to keep her of this world, lessen her pain.

Dayraven's cries were coming up short, not quite reaching his sense of hearing: *"Hadryn, please!"*

But, he was staring at her again. She was a monstrous Wyrm, but he saw Oshin who he'd always love in every action of that warring queen.

He didn't think he knew how to give up being human.

Hadryn saw himself as he removed the bandages over his chest. The flesh was discolored underneath, but his breasts were gone. He smiled. But, Time was unnatural, and his memories went in reverse. He saw himself first waking up from surgery, then his doctor prepping his instruments. His doctor was speaking silence, but Hadryn knew he was explaining the procedure. Then, Hadryn had awakened, and his mother had asked, *Are you ready for today?* They drove in a carriage together, and through one window, Hadryn had spotted a black bird perched on an unusual tree before they passed them both.

"Dayraven."

Hadryn reached for the Serpent, and one of his hands felt the soft plumage under his palm.

And, then, Hadryn Archidux and the Serpent Dayraven elongated as a spectrum of light, of colors variegated. The light abruptly began to tremble, quaking to the form of ringed shape. It expanded. It grew. It transformed into an eldritch cry. With it, reverberated the cawing of ravens, and indeed, the skies experienced a fluttering and ink-blotting darkness, as thousands of them were birthed from the bright fog.

The Angel turned from his bout with the The Conqueror Wyrm. He watched and felt he knew and didn't know what was to come.

The queen did not look. She disengaged from the blackened god, falling away from him. She gave to the heavens a broken ululation, and with her injuries, she sunk towards the muddied earth. She fell. Her knees caught her, then she collapsed to one side as a human being, and Oshin said – so softly that none but her Knight might feel her words: *"Hadryn, you promised me."* She, who was the blood-red queen, became lost in a daze, as though she could not bear to see Hadryn as he was. Her body panted with weakness. She stared at the ground she rested upon. The liquid once in her veins found the marl as well, and she was unsure if she was dying.

The kingly beast to raise its head from out the dissipating nebula was arrayed, from jowls to near the end of it, in a sleek plumage the hue of a starless night. The head of it was reptilian and the tail of it: bone, which formed a singular horn or tusk of sorts. The bone was ridged and curving. The creation birthed rippled to its full height, and the sun nearly could not reach over the top of it. The being had eyes with the quality of human to them and were mismatched, one being entirely white, and the other eye was shades of purple and blue entwined. As the creature experienced the first of its movements upon Earth, sound shifted with it, and the integument of soil gave reaction to this new presence by cracking and molting under the sheer weight of it. Slowly, the creature released its tail which had been held by the tip in its mouth.

It turned to face the Scourge Angel. It was the World Serpent, Uroboros.

"You are not real!" the Angel cursed Uroboros. Desperate saliva flew from the ends of his teeth. *"This world will never be enough to house something more than gods!"*

The great Serpent screamed and came for him.

Day shuddered and became night under the shattering movement of Uroboros. Shadows fell everywhere, like autumnal leaves being frightened from their branched homes.

On instinct, the Scourge Angel rose to his full height. By this, he salvaged his life, for the jaws of the creature came down upon him, but the teeth of the beast stopped in his shoulder. There was, simultaneously, a glass-like cracking sound, as the chalcedony upon his shoulder crumbled easily under the might of Uroboros.

The Scourge Angel's head was bowed to keep from being decapitated by the Serpent, and his eyes darted here, then there, at the teeth of the creature to surround him – *him,* a god. A tremor overtook the Angel, as he realized the incredible proportions of the World Serpent. From his shoulder, he bled. He saw his own blood.

The maw of the beast came away from him, and the creature rose up, bristling its feathers to show hues of gold, orange, and crimson closer to the roots. Mesmerizing were those coruscating colors, like the promise of stars which descend in streaks to make a night of wishes.

Ardyce and the other watched the contention of the mighty creatures. Their rushing blood and hammering hearts kept them silent. They had to remember their breath; it was important. Thaddius was shedding tears. She cupped a hand over her mouth to restrain crying out to her dearest friend. She muttered words for him; they were this: *"Idiot. Do not forget how you are loved."*

The Serpent's gaze was nudged in direction of the Drakes with humans, then its attention flickered back, and it rushed the Scourge Angel, again. With it came dawn at its back, hurrying the moon from her high balcony.

A sound of terror came from the coal-black god. Wildly, he discharged grim-fire from his throat, and the eruption of it blasted away a chunk of steaming meat from the Serpent's body – black feathers leapt in the air and a little blood entwined with them. But, the blow did not slow Uroboros in the least.

The Angel of Scourge had to pivot away from the flight of the beast to preserve himself, but in that turning away, he felt an unusual, sickening sensation of lightness overcome him. He was yanked once, rudely, he felt, then he fell to the marl – an immortal with mire thrown over his face.

Within the World Serpent, still retaining pieces of his consciousness, Dayraven swallowed.

Hadryn chocked, trading air for something despicable.

The Angel was huffing with breathlessness. He looked down at himself, and his tail had vanished. The bones of his remaining vertebrae were partly-sheathed in gore, and it wasn't until seeing it that he felt the torment of his loss. The Angel bit back his pain and sought to further his escape.

There was blood at each corner of Uroboros' mouth. The stump left to the Angel flailed about, whipping vermillion streamers into the air, as the god said weakly, *"No."* He clambered to his feet and urged the lightning to return to the lands and vanquish the feathered beast from his presence. The welkin heaved with threads of brilliance, answering him.

Dayraven was soused in the blood-rush which is battle, yet beyond it, he could see the edge of another era. It wore the blush of innocence, blood kept under the skin, and its vanity was peace without the knowledge of war. It was the vision for which he fought. Dayraven fled towards the Angel god.

Hadryn's head hurt, producing in him a strange torpidity which was, contrastingly, full of power. He struggled for his breathing, to ensure himself he was still drawing breath, and Hadryn swallowed, again. In front of him was an animal who was missing one of his legs – perhaps, another limb, too, but Hadryn could not tell if he had been born like this. The animal was all black and partly dragging himself along the ground.

"Do not kill me," said the animal.

And, night fell, once more. The days were toppling over each other with every action of the World Serpent. Time had become demented, disoriented. It accelerated.

Oshin, where are you? Hadryn asked himself, in his own mind. He looked as far as he could, in either direction.

There was a bellowing scream – that of immense pain.

Hadryn was so disoriented, he swallowed yet again.

Fleetingly, he saw the animal had lost both his back legs. He was crawling through the loam – through his blood and scrap pieces of his own tendons.

Hadryn's attention strayed from the suffering animal. He witnessed the sky and toppled trees, but they seemed to be in the wrong places, one up and the other down, when that was not quite right. He shook his head and feathers skirted his view at the sides. Hadryn looked, again. He saw Ardyce, lying on her side. Her eyes were open, but opaque, and she gasped thin, short breaths, as Nandenia cried and tugged at her, begging for a response. Mohonia fought to soothe their child. Like a chain with beautiful links, Hadryn saw LeShawn embracing Thaddius who held Chinami, and Chinami's arms were wound around Soo-yeon. Soo-yeon wept against the pale-haired woman, and Chinami allowed herself to be needed, to be loved. In that, she became more human – so human that she could see Hadryn within the depths of Uroboros, as the World Serpent stared back at her.

Chinami signed to him these words: *Accept yourself.* How he understood them, Hadryn didn't know, but he knew somehow that it was her last act as a goddess.

Hadryn looked away from her to see that sunrise was approaching, again. He searched. He found a sea of possibilities and realized he was staring at her he had been desirous to see.

Oshin was gazing at him. Her stare was locked in a dream. She wasn't saying anything, but his memory brought her voice to him: *'A million more days together.'*

Hadryn found his will.

"I don't want to die!" yelled the Scourge Angel.

And, the sunrise crept away to let the stars return to the sky. Evening and day merged, fused and confused by the entity to make entry to this world – a world with Serpent. A world in rings. The Rings spinning their revolutions.

Uroboros reared in the twilit night-day.

Hadryn's memory of Oshin continued: *'Wait for my next letter.'*

She was still staring at him, as the World Serpent drew closer to her, leaving that maimed god.

Hadryn, no! Dayraven's frantic words reached Hadryn, as the Knight's head cleared. *What are you doing!*

There was a glare of sun-brilliance, as a timeline regained itself, then bent and showed its belly for a backwards turn. Blood came, returning to the Scourge Angel. Flesh vibrated near him as individual molecules, then relented a form to him. The Angel looked down at himself, and against all understanding, one of his legs had been returned to him, as if it had never been torn from his body. He looked all around, but he was unable to perceive Uroboros any longer. He saw only the boy with heterochromatic eyes. Time continued against its nature, following its opposite direction. The Angel fought to resist this, the looping of events. He had killed the Wyrms, torn out the Up-Ended Trees, rid the world of Ardyce, Great Aegis of the Tree Crowns, and he had done these things to cease what he knew always occurred. He had done all of it in vain. Suddenly, the Angel knew. *"You,"* he said to Hadryn.

Time fled upon a backwards footprint. Ardyce rose up with helios-burn, battling with the Angel of Scourge, then she didn't, for Daofeng was dying in the River Orb. Except, this he could not. He would stand with his Higher Counsel of giants, because Wyrms were fleeing across all territories to escape the dark Angel, and war was everywhere.

Time. Time. It is not a clock, only the shape of it.

And, it's face changed by the hour. It was familiar and shifting all at once.

Then, abruptly, there was a banquet with oxen and their eyes glowed an electric blue. With them was a mysterious suitor who presented a treasured dinner in the back room of a grand estate, and the food was for two lovers, their meeting much overdue.

Hadryn stared at the things he saw. There was less and less he recognized. The room with the lovers was several levels up, for the windows of it looked out on a portion of the sky. He felt confused. Hadryn felt something being torn from his grasp. Dayraven was calling to him, but he couldn't answer him.

A morgue came next, and two military personnel were standing over a mangled corpse. They looked shocked. Finally, a man – himself, Hadryn saw – climbed upwards to read a letter under the eye of moon-glow. He unfolded the pages meant for him.

The night breeze moved through his hair. Around him, the city raised up tall and dark with buildings of various geometric shape. They were not the sprawling mansions belonging to denizens. They were skyscrapers aglow with the signage, advertising, and activity of commerce. A whirring of mechanical parts pervaded the environment, and Hadryn felt lost, but he continued.

Hadryn, as Uroboros, fled back through Time. He was a creator and a destroyer and a re-creator. Hadryn felt this now. He overpowered Dayraven, who was his recusant by every second and every fiber of muscle. Their wills vied for supremacy, yet so often has history witnessed Love – passionate, enamored, and sworn to eternity – subduing the iron staffs of Logic and morality.

Hadryn knew not else how to rescue those surviving and those lost. He knew of no other way to save Oshin but to return her to a time in which she did not need saving. He went back as far as he could, as far as Dayraven would allow him.

August 15th, the year 2048, began again.

Eryx had said, "It may be the crown of a tree."

"Floating in the sea?" Mei Xian asked.

"No," Naehska answered. "An island."

Mei Xian had never stared at the greatness of the ocean before. She hadn't had the time for such luxuries, but turning her back on war, she and the two others she stood with had discerned a farwary verdancy in what seemed to be the middle of the Deepest Mirror – the sea.

"Shall we go to it?" the human had questioned.

Then, Mei Xian had gathered them: one on her back and the other in her hands. She flew with them.

The small gathering of leaves seemed never to come closer to them. They flew for a long while, and at their backs there was a terrible brilliance. Eryx sought to turn to look, but Mei Xian refused her the movement.

"Look only ahead," the Tianlong said to them both.

They kept on.

She was tiring.

"Give me to the waters and turn back," Eryx told the golden Drake. "You've enough strength to make it back, Mei Xian. Release me!"

But, she didn't.

She flew still. She might have slept for seconds at a time as she did.

They'd lost sight of the greenery.

Mei Xian questioned what strength was left to her. She pushed at her weary frame. She pushed at each muscle of herself.

They fell.

"Mei Xian!"

She didn't know which of them had screamed her name, but then, they were tumbling through sand. It caught at the corner of their eyes, stinging. It flew up in arcs all around them. Then, their momentum came to a halt, and they were able to catch their breaths.

Above them, they saw the crown of the tree they had followed.

They laughed as one.

Yet, as the three of them righted themselves, they turned to look back on the world they'd left behind.

"What is that?" Eryx asked the other two. "How could that be?"

What they saw, in the long-ago distance that had been their homes, was not what had before existed there.

"Those structures," Mei Xian said, struggling to understand.

"Skyscrapers," Naehska told them. "Something's happened."

HADRYN
ARDYCE
OSHIN
CHINAMI
LeShawn & Thaddius
Soo-Yeon, Chinami, & Daofeng

Earth-fallower
Wyrm,
Earth Wyrm,
Water Wyrm,
Death Wyrm,
Armored Wyrm

PREVIEW OF:

SERPENT'S SYNDROME

PART 2:
THE CONSUMED WORLDS

SERPENT'S SYNDROME:

Again, the year is 2048.

In a separate timeline, humans live as Droids. These mechanical replicas are controlled by the people they are made to look like. They go to work, run errands, indulge in social relationships, take vacations, and tend to their families – all as robots, whilst the actual human of flesh and blood remains hidden away, keying in commands for their Droids on an electronic tablet.

The new world is one of ease and pleasure. Until, the Droids begin to malfunction one by one. Until, a Droid kills its human.

Technology was enjoyed, until it seemed to gain a consciousness...

~~~

PART 2 OF **THE CONSUMED WORLDS**
~~~

LOST CHAPTER

When something or someone comes for one's life, there is, at first, shock. A belief in disbelief. Our eyes open wide, to their limits, and possibly, they are burst open for the first time. Do we see differently then? As it happens? Or does sight fail the human being because it belongs only to one world and death is a separate planet, unearthly?

She'd been asleep.

She'd fallen asleep at work, but somehow ended up returned to her apartment.

She was awake now, in her own bedroom. The hours before were missing. Instead, she was nothing but the present, as if her life had begun here.

Ermaya Khanna's eyes were so wide, they shivered in their sockets from the strain. Her bed mattress was filling with blood, almost as if it'd always rested on a bog of her vital fluid and now, was finally submerging into the deep. She searched for pain because it was absent. But, the adrenaline might be stunting that. Then, Ermaya's body spasmed: one quick, flinching movement, and it seemed to return to her ownership, piece by piece – second by second.

The fingers going into her midsection, piercing flesh and muscle, were her own. She had a beauty mark on the inside of her right thumb. She could see this beauty mark now, as she stared down at the hand to murder her.

"No." She choked on a hoarse whisper.

Suddenly, the pain arrived, altering everything it touched. Ermaya cried out as her suffering became the entire room which enclosed her. She felt it stain the air all around her, and her nerves became the largest part of her person, abruptly overloaded with experience. The feeling was all razors.

"Stop!" she pleaded.

The hand went deeper. She only knew it by a sensation of heaviness that was increasing. Then, there was a wrenching motion within Ermaya's entire frame and a dull, cracking sound, as though she were underwater, listening as a tree limb snapped away from its whole in a muted storm that was her panic. What followed, she can only think of as a slow and languid rupturing within, like she was made up only of soap bubbles beyond her skin.

Ermaya's life could no longer be contained in her body. It drained into the basin of another world of which she knew nothing.

And, that was her final thought of who she was.

Ermaya knew nothing of herself, and she had killed herself with it.

CHAPTER 1

16 hours earlier
(In the year of 2048.)

The coffee had been weak, and after five sips, she'd left the mug at the edge of her walnut dresser to imprint a ring she would later have to scrub at to be erased.

The door to her apartment opened and closed, locking itself.

Then, the flocking to the subway. Courteously, everyone rushed. Polite smiles, well-mannered gestures. Each passenger was distinctive, eccentric, and awash with a carriage and comportment all their own. Each a thing of *beauty*. Absolutely handsome, as if they were a daring circus of performers snaking beneath the surface in underground cars that knew nothing of its guests' mesmeric pulchritude. A subway anywhere was old and had the grit and grime to match its years. But, beauty belonged to the people. Not even a dimple was out of place.

A text came through to her notifications on her wristband device. It was from her sister, who, a month ago, had said she was selfish.

Selfish.

They hadn't been arguing over anything. Her sister had said it without forewarning, like mentioning the weather. She'd said on the phone that day:

You think only of yourself. You're selfish.

Ermaya Khanna didn't need this today. Of all days. Not today.

She, herself, was dressed rather conservatively, but it was for work and not because she was boring, she said in her own thoughts. Her black, clinging dress was long-sleeved with mesh windows in the shape of large flower petals over her thighs and a smaller mesh window in the cutout of a budding flower just above her breasts. Her hair was the color of dark chocolate, wavy, and she'd once been told her skin tone was that of pecans.

Ermaya was just as lovely as everyone else. Even as she was frowning at the silver band around her wrist.

For several seconds, she was angry with her sister for contacting her, even without yet reading the message. She felt an unusual urge to call her sister and tell her that she would not do this to her *today*.

But, the doors to the subway opened at the next stop with an extended mechanical sigh, and despite the habiliment or trappings of an individual, there was cordial pleasantry. She, herself, conjured a warm smile and walked with everyone else onto the platform for departures. The hurry of the morning routine resumed, but each of those around her were exceedingly proper – nothing less than charming, as though they would acquire the best marks from parental or authoritative onlookers.

Graciously, she laughed as one of the speeding passengers bumped into her from behind. She pardoned herself, and her manner was mirrored by the one to jostle her.

Ermaya walked most of her way into work; she liked it that way. After a half mile, she had passed mostly restaurants and cafes. Everyone ordered their food to go, plastic rustling. Then, a few more steps and the marquee to the largest scenario house in the city rose above her, like a modernized kingdom in the midst of downtown traffic, shopping complexes, and travel agencies. 3D images projected from the marquee, advertising faraway lands, fantastical places of imagination, and environments of the most popular cinematic experiences. She wove and cut through queues of people waiting to pay admission. The scenario house was like this, day and night. Some people seemed to live here on the eight city blocks that made up the business and left only when their bank accounts withered to a weakness that could no longer keep them upright or fed.

"Weijia!"

Ermaya stopped abruptly because she had run into something, knees bumping softness. Or, something had run into her.

"Please, hold onto her, miss!"

A couple, the man Caucasian and the woman Chinese, ran at her, and Ermaya panicked for a moment, then looked down towards her feet. A child in a pale blue fleece jacket stood in front of her, nearly standing on the tips of Ermaya's kitten heel pumps. The girl shouldered a yellow backpack, and she looked scared, so Ermaya kneeled to her level. She was, perhaps, six or seven-years old.

"They aren't my parents," the child whispered to Ermaya.

Alarmed, Ermaya held at one of her shoulders as the man and woman approached them. The girl whirled suddenly and screamed, frightening Ermaya.

"I want my real *Ma and Pop Pop!"*

The man frowned and bent at the waist to say to her, "Let's just go home, Weijia. You mustn't run away from us like that." Then, he looked at Ermaya. "She's at that age, you know? They can get like this."

Ermaya stared at the man. She nodded faintly, but her hand was still on the girl's shoulder.

"Oh, Weijia, you've upset this poor woman." The mother was kneeling, too, in front of the child. "I'm sorry, miss," she told Ermaya, reaching for the top zipper of the girl's backpack. "We *are* her parents. Of course, we are."

"You're not!" the child yelled again. "You're ugly!"

Ermaya glanced from the father to the mother. They were richly beautiful; she was envious of them for an instant. Then, the mother was holding the child's ID card up for her to see alongside her own ID. Their last names were the same.

"I wish she wouldn't do this," the mother was saying. "I'm so sorry to take up your time. You must be on your way to work."

Ermaya remembered her job and the day ahead. Awkwardly and not at all how she would have liked to imagine her handling an incident like this, she said to the parents, "I am. Excuse me. Have a nice day." She worried about the girl, but convinced herself she would be fine. It was merely a child's tantrum or fit to have made her say such things. Ermaya chose a brisk pace as she separated from the family, but her steps felt sticky, like she didn't quite want to leave.

She looked back once at the child. The girl was staring at her with large, dark eyes. She had a runny nose, and the father wiped at her face as they both gently lectured her. Or, comforted her. Ermaya couldn't tell, but they seemed like any other family.

Another twenty minutes, and she had arrived to the shuttles that would escort her to work. A man saw her enter the short lobby that led to the cars which specifically ran a 10-mile incline to the building where she was employed, and he tipped his pinstripe newsboy cap to her. She nodded at him, then entered the waiting cab. It wasn't unusual that onlookers gestured respect to those who were employed to this corporation.

SC/RG corporation all but ran the country.

Her smile slipped away, like a breeze casually overturns a severed, Autumn leaf. She wished she hadn't had the thought of the company's importance today. It tottered her nerves, but she was just as much ridden with anxiety at the thought of abandoning her venture. It was years overdue already.

Within the towering building, black as though it had been painted with soot, and past the security desk, she shadow-skirted into a crowded elevator after pressing the number of her floor. She fiddled with her wristband, then read the text from her sister. It was an apology for having said she was selfish.

Selfish.

She was nearly to her lab now.

She would forget all about that text in the next few hours. Today was full. She had her own agenda to care for. Ermaya pressed at small buttons on the device without even looking, then her wristband shown with subdued lights for a moment. The call was picked up.

"Even if I am selfish, I'm curious too, and that makes me human."

"You called. I wasn't expecting that. You sound agitated."

"Not everything about me is bad. I'm curious, too."

"What are you talking about? You're not making any sense."

She sighed. She shouldn't have called her sister. She said, "Never mind," and ended the call.

8:16 a.m.

Am I selfish?

11:09 a.m.

Curious. Not selfish.

1:47 p.m.

Curious and *selfish.*

"I'm going on break," the man beside her said.

"You can't go this late," Ermaya answered.

"I always go this late."

She knew that. She wanted him to go. Yet, she replied, "It's a wonder I don't report you."

If he didn't leave, she would have to abandon everything she'd plotted for this day.

"'Report me?' You like too much to keep things quiet around here." He laughed.

"I do," she agreed, and he left. She stared at the closed door to their lab.

Ermaya Khanna keyed in a request for the next Droid to service. She knew she would lose her job for this, if anyone even suspected what she intended now to do. Her career, really, she told herself. It was a *career* she had at the corporation's labs — one going on four years that paid well. She had benefits and a retirement plan; this was her livelihood. She felt she wouldn't be able to survive without the income it provided. What's more, she was certain her employers would arrange to have her reputation forever besmirched, if she were caught doing this.

And yet, she was risking it all and purely for the sake of curiosity.

I could stop. I don't have to do this. There's no reason why I shouldn't just continue to have a completely ordinary day.

Ordinary. Selfishness.

"Employee ID: EK97817091. Requesting Part +0 for implementation into Vessel 73738." Ermaya stood in front of the silver tank that was easily over 20 feet tall and emerging from the wall, like a giant space capsule. She could see the cold coming off it in drowsy clouds which rose into the air, then dissipated. She could hear its inner mechanics as it worked to fulfill her voice command.

If I do this, I won't tell anyone about it. It will just be for me. To know.

The lab Ermaya arrived at every morning was located on the second floor of the building which rose seven levels into the sky. It was the smallest in a series of labs, which occupied floors 2 through 5. The product, the Droids, came to them in these levels, and the toilers here gave the merchandise its foundation, its hard-wiring. The workers at these levels often said of themselves that they "hammered the nails and turned the bolts," but their work required advanced degrees in computer science and engineering. Finally, the two uppermost stories were where those who considered themselves "artists" labored, designing finishes that met each customer's demand and most trivial whim. The employees here tailored the physical appearance of the product, but not only that, they installed the "conditioning" of each of their "masterworks."

The flourish of the "personality" of a Droid emerged here and was painstakingly sculpted. One customer request: dashing and emboldened, yet sensitive to smaller life, like children and windowsill birds, but with a passion for Renaissance art and a shortcoming of doubting one's self in group gatherings. Another customer request: reserved and stoic, but emotional towards one's moral code, which surprisingly, was coupled with an aptitude for erotic dance and the desire to please others. People wanted complexity. They wanted their Droids to make convincing humans.

The sixth and seventh levels were, therefore, over-accommodating of the "artists," and they were laden with extra benefits. Ermaya was most envious of the rumors about the "bonus wages" given to those on the top-most floors, if customers praised their work. That and the paid "personal days," which could be taken to "uplift one's inspiration." But, Ermaya imagined the employees who had this leave mostly took it to wake up late, then scroll through "dating" apps for random sexual encounters.

Maybe she was envious. She and her co-worker contributed almost nothing at all to the elaborate dolls. What frustrated Ermaya most was that she had really no idea of what they did contribute, knowing only it was small: just one palm-sized piece to the whole of the Droids. *Part +0,* it was called. Maybe that's why she was destroying property that wasn't hers and possibly one that cost thousands of dollars.

In contrast to the other floors with their weaving lab stations, Ermaya's lab was aesthetically sterile and furnished as though self-abnegation was one of life's best virtues. She often thought those who designed this boxed room would have denied the employees chairs, if the corporation would have approved it. There was one, long counter in the space where she worked, and it was too high to sit at; one had to stand beside it to make any use of it. So, Ermaya often balanced the laptops they were loaned for work on her knees when she didn't feel like standing to check her e-mail. Or, she sat outside the lab, in the crowded breakroom, that was really more of a hall, where she saw too many people she didn't know and would never know – each of them flawlessly composed like different songs to the orchestra that performed only for beauty.

It could be she was a disgruntled employee. That would make more sense to her for doing this. She really *shouldn't* be doing this. And, at least, if she were going to go through with it, it should be for a better reason than simply wanting *to know.*

Ermaya wanted to know more and she didn't. She didn't want to do this. She wanted to stop and be a model employee. Gentle, demure, obedient, and kind. A quirky, yet endearing sense of humor. That was how she wished to have others speak of her, and yet, all of that would be impossible, if she were discovered and fired from the corporation.

"Neel?" Ermaya had asked at a secluded hiking trail located past the city limit where the corporation resided. She didn't know why, back then, she'd thought the distance would make it safe for her to speak about the thing which held her fascination. She sat at a park bench with a man, and they watched other people in yoga pants, taking big strides up a raising path. Rogue winds came to jumble their hair, so that Ermaya and the man were continuously running hands through their own dark clouds of hair in order to look at each other, unobstructed. They hadn't done any hiking, both confessing at the onset of their meeting that they had no interest in hiking.

"What is it?" he returned. They both spoke Hindi, so she didn't know why he was over-reliant on English, but she wasn't here to nag him. He said, "Don't talk about work. It is illegal for us."

There were only the two of them who worked in the small room with the one, long counter. They performed but one procedure: the insertion of a narrow, metal plate into the pelvic area of eerily-realistic, AI-governed Droids.

Ermaya didn't like the way the Droids came to them: fresh off the assembly line and lacking most features which so endeared them to the public. They had a human shape, more skeletal than not, and staring eyes, but that was all. The face of the Droids had a nasal cavity and a thin slit for a mouth, but the silicon shaping to give them depth and familiarity would come much later when they reached the sixth and seventh floors of the building. Most days, Ermaya could think of them as *items* or *things*. But, she'd had to stay late before and work into the night a few times, and then, it seemed the Droids glanced at her when she wasn't looking at them. They blinked at some of the words she said to Neel or in muttering to herself. It was something she knew she imagined catching at the corner of her eye, but she sometimes couldn't entirely convince herself that it was just her nerves making her see things.

Ermaya pouted and traced an imaginary pattern on the tabletop of the bench where they sat. Neel sighed, watching her.

"I don't even know why we're here, of all places. You always make us meet at that Reptile House you so adore."

She glared at him. "Because the zoo was actually serious when they asked that you not return because you keep screaming whenever the iguanas so much as blink, Neel."

"We *are* both talking about the same ferocious, miniature dragons, aren't we?"

She whined at him. "You're so stupid. But, still, I want to talk about work with you, okay? Please?"

"No."

They sat, muted and people-watching. They stared at the forest scenery, neither caring for trees or the view. Ermaya waited, knowing Neel would depart without saying more, as he often did when she bored him, or she wouldn't relent speaking of their work.

"We look at Droid junk all day," her singular peer finally said. "There's nothing to talk about. And, thank gods no one knows that or how would we ever go to the shopping complex on ground level? We would be teased mercilessly, unable to go make use of our 30% employee discount. *30%,* Ermaya. Do you know how much I've spent since starting work here?"

"No one knows what we do, Neel. Why did we have to sign forms instructing us to answer 'systems check,' if anyone asks what we do? We don't do anything remotely like 'checking systems' in the Droids. Our lab isn't even labeled like everyone else's is on the outside. I've had other SC/RG employees ask why I walk into the storage closet every day."

Neel frowned at her. He liked to repeat himself and repeat his work. He didn't seem to want anything more from his job. "We aren't supposed to be talking about this. That was in our forms, too. They'll track this conversation. We'll lose everything, Ermy."

"Do not call me that," she grimaced at him, then persisted. "But, you must wonder. Why haven't they told us anything about the insertions? They're kept cold, so they're preserving something."

"It's probably a back-up battery," he said.

"A battery kept cold?" she mused.

"Or something for when the Droids engage in make-believe sex. A separate program. Animal. Artificial pheromones, maybe."

She was excited. He'd thought about Part +0, too. "But, we know the Droids' sexual response is dependent on visual input and verbal consent. Their 'breathing' doesn't even accelerate, unless a number of sequences are set in motion. What would that have to do with Part +0? Part +0 doesn't even connect to the Droids' hardware, except the refrigeration line. And, why is it called 'Part +0?'"

Neel guffawed. "Most obviously, that is another way of telling us to mind our own business, Ermy. Anything plus zero is nothing. It's the same as it was before. *My gods,* you'll search the smallest thing, won't you?"

"It means something," Ermaya said to herself.

Neel was waving invisible things away from his head as if he were being attacked by flies. *"Hey,"* Neel interrupted her. "You do understand who it is we work for, don't you? SC/RG has more money, more power, more influence than Jesus Christ. Jesus, even if he was a rock star in an up-and-coming reality TV show."

"Neel, Jesus didn't have money—"

He made a motion to cut her off. "Please. Please stop talking about this."

And, Ermaya was frustrated with him, but avoided further talk about their mysterious work. She was sour she hadn't asked to meet at the Reptile House after all.

"Part +0." Some nights she couldn't cease milling over thoughts of what it could possibly be. It wasn't a computerized part, she knew that much. It wasn't linked to the Droids' intelligence systems. The palm-sized sliding door that led into the region in the pelvis where the device was installed opened and closed only once. After that, the metal plate was forever locked within, guarded against anyone tampering with it or even reaching it. Ermaya had used a compact's mirror to look inside the slot where the plate was fitted and determined that there was a narrow

channel, leading to the stomach cavity of the Droids. In fact, the stomach cavity and the slot for the piece she installed shared the refrigeration line. But, that was all she could determine in her four years doing the work that was her livelihood.

Every other department on each level of SC/RG Corporation had to train for a year to understand the most meticulous details and seemingly extraneous information of their part in the production of the unimaginably expensive Droids. But, Ermaya and Neel had trained for two weeks, then had been entrusted to work unsupervised, not withholding the mounted cameras that were found on every floor and in every small corner of the multi-faceted building. Indeed, Ermaya sometimes wondered why chimps weren't employed to do their work instead. It was nothing more than keying in an order to the automated freezer unit – it operated as a giant vending machine - for one of the rectangular pieces, then lodging them in their designated groove within the walking machines, connecting the refrigeration line, and ensuring, lastly, that all of it was done correctly.

The mechanical voice came out bracingly loud. *"I'm sorry. Command insufficient. Please clearly state Vessel number, again."*
Ermaya sighed, standing in front of the enormous capsule. She gave herself a moment, telling herself, again, she could back out of her own plans. "For Vessel number 73738." She could simply stop wondering. She could be like Neel, who she'd sent downstairs to the shopping complex for the latest print catalogue of upgraded Droid models. Maybe in a few more years, she could even apply for a promotion.
The rectangular plate inched down the chute, then it was fully visible to Ermaya and waiting for her to retrieve it.
She did. And, she purposively dropped Part +0 on the ground at her feet. A wide, sweeping metallic clang reverberated off every wall of the miniature lab, and though Ermaya had been practicing her acting, her cringe at the sound was genuine.
"Shit," she said loudly. Maybe too loudly, but she wanted the surveillance to pick up her reaction. She told herself thrice, in

quick succession, not to look at any of the cameras in the room which she heard whirring softly to focus on her. At least three tiny heads pivoted in her direction with their one, cyclopean lens to record her next actions. It might be questionable, if she glanced at them. Would the look on her face give her away?

Ermaya was a tangle of nerves. By now, both her and Neel's employee wristbands had been pinged with the warning of what had happened. She had to move quickly, but appear calm, as if she were following procedure.

Ermaya paused too long, staring down at the metal plate and her entire future there on the gleaming floor. *Maybe it* is *just a spare battery*, she told herself. But, Part +0 wasn't. She felt she knew that. She knew it was something that could possibly undo SC/RG Corporation in the eyes of the world. Maybe. Ermaya carefully knelt beside the little device. She gauged it was no more than two inches by five. By crouching over it, her long lab coat briefly obscured the fallen piece from view of the cameras, and Ermaya let the scalpel that was tied against her forearm, inside her sleeve, slip down a few inches. She pretended to be fumbling with the plate, trying to pick it up, and the small motions were enough for her to force the tip of the blade into the only groove she knew of on the device. She flicked hard with the instrument, hoping she would find entry.

Something popped. Audibly.

Ermaya lifted her eyes, peering out from the length of her bangs. There was suddenly a loud mechanical drawl in her ears. She saw the cameras had a feature she hadn't known before: they could extend out of the walls where they were mounted. She gasped, as they dollied in closer towards her. Now, she couldn't stop herself from looking. She surveyed the room and saw that there was one camera in front of her and two behind her that hung, suspended, in the air on long metal arms with joints which allowed them to inch in still nearer to her. Like hovering vultures, their shadows fell over her.

Ermaya spoke now, knowing the footage would surely be reviewed. "I think it's fine. Just fine. See?" She held up the device, upside down, and a flutter of excitement went through her as whatever was housed inside of the slender plate fell down her sleeve, just as she'd planned, and came to rest against her elbow. It was an idiot's gamble, but genius as well, she felt. For a split moment, Ermaya feared whatever it was she'd now stolen was liquid and evidence of her theft would leak through her coat to reveal her, but she felt it again and the thing had shape and solidity. It was ice cold, but not liquid in the least.

She forced a little chuckle, mimicking innocence. "Oops, it's upside down." Ermaya lowered Part +0 from view to grasp it in two hands. She slid her finger over the tiny door which she'd popped open, closing it, and had no choice but to press one fingertip against the point of the scalpel to lower it back into the concealment of her clothes. She should've thought of how to retract the scalpel, but it was too late now.

Ermaya showed the pristine, metal device to the cameras again, this time right-side up with the small port for the cooling element to attach to it at the top of the unknowable part. "There we go." She smiled into the reflective lens that came straight for her face.

The door to the lab burst open, making Ermaya balk with muscles that went from weak to pulsing with tension in a matter of eye blinks. Then, she realized it was Neel at the entrance and not someone with termination forms for her job. Ermaya sighed as he rushed to her side.

"What the hell are you doing? How could you drop it?" he asked in a tone like she'd murdered someone. He was horrified. "A report already went to Upper Management." His hair was now blonde, and Ermaya stared at it for a second.

"What?" His words had rushed past her without her understanding them yet. He grabbed her wristband to show her the face of it, displaying his alongside hers. Both flashing screens read exactly as Neel had said.

PREVIEW OF THE UPCOMING
NEW SERIES:

ONE SPHERE, THREE REALMS

BOOK ONE of *ONE SPHERE*

ONE SPHERE, THREE REALMS:

Into the night, Lucifer fell.

It was a night darker than missing dreams, upon an hour before Time, and a purloined moment that became the history we never had.

It was the beginning of the selves we lost in Hell.

That banished angel fell, and as the depths swallowed the truth of the devil, *Satan* awoke.

And, we were all cast in sinful light, and Satan was made The Goat, the ever-scapegoat, to reflect the "blackness" in every one of us.

Now, Heaven and Hell will clash with the realm of mortals in between, and The Goat will rise to tell the story that was never born.

~~~

BOOK ONE of **ONE SPHERE**
~~~

PROLOGUE

GENTLY, may Those Remaining sing threnodies for thy life henceforth shucked. They bury thee, and Time becomes a rotation which has forgotten thy name.

In a hewn tree, in a hinged tree, arrive thee to the soot-stained Dark. Succumbed to earth, the worms burrow their faces into thee, until their writhing faces thee become.

Wherein, thou art freed.

Sally forth, upon a feathered flight.

And, trust this voyage anew.

Now, espy the pale sun with her crown of rime waning to pinpoint of firefly's glow, and sleep anon, for thou art held within the eyes of the Crane and at the depths of dreams that dreamers shall never know. By winged transport, are thee shorn from the reach of the MidWorld, and when thou cast thy arrowed gaze piercing heavenward, an inversed apex is revealed. A gorge hast swallowed thee whole and the stony arms of walls tremendous push even the clouds away.

Blink away that wakeful world, for as thine eyes darken to death, by some other sight dost thou witness the hush-whispering fields of the Reaper *Grim Mortis.*

Now, hast thou descended.

Fallen.

Like hourglass sand, which both counts and buries.

Slowly, upon one's own stride, dost this death become thee. It is an ending which traces back to the Beginning.

There is but one egress, and the hamlet's bleak sparsity fills with thy little steps, adopting the likeness of parchment fulfilled by ink spill. Thy penmanship creates anew a story yet told.

Begin shifting thoughts away from the hemisphere thy hast trowed.

At first, there is Fear.

The breathing mind makes orbit out the rotations of the living rondure, as is its wont – becomes a hollowed lung sack. There, clung to the First and Last Breath, the ancient fables doth linger at the failing consciousness in singular and mountainous dread that we shall be sank to the cramoisy holds of Hell. Tellus Mater, so motherly familiar, will not reach us in the swarthy face of the deadlands. All sunlit matters and visages of verdure decline every wish to show appearance and stand, imprisoned, beyond a shroud made of the backs of blackened fiends.

Yea, these old thoughts challenge us, so that we strive and make ambition to grasp every final cordage which may allow us tie to the planet of begotten Life. For we have propagated deep fiction of the horrors of that waiting realm below. The guilty do imagine punishment and torment to break the body in repetition illimitable. The forlorn fantasize piercing anguish and their cries which never reach ears of those forgiving or merciful. The lonely convince themselves surrendered to cavities endless in isolation.

But, what thou shalt see, as a Darkling, will be the labradorescence of Heaven, turned within out.

Now, then. Thou hast ended.

And shall share a tale with the most notorious of angels.